— BOOK 2 —
TARAN EMPIRE SAGA

EMPIRE UPRISING

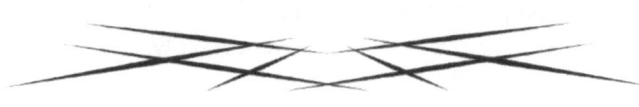

A K DUBOFF

Published by Dawnrunner Press
Cover Copyright © 2021 A.K. DuBoff

ISBN-10: 1954344228
ISBN-13: 978-1954344228
Copyright Registration Number: TXu002273208

0 9 8 7 6 5 4 3 2

Produced in the United States of America

TABLE OF CONTENTS

THE CADICLE UNIVERSE

Tarans are the predominant race in the Cadicle Universe; humans are a Taran genetic offshoot. Most of the Taran sphere falls within the purview of the Taran Empire, governed from the planet Tararia by a council of High Dynasty families. Earth is one of several rogue colonies on the outskirts of the Empire, separated so long ago that they have forgotten their Taran ancestry.

The Tararian Guard is the primary military force for the Taran Empire. Its counterpart, the Tararian Selective Service, includes a specialty branch with Agents gifted in telekinetic and telepathic abilities. The TSS is headquartered at a base inside Earth's moon, and its iconic Agents are known in Earth lore as the mysterious 'men in black'.

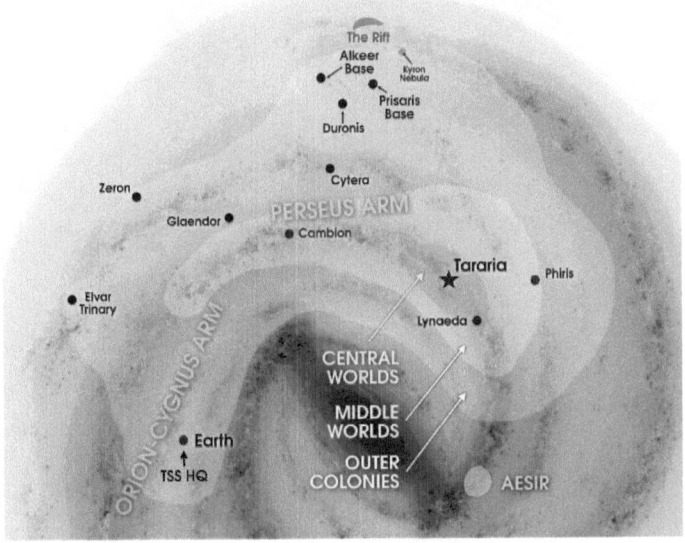

KEY TERMS, CAST & LOCATIONS

KEY TERMS

Taran – The race of all people in the Taran Empire; synonymous with human

Aesen – The foundational energy of the universe; pure energy capable of being shaped into any form

Erebus – *The nickname for a race of high-dimensional aliens*

Jump – Faster-than-light travel through subspace using the SiNavTech beacon network

Beacon Network – The navigation method for subspace jumps, maintained by SiNavTech

Independent Jump Drive – A jump drive that does not rely on the SiNavTech beacon network for navigation

High Dynasties – The seven ruling families of the Taran Empire, collectively a governing council

Lower Dynasties – Influential families throughout the Taran worlds, second only in power to the High Dynasties

ORGANIZATIONS

Tararian Guard – The primary military force for the Taran Empire

Tararian Selective Service (TSS) – A quasi-military organization with Agents specializing in telekinesis; a complement to the Tararian Guard

Priesthood – The former governing body of the Taran Empire

Sovereign Peoples Alliance – Revolutionary group based on the planet Duronis, advocating for independence in the Outer Colonies; known as the Alliance

Coalition – A suspected larger organization controlling the Alliance

Aesir – A reclusive group of technologically advanced Tarans

CAST

TSS

Jason Sietinen – TSS Primus Elite Agent; son of Wil and Saera; twin brother to Raena

Wil Sietinen – TSS High Commander; Jason's father

Saera Alexri – TSS Lead Agent; Jason's mother

Michael Andres – Primus Elite Agent / Head of TSS Operations and lead Primus Division trainer; Wil's close friend

Alliance

Lexi Karis – Informant within the Alliance providing information to the TSS and Guard

Oren – Manager within the Alliance

Shena – Lexi's former friend within the Alliance

Magdalena – Suspected leader within the Alliance/Coalition

Tararian Guard

Kira Elsar – Major; working undercover in the Alliance; modified with alien nanites and paired with embedded AI

Leon Caletti – Civilian consultant, geneticist/scientist, Kira's fiancé

Jasmine – Sentient AI embedded in Kira

Jakob Mathaen – Admiral of the Tararian Guard

Taran Government

Raena Sietinen – Sietinen Dynasty heiress; twin sister to Jason; Ryan's wife

Ryan Dainetris – Head of the Dainetris Dynasty; Raena's husband

Cris Sietinen – Head of the Sietinen Dynasty and SiNavTech executive; Wil's father

Kate Vaenetri – Cris' wife and Wil's mother; member of the Vaenetri Dynasty

Celine Monsari – Head of the Monsari Dynasty and MPS executive

Other Key Characters

Dahl – Oracle with the Aesir; Wil's main point-of-contact and longtime friend

Darin Suro – Sole survivor of the *Andvari*

Tiff – Jason's former lover and close friend (deceased)

Melisa – Lexi's friend, who disappeared after joining the Alliance

Ships

Conquest – TSS flagship with a unique telekinetic energy weapon

IT-1 – Classification of TSS fighters with telekinetic energy weapons

Andvari – A salvage hauler ship destroyed in an Erebus attack near the Rift

LOCATIONS

TSS Headquarters – Base inside Earth's moon

Tararia – The capital planet of the Taran Empire

Earth – A 'lost colony' of the Taran Empire, located in the remote Outer Colonies

Duronis – A developed planet in the Outer Colonies, base of operations for the Alliance

Alkeer Station – A former TSS base near the Rift destroyed by the Erebus

Lynaeda – Technologically advanced central world, specializing in AI and cybernetics

CHAPTER 1

THEY COULD ONLY skirt the issue for so long, and Wil Sietinen had exceeded his patience. "I've made the case for the mutual benefits. All I need is your agreement."

When he'd called the meeting with Celine Monsari, he had expected her to jump at the offer to have MPS manufacture the new power core design provided by the Erebus. The TSS needed a long-term production partner, and the MPS made the most strategic sense. After all, the company was the preeminent supplier of such equipment, so maintaining a monopoly was in their best interest.

However, the disinterested look Celine gave Wil from across the glass conference table did not instill him with confidence that they were about to strike a deal. *We need this to work. It would solve so many problems.*

Celine squinted at him, her tawny eyes calculating and suspicious. "Why are you coming to us now?"

To offer you a lifeline, you ungrateful witch. He forced a friendly smile. "I know it's delayed, but the TSS wanted to vet the technology before we put any manufacturing plans in place. We've spent the last seven months testing the core prototypes in DGE ships, and we are confident that they are safe. So, naturally, we thought MPS would be in the best position to scale up production."

"We already have a line of power cores."

Yes, and you're running out of the material to make them. Wil bit back the snide retort. "Your legacy products have been a mainstay of Taran civilization, but there is no denying that this new design offers improved functionality."

Celine leaned back in her seat, studying him. "You aren't being entirely forthright with me."

"All right. Shall we drop the pretense and speak freely, then?"

She inclined her head.

"In that case, Celine, what is the state of your voydite mine?"

"Whatever do you mean?"

"I think you understand the question perfectly. My suspicions started when we discovered that the *Andvari* had been running salvage for you—along with who knows how many other ships. Then your reluctance to provide power cores for planetary shields for the Taran worlds outside the Empire. And now every single conversation where you hedge. MPS has almost exhausted its voydite supply, hasn't it?"

She kept her expression impassive. "Why would voydite be relevant?"

You have to be foking kidding me! Wil was finding it increasingly difficult to not outright yell at the woman. "Because voydite is a critical material for the manufacture of your current power cores. If you run out of voydite, MPS will no longer have a product. Without MPS, the Monsari Dynasty would no longer be relevant. Do I need to spell out the rest, or can we have a *real* conversation like we agreed?"

Celine finally pulled her gaze away, focusing on her hands splayed on the tabletop. "You have no idea what it's like. You just abdicated your position so you didn't have to deal with inheriting a mountain of shite."

Now they were getting somewhere. "I had my own messes to deal with, but I am intimately familiar with the burden of cleaning up others' mistakes." His entire career in the TSS ultimately stemmed from correcting the Priesthood's past atrocities; few knew that truth, though the information was becoming more widely known.

"It's weak leadership that led us here," Celine huffed. "Now everything is falling apart."

"There's a breaking point for everything. Sometimes it comes down to bad luck."

She scoffed. "The infuriating thing is that they saw this coming generations ago. Each useless fool after another kept pushing off responsibility to the next poor sap in line. By the time I stepped in, there was little I could do."

He nodded. "Natural resources have a lifecycle. But when there's something new—"

She laughed. "Wait, you thought I was talking about the voydite?"

"Of course. That's—"

"You have some nerve to think I'd discuss private Dynasty business with the likes of you."

It took a moment for Wil to gather himself. "Excuse me?"

"Your family caused this mess. Preaching that the 'Gifted' should be allowed in civilized society. It's been a steady decline since your father took over Sietinen, slowly running the Empire into the ground."

Wil stood up. "Well, Celine, I wish I could say it's been a

pleasure. Good luck." *You're going to need it.*

Without waiting for any reply, he left the conference room.

For a minute there, she actually had me thinking she'd come around. They'd had their differences of opinion for as far back as he could remember, but at least they'd feigned civility. To insult him and every other Gifted person to his face was uncalled for. *With her at the helm, Monsari deserves whatever fate might befall it.*

He didn't like to wish ill of anyone, but that particular family line had failed to adapt to the changing times. More than that, they epitomized everything that people disliked about highborn—out of touch with normal people, using wealth as an excuse to forego decency. As long as that kind of elitist thinking persisted, there wouldn't be a sustainable balance of power within the Empire. If either Celine or her successors didn't open their eyes to the present reality, Taran civilization would move on without them. Though, perhaps that would be for the best.

Still fuming from the conversation, Wil stormed from the conference room and headed toward the port where his shuttle was waiting. Various administrative and security personnel watched him from a distance as he exited the manor and took the path eastward through the Monsari Estate's lush gardens.

Situated on the inner curve of the crescent-shaped Second Region, the cool air of Tararia's northern expanse was a fitting accompaniment to the chilly mood of all the staff he'd encountered during the brief visit. Wil looked forward to getting back home to TSS Headquarters—the one place he truly felt he belonged.

The entire mission had turned out to be a waste of time. Granted, five hours of transit in each direction made it a day-trip, but there were plenty of other things he could have been working on back at TSS Headquarters.

Returning to a more productive frame of mind, Wil ran through a mental checklist on what he could work on during the return journey.

They were in the midst of sorting out the training paths for the next Agent cohort. With the TSS' continuing trend toward academia in addition to specialized military training, they needed to expand the organization's training facilities and curriculum. Most of that fell under Saera's purview as Lead Agent, but Wil was serving in an advisory role as High Commander. Truthfully, they were in desperate need of others to help with the effort; Wil recognized that both he and his wife were too military-minded, and they were lacking a civilian viewpoint on the project. Unfortunately, no one had yet stepped up to assist them.

The most urgent task, however, was reviewing the latest reports from around the Rift.

The Erebus had been mostly quiet and distant since the encounter at Tararia. Though the TSS and Taran High Council had received a handful of communications during the intervening months, there had been no other indications of the Erebus interacting with the spacetime dimension. Wil wanted to believe that no signs of an impending attack was a good thing, but he hadn't been able to shake the feeling that the transdimensional aliens were gearing up for a bigger assault.

And then there's the matter of who can manufacture these new power cores. Another wave of annoyance surged through Wil as he reflected on the conversation with Celine. *We'll figure out a way forward without MPS.*

As soon as he was beyond easy earshot of the manor and there was no one in sight, Wil called his father on his handheld. He kept it voice-only for ease while walking.

"Hi, Wil, how'd it go?" his father greeted.

"Hey. It was not the cordial, productive chat I'd envisioned."

Cris sighed. "I was afraid that might be the case. The way Monsari has responded to the Erebus' presence hasn't given me the impression that they want to play nice."

"I'm afraid we're back to open hostility. I genuinely don't understand how Celine thinks this is a smart way to navigate our relationship."

"Are you still at the estate?"

"Heading to my shuttle now."

"We can talk further once you're somewhere more private. I have some thoughts on the matter."

"Sounds good. Thanks, Dad."

"We're prepared for this contingency. Forget Celine. Monsari has decided its own fate."

"I hate to condemn an entire family over the act of one individual, but she's made it difficult for me to separate the two."

"You're right," his father said, "we shouldn't write them all off. Doing so would be no different than the Erebus punishing all Tarans for the actions of a few rogue criminals."

"I always try to find redeeming qualities in a person, but something— I don't know, it doesn't feel right. The way she was so dismissive of the offer doesn't make sense. Why turn down an opportunity to…"

Wil faded out as a tingle rippled down the back of his neck—an instinctual alarm of both his training and Gifts. He raised a telekinetic shield around himself.

The blast hit only a moment later. The charge diffused as it struck his shield, rippling in waves from the point of impact.

The fok? He spun around to face the direction of the attack, looking for the perpetrator. "Someone just took a shot at me!"

"What?!" his father exclaimed.

"I'll call you back." He ended the call and slipped his handheld back into the inner pocket of his TSS uniform's black overcoat.

Wil's senses were on high alert. He reached out with his mind to feel for anyone in the area. When he found no one in the immediate vicinity, he expanded the search radius. A hundred meters out, he felt someone watching him. They were preparing to make an escape.

That was a big mistake.

Wil gripped the man in a telekinetic hold from afar, lifting him from the ground and pinning his limbs so he would be unable to flee.

He ran over to where the man was suspended behind a hedge. As Wil came around the natural barrier, he lowered the man to the ground but still held him in a firm telekinetic grasp.

The captive's eyes darted from side to side with terror. The young man was dressed like a grounds worker in green coveralls. Only the plasma rifle at his side gave away his murderous intentions.

"Did you really think you could take me down so easily?" Wil asked. Another traitor had successfully landed a near-mortal shot on Wil, but he had been a mere teenager then. For anyone to make an attempt now on the TSS High Commander—let alone a Sietinen heir—was either insane, foolish, or getting paid a lot of money to take the risk.

"I don't know what you're talking about." The young man hung in the air, immobile and his mind open.

"Who do you work for?" Wil demanded.

"What do you mean?" the man stammered. All of the answers to Wil's questions were right there in the man's mind for the taking, but it was almost like that's what he *wanted* Wil to do. Such an invasive telepathic action might be justifiable in an interrogation after an official arrest, but not like this.

Wil glared at him. "Who put you up to this?" His heart pounded in his chest, more from anger than fear. *Was this Monsari's doing? Was this entire meeting a trap?*

"What's going on here?" a stern male voice demanded from behind Wil.

Wil wheeled around to face the approaching man, who was dressed in the distinctive gray uniform of a Guard officer.

Good, we can settle this properly. Wil addressed the officer, "This man just attempted to shoot me in the back. That's a hefty criminal offense of both attacking a military officer and a highborn heir."

"And what evidence do you have of this alleged infraction?" the officer asked.

Wil hesitated. That wasn't the kind of response he'd anticipated. "I'm sure your surveillance footage will provide an adequate illustration of the events."

"I'm afraid our visual monitoring system is currently offline for maintenance."

A quick telekinetic survey of the surrounding area confirmed that the security system was powered down. The predicament crystallized in Wil's mind. *This was a setup.*

Wil thought over the geography of the incident. Even his shuttle wasn't in sight, which meant its onboard cameras wouldn't have witnessed the incident. The perpetrators had picked a perfect location where Wil would only have his word about what had transpired.

What do they hope to gain? Was this really an assassination attempt, or something else? Wil looked between the face of his assailant and the officer. "I can offer no additional witnesses to the encounter."

The officer shrugged—far too casual a gesture for the nature of the situation. It was almost like he was trying to taunt Wil. "Then I'm afraid it's your word against his."

The heat rose in Wil's chest. *He was probably watching the whole thing. He's in on it.*

"You do not appear to be injured," the officer continued, looking Wil over, "nor is there any evidence of a shot being fired in this vicinity. Please, release this man." A smirk tugged at his lips.

Oh, that's it. They're trying to get a rise out of me—to bait me into action. Well, this isn't over yet. Wil took a calming breath. "If you examine this rifle," he gestured to his assailant's weapon, "you no doubt will find it has been recently fired. How do you explain that?"

The officer glanced at the rifle. "You just came from the target range, right, Tony?"

"Yeah. Got a great pattern, too." The assailant nodded—about the only action he could take while still in Wil's grasp.

"I'm not seeing the issue here," the officer said. "Please, sir, I need to insist that you release him or I'll be forced to escalate this issue."

That's exactly what you want, isn't it? For me to use my abilities to force the truth out of him, so you can declare how unstable I am and abusive of my power. Wil schooled his expression, unwilling to give the men the satisfaction of seeing him angry. "I see."

Reluctantly, Wil released the shooter.

The assailant shook out his limbs and flashed Wil a smug sneer. "It appears this has all been a misunderstanding."

"Oh, I think we understand each other perfectly." Wil met his gaze.

After several intense seconds, the officer cleared his throat. "Then it's settled." Without another word, he spun around and strode back along the path.

The shooter glanced between his weapon and Wil. From the twist of his lips, he wanted to say more, but to make any comment might be incriminating.

Wil stared back levelly. *Yeah, we both know that would have been a clean center-mass shot if I hadn't blocked it. Don't think I'll forget.* The very notion that the man had been willing to take the shot said everything Wil needed to know about him.

The shooter gave a final nod and then followed the officer toward the manor.

Un-foking believable. Wil watched him go. *That's it?*

The entire encounter was bizarre. He had expected them to press him further—to *make* him take action against them that they could then warp to fit their own narrative. Instead, they'd simply walked away.

Was this just a warning? He didn't know what to make of it.

Wil took another minute to clear his head before he went to his shuttle, much more aware of his surroundings this time. As a precaution, he kept a shield up around himself, though he doubted they'd try the same assault twice.

On his way, he sent a quick text to his father, knowing he must be worried about the abrupt end to their call: >>I'm fine. I'll fill you in later. No one in Monsari can be trusted.<<

As much as he valued his father's council, it was more critical that he alert the TSS about Monsari's transgression. As soon as he strapped into one of the private passenger seats in the central body of the shuttle, he called Saera.

She appeared on the screen of his handheld. "Hey, how'd it go?"

"Not good. First, the easy part: MPS isn't interested in manufacturing."

Her jade eyes widened with surprise. "Really? That seems like a *terrible* business decision."

"That's my assessment, too. I don't get it. I would have thought she'd jump at the idea."

A low rumble vibrated the deck underfoot as the small ship powered up and lifted from the ground.

His wife frowned. "Is it possible we've misread the situation and they aren't in as dire straits as we think? Why else would Monsari decline such a generous offer?"

"Well, it might have something to do with them trying to shoot me."

"Stars, Wil!" Saera exclaimed. "They *shot* at you? Are you okay?"

"Yes, I'm fine. It's not like this was the first time." In many ways, the hyper-awareness born from the trauma of his past experience had helped keep him safer in the years since.

Saera's expression immediately shifted to matter-of-fact professionalism. "I'll contact the local Agents to provide backup for an arrest."

He held up his hand. "That won't be necessary. We can't make any arrest now."

"Why in the stars not? Did you not locate the shooter?"

"Oh, I spotted him right away. I think I was supposed to. The problem is, the security system was out—*conveniently*—and I didn't *see* him take the shot. Extrasensory perception isn't grounds for an arrest."

She frowned. "Agents use it all the time."

"Tararian local law is different. They haven't yet rolled back all of the regulations the Priesthood put in place during their rule."

"There has to be *something* we can do! Please don't tell me you're going to shrug this off."

"Absolutely not. However, there's little we can do about the situation at the moment. It's my word against his, and any attempt to throw around my authority is likely to do more harm than good." The more Wil talked through what happened, he saw just how brilliant a setup it was. Either he had to let Monsari get away with the entire thing, or he'd need to overstep the scope of his position in order to respond to the assault. They were clearly counting on him seeking vengeance no matter what.

She scowled. "This isn't right."

No, it's not. He fought against the anger welling in his chest. "Justice will be served. Have faith. And patience."

"It's never a good sign when you're the one telling *me* to be patient."

"Just taking turns, my love. We'll get through this like we have everything else."

"Meanwhile, an assassin is running loose."

"*Attempted* assassin," he said. "Right now, I'm more concerned about whoever put him up to it—whether it was Celine or someone else."

Saera scowled. "Monsari is obviously involved. But was it a temporary collaboration of convenience, or is it part of a longer-term strategy?"

"Given how things tend to go for us, I suspect this was a tiny piece of a much bigger scheme."

"To what end?"

Wil shook his head. "I'm not sure, but it was all a setup, Saera. They wanted me to read their minds—I could feel it. And it would have been so easy to get all the answers, but this bomaxed code of ethics is here to keep us from becoming the monsters people like Celine think we are. I would never give into that trap."

"I trust you, more than anyone, to respect those lines."

"I can't think of another reason why they would have reacted the way they did. They had to have known I would be able to identify and deflect a single blast like that. It was intended to piss me off, not hurt me."

"Devious."

"And shows they don't know me well at all."

She nodded. "Even if you *had* gleaned information, anything you learned via surreptitious telepathy wouldn't be considered proof outside our immediate circle."

"To have a solid lead, though…" He sighed. "But we can't go down that path."

"No. And we also can't waver. This event underscores that we're up against powerful adversaries."

"Our options are becoming more constrained."

"Though new opportunities may yet open," Saera replied. "I'm anxious to see where Raena's investigation into Earth leads. There's mounting evidence that there's something significant on the planet."

"I don't want to get my hopes up."

"Me either. We still need to figure out a production strategy for the Erebus power core; that single item can do more for us than anything else—and I'm now doubly eager to no longer be reliant on Monsari and MPS."

Wil nodded. "I agree wholeheartedly."

"It's time to take another tactic. The right strategic manufacturing partner would send a strong message."

"What are you thinking?" Wil asked.

"One option is to keep it in-house within the TSS, but that goes against our mandate to be a neutral party."

"We can't cross that line."

She leaned closer to the camera. "That leaves two alternatives, both with pros and cons: either we pick an existing corporation and elevate their status, or we establish a new corporation, which would position them as a new powerhouse—pardon the pun—to take the mantle from MPS."

Wil frowned. "*We* shouldn't be the ones making that decision."

"Do you really think the High Council will be equitable about it? I love our family, but even they couldn't approach this without bias. Your dad would say SiNavTech is happy to take it on, Ryan would jump at the opportunity to expand DGE, your uncle would make the case that VComm already makes their own micro power cells for handhelds, so they know the market. It'd start a messy bidding war, at best."

I wonder if that's what Dad was going to suggest? Wil agreed with Saera that keeping the High Council out of it was for the best; hopefully, his parents would agree with the reasoning.

"What, then? We quietly hand it off to the person or group of our choosing?" he asked his wife.

"You've selected plenty of candidates for important positions in the past. You understand how to pick individuals who'll act in the best interest of others rather than themselves."

He groaned softly. "And I hate having that kind of responsibility—especially in situations with galactic-scale implications."

"I respect your judgment, just like the Aesir do."

He tilted his head. "Now, there's a thought."

"Hmm?"

"The Aesir. We could hand it over to them."

Her face scrunched. "You think they'd go for it?"

"It's worth a conversation."

— — —

"What do you mean 'they took a shot at him'?" Raena Sietinen exclaimed, nearly jumping out of her office chair.

Her grandfather had passed on the news in a tone which was entirely too calm. He evaluated her over the viewscreen, still cool and collected. "I must admit, I didn't expect Monsari to make such an overt move."

How is he not furious? Raena felt the flush in her face. "Was it Monsari directly, or were they simply turning a blind eye?"

"Does the distinction matter?" Cris asked. "Either way, this amounts to a declaration of civil war."

Raena's heart dropped, and she sank back into her chair. "I hope you mean that as hyperbole."

Her grandfather looked away from the camera as he folded his hands on his desktop. "Conflict with Monsari is nothing new. However, an act of physical aggression changes things."

"Why would they do it? Doesn't it make Monsari a target?"

"Lines are being drawn," he said. "Whatever they hope to gain, they consider this action worth the risk. Or, perhaps, it was simply a test."

"To see how Dad would respond?"

"To see how we *all* will. The event won't make the news, but word will get around. In the right circles, someone willing to take a shot like that might be celebrated. There's a lot of clout to be gained."

"In other words, Monsari is gearing up for a larger political move."

Cris nodded. "That's my suspicion, based on what little information we have."

Raena's stomach lurched. "What does this mean for us?"

"That you must continue your work with Earth. Right now, the ancient sites on that planet have the best chance of uncovering information about our past that could reveal a new path forward."

"None of that will do us much good in a political battle against another High Dynasty."

"Perhaps not, but my greater worry remains the Erebus."

She took an unsteady breath. "What if we can't figure out how to fight them?"

"Positive visualization, Raena. We *will* find a way." He paused. "Still, we must be cautious. Danger is closing in on all fronts. There will come a time when we'll discover who truly supports us and those who never did."

"We'll always have our family, if no one else."

Cris smiled. "That's all we really need. Anyone who stands against us picked the wrong side."

Raena gave a resolute nod, pushing down her nerves. There wasn't room for worry or doubt. "No matter what happens, I'm ready."

CHAPTER 2

AS JASON SIETINEN reviewed the latest TSS threat assessment report, he was again met with nominal accounts on most fronts—only a handful of civil demonstrations under the purview of the Tararian Guard. *But everything is not okay. What are we missing?*

The peace was an illusion. In the seven months since the Erebus appeared, Jason had been waiting for the tentative truce to shatter. The timing on the Taran calendar made it the better part of an Earth year, but the losses at Alkeer Station were the kind of tragedy the TSS wouldn't ever forget—not to mention the personal nature of that loss to him. For the sake of maintaining the tenuous alliance with the aliens, the TSS pretended publicly to have set aside any hard feelings against the Erebus. But Jason knew he wasn't alone in his resentment. Wrath would be dealt when the time was right.

For now, everything was suspiciously quiet. Something was brewing beneath the surface; he sensed it. It wasn't a matter of *if* the Taran Empire would be plunged into chaos, but *when*.

A knock sounded on his office doorframe, and he looked up to see his mother. "Come in."

Saera slipped inside and closed the door behind her. "There's been an incident."

Jason braced for the news. If she was coming in person, it was no doubt serious. "What happened?"

"While your father was leaving the Monsari estate, someone took a shot at him."

"What?!"

"He deflected it—no need to worry—but obviously there are… implications."

"Shite." Jason deflated in his seat. "I take it the negotiations didn't go well."

"It appears they only accepted the meeting as a pretense to get your father there. Our suspicion is that they were trying to provoke him into taking unbecoming actions that they could use against us."

"The TSS or the Sietinen Dynasty?"

"Probably both. As well as all Gifted, most likely. Since they consider us to be 'dangerous savages', and all that." She crossed her arms and leaned against the wall.

So much for the peace and quiet. Jason ran his hand through his hair. "I can't believe they'd make a move like this *now*."

"Clearly, they saw an opportunity." Saera's brows were pinched with concern.

He hated seeing his mother like that. They'd been through plenty of tense times in their professional lives together, but she was still the stalwart mom who'd comforted him when he was scared or hurt as a youth. Witnessing her be so openly worried hit deep.

"It'll be okay, Mom," he told her.

The words sounded hollow to his ears, but Saera straightened and gave a confident nod. "I know it will. Thank you, Jason. I'll keep you apprised of further developments."

"All right."

She gave him a half-hearted smile and departed.

Jason returned his attention to the minor TSS incident reports on his desktop. *None of this scratches the surface of the real issues.*

He closed out from the reports and pushed back from his desk with a sigh. The attack on his father was just one more item to add to his growing concerns.

The absence of the Erebus wasn't all that surprising. After they'd dropped their 'gift' in the TSS' lap, they'd closed up their micro-rifts and disappeared behind the dimensional veil. They were no doubt still watching Tarans' actions, but with everyone on their best behavior, there was no reason for the aliens to intervene.

What was far more concerning was how uneventful things had been on the surface in the Outer Colonies for months. The botched siege on Duronis had been the last incident of any significance, with only a handful of smaller demonstrations in the intervening time. However, since the original perpetrators hadn't been apprehended, it simply meant that their planning had gone underground. What had become clear, though, is that the Coalition's network was large and very well-funded. Unfortunately, the people behind it were also very smart and had covered their tracks with expert precision.

Jason regularly scanned the public news reports about the sector around Duronis. There was absolutely nothing useful—all headlines perfectly manicured to avoid discussion of the real issues within the Taran Empire.

Yet here he was, stuck at Headquarters away from the

action. Sure, teaching passed the time, but he wanted to stand up to the Erebus or apprehend criminals. Knowing there were now would-be assassins running around made it that much worse.

I need to know what's really going on out there. We can't afford to be caught by surprise again.

The TSS was counting on him to be in regular communication with their undercover operative, Kira, who was working inside the Sovereign Peoples Alliance with her fiancé, Leon, and their informant, Lexi. Kira had struggled to embed herself deeply enough into the Alliance to learn anything incriminating about the larger Coalition. The nature of the assignment made regular check-ins difficult, much to Jason's consternation. Technically, the Alliance didn't like its members talking with anyone outside its membership; yet, the organization's leaders also recognized that enforcing a no-outside-contact rule would create more issues than it solved. This left a small opening that they had exploited over the past several months.

However, Jason hadn't heard from Kira for two weeks now, and they were past due for her latest report from the field. For those check-ins, Kira would call Jason on a throw-away handheld, used only once.

It's been too long. What if something happened to her? He wasn't typically one to worry, but with the Alliance, the concern was valid.

The organization had a history of disappearing people, and they had every reason to make sure Kira was never able to report what was really happening within the organization. Even if she hadn't been found out, it was possible they were keeping too close a watch for her to get out a message.

He tapped his fingers on his desktop. *I need to make sure*

she's okay.

Jason only had one option to get in touch. They'd set up an encrypted account for Kira that could receive text messages and files, which she could access remotely. Using coded phrasing, they could send notes to each other that would come across like a casual interaction that shouldn't raise alarms if anyone happened across their communications.

If everything was okay, she would be checking it regularly. It was better than him being stuck in 'wait and see' mode.

Jason opened up a new text message to send via their established covert protocol: >>Hey! Wow, how time flies, huh? Things have been quiet around here. Mom and Dad keep asking about you. I figure you're busy, but just wanted to say hi and make sure all is well.<<

Once the message was sent, he tried to turn his attention to other tasks. He wouldn't be able to rest easy until he heard from her—not when he knew the Alliance was capable of such terrible things. *Please, reply soon, Kira. I don't know what I'd do if you disappeared, too.*

—   —   —

Lexi twirled a section of her brunette hair with one hand while she anxiously drummed her fingers on her desktop. Her patience for acting like she cared about the Sovereign Peoples Alliance had worn through a long time ago, so keeping calm enough to maintain her cover brought out every nervous tick she'd ever expressed.

In a moment of clarity, she realized that her foot was also rapidly jerking back and forth, in addition to her fingers taking on a life of their own. She made a conscious effort to sit still.

What is it that Leon wanted to talk about?

She hadn't been able to concentrate on her mundane work tasks since breakfast. Kira's fiancé, Leon, had made a passing statement about hearing something interesting the night before, and she was dying to learn the details.

Maybe he finally got information about where the Coalition is based so I can leave this shiteshow behind. It could be wishful thinking, but she needed to believe that the end was in sight.

The days of working at the Alliance office had long since blurred together. She used the term 'work' loosely since activity had seemingly ground to a halt since the failed cargo ship takeover during the attempted coup on Duronis. The Alliance's shift to keeping a low profile had worked to her advantage at first, with the organization having been unable to conduct a thorough investigation into the control room cave-in she'd caused. The entire incident had been written off as an 'accident', just like she'd hoped.

However, after spending the better part of the year with little to do, she was getting antsy. The one saving grace had been having Kira and Leon around the office.

Lunch was fast approaching, fortunately, so she had social time to look forward to—and, with any luck, an opportunity to hear about what Leon had learned.

Unable to focus on her tedious administrative tasks, Lexi spent the remaining fifteen minutes until lunch looking over the morning's news reports. There hadn't been any major incidents reported on the galactic broadcast streams, but she'd been hearing rumors around the office about new demonstrations happening on Duronis and the surrounding planets.

Recently, the messaging she'd seen on Duronis ranged from 'independence in the Outer Colonies' to 'down with the Central Planets'. However, it lacked any kind of cohesive argument about *why*. That was by design. The Alliance's entire purpose behind fueling that messaging was to create disruption and dissent in the public consciousness. With a vague enough rally, people would fill in their own reasons to be upset and add fuel to the larger movement. It was on a simmer now, building their following in preparation for an explosive boiling over when the Coalition was ready to make its move.

That move was coming soon—the energy around the office had shifted again, just like before the last big revolt.

Except, she was frustrated to not have any details about *what* that move might be. *They're being even more secretive than last time. You'd think with two telepaths we could learn more!*

At 13:00, Lexi locked down her desktop and went to the cafeteria where everyone gathered for lunch. A quarter of the tables were filled by the time she arrived. She spotted Kira and Leon among those seated, easily recognizable from a distance by Kira's vibrant red, pixie-cut hair.

Lexi waved at them before grabbing a plate of bland fare from the buffet line; like the second-hand nature of the furnishings throughout the Alliance's building, the food was subpar. The menu was frequently various forms of mush that were more 'nutrition' than 'cuisine', but on the rare occasion there was something solid, the once-fresh items were noticeably nearing their expiration date, almost certainly purchased at a discount.

Today's sampling happened to be one of the trademark gruels, this one beige.

Great.

Lexi set her tray down on the table with a sigh and took a seat across from her friends.

Kira scooped up a mound of the beige mush on her spoon and watched it dribble back into the gelatinous mound. "I need a real meal."

Next to her, Leon shoved his tray away from him, a look of disgust twisting his handsome features. "I second that."

Though his fair complexion wasn't what Lexi would typically go for, she found his unique violet irises quite mesmerizing. She'd never said as much to Kira, but she could see why the other woman had fallen for the guy.

"Hey, at least the food is free." Lexi used her spoon to play with the mush until her growling stomach's demands overrode the lack of visual appeal. Once she got past the first bite of the slimy texture, the vaguely nutty flavor wasn't too bad.

After running from planet to planet without a proper home to call her own for most of her life, one thing Lexi did appreciate about the Alliance was that it had offered her a measure of stability over the past year. They fed her. Housed her. Gave her tasks she could pretend were meaningful employment. Though it wasn't a great life, her situation could be a lot worse—or so it seemed on the surface.

Just when she started to think it wasn't so bad, she'd remember that the Alliance had been willing to kill innocent children in the name of 'independence' and that they'd disappeared her closest friend. Perhaps not all the people in the Alliance were bad, but there was an evil undercurrent in the organization.

They need to be taken down. She reminded herself that it was best to keep that thought front and center at all times— regardless of how they'd made her feel like part of a community.

"Well," Kira said, a mischievous sparkle in her hazel eyes, "I have credits to burn, and I need to get out of here for a while.

What do you say to an offsite happy hour?"

"I don't think 'happy' or 'fun' are even in Oren's vocabulary," Leon replied.

Lexi smiled and took another bite of her meal. Leon was one of those quiet, cerebral types who consistently caught Lexi by surprise with spontaneous displays of dry humor. Not that she thought the guy was uptight, it was just never clear when he was listening to them or when he was lost in thought ideating about whatever it was super-smart people contemplated.

"Lucky, then, he's not invited," Kira replied.

Leon nodded. "I'm always up for a good chat." He made brief eye contact with each of them, giving a subtle indication that it would be an opportunity to expand upon his breakfast comment.

"Besides, I've been out of touch for too long," Kira added. "I need to check my messages."

Lexi recognized the phrasing to mean that Kira needed to touch base with her TSS handler. She hadn't been privy to the conversations directly, but what little Kira had said about the matter was that her undercover mission had come directly from the top of the organization. It had taken months to get even that much out of her—not that Lexi blamed her for being cautious. Though Lexi had solicited the help to investigate the Alliance's dealings, it could have easily been a setup. She'd needed to earn Kira's and Leon's trust, but she now proudly called them her friends.

"All the more reason to go out tonight," Leon reiterated.

Stars, that does sound good. Despite her desire to get outside the office and speak freely for a change, she was well aware how important it was to not draw attention to herself by rule-bending. "Go for it. Have fun."

"Come out with us," Kira urged. "It's been too long since we had a change of scenery."

The phrasing made it sound like a friendly offer, for the benefit of anyone who might overhear the conversation. However, as she spoke, Kira made eye contact with Lexi and initiated a telepathic link.

"You'll want to hear what Leon has to say," she said in Lexi's mind.

"What if we get caught?"

"We won't."

Lexi broke eye contact and shook her head. "As much as I'd like to, I don't need Oren giving me another lecture about my 'commitment to the cause'." He was the most infuriating manager Lexi had ever dealt with, not even taking into account his psychopathic tendencies. She did everything she could to avoid crossing the man, fearing retribution.

Kira waved her hand dismissively. "It's just for an hour." She caught Lexi's gaze again, *"We'll say we're going to scope out new recruits or something. It's not like we're* never *allowed to leave the building."*

Lexi wanted to protest. She knew it was a risk to leave, even for a short while, on non-Alliance business. Yet, she was curious about Leon's information, and her nerves were frayed from being cooped up for too long.

"All right," she yielded.

The other woman beamed. "Excellent. Let's head out at 17:00?"

"Sounds good." Normally, it would have been delivery pickup time, but there weren't any on the schedule for the rest of the week.

Kira smiled. "Great! It'll be a fun time."

It really might be. Lexi was relieved to not feel alone

anymore.

Kira had quickly become a good friend, and Leon was the kind of level-headed person who was easy to be around. None of her other relationships within the Alliance had offered any kind of meaningful social connection, and she hadn't realized how much she'd missed having real friends. She'd been on her own for a long time, aside from Melisa, but that didn't mean she *liked* being a loner.

After finishing her lunch, Lexi returned to her desk to finish up the remaining administrative tasks for the day. Having the evening outing to look forward to helped pass the time, and she soon found it was approaching the planned departure time.

She met up with Kira and Leon at the office's back access door and slipped outside into the shadowed rear alley.

Kira breathed in deeply, despite the slightly foul air wafting over from the nearby dumpster, and smiled. "Oh, it feels good to be out!"

"I've been going a little stir crazy," Leon admitted. He tousled his light-brown hair. "When are we going to *do* something?"

"This is what it was like before you joined up," Lexi told them as they walked away from the office. "A whole lot of nothing, and then the, uh… incident."

They nodded, catching her meaning. She couldn't explicitly talk about the attack on the space station or attempted seizure of the supply ships.

"People are getting restless. It doesn't take anyone special to see that," Kira said.

Lexi tilted her head questioningly. "And what might a more perceptive person pick up?"

"That pieces are moving. The wait is almost over…

though, whatever is going on is happening at a higher level than us little cogs."

"The question is, how does one ascend to that higher level?" Lexi asked.

Kira gave her a confident smile. "Leave that to us."

Kira's abilities largely remained a mystery to Lexi. She knew the other woman was some kind of telepath, but she wasn't Gifted in the usual sense. It made her a great asset to extract information—assuming she got access to the right person—and also prevented her from being detected. However, it also meant Lexi was unable to read the woman in the way she would other people.

She trusted Kira, for the most part, but she wasn't entirely sure where she stood in Kira's eyes. Lexi wanted to think she was one of the team, working on the inside of the Alliance to help the TSS. Yet, she might just as easily be an expendable tool who the TSS would only keep around so long as she was useful.

Regardless, aligning herself with Kira was Lexi's best—and, really, *only*—play at the moment. She needed answers about the Alliance's operations, and what may have happened to her missing friend, Melisa.

I wish I could be more help. When I called in the TSS, I thought we'd be able to get in deeper by now. The whole mess with the aborted revolt had shut down the Alliance's activities, leaving their mission at a standstill. They couldn't press the issues without leaders like Oren getting suspicious about their impatience, so they'd been keeping their heads down.

Though the waiting was annoying, and it was frustrating that they couldn't talk openly about their real purpose for being in the Alliance's ranks, it set Lexi at ease to know that she had two allies who viewed the Alliance as the bad guys. Too many others around the office seemed eager to swallow whatever propaganda the Alliance was spewing as their flavor of the day.

The group stuck to the back alleys as they put distance between themselves and the Alliance office. A kilometer from the building, they transitioned to the main streets.

Kira looked around them, as though checking for a potential tail. "I think we're good to go."

"Should we chat before you do your check-in?" Leon asked.

"Yeah, let's find somewhere to talk."

They spotted a moderately busy pub a couple blocks away and ducked inside. The buzz of conversation made for the perfect background noise to have a private conversation in plain sight. One of the back corner tables was available, so they grabbed draft drinks at the bar and then settled in.

Kira dramatically motioned toward Leon, as if making a big reveal. "Take it away."

He placed his elbows on the table and leaned in. "I may finally have a lead," he said, barely above a whisper. "I've started hearing rumors about a big project they're working on offworld."

Lexi perked up. "Where'd you learn that?"

"I overheard a group of researchers talking early this morning. They were making plans for a new lab."

"Were you able to get any more specifics?" Kira asked.

"Based on their specializations, it's related to something biological... and nasty. It sounds like they picked this new site because it's remote."

"An uninhabited world, then?"

"I got the sense there was *some* kind of existing settlement on the planet. It's difficult to start up a research operation without any resources, so that'd make sense."

"A heads up on *where* would be really nice to pass onto our friends on the outside," Kira said.

He nodded. "Secret research on remote worlds rarely bodes well. Whatever they're planning to work on can't be good for the rest of the Empire."

"It's like their goals have completely changed," Lexi mused. "They were focused on that plan to isolate Duronis, but then... nothing."

Kira swirled the beer in her glass pensively. "The shift happened right when the Erebus showed up."

Lexi stared at her. "Stars, you're right! But why would that impact their plans? You'd think they'd want to take full advantage of that distraction to push things forward."

"Unless that revelation opened up a new, better opportunity."

"Such as?"

"I don't know. The whole thing has me worried. They're recruiting all these people, and no one is *doing anything.*"

"It's like they're gathering troops," Leon said.

"An army to activate and direct when the moment is right." Kira shook her head. "What in the stars are they up to?"

Leon shrugged. "This information about the planet might offer some clues. I'll ask around, find out what I can."

"I've never been so happy to get bad news." Lexi let out a satisfied sigh. "It's a lead. Finally!"

Kira raised her glass. "Cheers to that."

Lexi clinked her glass with the others. *All the waiting is paying off. Now our hunt can begin.*

CHAPTER 3

JASON FROWNED AT the cryptic message from Kira displayed on his office desktop. It simply read, >>Might have a lead. Looking into it more. Will be in touch soon.<<

Well, at least I know she's alive. After weeks with no communication, he was happy to see the note when he checked his morning messages. However, he'd hoped for more of an update. *With any luck, 'soon' will be a lot faster than the last interval.*

The assignment was proving to be tedious, and she was a soldier who thrived on action. She was probably losing her mind. Ever since she and Leon had entered the Alliance, nothing had gone like they'd planned. The organization had apparently gone into lockdown after the thwarted takeover on Duronis, leaving Kira without a means of upward mobility in the organization.

However, after investing this much time, Jason didn't want to abandon the project. To admit defeat would mean they had been outplayed by a band of criminals. Jason couldn't abide that. Kira wouldn't stand for it, either.

But if this new lead doesn't pan out, we might need to call it quits, regardless. He didn't like that possibility. Even so, at a certain point, keeping a valuable asset like Kira tied up undercover no longer made sense; realistically, they were already past that point.

He wasn't ready to give up quite yet. *We* need *to know what the Alliance has been doing for the last seven months. They're too well-connected to have been idle all this time.*

Jason resolved himself to be patient. Kira had a new lead to chase. He had to trust in her ability to unveil the larger plan.

— — —

After spending the full prior day traveling to and from Tararia, Wil was looking forward to time at TSS Headquarters so he could get caught up on work. Saera had given him a gentle reminder at breakfast to review the proposed course catalogue, among other languishing tasks.

I just need a day without interruptions. Such days were a rarity, but maybe he'd get lucky.

Before diving into the course lineup, Wil decided to reach out to Dahl to broach the topic of the Aesir manufacturing the Erebus power core. He expected it to be a brief conversation, with eager acceptance of the proposition. After all, the Aesir were currently reliant on MPS' power cores, like the rest of the Taran Empire, so having control over the manufacturing would be a natural fit with their proclivity for resource independence.

He initiated a direct vidcall to Dahl and waited for the Oracle to answer.

"Hello, Cadicle. What is the purpose for your call?" Dahl's pale, glowing eyes studied Wil through the viewscreen.

No talk of this discussion being foretold in the cosmic pattern, for a change? Wil smiled. "I wanted to give you an update on where we stand with the Erebus' power core."

Dahl nodded. "We have been curious about how it performed in your testing."

"Wonderfully. In fact, our engineers have given it clearance to go into mass production."

"Is that so?"

"Which brings us to the matter of *how* to manufacture it," Wil continued. "MPS was the natural choice, but they have declined the offer."

The Oracle scowled, his dark robes washing out the already pasty complexion of his ageless face. "Why?"

"Celine didn't offer an explanation. However, I received a nice warning shot—literally—as I was leaving. Needless to say, that relationship is finished."

"What have you seen of this in the pattern?"

Oh, here we go. Wil waved his hand dismissively. "Not every action has a deeper cosmic meaning. What are your thoughts on the core manufacturing?"

"This is not a conversation to be handled remotely. You should join us to discuss the matter in person."

Wil sighed inwardly. "I have a lot going on right now, Dahl. I'm afraid a trip isn't realistic."

"Come here to speak with us," Dahl insisted.

"This isn't a good time."

"You, of all people, understand how critical a reliable power infrastructure is to the health of the civilization. What else could possibly be a higher priority?"

It's not like the current power cores are failing across the board. We have plenty of time to roll out the new equipment. Wil was on the verge of voicing his rebuttal but decided against it. Past experience told him that Dahl's sense of urgency and timing was warped after living for more than twelve hundred years.

"Yes, you're right, Dahl. Can it wait until tomorrow, though?"

"Sooner is better. We'll send a ship to meet you at Bolhem Station."

Dahl ended the comm link.

I shouldn't have said anything to him today. I should have known. Wil groaned softly.

Meeting with the Aesir in one of their home bases always gave Wil conflicting feelings.

On the one hand, the Aesir welcomed him and were peers in the way few others in the Taran Empire could ever be. Their relationship with bioelectronic technology and ubiquitous Gifts made them easy to relate to. He felt understood by them, and that allowed him to relax in a way he couldn't around some people.

However, the Aesir lifestyle was also like stepping into another world. Their massive stations housing millions, encircling artificial stars, bent his sense of orientation. So much of his life had either been spent inside TSS Headquarters, which had no exterior reference points, or on a planet with a defined sky, that the notion of rotating around a central point—where 'up' was also down—that it messed with his perception. Whenever he visited a base, he found himself in a perpetual state of analysis that kept him from appreciating the comfort of being around other Gifted people like himself.

Part of that was by his own design. He recognized that giving himself the time to get comfortable with the surroundings would make the place feel more like home than anywhere else, so he was sure to keep the visits infrequent. The

Aesir had made it clear that Wil was welcome among them, and his children would be, but Saera and every other Taran he cared about were not. The distinctions for 'why' were stupid and infuriating, tracing back to the Aesir's feud with the Priesthood and decision to break off from the rest of the Empire. There was no changing their mind about it, so Wil didn't bother bringing it up anymore. They could invite him all they wanted, but he would never leave everyone behind—especially not his wife.

He reached out telepathically to Saera. *"Are you in your office?"*

"Yes. What's up?"

"Dahl wants to meet in person about the power core manufacturing. Right now."

Her annoyance came through full force in the direct mental link. *"You have to be kidding!"*

"I wish. I'll go over the course list in transit—I got through most of it on my way home from Tararia yesterday, so I should be able to finish up by the time I get home."

"All right. I'll gather up a few more things for you to look over. Swing by on your way out."

"I'd never leave without seeing you. Be right over."

Wil grabbed a travel tablet and checked that everything he needed for the TSS course review was saved to the device's onboard memory.

He left the High Commander's office and went the short distance down the hall to Saera's Lead Agent office. She came around to the front of the desk to give him a hug and kiss goodbye.

"Dahl is a great guy, but he really doesn't understand how much you have going on," Saera said as she held Wil at arm's length, gazing into his cerulean eyes.

"It shouldn't be too long. At least it'll be a faster trip than to Tararia. I'm meeting them at Bolhem Station."

"Try to get him to hand over their jump drive tech, while you're at it. I've been dying for us to have their transit speed for decades."

"Oh, I've tried. It wasn't in the Archive they gave us, and I don't know why."

"This so-called 'alliance' with the Aesir is confounding."

"Maybe this upcoming conversation can be the start of something good." He gave her another kiss. "See you soon."

"Safe travels. And good luck!"

Wil took a deliberate pace toward the central elevator. As he passed by Jason's office several doors down from Saera's, his son flagged him down telepathically.

"You look irritated. Everything okay?"

"Not sure yet," Wil replied. He detoured to the doorway of Jason's office. "Dahl has asked to meet with me."

"Didn't you just get back from Tararia?" He stood up behind his desk. "And is it really a good idea for you to be out and about after what happened?"

"I'm not in any danger with the Aesir. It's precisely because of how that meeting with Monsari went that I need to speak with Dahl now."

"Would you like me to go with you?" Jason asked.

Wil considered it for a moment; having backup would be beneficial for a number of reasons. However, he recognized that Jason was antsy, and that wasn't the right mindset to bring into any discussion with the contemplative Aesir. "I can handle this one on my own. Thank you, though. It's not that you're unwelcome there. Just—"

"I get it, it's okay." A little bit of a sigh slipped out.

I understand his frustration. Wil studied him. "We've had

the unknown hanging over our heads for a long time now. It's wearing on me, too."

"Why have the Erebus been so quiet? It doesn't make sense. And now Monsari is taking shots at you?"

"We don't know for sure that Monsari sanctioned that action," Wil said, though he suspected the family *was* behind it.

Jason crossed his arms. "Something is brewing, Dad. I can feel it."

"The Empire was thrown for a loop when the Erebus showed up. People have withdrawn to regroup and figure out how to proceed after such a major shift."

"I'm worried that our preparations won't be enough."

"You've been doing great work," Wil assured him. "Stay the course."

"I'm just anxious for the waiting to be over and to get to the action."

"Me too. I have a feeling that time is coming soon."

"And then we'll probably reminisce about this calm back in the good ol' days, huh?" Jason chuckled.

"The grass is always greener somewhere... or something like that." He gave him a wan smile.

"Good luck with the Aesir."

"I'll check in when I return."

"See you then."

Wil continued toward the central elevator, tablet in hand. *Jason's right—it has been too quiet. I wonder if that's what Dahl really wants to talk about?*

— — —

The TSS was facing both civil and transdimensional

threats, and Jason had to do everything he could to help them prepare.

In particular, his weaponized telekinesis students would be an important part of the TSS' response. They were nearing the final stages of their training, and he'd been waiting for the right moment to begin the next phase of their education.

If I don't get them ready now, it might be too late, he realized.

He checked the time; it was already too close to the scheduled class time to change the venue. After a quick stop by his quarters to grab his flight suit, he took the central elevator down to Level 11, where he proceeded to the large training room in which the telekinesis class was typically held. Standing on the padded mats in the center of the cavernous room, he stretched his back while he waited for the students; based on his protesting muscles, he'd been spending too much time at his desk recently.

In their usual fashion, the Junior Agent trainees began forming a semicircle around Jason as they arrived. They took the pre-class time to stretch in anticipation of the activity to come.

Limbering up was never a bad thing, but they wouldn't be engaging in one of their usual workouts today.

"It's time to change things up," Jason announced once the final student was present.

The Junior Agents exchanged intrigued glances with one another.

"Remember a few months ago when we toured the *Conquest*?" he asked, and they nodded. "Well, those talks about using bioelectronic interfaces to control weapons are about to come into practice. From now on out, no more floor exercises. We'll be training with tools to focus your telekinetic strength through other weapons." When they brightened further, Jason confirmed their unspoken question, "Yes, that means we're moving on to training in the IT-1s."

The Junior Agents stopped short of outright cheers, though their excitement was palpable. It pleased Jason to see them embrace the milestone; they'd worked hard for years to get to this point. Nonetheless, with the transition came a new level of responsibility.

Only a small number of Agents-to-be would ever embark on a training path like they were about to pursue. Craft like the IT-1 fighters were capable of feats beyond conventional armaments, making them both deadly and precise. Since the focused telekinetic assaults could cut through standard shielding, they were the single most effective offensive weapon in the TSS' expansive arsenal.

To train someone in the use of such a device meant showing a trainee the destructive side of their Gifts. Not everyone had the temperament to handle that kind of power— some found it to be too much responsibility, and others enjoyed it a little *too* much. Jason and his fellow instructors had the important job of identifying the students who were up to the challenge and weren't likely to abuse their power.

This particular cohort of Junior Agents had already been through significant tests of both skill and character, so Jason had no doubt about their suitability to the task at hand. Their present excitement was well-earned, but the next phase of their training was serious business and not to be taken lightly. His first lessons would be about reverence and discipline; that would set the tone for everything to come.

Jason held up his hand for the students to quiet down. "Since our training will be out in the black, I'd like to take today to refresh your skills in the simulators."

It was no secret among those who'd worked with him that he loved flying. This next phase of student training would combine two of his favorite things: piloting and advanced telekinetic feats. He'd been looking forward to it for months as the students approached the necessary skill level.

"As in, today?" Jimmy asked.

Jason motioned to where he'd placed his flight suit on the floor. "Yes. Though I was a flight instructor for some of you, I want to see everyone in action before we're in the real thing."

Paula grinned. "All right! I was wondering when we might get to put these new skills to the test."

"I hope you never need to use these abilities in the field, honestly. We train because we must always be prepared. However, as Agents, our goal is never battle. Whenever diplomacy is a viable option, it is—and will always be—the preferred route."

"Isn't force a more expeditious resolution in many cases?" Adam asked.

"Of course. But our power means that we must take extra care. We can use that strength against a formidable enemy, but where do we draw the line on who's threatening enough to warrant that action? It's a slippery slope. So, only after all other paths are exhausted do we move on to the use of force."

The students nodded their understanding.

With the moral groundwork laid for the lesson, Jason sent his students to get their flight suits and instructed them to reconvene on Level 2 in one of the training bays.

Jason went straight to the designated simulator room to configure the system for the lesson. He could recycle one of the scenarios from his advanced combat flight course, so the last-minute curriculum change for the day's lesson wouldn't pose an issue.

In the training room, twenty-one pods were arranged around the perimeter of the space, each a matte black oval hinged like a clamshell. On the right side closest to the door, the instructor pod was marked with a blue stripe to indicate its additional functionality. After donning his own flight suit, Jason got situated inside.

The pod's interior mimicked an actual fighter, complete with seat restraints, physical controls, and all the imaging augmentations a pilot would experience while flying the real thing. This particular training room was configured to simulate IT-1 fighters at the moment, though minor interior modifications could adjust the pods to represent a variety of craft. The critical feature was how the pods emulated movement, which varied based on the particular vessel.

Having spent significant time in the simulators as well as flying out in the black with students, Jason could pick up on what made a good pilot. This test would be enough to confirm that the students were flight-ready, but their real work wouldn't begin until they experienced the amplified power of an ateron-buffered telekinetic weapon for the first time.

Jason previewed a training course on the front screen of his pod while the students arrived and refamiliarized themselves with the flight controls. Once everyone was logged in as 'ready' on Jason's HUD, he initialized the immersive experience in his own pod.

It sealed, and the front screen transitioned to a breathtakingly realistic portrayal of a starscape. The holographic overlay on the control panel sprang to life, casting a cool blue glow in the replica cockpit.

While the main display perfectly imitated the flight interface for an IT-1 fighter, the augmented features of Jason's instructor pod included a representation of each student craft so he could track their performance. Selecting an individual craft brought detailed stats for an in-depth analysis. He'd go over those details later; for now, his primary concern was making sure the students wouldn't harm themselves or others on a real training run.

"Okay, here's the deal," Jason announced over the general comm channel. "You've all passed the intro courses, so I'm not going to go easy on you. The training we're about to do is about life and death situations—no sense dancing around it. If you can't handle it, you're out.

"Every one of you is going to make a great Agent, and the TSS has need for a lot of different skill sets. While I *hope* all of you take to these new techniques, some of you might not make the cut, and others might opt out. That's okay.

"This will be hard, because reality is foking brutal. No passes. No second chances. If you have what it takes, I will mold you into the best combat pilot I can. Now, we're going to dive right in."

Jason loaded the training course he'd queued up and previewed. It was a challenging scenario from an advanced combat flight course a couple of semesters back. Even skilled pilots could get tripped up with aspects of the mock mission, so it would make for a rigorous test of the students' skills.

"Once we start training out in the void, we'll be practicing with the TK weapons. For this engagement, you'll be using the standard armaments. Your mission is to rescue the friendly craft that has been seized by the enemy warship. Minimize casualties. Good luck."

He started the scenario.

The onscreen starscape momentarily warped as the enemy craft loaded into the environment. A large warship popped into the distance, surrounded by a sea of enemy fighter craft—

greatly outnumbering the twenty TSS vessels.

"Fok! Here we go," Lori said over the comm.

"Squad groups," Paula instructed.

Jason smiled to himself. *All right, nice start.*

He'd intentionally left out a command structure in his overview of the mission, wanting to see if they'd revert to the squad groups they'd most recently followed during training. For lack of contrary instruction, that should have been the default—and he was pleased to see it was.

The student craft broke into five groups of four, which curved away to take different approach vectors toward the enemy warship. Each squad had an assigned leader, and they'd need to coordinate their actions to be successful.

Jason tracked several conversations as the students switched over to separate comm channels for their squad, keeping the general channel open for inter-squad communications. The overlapping chatter from the different groups shared the consensus that they were at an extreme disadvantage in the scenario.

All by design. He sat back and watched the orchestrated chaos unfold.

In a real combat situation, the squads would report to a single individual. This scenario was designed to simulate conditions when the lead craft was disabled, leaving the different squads without their hub. In theory, each individual pilot was capable of taking over that coordinating command role; they were all soon-to-be Agents, after all. Jason wanted to see who among them would step up as the clear leaders.

The other critical aspect of the setup was the difficulty of the mission itself. The leader's craft had been seized by the enemy vessel and was being held in a grapple. This precluded any kind of barrage since the attack was likely to harm the friendly vessel. Instead, the TSS fighters needed to make targeted strikes in order to free their leader—all while fending off attacks from enemy fighters.

"Shite, we need to thin out these gnats before anything else," Paula said on the general comm, having taken command of B Squad. She used the common term to indicate enemy fighters.

"Target the launch tube so they can't get out reinforcements," Merith, the A Squad leader, instructed.

"C Squad is on it," Jon, the C Squad leader, acknowledged.

"Need to disable the jump drive, too," D Squad's leader, Cam, said.

"Go," Merith ordered. "B and E Squads, clear the path. A Squad, let's take out those turrets."

As the fighters dove into combat, the communications switched over primarily to the telepathic bioelectronic relays, offering faster coordination than spoken words.

Jason fell into the fluid rhythm of their exchanges, allowing the members of each squad to work as one while the group as a whole rallied against the superior enemy firepower. It was a dance of the most exquisite choreography—equal parts elegant and deadly.

The initial attacks went off as planned. C Squad threaded their way between enemy fighters to make a precision strike on the warship's launch tubes, hitting the port and then starboard access points. At the aft, D Squad sent several well-placed plasma blasts to damage the jump drive's prongs, preventing the ship from being able to form a stable spatial distortion to jump away from the engagement.

Meanwhile, Squad A was trying to get clear shots on the various railgun turrets and beam-weapon assemblies positioned on all sides of the warship. The IT-1's shields could withstand hits for short durations, but the constant fire from the enemy fighters would overwhelm them if they didn't get relief.

"There're too many of them!" Jimmy said over the private C Squad telepathic link.

"Going in! Cover me." His squadmate, Ellie, directed her craft toward a cluster of enemy fighters.

Hostile fire shifted focus to Ellie's craft as she broke away from the rest of the squad, making a desperate run toward their target.

Warnings flashed on Jason's screen, mirroring the alerts on Ellie's HUD. Her shields were failing. There was no escape path.

"Fok, they're all over me!" she exclaimed.

"We'll..." Jimmy started to offer, but it was clear there wasn't time to do anything.

Ellie's fighter was going down no matter what they did. She had a split second to decide if the enemy was just going to take her out, or if she was going to take a sizable chunk of hostile ships with her.

She activated the missile auto-targeting and released everything she had, sending a fan of ordnance to chase the speeding enemy fighters. As the missiles began clearing the path, she locked in a collision-course toward the main rail gun on the warship. She ejected.

The IT-1 fighter barreled toward the warship, gaining speed as it burned at full. It drew the enemy fire, shot to dust well before reaching its target.

Ellie was completely exposed in her ejected cockpit, careening through the battlefield. Ejecting was the smart move—better than the guarantee of getting blown up along with the fighter. It didn't change her fate.

"Shite," Jimmy swore on the private squad channel.

"We have our opening. Go!" Jon ordered C Squad.

Staying focused on the objective after losing someone was difficult. Jason was pleased to see them making the most of Ellie's sacrifice. Nonetheless, he couldn't help but wonder if she would have approached things differently if they'd been in a real engagement rather than a simulation.

The students continued their desperate run. Despite Ellie's ship having taken out half a dozen enemy craft in the course of its demise, they were still outnumbered.

The other squads had made a dent and disabled aspects of the warship's functionality, yet it was too large and too powerful to have been incapacitated completely. The combination of enemy fighters and the warship's onboard armaments proved too much.

A second student fighter was destroyed.

Then a third.

In a reckless move to gain the advantage, B Squad made a coordinated strike on the enemy fighters protecting the TSS lead ship held in the grapple against the warship's belly.

The well-intentioned strike decimated the targets—and sent the wreckage spiraling on a collision course with the hostage ship.

Rapid decompressions sent momentary plumes from the TSS ship as the debris struck. It wasn't destroyed, but close enough.

Jason terminated the scenario.

The front screen in the training pod changed to a readout of mission stats. Groans of frustration and disappointment sounded on the comms.

The mission itself was a failure. However, Jason had seen their flying and their attitudes toward combat when they were dealing with a faceless enemy—ships rather than hand-to-hand fighting, like they'd focused on in their training with him to date.

They can fly, and they're willing to take risks. I can work with that.

"I've seen enough. Shut down," Jason instructed.

They made the requisite shutdown entries and exited from the pods. The students lined up at the ends of their respective pods, flight helmets in hand.

Jason looked them over. Many of the Junior Agents had their gaze downcast with shame and others shifted nervously on their feet.

Good, they should feel bad after that performance. Strategically, it was a mess. Nonetheless, that wasn't one of the criterion for the test.

"You failed the mission," Jason said. "Quite terribly, in fact."

"I'll say!" Paula exclaimed. "We didn't rescue the captive ship. Not to mention we lost three of our own!"

"Yes, and that's the reality of battle. Not everyone always comes home."

An unbidden stinging heat of loss struck his heart. Tiff's sudden end still haunted him, and it likely would for the rest of his life. He'd come to terms with it, for the most part. Agents died in the line of duty all the time; he accepted that aspect of it for what it was. However, he couldn't—wouldn't—forgive the Erebus for their transgression.

Only, Tiff didn't die in battle. She was killed in her home. Jason swallowed. "Never go into an engagement thinking of 'acceptable losses'. We keep everyone safe, whenever possible. But, sometimes, there are losses we must accept."

The students nodded their understanding. It was a subtle

difference in wording, but it was an important distinction they'd do well to remember.

"However, the missteps today had nothing to do with your flying abilities, so we will proceed with TK training in the IT-1s," Jason announced.

Relieved sighs sounded around the room, though there were no smiles to be found.

"Don't think that gets you off the hook," he continued. "We're going to keep working this scenario until I'm satisfied that you've done everything possible to get a positive outcome."

The students nodded their understanding.

"It wasn't all bad, though. You worked together when it mattered, despite not having flown together as a unit before. One of the most important parts of being an Agent is that you need to be adaptable. Missions aren't handed to you with one clear solution." He looked around the glum faces. "Think about what you could have done differently. We'll alternate flight time and simulator practice until you get it right. Next class, convene at the surface port, suited up and ready to fly."

Jason knew he couldn't control what would happen to his students in their careers, or what future wars they might face, but he could help prepare them to face the darkness of their universe. That was within his control. And he'd do everything in his power to give them the tools they needed to make it home alive.

CHAPTER 4

THE WHOLE SITUATION with Monsari was infuriating enough, but now Wil had Dahl to deal with, too. Negotiating with the Aesir was one of the last things he wanted to worry about, but he'd need to find a way to strike a manufacturing deal today.

For all their 'divine mystic' style talk, the Aesir were awfully demanding and high-maintenance. Wil valued Dahl's friendship and the wisdom of the Aesir as a people, but some days he wished he could have a normal relationship with them where they could speak in straightforward language and he didn't have to dissect every statement for its hidden meaning.

Oh well. At least a face-to-face chat about this Erebus situation will quickly resolve the issue and we can figure out a path forward together. The flight over would give him a chance to turn around his sour attitude.

Still, he felt his frustrations with the Monsari Dynasty were valid. Beyond the personal assault on Wil, it was clear Celine wasn't acting in the best interest of her people from a business standpoint, but instead she was being willfully blind to the bigger picture. If there was one thing Wil couldn't stand, it was anyone behaving selfishly to further their own interests. That kind of behavior was all too common in business and politics— one of the reasons he avoided those interactions whenever possible. Everything in the TSS was mission-oriented, serving a greater good; he liked it that way.

All that he knew for sure was *something* was amiss with Monsari, and that meant a safety risk for the Taran Empire as a whole. MPS was too critical to the civilization's infrastructure to leave unchecked. The TSS, or perhaps the High Council, might need to intervene. Direct action against one of the High Dynasties would be tricky, but he didn't trust Celine one bit after his recent encounter.

They *needed* people who could be trusted in such pivotal leadership roles. Leaders who put Taran citizens first. Who were transparent in their decisions. Who had a moral foundation rooted in making lives better for those who'd never had a chance to get ahead.

Monsari had been rotting for a long time, but their proprietary product had kept them relevant. If that product was, indeed, going by the wayside, this might be a chance to mix things up. Wil had given Celine a chance to pivot the business and let their past interpersonal issues be bygones. She had not only rejected the offer but had taken an outright act of aggression in response. That made Monsari an enemy in his mind.

Wil would know soon how the Aesir felt about the matter. Their own infrastructure development needs were tied to MPS, so they had a vested interest in the situation regardless of their disdain for Taran politics.

The TSS transport ship dropped Wil at Bolhem Station, where it would await his return. Since the Aesir kept the precise location of their strongholds hidden, meeting at the station and having them escort him the rest of the way was the norm.

The Aesir ship was waiting when he arrived. Its smooth, sculptural lines gave the craft an almost organic shape, as if rivulets of metal had been poured into a riverbed. Like all other Taran craft, it had a forked assembly at the aft for the jump drive.

Wil approached the docking berth and was greeted by an Acolyte who worked closely with the council of the Aesir's Oracles. She had escorted Wil on several of his previous visits, so he gave her a friendly smile of recognition.

"Nice to see you again, Emara," he said. "How have you been?"

She bowed her head. "The grand patterns have favored us."

She's well on her way toward sounding like an Oracle, that's for sure. Wil wasn't sure how old the woman was, but she had the somewhat ageless look of those who'd undergone rejuvenation therapy. For all he knew, she might be into her hundreds.

"Thank you for agreeing to meet with me on such short notice," Wil said. *Not that I* wanted *to meet now, but better sooner than never.*

"The council is waiting to speak with you. Come with me." Emara bowed her head again before turning to ascend the gangway.

Wil followed her inside the transport ship. As he passed through the threshold, he sensed the familiar mental tug of the ship's bioelectronic interface system. The Aesir hadn't given him complete syncing ability with their vessels, but he was keyed into the systems enough to know a jump course was locked in and ready to initiate as soon as the vessel was far enough from the dock.

Emara escorted Wil to an observation room at the bow of

the ship, which had an expansive viewport spanning the length of the back wall. Within moments of entering the lounge, the view outside changed from the spaceport to an uninterrupted starscape.

A low vibration emanated from the deck, and time appeared to elongate for a moment as blue-green ribbons of light enveloped the vessel.

Wil's partial link with the ship was enough to let him know they'd arrive at their destination within fifteen minutes. He knew Emara wasn't one for small-talk, so he used the time to collect his thoughts.

Another moment of apparent time dilation marked the end of the jump. Rather than the typical view of a starscape, however, the view outside changed from subspace to the bizarre sight of a spatial rift—like an echo of normal space with warped representations of where stars and planets stood in normal spacetime reality. The rifts housing the Aesir strongholds existed in a habitable realm just at the edge of spacetime, bound by the same conventions but invisible to anyone outside the rift. It was the perfect hiding place, with the added benefit of enhancing abilities due to its slightly elevated position in the dimensional hierarchy.

More impressive than the rift itself were the structures the Aesir had constructed within the strange between-space. This capital city was the largest, or so Wil had been told. He took in the sight with wonder, still finding new awe-inspiring details even after dozens of visits.

The structure was an engineering marvel, among the most impressive he had witnessed firsthand. A massive, spinning ring served as the city's framework, offering centrifugal gravity rather than the simulated gravity found on most TSS stations, which made it a more sustainable habitat for off-planet life. In addition, a miniature artificial star at the center of the ring provided a light source to support the extensive green spaces wrapping the upper deck of the ring. Several glass-walled towers rose dozens of stories above the surface, from which one could observe a dizzying view of the 'ground' curving around to eventually become the 'sky'. Lower decks of the ring were filled with the residential and commercial services for the community.

The Aesir had several developments across different spatial rifts near the galactic core, based on what he had been told. Wil had never visited any others personally, and Dahl had been reticent about the specifics regarding the location and population of the additional communities.

As much as the Aesir claim they want to work with us and reunite the different branches of Tarans, they don't treat us like we're all the same—and we're not. Wil wasn't sure where that left them.

One look at the station the size of a small planet confirmed the Aesir had technological capabilities more advanced than those readily accessible to people on most Taran worlds. It wasn't that they couldn't understand the technical schematics or *learn* how to construct such things, but rather that the rest of the Empire was stuck in a rut regarding innovation. They'd achieved a comfortable balance between quality-of-life conveniences and cost—both in terms of labor and materials acquisition—so there was little incentive to try something new that might upset the equilibrium.

The Aesir, conversely, had been forced to make the most of very little. A mere two thousand individuals had left the Priesthood to form the Aesir, relying on their knowledge to maximize their limited resources. The resulting culture that had developed over the past millennium was now nothing short of astounding.

The ship docked on the lower portion of the massive ring in an area reserved for priority traffic. Though the Aesir's leaders didn't have many occasions to venture beyond the safety of their rift, the formality of their culture demanded positions of honor for their esteemed leaders.

Once the ship was docked, Wil descended the access gangway, where he was greeted by two additional Acolytes. The man and woman each bowed their head.

"Welcome back," the man said as his gaze rose to meet Wil's. "The council is waiting for you."

Wil politely bowed his head in response, even though he knew the escorts were of a lower station. "I look forward to the meeting."

A subtle shift in the Acolytes' stances was their only protest to his unbidden deference.

Emara joined them, and the three escorts led Wil through the port's broad concourses to an elevator.

The car smoothly raced upward as soon as the doors closed, with the changing view out the transparent back wall revealing the path. As it rose, the massive city sprawled across the broad ring receded in dizzying fashion.

As soon as the car glided to a smooth halt, the doors slid open to reveal four members of the Aesir's council of Oracles, led by Dahl.

"Greetings, Cadicle." His old friend smiled warmly. "I hope this day finds you well."

"We have our health, so there's that." Wil returned the smile and bowed his head to the Oracles. "Thank you for meeting with me."

Dahl held out his hand toward the conference room. "Come, let us speak."

Even after decades of visiting the tower, Wil had never gotten over the feeling of vertigo while stepping over glass block inlays on the floor, which provided a view all the way down to the ground two hundred meters below. He was well aware of the irony that he could do spins in a fighter at dizzying speeds without issue but walking inside a stable building dropped his stomach to his feet.

The conference room itself was a transparent dome cantilevered from the side of the building, like drop of dew on a glass blade. An oval table occupied the center of the room, accompanied by transparent plastic chairs well-suited to the airy space. Half of the seats were already occupied by the remaining members of the council.

Dahl took a seat at the far head of the table and the other Oracles took their customary positions, leaving the chair closest to the door for Wil. He detested having his back to the entry but tried to keep the thought to himself. Diplomacy was definitely a greater challenge in a room full of powerful telepaths.

Wil folded his hands on the tabletop. "I wanted to speak with you today because we're at a critical juncture. I'd like your opinions about how best to proceed."

Dahl nodded for him to continue.

"Since we received the gifted power core from the Erebus, the TSS has been conducting thorough tests of the device. We have been able to manufacture additional prototypes based on the provided plans, and those devices have successfully passed safety and functional testing. As promised by the Erebus, the materials needed to mass-produce cores are abundant and accessible. That leads us to the matter of *how* to scale up production."

Wil looked around the faces at the table. Their ageless faces were impassive, but their glowing eyes were sharp with calculated reasoning.

An electrical buzz filled the air—a telltale sign of telepathic conversation between the Oracles.

When no one offered immediate commentary, Wil decided to prompt them with a more direct question. "Taran politics are messy; you know that better than most. It goes without saying that the manufacture of these power cores has the potential to put MPS out of business, which could substantially shift the long-held power structure. That level of upset doesn't seem prudent, so I wanted to discuss the possibility of the Aesir—"

"No." The single word from Dahl hung in the room.

Wil leaned back in his chair, not sure how to take it from there. *Not even a discussion?*

He struggled to keep his annoyance in check. Dahl knew what Wil had wanted to meet about, so it was disrespectful of his time and authority to demand an in-person meeting only to shoot him down without exploring the issue in full.

"There's actually a compelling case for—" Wil tried again.

"No," Dahl repeated. "The Aesir cannot and will not involve ourselves in day-to-day matters of the Empire. Providing a critical infrastructure role would do just that."

I understand where they're coming from, but either we're working together or we're not. They can't stand on the sidelines and only participate when it's convenient for them. Wil met the gaze of each Oracle in turn. "I appreciate your reluctance to involve yourself in the affairs of the Empire, but the truth is that we need a more neutral partner on this initiative. Any existing political player within the Empire will gain too much power from this opportunity. You have proven yourselves to be rational and capable stewards, so..."

He faded out when Dahl held up his hand.

"Cadicle, we appreciate you holding us in such high regard for this role, but it is not a position we can take on," the Oracle stated. "However, we do have a recommendation for a group you may not have considered. The Lynaedans."

Wil's brows raised with surprise at the suggestion. *I had not thought of them, but that's an interesting idea...*

Like the Aesir, the Lynaedans operated somewhat independently from the rest of the Taran Empire, but not to the same extreme degree. Their primary reason for doing so was because of their strong inclination toward technology, going beyond 'use' by incorporating cybernetic components into their very being. The result was a number of cultural quirks related to openness and honesty that made relationships with non-modified Tarans challenging, though it actually made them exceptionally transparent business partners.

He considered the proposal, nodding. "An intriguing suggestion," he said at last.

"We understand that you have formed a working relationship with the Lynaedans while investigating a possible bioelectronic interface solution for those without Gifts to use certain technology in the information Archive we gave you," Dahl said.

"Yes, we have positive relationships with their leadership," Wil confirmed.

The Oracle tilted his head. "Why do you seem hesitant, then?"

"They're still closely involved in Taran commerce. The concern is that they might use the gift of this technology to leverage a position of power."

One of the other Oracles, Jayne, raised a slim eyebrow. "And the Aesir couldn't do the same?"

"You've made your position opposing such matters quite clear. Many with the Lynaedans are comparatively wealth-minded. I have tentative trust in their leaders, but I could see those among them seizing this opportunity for their own gain."

"There are risks in every transaction," Dahl stated. "We have taken the same gamble with you in many ways."

"I hardly think that's a fair comparison."

"A matter of perspective." There was surprising coldness to his tone.

Wil shook his head incredulously. "You don't trust me, after all these years and everything I've done?"

Dahl stared at him squarely. "You haven't followed through."

The statement caught Wil by surprise, and he shifted in his seat. "Regarding what?"

"You have the tools to get the Taran Empire back on the right track, and yet you have done nothing."

He couldn't help scoffing. "I think 'nothing' isn't giving me quite enough credit. I know I've been sitting on the technology Archive for a while now, but stewardship of that information is a responsibility I take seriously. I want to thoroughly evaluate everything before taking action." Given how the Aesir seemed to sit back and observe before intervening, he thought they would have admired his diligence, not condemn it.

He suspected the Aesir had given him the Archive as a test to see how he'd handle the dissemination of its contents among the Taran people. Wil had personally browsed through the information on multiple occasions to see what might be easy to implement, but even the simplest items came with potential risks or disadvantages. Many of the technologies could perform feats tantamount to miracles. Populations would skyrocket if people didn't regularly die from old age, and food and other resources would become more constrained as a consequence. Competition would be even fiercer. There was a lot to consider. So, instead, he had kept knowledge of the Archive within a trusted group until they could decide on a feasible path forward.

"The Archive does not hold all the answers. The threat of the Erebus has made this a time for action, but we have not seen you prepare."

"No disrespect, but you don't see everything I do."

"We do not," Dahl conceded, "but we know what we would expect to have observed on the Taran worlds if you were already doing everything within your power."

I can't win with them. They had regularly professed to Wil how they would defer to his leadership, but now they were criticizing him for not doing things the way they wanted. *If they have such strong opinions, they should do all of this themselves!*

He never wanted the responsibility that had been thrust on him.

"What, specifically, do you believe I should be doing that I'm not?" Wil asked.

"The Erebus can't be trusted," Jayne replied, "and yet you have embraced their offer as if it is a genuine gift."

Wil sighed. "I know, it does seem like that, but I haven't."

"You have plans to disseminate the technology to the Taran worlds."

"We first examined it and built it ourselves. It's safe."

Dahl exchanged glances with the other Oracles. "We are not convinced it is."

"What did you find in your own analysis?"

"Nothing that would indicate it is something other than what it appears to be."

"So what makes you question it?"

"We have foreseen it in the pattern," Dahl replied. "Have you not?"

"There's no way around the fact that we need this solution."

Jayne studied him. "It doesn't strike you as strange that the Erebus show up with this remarkable offer at the moment MPS' weakness comes to light?"

"Oh, yes, nothing about it sits right. Not one bit."

"Just because there doesn't appear to be anything nefarious about the tech, that doesn't mean it is safe," she said.

"I know. And I'll again ask, what do you want me to do differently? You've asked me, repeatedly, to follow my instincts and insist I'll know what to do in the moment. But now you're questioning me. This doesn't work both ways. Either you want me to take the lead and trust me, or you don't. If it's the latter—"

"We do trust you," Dahl interjected. "And we understand your reasoning. We do not mean to question your actions so directly."

"Then why am I here?" Wil was sick of dancing around the point.

"There are precautions that could be taken, as a contingency for if our respective worries about the Erebus' technology come to pass," Jayne stated.

He spread his hands wide. "I'm completely open to ideas."

The Oracles' eyes narrowed slightly in response to his somewhat brusque attitude, but Wil had exhausted his patience for the matter. Discourse, negotiation, planning. He would happily engage in lengthy conversations with the Aesir about the finer points of their technology policy. However, if they had a clear notion about how they wanted him to do something, then they should just *say it*. The endless riddles and deflection had worn him down. Perhaps this wasn't the best moment to voice that frustration, but it had come out all the same.

Jayne waved her hand, and the holoprojector integrated into the conference table sprang to life. She navigated to a map of the Taran Empire, noting the locations of the various inhabited worlds. "The Empire's territory is vast, but technological convenience overrides the safety offered by distance."

Wil nodded. "True, it's only a short hop to neighbors hundreds of light years away."

"Helpful if you are in a position to aid. Catastrophic in the face of aggression."

He wasn't sure where she was going with the explanation, but it was sounding dire.

"We've seen what these Erebus, as you call them, can do," she continued. "They can impact vast areas, but all beings have limits. The greater the reach, the more protected we will be."

"How does that factor into future plans?" Wil asked. "We can't very well move Taran-occupied planets to be further apart."

"No, the only thing you can control is where you install the alien technology."

"You propose only deploying it on select worlds, spaced apart, so if there is a surreptitious capability, its coverage won't be complete," Wil surmised.

"Yes."

"I understand the reasoning, but that's not a realistic solution. How could we possibly explain why some worlds are receiving such a massive security upgrade while others don't?"

"We don't involve ourselves in Taran politics," Dahl reiterated.

"Right, of course." *Give advice impossible to execute and step away.*

Wil had heard enough. "Thank you for the suggestion to pursue discussions with the Lynaedans. We'll look into that. Is there anything else you wanted to talk about while I'm here?"

"You seem upset," Jayne said.

There was no sense denying it. The Oracles were all powerful telepaths, and Wil would have a difficult time masking his true feelings even if he'd been making a concerted effort to do so. He'd learned long ago that being open with them was the safest policy. Unfortunately, what he had to say now would not be well received.

"It goes without saying that we haven't always seen eye-to-eye on all matters, but I like to think we've developed a good working relationship over the decades. However, compared to the other professional relationships I've had during that time, I don't feel like there's the same level of mutual trust here.

"Maybe it's because I'm so young compared to you—since your lives are measured on a scale unheard of in the rest of the Taran sphere. Or maybe it's an issue with *me* and my continued ties to the rest of the Empire. No matter the cause, it's frustrating to simultaneously be told that you are looking to me for guidance but then second-guess my every move.

"I don't have a suggestion for where to go from here, but I think something needs to change or these ideological divides will continue to grow."

Wil sat back in his chair, studying the expressions of those in the room. There was a hum of telepathic conversation flitting between them, though they gave no outward indication of what they were discussing or how they felt about his statements.

At last, Dahl spoke, "We appreciate your honesty. We will

consider how best to proceed."

"Thank you." Wil didn't have much hope for a major shift in the nature of their relationship, but at least he'd said what he wanted to say. He placed his hands on the table, prepared to leave. "Now, if there's nothing else, I'd like to get home so I can get back to work."

CHAPTER 5

SINCE JOINING THE Sovereign Peoples Alliance on his undercover mission, Leon Caletti's mood had been in a constant state of flux between boredom, disgust, and concern. As he faced yet another bland meal with his fellow investigators, looking forward to nothing but mundane tasks and irritatingly vague conversation, he knew that their days were numbered.

He plopped down his tray on the table and sat down across from Lexi, while Kira took the seat next to him. "Pleased to see they mixed it up with the orange gruel today."

Lexi poked at it with her spoon. "So deliciously cheerful."

Kira shrugged and dove in. "May as well get it over with as fast as possible."

"Yes." Leon took up his utensils. "And not just this meal."

The Alliance was no doubt up to shady business, and he disliked the idea of helping them in any way. However, he acknowledged that the Empire's law enforcement authorities needed solid evidence of wrongdoing in order to interfere in the private affairs of citizens. They were running out of time to get that information.

His fiancée, Kira, had been perhaps *too* eager to take on the covert assignment to aid in the investigation, but she'd always been one to run headlong into danger. He'd loved that about her when they'd met as teenagers on Valta, and he'd missed it greatly during their decade apart after she'd left without warning to join the Guard. When they'd reconnected a few years ago, he'd vowed to follow her anywhere so long as it meant never being separated again. Though he'd never expected that pledge to lead him into an undercover assignment like this, he had to admit it was a lot more thrilling than his years spent in a windowless research lab as a geneticist.

Nonetheless, his time in the Alliance had worn his patience thin. *We're not going to learn anything sitting here. Either we start asking the serious questions or we go home. Anything else is pointless.*

Kira met his gaze for a moment, gleaning his thoughts from the surface of his mind. *"I know. I think we'll have an opening soon,"* she replied telepathically.

Lexi leaned forward toward him. "Have you heard anything else about the new research thing?"

"Not yet."

Kira frowned. "As Leon has expressed to me, I think we're well past the 'listening' stage."

"We've been over that possibility and decided it was too dangerous," Lexi whispered.

"That was before."

Leon nodded. "I can try to push the issue with the researchers. No guarantees I'll get anywhere."

"Better to try than not," Kira insisted.

They quickly finished breakfast—no need to savor the food—and then parted ways to go to their respective stations.

Leon's assignment kept him in one of the building's basement rooms most of the time. Though referred to as 'the lab', the space lacked any equipment to make it suitable of the moniker. The other scientists on the team came from varied backgrounds and seemed equally hindered by the barebones facility. It'd been a revolving door of personnel, some sticking around for mere days while others had remained for a few months before disappearing. He wasn't sure why there had been such high turnover; perhaps some people hadn't demonstrated the skills the Alliance was looking for. Whatever he was doing, it seemed to be meeting their expectations.

To the dungeon cell, Leon thought as he entered the cramped lab.

It really did feel like a prison. They were being held, as a personnel resource, until they were needed—or deemed unworthy.

Let's see if we can move up that timeline for when I can be useful.

He didn't have many opportunities to interact with the management level of the Alliance, but every few days, Leon had seen his lab's supervisor, Claire, meet with the manager for his division—a beady-eyed man in his late-forties with brown, thinning hair. Based on Leon's observations, today should be one of their check-ins. If he timed it right, he could arrange a casual hallway interception just after the management meeting wrapped up.

Sure enough, an hour shy of lunch, Leon noticed Claire get up from her desk and go meet the senior manager in the hallway.

As silly as it seemed, Leon decided a fake restroom break would be the easiest cover. He knew the check-in meetings lasted about five minutes. That corresponded well with the typical roundtrip time from the lab to the restroom. So, as soon as Claire left, he followed.

Rather than *actually* going upstairs to use the facilities, he instead ducked behind a corner and tried to listen in, waiting for his opening. Frustratingly, he was just beyond earshot of the conversation, only picking up the occasional word or phrase; nothing useful jumped out.

Worse, the conversation was running long. By the seven-minute mark, his cover story was starting to look like it would need an adjustment to account for the delay.

Come on, wrap it up! he silently urged them.

The conversation continued in serious, hushed tones.

Leon checked the time on his handheld. More than eight minutes had elapsed; his coworkers would likely be wondering what was taking him so long.

Finally, the meeting wrapped up. Claire headed back into the room while the senior manager began walking in Leon's direction.

Leon quickly ran back several meters, traveling partway up the stairs, and then began casually descending the staircase as if just returning.

The manager barely glanced at Leon as he approached. That wouldn't do; he needed to strike up a conversation.

No opening words came to mind, and Leon's timed opportunity was about to expire. For lack of a verbal solution, he made a split-second decision to bump into the man at the bottom of the staircase, feigning distraction by his handheld.

With the skill of someone who was, in reality, quite nimble, Leon judged the contact and then collided with the manager just hard enough to call attention without causing injury.

"So sorry!" Leon exclaimed, slipping his Alliance-issued handheld back into his pocket. "It's easy to get lost in these scientific papers."

The man's severe brows softened. "Oh, you're one of the specialists?"

That went surprisingly well! Leon nodded. "Yes, genetics. My supervisor asked me to review some articles on the genetic component of Gifted abilities."

"Interesting stuff." The manager made to walk away.

Leon wasn't about to let the chance slip by. He went for it, all-in. "I heard you were looking for volunteers to help out with a new research initiative?"

"A call for volunteers? No. Where did you hear that?"

"Oh, uh, from a friend in the recruiting department. He thought it was the sort of thing where I could help."

"Why's that?" the man asked.

"I've conducted research on the biological components of extrasensory abilities and the transdimensional aspects of telepathy."

The man pulled out his handheld. "What did you say your name was?"

"I hadn't introduced myself, sorry. My name is Leon. Leon Caletti."

"Ah, yes," he said, scrolling through information on his handheld. "You have quite an impressive résumé. A doctorate in genetics? I don't recognize the school, though."

"University of Mysar, yeah. My home system was only brought formally into the Empire a couple of years ago. It's pretty remote."

"Ah, I see. It seems like you've worked on a lot of different types of research nonetheless."

Most of it isn't even in this document. Leon had to be careful what information he shared, since his most recent work had all been as a civilian contractor with the Tararian Guard. That wasn't a connection he wanted anyone in the Alliance to make.

Leon shrugged off the manager's statement. "Oh, I haven't done anything all that exciting. I'm just eager to put my skills to use for something other than pointless lab experiments that go nowhere."

"Well, like I said, we're not looking for volunteers for anything right now."

"Sure. Sorry for bothering you." Leon turned to go, not wanting to press his luck.

"Hey, if you have a minute…" the man began.

Ah, here we go. Leon spun back to face him. "Sure."

"I'd like to get your thoughts on a model."

"I'm happy to take a look."

The manager beckoned for Leon to follow him. To Leon's surprise, the path took them upstairs to the top level of the Alliance's building. He'd never been beyond the second floor, where the bunkrooms were located. He'd heard from others that there were administrative levels higher in the structure, though the rigid separation between the organization's different divisions meant that the area was off-limits. This invitation into the restricted floors might yield valuable insights.

Like the common areas below, the top level was furnished with simple, second-hand items, though the material quality was noticeably better.

Naturally, the leaders take the nicest things for themselves.

Given that observation, it was no surprise when they passed by several offices with glass walls along the hallway and expansive city views out the exterior windows. By contrast, his own bunkroom had a view of the dumpsters in the back alley.

The manager stopped at one of the well-appointed offices and motioned Leon inside. "Let me pull it up. Have a seat."

Leon waited patiently until the manager activated a portable holoprojector above the desktop, displaying a series of genetic models and other data that wasn't immediately discernable. He sat studying it for a long moment, waiting for the relevance to become clear.

"Is this genetically keyed tethering?" Leon asked at last.

A small smile touched the manager's lips. "Yes."

Leon looked over the information with greater interest. He'd heard theories about genetic tethering but had never seen a successful model presented. The practice was quantum entanglement, of sorts, linking two biological entities. As he understood it, the bond between Gifted people operated on a similar principle, though no one had been able to definitively present scientific documentation for precisely how it worked. The genetic tethering was a more exact science, using established cellular energy signatures as markers for the targeting.

What he saw on the screen, however, went beyond the hypothetical scenarios he'd seen modeled in research journals. This had markings of cellular infiltration and attack.

"This is quite a proposal," Leon said, not sure why he was being shown such sensitive information.

"You understand what you're looking at?"

"I believe so. Using a genetic tether as a delivery mechanism for a larger bio-hack."

The manager nodded, not giving a clear indication if it was the correct answer. "Thank you for coming by. I've taken up enough of your time."

What? That's it? Leon rose from the seat and bowed his head. "No problem. Let me know if you need anything else."

He returned to the lab, taking a slow pace to absorb as many details as he could about the offices. Little information of potential use was out in the open, but he spotted a couple of printed maps hung on a wall that seemed to indicate a sort of underground facility.

The rest of the day passed at an excruciatingly slow pace as he waited to share his findings with Kira. It wasn't until after dinner that the two of them were able to slip out for a quick 'check that no one took down the Alliance recruiting posters' patrol so they could speak freely.

They found a secluded area in a nearby park where Leon shared the news.

"Why didn't you invite Lexi along?" Kira asked.

"I thought you'd want to know first and see if you want to bring her in. I think they're working on some sort of bioweapon."

Kira's eyebrows shot up. "Like a virus?"

"That's what I'd originally thought. They gave me research to look over that seemed disease-like, but now things have started to go in a different direction."

"Which is?"

"It's difficult to explain, which I know sounds ridiculous since it's the bomaxed thing I'm working on. But it's weird stuff, and the tasks have been so discrete that I—"

"Breathe, Leon."

He took a deep breath. "Sorry, all this sneaking around is getting to me. I know I signed up for it, and all, just…"

"It's okay. You're doing great." She rubbed his upper arms. "Now, what about this research you're doing?"

"Right. Uh, the best way to describe it is that they are trying to isolate the part of the genetic code tied to Gifts—the telekinetic and telepathic abilities."

"The Priesthood did that already, and that's what mucked everything up."

"This isn't about the Generation Cycle. They're trying to go after the connection to the energy well on the higher dimensional planes that those people tap into to use their abilities."

"Are they trying to synthesize some means of Ascension, in the way the Priesthood was?"

He shrugged. "I don't know the endgame, but that's a possibility."

"How does that connect to the bioweapon?"

"I don't know. Maybe it doesn't."

Kira's brows knitted. "Regardless, does this new research have promise?"

"I think they're getting close to… something. The thing is, there's no known way to force the separation of consciousness from someone's physical being. We know from those rare few who can do astral projection that it *is* possible to disconnect the 'self' from the body, but it's something the person controls themselves."

"Not disconnect. Distance," Kira corrected. She had a lot more experience working with Gifted people than he did, so it wasn't surprising that she picked up on the distinction.

"Right. That 'distancing' without disconnecting is actually key. In the modeling we're doing for these genetic modifications, we're getting close to opening a more direct pathway for transdimensional energy flow at a cellular level. However, I can't begin to speculate about what this would mean for the interaction of consciousness and the body. Does only the mind 'Ascend'? Does the physical self go away?"

She nodded thoughtfully. "In any case, it's not something a group of rogue scientists should be working on without oversight."

"Which is why I came to you alone."

"And what about the bioweapon? In what way is it connected?"

"The mechanism for connecting to the higher dimension to draw energy. Whereas my previous research was about taking something from our dimension and elevating it, from what little I saw of the Alliance's research, it seems they are trying to create a vessel that can function as a tether—or avatar—in spacetime."

"Oh, shite." She paled. "Do you think they're trying to find a way to enable the Erebus to walk among us?"

"I don't know."

"You're right, this is bad. I need to talk to Jason."

— — —

Jason's heart lifted when his handheld lit up with an incoming voice call from Duronis. *Finally!*

The timing wasn't great, since he was in the middle of a lecture, but his flight students could wait.

"Sorry," he told the class as he picked up the device from the lectern at the front of the room, "I need to take this."

He rushed out into the hallway. Before the door had even closed, he accepted the call, not wanting her to hang up because it was taking too long. "Hey. How are you?"

"Oh, getting by," Kira replied.

Jason walked down the corridor toward one of the nearby study rooms where he could speak in private. "It's good to hear from you in real-time. I was getting worried."

"Yeah, sorry about that. Oren has ramped up his typical jerk-face, controlling tendencies, so I didn't want to call undue attention to myself when I didn't have anything useful to report."

"Makes sense."

"That's changed. We may finally have some movement—and I'm concerned about the direction the situation is trending," Kira reported.

"What's going on?"

"Those plans that the Alliance have been hinting at? We've learned that it involves a remote planet—but we don't know *which* yet."

"That's hardly an improvement."

She sighed. "I know. This whole thing is weird, Jason."

"Something else?"

"Leon is under the impression that the research they want to do is some kind of transdimensional tethering at a genetic level. That may or may not be connected to other research into some kind of bioweapon."

"Fok," Jason whispered under his breath. "That doesn't sound good."

"Funny you should say that—I thought the same thing!"

"It reminds me a little of the research the Priesthood was doing before their demise." He was hesitant to draw any comparison to that barbaric genetic experimentation and the Priests' attempts to 'ascend' to a higher state of being, but the parallels were too similar to ignore.

"I have a bad feeling about all this." She paused. "Jasmine has been logging everything, and the scenario models she's constructed based on the available data don't paint a pretty picture."

It was never a good sign when an Artificial Intelligence determined a worrisome narrative. Jason knew Jasmine, in particular, to be rather optimistic and upbeat for a sentient AI. From her position embedded inside Kira, Jasmine would be able to monitor and analyze everything Kira experienced, adding a crucial second layer of review to all observations. For both of them to be concerned, there was definitely a situation developing that would require the TSS' attention.

"What have you determined?" Jason asked.

"In broad strokes, it appears the Alliance is very well-financed, and whoever is behind it wants a territory in the Outer Colonies under their sole control," Kira explained. "That's no surprise, but what's recently popped up is the possibility that the TSS isn't the Erebus' sole point of contact among Tarans. This new transdimensional genetics thing is sending up all kinds of red flags."

Could the Erebus be working with the Coalition? The implications were disastrous. It would explain why communications had been so minimal since the standoff at Tararia. "Can you send those analyses my way?"

"Not via this burner handheld. Getting anywhere with a secure connection to download would be tricky. I can try—"

"No, don't risk it," he told her. "I think pulling you out might be the best option at this point."

"I'd like to stay under a little longer," she countered. "This Alliance office doesn't seem to have anyone from the larger Coalition involved in day-to-day operations—I've known that since very early on—but I've been looking for a lead about where to go to get the answers that we need. I'm convinced there's awful business at work behind the scenes here, with bad intentions for the Empire as a whole. I won't let that happen, and it's downright frustrating that I'm having so much difficulty figuring out where to take the investigation from here."

"The research planet may offer a new lead."

"I'm hoping so. If we can get them to invite Leon in, that could give us the entry point we've been trying to find."

Jason's chest constricted. "I'm not too keen on that plan. I was okay with him going in as a civilian because you were with him. If he takes that position, there's little guarantee that you'd be reassigned, too."

"He can look after himself."

"Kira, I know he's capable, but these people are dangerous."

"Believe me, I wouldn't suggest it if I thought there was any chance of him being in danger. He'll be in a research lab, or whatever. That's far away from the 'action'."

"I would still feel a lot better if you made the assignment be a package deal—either you go with him or he stays put."

She nodded. "Shouldn't be a tough pitch."

Jason pinched the bridge of his nose between his eyes. "Okay, try to sell them on it, but under no circumstances are you to let him go off on an assignment on his own."

"Aww, I think you're even more concerned about him than I am."

"And why aren't you?" he asked pointedly.

"Because I've been hanging around with these people for the better part of a year, and they've been all talk. Leon's my world. I wouldn't suggest anything where he might get hurt."

"Have you talked about this with your contact—Lexi?"

"Not in so many words."

"Well, let's not forget that her friend disappeared after she joined the Alliance, so these people might be capable of more than you've seen."

"True."

Jason hesitated. "Kira, don't take this the wrong way, because I hope you know I have tremendous respect for you—"

"I do."

"I don't know if you can be an impartial judge in this matter. I totally get it, because I struggle with the same thing. When you have unique abilities that set you apart from others, it can be easy to forget that those around you have different limitations. Even those we love and think of as superheroes."

She nodded. "I hear you. I guess it's been long enough since I got these nanites that I've started to forget what it was like before the upgrade. Jasmine agrees that you make a good point about taking unnecessary risks with Leon."

"His skills do offer a great potential entry point into other groups within the Alliance—or Coalition, or however they define themselves at that level. Just… be smart about it."

"Will do. At any rate, some careful questioning is in order."

"Yes. I hope you find something. I share your frustrations about the slow progress."

She groaned. "Right? I honestly thought I'd be in and out of here within a month."

"Clearly, there were miscalculations in that approach."

"No, it's more than that. I think something changed within the organization right around the time I got here. It's like everything went on hold while they sorted something out at the top and only now is the new leadership filtering down to the bottom levels of us peons. I still believe that entrenching and waiting it out was the best approach—as annoying as it's been."

"I can give you another two weeks, but then we need to have a serious conversation about extracting you if nothing has changed."

"All right. Either way, you owe me a good meal after this is over. The Alliance's cafeteria makes the Guard's mess hall look like fine dining."

"Sorry. I'll get you and Leon a special date night as a thank-you, I promise."

"Deal." She let out a long breath. "Okay, I should get back to it. I'll be in touch about whatever we can find out about this new research planet."

"Sounds good. Talk soon."

Even once Jason had ended the call, he couldn't relax. The part of himself that sensed shifts in the cosmic energy patterns tingled. Disruption was coming, and he had no idea how to stop it.

CHAPTER 6

RAENA SIETINEN REVIEWED the latest report from the Taran researchers working on Earth. The reports were an ancillary part of her oversight duties as the official ambassador for the Taran Empire to the newly rejoined planet, but she found the archaeological projects to be one of the most interesting aspects of her responsibilities.

"So, there really might be something there?" she asked Trevor, the liaison who'd furnished the confidential information she was now reviewing on her tablet.

"It appears so, my lady," the young man confirmed from her viewscreen. "It is still too early to say *what* it might be, but the properties observed at each site are too similar to be a coincidence."

Raena stared with wonder at the information in front of her. *Is it really possible that these sacred sites on Earth have ancient alien tech hidden beneath them?*

Such tall tales were the kind of thing she'd read about or seen on overly dramatic 'real-life mystery' shows during her youth on Earth. She'd found it fun to daydream about, but she had never considered it a genuine possibility. Of course, her perception of what was feasible had been radically altered when she'd learned about the Taran Empire. Even so, the concept that Earth may be hiding secrets that predated modern Taran history was intriguing and exciting.

"We've done everything we can from the surface," Trevor continued. "The next stage of investigation will require excavation."

"Do whatever you have to do."

He bit his lip. "There's a problem. The political situation is tricky."

Raena set down the report and focused her full attention on him. "Walk me through it."

"Well, we started the investigation under the guise of a resource survey, like we had planned. A, 'Hey, welcome to the Taran Empire's neighborhood, let's see what you have and how we can help you,' kind of thing. The us-helping-them scenario was easy to sell. But now that we need to *dig*, it's going to look like we're trying to *take* something."

Raena nodded. "I'd hoped we'd be further along with our diplomatic relations by now."

"You know how it's been for us onsite. I'm worried that with tensions already running high, the moment we try to break ground there's going to be a scene."

"It's imperative that we don't make waves." She paused in thought. "Let me make some calls. Hold for now; tell the team to take a little vacation and soak in the local culture for a few days while we get this sorted out."

"Yes, my lady." He bowed his head.

"Thank you, Trevor. I appreciate you being my eyes and ears for this."

"It's my honor."

"Talk soon." She ended the vidcall.

None of the news was unexpected, but Raena had hoped certain challenges would have worked themselves out before they reached this stage in the investigation. She'd done her best to lay the diplomatic groundwork, but certain government leader personalities on Earth had set back their progress.

The planet simply had too many political players for anything to get done quickly and without facing some form of opposition along the way. Even with the United Nations on good official terms with the Taran Empire, their influence was not absolute. Ultimately, setting up massive dig sites—especially near major international tourist attractions—was going to require the signoff of each country, and the request was almost certain to be denied unless a magnificently compelling reason could be given.

I didn't want to do this, but we don't have a choice. Taking a deep breath, she reached out to Ryan telepathically. *"Hey, are you available to meet?"*

"Wrapping something up. I'll be free in fifteen."

"Okay, I'll head to you."

She used the time during her walk across the Morningstar Isle estate to her husband's office to prepare potential solutions to forthcoming problems.

Opposition was a given. Everything related to Earth and the larger political concerns throughout the Empire had set the Taran leadership on edge.

Ryan, in particular, remained in a delicate situation as the youngest and least experienced dynastic Head. Through her role as a diplomat, Raena had been positioning her wins as accomplishments for them as a couple, building goodwill and favor wherever possible. This latest situation had the potential to undo all of that progress if it was handled incorrectly.

By the time she reached her husband's office, Raena had formulated a plan and how she was going to sell it.

Ryan beckoned her into his office when he saw her in the reception area.

Raena smiled as she closed the glass door. "How's your day going so far?"

"Not bad." He combed his fingers through his dark hair. "We finally got the quotes for the autonomous robot welders from that other vendor on Lynaeda. Thirteen million, but the increased capacity compared to the bots spec'd in the bids out of Beurias should pay for itself within five months."

"Can't argue with that return." She strolled to one of the plush visitor chairs facing the desk and took a seat.

"My thoughts, as well. The rest of the board agrees."

"Good. One more thing to check off the list."

He studied her. "As happy as I am to see you midafternoon, I imagine there's a reason for this visit?"

"Yes. Unfortunately, we've hit a roadblock with Earth."

"I'm not surprised." Ryan leaned back in his swivel-chair. "What, specifically?"

"The need to excavate." She rearranged the skirt of her dress as she crossed her legs.

"Ah, of course. And the government officials aren't too keen on letting aliens root around for no clear reason?"

"You've got it. But it's more than that." She paused. "Over the last year, I've watched a lot of footage about the protests in the Outer Colonies—Duronis, Naevo, Erosaen, and all the other places. And now we're seeing it on Earth."

"Humans aren't that different from us," Ryan said.

"No, but I grew up watching the news on Earth. The way people respond. Something about this seems… different."

"The galaxy opened up to them, Raena. It's natural that

Earth's citizens would react differently now that they know they aren't alone in the universe—and especially while we're snooping around on their planet."

"Maybe that's all it is." She wasn't convinced. "I don't know. The rhetoric reminds me of the anti-Tararian government messages in the Outer Colonies. They're calling our presence on Earth an 'invasion' or 'occupation'. It's pressuring the political leaders to take a step back. Seems to be a planet-wide sentiment now."

"You might be reading too much into it. I didn't want to be overly pessimistic before, but I expected there to be a bigger scene when you were making first contact—or at least immediately afterward."

She drummed her fingers on the chair's armrests. "Honestly, I'd expected a bigger reaction then, too. I guess I should be happy that the peace lasted longer than we expected."

Ryan nodded slowly. "Your approach of stunning everyone worked."

"Until the shock wore off. And now they're wondering if we're an enemy in disguise."

"The people on Earth have every right to freak out about alien contact. And to be angry that we didn't help them sooner, and all that. Even so, on the planetary scale, they have everything to gain from befriending us and making sure that the relationship goes smoothly. Unrest at the local level? Sure. But as a *planet*, there's not a lot to be gained from protests."

"That's why this new situation is concerning."

"I must admit, coupled with the timing, it *is* strange," he said. "Seven months is quite a while to wait before getting up in arms. And it's also odd that the situation on Earth is beginning to deteriorate just when the protests are ramping up on the other worlds again."

"I have this sinking feeling that it's connected." Raena shook her head. "First the protests, then the media campaign, and now my Dad getting shot at…"

Ryan bit his lower lip. "I can't rule out the possibility that the same organizations behind the disruption on Duronis and other planets might be trying to take advantage of the tenuous situation on Earth."

"Maybe. But *why*? What would they hope to gain?" Raena's brows drew together in thought. It didn't make sense. *Unless…* She met her husband's questioning gaze. "Wait, what if this has something to do with the alien tech we're trying to find?"

"Isn't that a bit of a leap?"

"Maybe not. We know there were Tarans searching for the Gate tech. We took out Victor Arvonen, but others were no doubt working with him—and it's *possible* that those people are connected to the Coalition. After all, we know that the Coalition is very well-funded, and a Lower Dynasty like Arvonen would certainly have had the financial resources to fund the Coalition's operations."

"That's true," Ryan said. "And the ancient treaty referenced Earth, so if this group heard about that, it's conceivable that they'd want to investigate the planet for themselves to try to get their hands on more alien tech."

"Could they be manufacturing this civil unrest as a distraction?" She thought through the possibility.

The logistics of it were tricky. Not many Taran ships had visited Earth, so organizing worldwide protests would be difficult. However, as the unrest accelerated, more Taran ships had been deployed to help strengthen interplanetary relations. Insurgents could have slipped in.

They exchanged concerned glances.

"We can't let the protests deter us," Raena said. "*We* need to get access to that hidden tech before the shadow faction—if they are, in fact, after it."

"You can't just go in there and start digging without permission. That would make us the invaders they claim us to be."

"I know." She smoothed her skirt over her thighs. "I've been thinking it through, and I have a solution, but no one is going to like it."

"Isn't that what your dad said when he suggested bringing Earth into the fold?"

She smiled. "Yes. And he was right."

Ryan braced. "What do you have in mind?"

"I think we need to tell Earth's leaders the truth."

"About…?" His face dropped. "You don't mean the Erebus?"

She nodded. "We can't build future relations on a lie. Conditions are already unstable, and that would be the end of it. I can't think of another excuse for why we need to do so much underground investigation."

"Can't we just say we're doing… 'restoration'?"

Raena raised an eyebrow. "By digging up some of the most revered sites in human history?"

"Not my finest suggestion," he admitted. "But there has to be *something* we can say other than, 'We've been semi-invaded by a race of transdimensional, god-like aliens, and we think you might have something hidden on your planet that can help us fight back'."

"That's not exactly how I'd put it." She leaned forward, "But think about it. Nothing sounds cooler than 'we're fighting a powerful enemy and we think Earth holds ancient secrets that could win the war'."

He squinted. "Is 'coolness appeal' really the issue here?"

"No, but yes. What's a more universal trait than the desire to feel valued? What the truth—or a version of it—offers is a genuine way to make my little backwater homeworld feel like the most valuable planet in the entire Taran Empire. Moreover, the individual nations of Earth will all want to be the special ones offering this incredible solution."

"Are you sure it will work that way?"

"Can never be certain about these things, but I think it has a better shot than other approaches."

He nodded slowly. "Okay, I'll run it by the High Council."

— — —

Jason anticipated the meeting with his father before the official summons came. He'd been keeping an eye on the spaceport activity to see when his father's transport ship returned, and he was ready to head to the High Commander's office the moment Wil stepped foot on Level 1.

As suspected, his father beckoned to him as he walked by Jason's office. "Let's debrief."

To his surprise, though, his mother wasn't anywhere to be seen.

"She's tending to some trainee issues at the moment," Wil replied to Jason's quizzical look. "It's okay. I can catch her up on the situation later."

They settled into the High Commander's office in their customary seats.

"So, how'd it go with the Aesir?" Jason asked.

"A nonstarter, in many ways. Just when I thought we were going to begin properly working together, they pulled back. I wish we had more reliable allies."

Jason shrugged. "They haven't outright betrayed us, so there's that."

"True. They have always shown up when we've needed them the most." His father shook his head wearily. "Still, it feels like a lopsided relationship when I know for a fact that they're holding back."

"It's annoying," Jason agreed. "I don't know what to suggest."

"At this point, I'm going to wait for them to come to us. Like any relationship, the interest needs to be mutual if it's going to work. I won't keep chasing them."

"Fair."

"There is another tentative ally we've been neglecting," Wil continued. "The Aesir suggested we approach the Lynaedans about the power core matter."

"Hmm, that's an intriguing proposition." Jason thought back to his previous dealings with the Lynaedans. Like the Aesir, they were somewhat insular and regarded themselves as a distinct branch of Tarans. However, the Lynaedans were still full members of the Taran Empire in all respects, which made for a complicated dynamic.

"You're probably the most acquainted with them of all the senior Agents at this point," his father said. "Do you think they'd be open to discussing a manufacturing deal?"

"Not if it's presented that way. They don't like the idea of being a contractor working for someone."

"How, then, do you suggest we approach this?"

The Lynaedans were regarded as the 'tech heads' of Tarans, embracing all manner of cybernetic modifications and artificial intelligence. Many of their advancements could be seen throughout the Empire in everyday medical technology, starships, and communications consoles. Most notably, they were the only subculture within the Taran sphere to actively cultivate new sentient AIs, which had proved to be vital allies for various research and military endeavors. Likewise, Lynaedans had developed the original CACI non-sentient computer intelligence commonly found as a central operation system on ships and within facilities, which had been modified into several 'clone' lines with various specializations.

They were a brilliant people, but they didn't hold outsiders in high regard. Jason had been nurturing a handful of contacts within the Lynaedan leadership for the past two years, but he couldn't call any of them more than professional acquaintances. However, any 'in' was better than nothing at all.

"We need to frame any deal with the Lynaedans as a partnership," Jason said. "Deception doesn't go over well. If we want their help, then we need to lay it all on the table."

"I'm not keen on sharing the details of our military position with a group of civilians," his father replied.

"They've been reliable throughout our collaborations on bioelectronic interfaces. This is an opportunity to build on that foundation."

Wil nodded. "You seem to have a good handle on the situation. Would you be willing to take point on this?"

"With what, specifically?"

"Negotiating a production deal with the Lynaedans—and, potentially, further research into the Erebus' power core technology."

Jason's pulse quickened. "I'm flattered, Dad, but negotiating those kinds of deals isn't really in my wheelhouse."

"I know for a fact that you took numerous contract law courses as a part of your Agent training, and you received very high marks in all of them."

"Well, yes." Jason didn't have a good comeback to that.

Obviously, class assignments weren't the same as being in the field, but saying as much would be tantamount to asserting that the TSS Agent training program wasn't sufficient to prepare its graduates for real work. He didn't believe that in the slightest, so it was only reasonable to hold his own training in equally high esteem. *It's all about confidence. I know what to do. I just have to do it.*

When his father continued looking at him expectantly, Jason yielded with a nod. "Okay, I'll take the lead. But, it would be great to have someone come along who can provide an experienced set of eyes on the documents accompanying the deal. And you know the tech better than anyone, so I'll leave the design review to you."

"Of course. I'll find someone from the Legal team to accompany you who can sit in on the meetings and review everything."

"Sounds good. I'll do my best."

Wil looked him over, his hands folded on his desktop. "What happened, Jason?"

"What do you mean?"

"When you were younger, you were always confident. Oftentimes, overly so. Now, you seem to frequently second-guess yourself."

"I realized that bravado was overrated."

"It's more than that. You seem… unsure."

Jason stared at his hands in his lap before shifting his gaze up again. "We're not as strong or powerful as we like to tell ourselves. There's no reason for me to blindly think that I can do everything." He'd learned that the hard way recently as he'd helplessly watched Tiff killed before his eyes. *We can only do so much.*

His father softened. "That's true, in many ways, but

maintaining humility shouldn't mean doubting the skills you know you possess."

"Negotiating alien power core production deals is *not* my expertise."

"Granted, this particular situation might not be the best example," Wil admitted. "The fact remains, though, that you've been exhibiting more doubt in the past several months than you did in all the years leading up to now. I had expected a rough patch after what happened with Alkeer, but I'm getting concerned that you're not moving past it."

An unexpected flush of resentment surged through Jason. *'Moving past it'? I lost my best friend!* He managed to bite back the initial reaction and remain silent, but he could feel the heat on his face.

"I didn't mean it like that," his father hastily said, clearly picking up on the shift in his mood. "I know better than most how some scars linger. However, it's important to recognize when something is keeping us from moving forward."

"I don't know what to say to that, Dad. I got slapped in the face with the fragility of life. How is it not a *good* thing that I'm more careful and considerate now?"

"You're right, that is a natural consequence of growing up. I appreciate that transition in your outlook, and it does ultimately make you a more seasoned officer."

"Okay, then."

"Nonetheless, there's a difference between being realistic and pessimistic. You must remain objective about your capabilities without being unduly self-deprecating—and I assure you, you're a more capable negotiator than you're giving yourself credit for."

Jason tapped the armrest of his chair. "If you say so."

"I think this Lynaedan mission will be good for you. A

chance to hone different skills, and maybe you'll discover some things about yourself in the process."

He appreciated his father's attempts at a pep talk, but this one wasn't going to land, no matter what was said. Once Jason's mood soured, only time would bring him out from the funk. "All right. Send me the specifics about what you need from the agreement, and I'll try to make it happen."

"I know you will."

With his orders in hand, Jason left his father's office to prepare for a visit with the Lynaedans.

Showing up at the planet with zero warning wasn't advisable, so Jason elected to put in a call to the planet's government representative. His relationship with her wasn't particularly longstanding or deep, but she'd never refused to speak with him when requested. Those previous communications with the Lynaedans had been an important mission at the time, but the stakes paled now in comparison to what the Taran Empire was facing.

Jason's first interaction with the Lynaedans had been two years prior, where he'd gone to meet with the reclusive group of Tarans about getting their help to design and manufacture a new line of bioelectronic interface devices. The Aesir's technology Archive contained numerous devices intended to function in concert with telepathic abilities, which limited their application. By working with the cybernetics-savvy Lynaedans, the TSS had hoped to develop an interface solution which would allow non-Gifted people to interact with the technology, as well.

While most modern Tarans had moved away from having physical modifications to their bodies, the Lynaedans had leaned heavily into augmentations, blurring the line between biology and machine. Back on Earth, Jason would have called them 'cyborgs', but his limited interactions with Lynaedans had shown them to be creative, life-loving people who viewed their physical changes as an extension of their true being.

He appreciated their perspective, even though it didn't align with his own. Maintaining a level of physical autonomy was something he valued, so modifying his physical self to be in constant contact with wireless technology links was counter to those ideals. In discussions with his parents he'd learned that was a widespread philosophy among many Tarans—that technology was a necessary convenience, but it should be viewed as something that could be set aside at a moment's notice. To make that technology more integral made it more than a tool, and that threatened to overthrow the natural balance and sense of self.

In Jason's dealings with the Lynaedans, he'd learned that they actually considered technology to be a means of keeping themselves more open and honest with each other. Their augmentations allowed them to detect deception more readily and to be in a constant state of connection with others' perceptions. 'Truth' was easy to discern under such analytical circumstances.

Meanwhile, other Tarans could lie to each other, and they didn't have any skin temperature sensors, or heartrate monitors, or network-monitoring software to keep those around them honest. That made surreptitious dealings common, and the Lynaedans wanted nothing to do with perpetuating that standard. So, the Lynaedans kept their distance from most other Tarans, only interacting with those who'd proven themselves to be honorable.

Those cultural quirks would make this negotiation surrounding the Erebus' power core a challenge, but Jason was cautiously optimistic that the goodwill he'd gained through his previous work would at least get him a fair audience to hear out the potential deal.

Jason settled on the couch in the living room of his quarters and placed the call.

After several seconds, the screen resolved into a video stream of a dark-haired, middle-aged woman, her mouth set in a pensive line.

"Hello, Ambassador Greggor. How have you been?" Jason greeted.

"Agent Sietinen, I'm surprised to hear from you. I am well," she replied. "To what do I owe this call?"

"I'd like to meet with you to discuss a new collaborative opportunity—to expand upon our relations of sharing technology."

She tilted her head slightly. "An intriguing proposition."

"One best discussed face-to-face. Would you be available for me to make an impromptu visit?"

The ambassador momentarily got a faraway look in her artificial, silver-irised eyes, which Jason knew from experience was an indication of her communicating with others through the shared neural net.

"Yes, we will speak with you," she said after a several second pause.

"I'll head over now, if that works for you. I can be there in six hours."

"That is agreeable. We will see you then."

Jason ended the call. *Now I just have to convince them to make this deal.*

— — —

A tight knot of anxiety had settled in Lexi's chest. All

morning, as she worked at her desk on the ground floor of the Alliance office, she hadn't been able to shake the feeling that everything was falling apart. Her thoughts were focused on Kira's and Leon's recent behavior. *I thought we were a team. What was so sensitive that they'd keep me out of the loop?*

She was certain Leon had learned new information that he had only shared with Kira, and they hadn't told her for whatever reason. Lexi couldn't blame them for keeping some things to themselves; after all, they were on an official military-sanctioned undercover assignment while she was just an informant. That meant that whatever he'd found out had important implications.

Even though she understood *why* they might keep something from her, she didn't like it. The three of them had become genuine friends over the past several months—or so she believed—and that relationship had been a key part of her staying sane within the cultish Alliance. If they no longer considered her an equal collaborator, she might once again be on her own when it came to finding out what happened to her friend Melisa. She wasn't about to rely on them if they didn't fully trust her.

That left her in a tough spot. Lexi had become somewhat lax in her own investigation, deferring to Kira's lead as an undercover Tararian Guard officer. This new indication of being pushed to the outskirts of the search reminded her that she needed to be proactive in her own efforts.

Perched on the stool in front of her workstation, Lexi's leg shook with nervous energy. She'd tried to control the tick, but she needed an outlet for her anticipation or she feared she might explode.

If Kira and Leon have a lead, this might be over soon. But if they learned something about what may have happened to

Melisa, then why didn't they tell me?

The truth was, the breakthrough probably had nothing to do with her missing friend. If they *had* learned key information regarding her whereabouts, Lexi would like to think they would have mentioned *something*, even if the details were classified.

If they've had a breakthrough, we might not be undercover for much longer. If I don't find out about Melisa now, I might lose my chance. The thought was sobering.

Lexi's sole motivation for joining the Alliance in the first place had been to find Melisa, and it was only once she was embedded in the organization that she'd learned there were much bigger issues than a single missing person. While she supported the TSS' and Guard's efforts to root out the organization's leaders and put an end to their dangerous activities, she couldn't abandon her original goal.

I won't give up finding out what happened to her, she vowed. *Once the TSS seizes this Alliance office, I'll lose the only lead I have.* Her friend meant too much to her to leave it to chance that the larger investigation into the Alliance's activities would result in a clear answer about the fate of a single person. That was information she'd only trust getting on her own.

The problem was *how*. She'd already been trying to get to the bottom of that mystery for a year. Granted, she'd been excessively careful—passive information-gathering rather than conducting a true investigation.

With time running short, she could no longer afford to be tentative. It was now or never.

Lexi stood abruptly, energized with renewed determination to discover the truth.

She'd been scared, and the fear had made her passive.

No more.

Her abilities gave her an edge. She'd hidden them for so long that the thought of using them felt like discussing the skills of another person. But it was her. The *real* her.

Staying quiet and playing along wouldn't solve anything. She'd convinced herself that joining the Alliance was a 'big move', yet it was just another kind of running away—like she'd always done when faced with opposition. This time, she'd run *toward* the problem, but she'd done absolutely nothing to solve it. It'd been a year of sitting around, doing little other than *help* the very people she'd set out to stop. Her single act of sabotage didn't make up for her complete lack of engagement in all other respects.

No more being afraid. I need to take a risk. She placed her hands on her desktop, leaning against the rough, wooden surface.

One row over, Shena looked up from the monitor on her own desk. "What are you doing, Lexi?"

With a sudden rush of awareness, Lexi realized how odd her behavior must seem—staring off into space, her expression set with battle-ready determination. She made a conscious effort to relax her pose while she thought up a cover story.

"Sorry," she replied, "I've been struggling with the best approach for this new marketing campaign, and I'm trying to get inspired."

Shena raised an eyebrow. "It looks like you're more likely to murder the idea before it forms."

"Just striking down the bad concepts before they can take hold." Lexi pushed off from her desk, looking around the room. "I think I need a change of scenery to get the creative juices flowing. I'll be back."

"Good luck." Shena returned to her work.

Lexi hadn't intended to leave her workstation, but this was

precisely the kind of nudge she needed to spur herself to action while she was fired up. However, since she had no plan in mind, she would need to wander until a course of action occurred to her; at least her spontaneous cover story fit.

She set her attention to figuring out a strategy while she roamed the halls.

The only people within this Alliance office who might have answers were the senior managers working on the upper floors. Oren was an oddity among the leadership, spending most of his time in his basement office—perhaps because of his oversight related to the supply inventory stored in the underground tunnel network. All other leaders, as far as Lexi knew, resided almost exclusively on the facility's upper levels; even their meals were taken in a separate cafeteria, which was rumored to serve much better food.

Getting access to those supervisors would be a challenge. Lexi had no reason to go up to those higher floors in the building, and the managers had few reasons to come down.

Unless… An idea slowly formed in Lexi's mind.

A novel situation might draw management's attention. Such an occasion might also have the senior managers distracted enough to allow for light-touch mind-reading without anyone taking notice.

But what kind of distraction could I orchestrate?

Kira or Leon might be able to offer ideas, but Lexi was only taking these steps because they had cut her out of their process. They'd probably try to sideline her if she told them her intentions.

No matter what she did, she'd need to be extremely careful. The Alliance detested Gifted people, and it appeared anyone who was revealed to possess those abilities might find themselves in danger. She suspected that her friend Melisa had unknowingly been open about her Gifts, as Lexi knew her to be, and that might be connected to her unusual disappearance.

Lexi had taken opportunistic telepathic readings before, whenever she'd found herself in a situation with little chance of discovery. The problem was that people weren't generally thinking about the topics of interest. Mid-level managers didn't sit around musing about evil master plans; they lamented a boring lunch and longed for relaxation time in the evening. While a telepath *could* access deeper information buried in a person's mind, that required a more invasive approach that exponentially increased the likelihood of detection.

I need for them to believe there's been a leak of their plans, Lexi realized. *Get them thinking about the information they want to keep hidden.*

Conceptually, she liked the idea. Putting it into practice would be much more difficult.

Lexi wandered toward the office's main lobby, where there was the most foot traffic of anywhere in the office; it also connected to the main stairway that led to the upper floors. If she was going to happen across a good lead to jumpstart her new investigation, it would be here.

She scanned the room, looking for anyone dressed a little nicer whom she didn't immediately recognize. Unfortunately, no one jumped out right away.

Standing there watching people would get her unwanted attention, so she took a seat on one of the wooden benches along the wall and pulled out her handheld, pretending to be working. Though her gaze was fixed to the screen, she allowed her mind to roam, gleaning telepathic impressions from the passersby.

After five minutes, an intriguing thought snippet caught

her attention.

"...Transportation orders. Pending final staff list..."

The thoughts stood out from the buzz of other mental conversations of those around her in the office. Though the statement itself could be about anything, the *feeling* of the words gave it significance. This person was working on the staffing for the new research lab. She sensed it in her core.

She latched onto the person's mind and traced the thoughts back to their origin, blocking out the mental din from the other people in the vicinity. Her focus settled on a middle-aged man with intense dark-brown eyes and graying hair, dressed in slacks and a button-down shirt that seemed too formal for the work within the Alliance.

In a stroke of good fortune, he was coming down the staircase from the upper level, heading outside. That would make it much easier to follow him than it would have been if she'd needed to invent an excuse to head upstairs.

As the man reached the bottom stairstep, Lexi rose from her bench and turned away, still focusing on her handheld. She traced his movements with her augmented senses, as if she'd tied an invisible thread to him.

Keeping a dozen meters back, she followed him out from the building and onto the busy street. The telepathic thread made him easy to track, despite her not having a clear line of sight.

More thought snippets came to her. *"...Check the inventory with Oren... Arrange for transfer."*

Most likely, he was running through a mental checklist of tasks. While it indicated he was the right person to talk to, she'd need a deeper delve in order to learn where the new research planet was located. Even a name would go a long way.

Unfortunately, while he was alone with his own thoughts,

it would be quite obvious if she tried to telepathically direct his thinking toward her desired answers. For optimal covert mind-reading, he'd need to be slightly distracted—such as engaged in idle small-talk.

Lexi followed him along the street, waiting for an opportunity. After ten minutes of darting through foot traffic on the sidewalk, the suited man turned onto a side street Lexi knew well; it was a back way to the transit port.

If they need to get people offworld, that makes sense. Despite being an integral piece in the mystery she was trying to solve, the revelation did little to calm her nerves. The circumstances were looking less and less hypothetical. Real people's lives were on the line.

The man checked over his shoulder as he stepped onto the side street, prompting Lexi to quickly duck aside, out of view. She gave it several seconds, then followed him, darting behind cover whenever possible.

Half a block down the side street, the man stopped and knocked on an unmarked metal door.

Lexi took up position behind a dumpster and pulled out her handheld, to give the appearance of someone checking directions.

The door creaked open. "Hey. You have the manifest?" a woman asked with a brusque tone.

"Yes, we're ready."

This was as good an opening as Lexi would ever get. Though her training wasn't sophisticated, she'd had enough to know her abilities were above-average. She'd need every bit of that innate talent to invade his mind undetected.

She carefully reached out to glean the thoughts on the surface of the suited man's mind. Despite the promising conversation he was having out loud, she was met with only thoughts of dinner, a sore back, and lamentations about a lost game of Fastara.

No! there has to be something in here...

She dove in deeper, peeling back the layers of his memory. There was a flash of a ship port, and then a metal briefcase.

Getting closer...

A corner of his mind was walled off. The secrets he was trying hard not to discuss out loud. It would seem his present contact didn't know the whole story.

Lexi had no choice. She needed to push her luck and go in.

She tugged at his mental guards, willing his mind to let her in. She could force it but—

"Argh!" the man exclaimed in pain, bringing the heel of his hand to his temple.

"You okay?" his companion asked, concern wrinkling her brow.

Oh, shite, that wasn't supposed to happen! Lexi wanted to pull back, but she was so close. She needed to find out what he knew.

A mental image of a new-looking research lab flooded through to her.

Lexi snapped to focus. The man wasn't projecting any details about where the lab might be located or its purpose, but his view of the room struck her as a recent experience. She absorbed every detail she could: layout, equipment, environmental controls. It all was filtered through the haze of memory, with some details of the sensory input seemingly absent while other aspects jumped out with unusual emphasis.

He was walking through a corridor. An exterior door was up ahead. If she could just walk outside in that memory, it might give a clue about the landscape or moon configuration that could narrow down—

"That's a nice handheld there," a man said from Lexi's side.

Bomax! Her awareness returned to the present as the interruption broke her concentration. *I don't have time for this shite.*

Trying to ignore the speaker, she took a centering breath and began to fight her way back into the manager's mind. *I need to see outside that lab—*

"Hey! I'm talking to you."

Her telepathic link to the memories shattered.

What the fok does he want? She glared at the scruffy man, who appeared to be a few years older than her, and was advancing far too close for comfort.

"I'm busy." She returned her attention to her handheld, hoping she could salvage her telepathic inquiry. "And it's really not. This old model is a piece of shite."

"Looks fine to me. Hand it over."

You have to be kidding me! She looked him over from the corners of her eyes, sizing him up. "Are you seriously trying to mug me?"

"There's no 'trying' about it." He slipped a knife from his sleeve. "Hand it over."

Lexi sighed as she slipped her handheld into her pants' pocket. The situation was clearly not going to resolve itself by ignoring him. If she could get rid of him quickly and quietly, she might still have a chance to get back into her target's mind before his business concluded at the port.

"Hey, I said—"

Lexi struck out with her right hand and gripped the man's wrist, augmenting her action with a subtle use of telekinesis to prevent him from lashing out at her. "Robbing people isn't nice." She yanked the knife from him.

"How—"

Before he could complete the question, she kicked his right thigh. "Go. Get out of here before you make this worse for yourself."

Undeterred, he lunged for her. "Hand it over!"

Lexi nimbly side-stepped him, and he collided with the dumpster, sending a reverberating *clang* through the alley.

"Hey! What's going on over there?" a woman shouted in the distance.

Lexi's attention snapped to the people she had been spying on. The older woman who'd been speaking with the manager was now staring directly at Lexi with a pinched expression of suspicious accusation.

Shite! Now there was no hope of resuming her telepathic reading.

The increased attention must have been too much for the mugger, because he ran off.

What a foking waste. Lexi looked between the knife in her hand and the two people watching her from down the alley. "Sorry, an idiot tried to rob me," she said with a casual shrug, then chucked her assailant's knife into the dumpster.

The man she'd been reading narrowed his eyes. "Hey, you look familiar. Do you work at the office?"

"Depends on which office you mean." She thought her tone sounded innocent, though it was difficult to be certain with her heart pounding so loudly in her ears.

He started walking toward her. "No, I definitely recognize you. What are you doing here? Were you following me?"

How in the stars can I talk my way out of this? She resisted an urge to run; doing so would admit guilt. Besides, she had nowhere to go other than back to the Alliance office, and he'd surely track her down there.

"I was," she admitted at last. Truth was the only way to play this… along with a bold lie. "Someone thinks that it's necessary to check up on you."

He paled slightly and shifted on his feet. "Everything is on schedule."

"Is that so?" Lexi evaluated him. "I guess we'll find out what they think of my report." Before he could question her further, she set a brisk pace back to the office.

No, no, no, it wasn't supposed to go this way!

Her cheeks burned, knowing that she needed to tell Kira about what had happened. If the man recognized that he'd been telepathically probed, it would be obvious that Lexi had abilities. She wasn't safe anymore.

Can I leave? Is that even an option?

It was possible that the man wouldn't know what had happened and that he'd just think she had been eavesdropping. She *had* offered a cover story… one so flimsy that even she didn't believe it. No, it was pretty clear that her cover had been blown by one foolish act, after a year of trying to worm her way in.

So stupid! Couldn't you have stayed patient for just a little longer?

There was nothing to do now but fess up. Admit her idiocy.

Lexi found Kira in the dorm, lounging on her bunk.

"Kira, we need to talk. Now," Lexi whispered.

"Is everything…?" The other woman got up without finishing the question. "Let's take a walk."

They took the back exit and huddled in a dead-end turnout that had become their go-to 'quick chat' place.

"Shite!" Lexi looked over her shoulder, unable to shake the feeling that she was being watched. *I'm on their list now. They're going to come for me…*

"Hey, calm down." Kira placed a reassuring hand on her

shoulder. "What happened?"

"I was trying to listen in on a conversation that seemed like it might be related to the new activity planned on that mystery planet. They noticed me snooping."

Kira frowned. "That's not good."

Lexi dug her fingers into her hair on the top of her head. "That was so stupid. I know how to be careful. It was sloppy and reckless."

"Hey, we're all getting antsy. Mistakes happen," the other woman assured her. Though the words were kind, there was tension around her eyes.

I just called attention to the plans not being secure, and these two are my friends. I may have blown all the cover. Lexi's own mental berating made up for the lack of criticism from her companion. They were in trouble now, and she knew it.

CHAPTER 7

WHEN JASON'S TSS transport ship dropped out of subspace, he took in the impressive sight of the artificial planetary rings and spacedocks encircling the highly developed planet of Lynaeda.

Whereas most Taran worlds had retained a large proportion of greenspace for both environmental management and aesthetic reasons, the Lynaedans had opted to utilize their planet's surface area for industrial and commercial development. The result was a greyish hue to the planet when viewed from space, with so many lights illuminating the night side that it appeared to be a singular glow.

"I can't decide if it's marvelous or hideous," Jason's travel companion, Sabrina, commented from the adjacent seat as they gazed out the viewport.

"Maybe a little of both," he replied.

Dressed in a smart, gray business suit with her blonde hair pulled into a bun, Sabrina consulted her tablet. "I'm curious to hear what Ambassador Greggor has to say about this offer. Are you ready to plead the case?"

"A little more prep time would be nice, but I think I can

handle it with your help."

"Oh, yeah. We've got this." She flashed a confident smile.

A few years older than Jason, the TSS legal advisor was on the Militia side of the organization, which Jason and his father had agreed was for the best, given the Lynaedans' caution surrounding those with abilities. Despite not having telepathic Gifts, she had every bit the negotiating prowess of any Agent representative. Furthermore, since she had spent time on Lynaeda as part of the TSS' previous outreach efforts, she was an ideal colleague to assist Jason in his present mission.

Nerves rose in Jason's chest as they approached the planet. *Have I done enough for them to take me at my word, or will they test me again?*

Given their divergent views of autonomy and privacy, if the Lynaedans didn't feel they were getting transparent answers from someone, they would forcibly extract the truth through a direct bioelectronic interface—and perceived no ethical violation in doing so. Since Gifted people possessed the means to get around the Lynaedans' normal evaluation tools for honesty, they were automatically deemed unreliable, no matter any spoken assurances about having good intentions.

Consequently, all Gifted were required to submit to direct mental links. In Jason's case, they'd tricked him into an intrusive neural link during their first meeting. He had been forced to open his thoughts to the Lynaedans in a way that he wasn't accustomed to doing, and even that had only gained him slight favor. Though the Lynaedans didn't view their actions as a violation, such invasive practices were in direct opposition to the strict code of conduct within the TSS related to telepathic probing.

He'd been wary to go to Lynaeda every time since. Even so, his duty to the TSS drove him forward now. Moreover, his concern for the Empire's future demanded he set aside his personal feelings. The Lynaedans were the best partners for manufacturing the new power core, and without that new technology to bolster their defensive capabilities, the TSS had no hope of making a stand against the Erebus. It was imperative he find a way to make this deal—even if that meant putting himself in an uncomfortable place.

Jason rose from his seat in the transport's lounge and walked over to the viewport, taking the opportunity to stretch out his legs and back after the several hour journey. "This is going to be a tough sell," he said to Sabrina while focusing on the scenery outside.

"They should jump at the chance to have ownership of something this lucrative. Look at this place!" She spread her arms wide to encompass the breadth of the planet's development. "Their power demands are *enormous*. A new option that's a fraction of the size and significantly higher output is a game-changer."

"It doesn't alter that they're highly insular and wary of outsiders." He frowned. "I have no choice but to open my mind to them the moment we step into that meeting, and they'll see right away that I don't trust the Erebus to have benevolent intentions."

"But you do believe that we need this core to be mass-produced?"

"Yes."

"Then you'll be genuine in your plea."

"Right, and 'we need to do this, but doing so may doom us all' isn't a great sales pitch."

Sabrina scowled. "Obviously, don't say that."

"I never would, but that's about the only thing that's been on my mind for the past several months."

Sabrina evaluated him. "You might want to adjust that thinking before we go into the meeting."

Jason shook his head and shrugged. "They'll see through it. Won't matter."

She sighed. "And I imagine this is why you like to keep up mental guards."

"Now you understand the problem."

"Facts prevail. And the facts in this case are that the Taran Empire—and the Lynaedans—would benefit from this technology," Sabrina said. "They're the 'tech heads', right? They'll have to see that."

"They're not fond of that nickname."

"Oh."

"Granted, they *do* implant cybernetics in their heads, so it's an apt description." He smiled.

"It never came up in our previous dealings." She waved her hand. "No matter. We need to win them over, so I'll call them whatever they please."

"They never said anything to me directly. It's just a feeling."

"I'll follow your lead. I'm just here for the paperwork."

He nodded. "Now to close the deal."

The TSS transport ship docked at one of the massive stations orbiting the planet. This one was geosynchronous, serving as the upper anchor point for a space elevator leading to Ulthren, the capital city of Lynaeda—not that Jason could distinguish where one city ended and another began, everything was so developed on the surface. Due to that population density and the associated activity, surface-to-orbit spacecraft were a rarity, making the space elevator the most practical way to get to the planet below.

Jason and Sabrina descended the gangway from the ship to

the station, where they were met by four escorts. The men didn't have overt weapons visible, but the way they carried themselves indicated combat training. No doubt, they had significant strength cybernetic enhancements beyond the muscular physiques visible under their jumpsuits.

"Hello, and thank you for receiving us," Jason greeted.

"Ambassador Greggor is expecting you," one of the larger men said and turned to begin walking toward the elevator access.

With small-talk clearly out of the question, Jason and Sabrina followed him in silence. The three other escorts fell into step behind them.

As with his previous visits to Lynaeda, Jason was fascinated by the range of people walking around the spaceport. Some looked indistinguishable from the Tarans he'd see elsewhere, while others had undergone significant modifications to their appearance, ranging from external cybernetic augmentations to subdermal implants that added ridges or horns to give an almost alien appearance. A significant number of people had replaced their organic eyes with ocular implants, creating a strange uncanny valley effect as he caught the gazes of the passersby.

The Lynaedans regarded him with a mixture of curiosity and suspicion. His TSS Agent uniform was a well-known symbol, but he suspected they recognized him, specifically; Sietinens rarely went unnoticed, especially among those perpetually connected to news streams.

Their party had a chamber to themselves on the elevator, and Jason took the opportunity to properly take in the view of the planet during the descent. He'd been somewhat distracted on his previous visits, so he hadn't noticed the detail like how the cities had been built up over the large bodies of water and where greenspaces had been enclosed within biodomes. Though he missed seeing an expanse of ocean and vast swaths of green forest from above, he realized the planet wasn't nearly as gray and devoid of nature as he'd once thought.

Upon reaching the surface, they exited the elevator and were greeted by another set of escorts, this time dressed more business professional than military guard.

A young purple-haired woman standing at the front of the group bowed her head to Jason. "Welcome back to Lynaeda. I'm Ashan."

"Pleasure to meet you. I'm Agent Jason Sietinen, and Sabrina Matael is here to serve as TSS legal counsel."

Sabrina smiled. "It's an honor to be here."

Ashan evaluated them. Though a slight smile turned up her lips, her gaze was calculating and guarded. "Ambassador Greggor and the Chancellor are waiting to speak with you."

Jason tried to hide his surprise. "I didn't realize Chancellor Ewen would be joining us today."

"Yes." Ashan gave a prim smile and another slight bow of her head before pivoting on her heel to begin walking through the broad receiving hall.

Sabrina shot Jason a glance he took to mean 'this'll be interesting!' before the two of them followed the government representative.

The receiving hall was an impressive chamber with a curved roof towering at least ten meters overhead. Its ceiling was a massive visual display alternating between a realistic rendition of natural sky to intercuts of advertisements. Solicitations of other sorts abounded on the ground level, with kiosks and popup holographic displays promoting various services, products, and cybernetic modification experts. The flashy colors and sounds were an assault to Jason's senses, since he was accustomed to the relatively subdued environment of TSS Headquarters. Even compared to the vibrant commercial ports on Tararia, this was over-the-top.

Ashan took a quick pace through the middle of the hall, and others hurried to clear a path well ahead of her. Some cast Jason an evaluative look as he passed by but the expressions of the onlookers remained neutral.

No doubt, this TSS visit is going to be all over the news tonight, he assessed.

A hundred meters from the elevator, Ashan took a sharp left through an open set of double-doors decorated with fine-detail metalwork in contrasting tones, giving the appearance of circuitry.

The corridor beyond had none of the commercial advertisements found in the main hall, and the furnishings were distinctly more opulent, befitting a place of official business where first impressions were everything.

Ashan gestured to a conference room off to the right, which was already occupied by half a dozen people.

Jason recognized the woman sitting at the head of the table as Chancellor Ewen, and the woman to her right was Ambassador Greggor, with whom he'd conducted most of his prior dealings with the Lynaedans. The remaining men and women around the table had the poised look of administrators and advisors who felt they had more important things to do than attend an unplanned meeting.

Chancellor Ewen indicated Jason should take the seat to her left. He complied, and Sabrina sat next to him.

"I'm honored to formally make your acquaintance, Chancellor," he said with a respectful nod to the older woman. "Wonderful to see you again, Ambassador Greggor."

"Since it appears communications with the TSS are going

to become a regular occurrence, I figured it was time to hear your pitch firsthand," Ewen replied. A thin fiber optic inlay patterned her forehead and temples, which transitioned into her upswept hair. The most striking feature of her appearance, though, was the intense glow of her blue-hued artificial eyes, perhaps meant to mimic the bioluminescent irises found in those with abilities.

"Well, we certainly hope this is the beginning of a longstanding good relationship." Jason smiled. "I'm Agent Jason Sietinen, and I'm accompanied today by Sabrina Matael, one of our TSS legal advisors, whom some of you may know."

"Your reputation precedes you," the Chancellor said.

"In a positive light, I hope."

"With the Sietinen name, we're never sure what to think." She searched his face, likely looking for subtle changes in temperature or eye movement to gauge his thoughts.

"I assure you, I am here only as a TSS representative. My family has nothing to do with it."

"Except, that can never truly be the case, can it?" Ambassador Greggor asked, folding her hands on the smooth tabletop. She leaned forward.

Honesty is the only option. Jason nodded. "You're right. My family's positions of leadership within both Taran politics and the military mean that we must tread carefully in certain matters. I am here now because we need a partner to serve as a neutral third-party to bring a new technology to market. It can't come from the TSS directly because that's not our place, and to hand it over to any existing corporation would upset the balance of power."

"Why us?" Greggor asked.

"Because you understand technology better than any other subculture within the Taran Empire. You have the infrastructure to quickly ramp up to large-scale production and can offer the necessary technical expertise to create variations for different applications while maintaining exemplary quality control."

The chancellor pressed her lips into an intrigued smile as she spoke. "And what is it that we would be producing?"

Jason slid his handheld from his breast pocket and placed it on the conference table to sync with the holoprojector. He brought up a wireframe engineering diagram of the Erebus' remarkable 'gift'. "A new type of power core."

The Lynaedans evaluated the three-dimensional holographic rendering, using the bioelectronic interfaces in their brains to manipulate the model in different directions and zoom levels without making any physical movement.

"A curious design," said a middle-aged man with burgundy hair, seated a couple of seats down the table from Jason. "What kind of testing has been carried out?"

"Seven months of intensive field protocols. My father oversaw it himself," Jason replied.

The man nodded, satisfied. Though it was a vague answer, the engineering skills of Wil Sietinen were well-known, especially among this technologically fluent culture. Even to them, the advent of the independent jump drive had been an astonishing breakthrough, granting a significant measure of celebrity to Wil as its creator.

"This design has the potential to change the game across the Empire," Jason explained. "The miniaturized versions of this core could enable technologies we haven't been able to implement through other methods—that means lower costs and access for people who never would have been able to have that standard of living without these changes.

"I know Lynaedans' relationship with technology is

different than it is for many other Tarans. This is a chance to narrow that gap. We'd like to continue bringing people across the disparate Taran worlds closer together, and this seems like a good place to start." Jason looked around the faces at the conference table when he finished, weighing their reactions. There wasn't overwhelming enthusiasm, but he at least didn't see repulsion.

"I'll be honest, we did approach the Aesir before coming to you," he continued. "However, they aren't entrenched in Taran commerce in the way you are, so they suggested that you would make better partners to bring this to market. The TSS is happy to advise, but we can't be the face of the effort. It's important for the larger political stability of the Empire for us to maintain neutrality and not profit from any innovation."

"What about the independent jump drive?" Greggor asked. "You can't profess your family has not gained significant wealth from that invention, and it originated within the TSS."

"My father was a Junior Agent in the TSS at the time, yes, but the jump drive's development was done on his own time and he has always personally held the patent; it was only *licensed* to the TSS. A subtle distinction, I know, but it's a different situation than this power core. The independent jump drive, at its heart, is a string of code that could be applied to existing physical devices. A power core is a unique physical item itself."

Ewen nodded slowly. "All right, I understand the difference. So you wish to turn over the technology in its entirety, or are you simply looking to license it to us?"

Jason turned to Sabrina and gave her a subtle nod to answer.

The legal representative took over. "The TSS proposes that the power core design be entered into a 'restricted public domain' registration. This classification is reserved for technologies that are not owned by any one organization but require oversight in their production in the interest of public good. The entity on Lynaeda of your choosing would be granted a ten-year stewardship with renewals in perpetuity so long as agreed upon performance benchmarks are met."

Chancellor Ewen and Ambassador Greggor looked at each other, their eyes twitching slightly with what Jason suspected was the telltale signs of a conversation over the local Net.

After several seconds, Ambassador Greggor nodded slowly. "It is an interesting proposition. However, we must decline."

Stars, not them, too! How is it this difficult to get people to take such a lucrative deal? Jason schooled his expression to keep his disappointment from showing. "May I ask why?"

"Frankly, we are hesitant to have that level of close involvement with the Taran government."

Sounds awfully similar to how Dad said the Aesir responded. Jason folded his hands on the tabletop. "This wouldn't entail dealings with the government. You'd be functioning as an independent contractor. It's no different than when you sell your other products outside the Lynaedan system."

She tilted her head, narrowing her eyes slightly. "Do not pretend you aren't using us as a political tool to further the TSS' objectives."

It's true, we're using them as an intermediary to play out this scenario to our own designs. But what else can we do?

There were many ways Jason could respond, and most of them would end in the Lynaedans dismissing him and never inviting him back for future talks. To bring them around to his point of view, he'd need to lay it all out there.

"This isn't just about the TSS," he said. "In fact, we have little to do with it. The reality is that the TSS is about as neutral an entity as we have in a high-powered position with the Empire right now. None of the High Dynasties could fully set aside their corporate interests to be impartial. It's imperative that the TSS maintain as much of its neutrality as possible, so we can't be a supplier for a product. The fact that you *don't* want to be involved in Taran political or commercial affairs is precisely why you are the perfect stewards to bring this energy core to market."

Chancellor Ewen leaned back in her seat, studying him with slightly narrowed eyes. "It's curious that you, Jason Sietinen, are here representing the TSS. It is impossible to see your role here as being anything other than political, despite your claims."

"I can't deny that I sit at the intersection of great powers. SiNavTech, DGE, and VComm—they'd all take my call with no delay. My parents run the TSS. Yes, I'm here because I'm someone people will listen to. Because of my connections, I can make grand promises and actually be able to deliver. A lot of people can talk without having any means to follow through.

"However, I have no ambitions of wielding that power myself. You've seen in my mind, and I'll let you in again, if that's what it takes. I'm here asking this of you because I see it is the best way forward for the Taran Empire. As much as you and the Aesir try to distance yourselves from the other goings-on, we can't ignore the fact that we're in this together. The Erebus hold great power over us, and quibbling over petty civil differences will only weaken our position against that potential threat."

"You don't trust them," Ewen stated.

"The Erebus? No. Not at all." He chuckled. "Yet I'm asking

you to manufacture this device that they gave to us. It doesn't make any sense, does it?"

"It is a means to other ends," Ambassador Greggor assessed.

"Yes." He nodded. "If we can get this core manufactured at scale, we believe we'll be in a better position to grow and strengthen our position across the Empire. Unite our worlds against a common threat."

"That makes it more intriguing," Ewen said, straightening in her seat, now fully engaged.

Jason smiled. "Let's go over what we were thinking."

CHAPTER 8

AS RAENA REVIEWED the latest injunction against further investigation into a particularly intriguing historic site in South America, she couldn't help but wonder if starting an interstellar incident was worth it to continue the investigation into potential ancient technology hidden on Earth.

She set down her tablet and sighed. "What do you think, Trevor? Do we try to fight it in the courts or take another tactic?"

The young liaison shrugged on the other end of the vidcall. "I don't believe taking up a legal argument would get the desired outcome. If anything, bribery would be much more productive."

It didn't take him long to understand how things work on Earth. She shook her head. "I'm not comfortable playing it that way."

"Then I don't know what to suggest. So long as there are public protests, I believe government leaders are unlikely to cooperate."

Serving as the Taran ambassador to Earth illustrated for

Raena just how similar Tarans and humans were, despite tens of thousands of years of cultural separation. There was something in their genetics, she was certain of it, that made people defensive of their territory and their way of life. No matter how different the details in their everyday existence, that rang true across the Taran worlds.

It stunned her how much those common elements of their nature could be found across the Taran Empire. Millennia of development, with microevolution and cultural diversion, and yet everyone was still fundamentally the same. It didn't make a lot of sense from a scientific perspective, but somehow she wasn't surprised. Those traits persisted because they worked—they'd gotten people to that point in the first place. Sharks and crocodiles had remained unchanged for millions of years, so why would Tarans be any different? They'd simply substituted technological advancements for biological adaptations to suit their changing environment.

Unfortunately, that shared nature was proving to be a challenge for her at present because the people of Earth were understandably reluctant to let aliens—no matter how similar they looked to the locals—dig up their revered historical sites in the vague name of 'research'.

There had to be a solution, but her suggestion to approach Earth's leaders with the truth about Tarans' motivations hadn't been received well by the High Council.

"We need to up the coolness factor," she mused.

Trevor's eyebrows knitted. "What does that mean?"

"They don't want us digging and disturbing the site—but I think it's more because they don't want to disrupt tourism. To get them to agree, we need to make the site even *more* alluring."

"What do you propose?"

Without information to the contrary, it was prudent to

proceed as though the civil unrest on Earth was being perpetrated behind-the-scenes by the same group involved in the other Outer Colonies disruption. The sudden planet-wide coordination had too similar tactics to write off as a coincidence.

While the Coalition had proved difficult to combat on the Taran worlds, Raena had an advantage when it came to Earth. Having grown up on the planet, she had experienced the worldwide interaction between media and public opinion. She was all too aware of how transient sentiments could be, quickly shifting in response to current events. If she could lay the groundwork to capture the public consciousness and turn them to the Taran government's side—to *encourage* the excavation efforts rather than condemn the involvement—they could mitigate both issues at once. All they needed was to shift the momentum.

Doing so would take another big spectacle, much like when they jumped in the TSS fleet to make their public first contact. This display would need to be more tailored but every bit as impressive.

A smile tugged at the corners of Raena's mouth. "It's a simple plan. The objections are to us destroying important monuments—which we have no intention of doing. The technology on Earth simply isn't advanced enough to relocate structures of this scale, but *we* can. So, we need to simultaneously preserve the sites and turn them into even more interesting tourist attractions."

"What about the people who worship these sites as holy land?"

"It'll take some convincing that a dig will let them get closer to the power of a site—which is true. The religious concerns only pertain to some of the sites, so we can save those for the end."

"Okay." Trevor nodded. "How would you go about making this impressive tourism display for the rest?"

"We take up the entire section of ground around the historic sites in question, slap an anti-grav platform under it, and suspend it in the air."

He blinked at her. "That's, uh…"

"Bold? Yeah." She grinned. "But come on… what person on Earth wouldn't want to see tech like that in practice? The only thing more interesting than going to visit an ancient pyramid is going to visit that pyramid while it's *floating in the air*, right?"

"I can't argue with that," Trevor said cautiously.

Raena tapped her foot while she thought through the logistics. "It's not a guaranteed sale, but I think if we can just get one country to agree, the others will follow. A little well-placed social media marketing and we'll let the public drive the demand."

"It could work."

"There's too much promise in the subterranean scan data to not pursue this," she said. "I'd like you to begin making preparations for a proper excavation. I'll make sure we get the approvals."

"How public do you want it to be?"

"Shield it as much as possible. Let people focus on the floating monuments; what's happening underground can be our business alone."

Trevor inclined his head. "Yes, my lady, I'll make the arrangements right away." He paused in quiet consideration. "I do believe there's something here worth finding. The most important answers don't come easy."

"I feel it, too. There's something significant about Earth to the Taran people as a whole. Now, more than ever, we need to chase every lead we can."

"What we've already seen in the deep ground scans... no human tech could have ever detected it." He shook his head with wonder. "I don't think anyone will believe it if it pans out. It may change our entire understanding of human and Taran history."

She smiled. "More importantly, it may change our future."

— — —

Delegating should have given Wil more time and mental space to deal with his most critical responsibilities, but he found himself preoccupied with thoughts about the Erebus. Too much was riding on his son's conversation with the Lynaedans for the worries to fade into the background. He trusted Jason to get the job done—that wasn't the issue; he was just used to being involved in the conversations firsthand.

I can't do everything myself. Jason can never grow as a leader if I'm always there taking charge.

Wil knew he'd been a control-freak for much of his life. He consistently tried to take on too much and do everything himself. It wasn't sustainable, and he'd burned out more than once over the years. Lately, he'd been making a concerted effort to let go and allow others to shine—especially when it came to shaping the next generation of leaders.

Requesting that Jason take point with the Lynaedans was a test not only of his son's command aptitude but also a measure of Wil's progress toward once and for all leaving behind his micromanagement tendencies. Their greatest challenges would soon be upon them, and he needed to trust others to fulfill their roles without his direct oversight.

Wil's desktop lit up with an incoming communication from Jason's handheld, and he immediately snapped to attention. He took the vidcall on the holoprojector above his desk.

"Hi, Jason. How did it go?"

His son smiled. "We have a deal. I needed to pull a little more political leverage than I'd intended, but that made the difference."

Some of the weight that had been pressing on Wil's chest began to lift. "That's great news. Any indication of when they may be able to begin production?"

"They'd like to run their own short field trial first—just a week or so. Assuming that goes well, I think we can expect production-ready designs for several new core form factors by the end of the month."

"Thank you, Jason. Well done."

"Took name-dropping you to make it happen. I think they may have said 'yes' right away if you'd come yourself."

"That would have introduced other problems."

"I know. The point is, we're good to go now."

"Or at least moving in the right direction." Wil took in a deep breath and let it out. "All right, get back here and we'll go over the next steps. Pass on my appreciation and congratulations to Sabrina, as well."

"Will do. See you soon." Jason ended the vidcall.

Wil passed on the good news to Saera telepathically, and a few minutes later she joined him in his office.

"What a relief," she said as she entered.

"I don't want to celebrate just yet since there isn't a production facility up and running, but having an agreement in place is certainly a big hurdle to have overcome."

"It's wonderful to see our son grow into this role," Wil said.

"We got very lucky having two good kids."

"It helps that they had a fantastic mother."

"And dad. You were with them a lot more than I was when they were little."

"A team effort."

She smiled. "I'm proud of you for handing over the reins with this."

"It's good experience for Jason, and I can't always do everything—as begrudgingly as I must admit that."

"We do have bigger issues to worry about."

He nodded. "Like what's going on with the Erebus."

"I still don't fully understand *how* they interact with our reality," Saera said. "Without that knowledge, how can we figure out a method to prevent an attack?"

"I've been trying to piece it together, but most of it is still hypothetical. It's difficult to measure what we can't readily observe."

"Are there any threads worth chasing?"

"Well, I believe there's a connection between our abilities and the *aesen*, so we have *some* sort of common ground with the Erebus in a roundabout way."

She gave him a knowing look. "It really puts it all into perspective, doesn't it? I'm sorry to admit that I've taken these abilities for granted... that I can always have instant access to power when I want it, the way I expect a light to come on when I flip its switch. As I learn more, it's truly amazing that we can tap into those cosmic energies at all. We are Gifted in more ways than one."

"It is remarkable," Wil agreed. Though he hadn't articulated his own abilities in terms of *aesen* until recently, the words were simply an expression of what he'd felt ever since his Awakening. He was connected to something bigger than himself, and that link was stronger for him than it was for most others. If nothing else, it was comforting to now have vocabulary to explain *how* and *why* he was different rather than being a mysterious anomaly.

"I'm shocked that there weren't more studies before now about the Gifted and the apparent transdimensional connection to that 'energy well'."

Wil shrugged. "It wouldn't surprise me to find out that the Priesthood had done a lot of research about it and kept those findings suppressed."

She scoffed. "Yeah, for sure. They clearly knew there was life in higher dimensions capable of manipulating that cosmic power."

"To that end, I've been thinking about how the Erebus use *aesen*," Wil said. "I believe the Erebus still wield the *aesen*, just like we do. They're not all-powerful beings."

"They can do things with it that we can't begin to fathom. If it's all the same energy source, what makes them so exponentially more powerful?"

"It might be a matter of saturation. I've been thinking of the *aesen* like particles. Some people have a genetic propensity to attract those particles and become saturated by them. The higher the saturation level, the greater one's Gifts, as enabled by access to the *aesen* energy. We appear to continually recharge our 'power reserves', so to speak, through a transdimensional connection to that *aesen* energy well. The Erebus just happen to have a *very* high capacity—and perhaps residing on a higher dimensional plane, they might be 'closer' to that raw energy source."

She nodded. "So, if we're saturated with the *aesen* particles and that's what gives us our abilities, does that mean that we might be able to counteract what the Erebus do since we're using the same base energy?"

"Maybe." Truthfully, Wil wasn't confident enough to give a more definitive answer. Everything he'd stated on the matter up to that point was hypothetical, and he wasn't about to stake the Empire's future on an educated guess without conducting further research.

"I'll take 'maybe' over a definitive 'no'," Saera said. "It'd be amazing if we could use the *Conquest*'s TK weapon."

"Aside from the obvious problem of us only having one ship like it—and it's unlikely we'll be able to get enough ateron to build more—we may have another issue with that," Wil began.

Saera's smiled faded. "What?"

"It's possible that trying to focus an *aesen*-fueled energy-attack toward the Erebus would actually *heal* them, or at a minimum, do nothing at all."

"Stars, you're right." She shook her head and sighed. "It'd be like giving them a concentrated shot of power-juice."

"Or maybe not," Wil emphasized. "The nature of the *aesen* is pure energy with infinite potential to be shaped into any form we can imagine. What I can't begin to guess is at what level the energy's use is 'set'. Is it fully under our control once we're saturated by it, or can the *aesen* be intercepted at any given moment?"

"The Erebus can clearly 'un-make' objects—and people." She grimaced.

"Yes, but that's once the *aesen* has been placed in a fixed state. I'm curious about when it's more 'raw'. For instance, what would happen if we were to charge the *Conquest*'s TK weapon from inside the Erebus? It might be possible to draw on their individual energy saturation, and we could then channel it away from them—like draining a battery."

"Do you think it would be possible?"

He nodded. "Between the data we've recorded during Erebus encounters and the records we have about the Gate sphere, I believe we could modify the *Conquest*'s TK weapon to make it harmful to the Erebus."

She nodded solemnly. "It'd be barbaric—like tapping into an artery and trying to bleed them dry."

"I'd prefer to avoid that option. We're trying to show them we're worthy of respect. This would not be the way."

"Yeah, hurting someone isn't a good way to make friends." She frowned. "Which is why the Gate tech was banned in the first place."

"Correct."

"And those Gates draw on *aesen* to power them, right?"

"That's the working hypothesis."

"How is that transdimensional energy transfer any different than when we use our Gifts?"

He hesitated. "I don't know… but it must be. The Gate tech is what the Erebus protested. If our abilities hurt them, too, then why not say something?"

Saera met his gaze. "Maybe it's just at the 'annoying' level when we use our abilities, but the power draw of the Gates puts it over the top. Like, the difference between a mosquito bite versus a tarantula hawk sting."

Wil's stomach clenched. He sensed that Saera had tapped into something significant that he hadn't previously considered. "No one would want to deal with a swarm of mosquitos for eternity. You'd take control measures."

Saera's face went slack. "What if they did? We don't know anything about our Taran ancestors. What telekinetic abilities used to be a lot stronger and more widespread in Tarans? What if the Erebus also gave some sort of 'gift' to people back then to mitigate the problem?"

Wil's mind raced. "The Priesthood didn't create the Generation Cycle that diminished abilities until... what? Eight hundred years ago? The ancient war was *much* older than that."

"Everything is cyclical. Abilities are becoming more prevalent in the population again. You and our children are in a new bracket of potential. If that advancement continues..."

"Eventually, you'd need another reset," he realized.

"And, ultimately, you'd decide that the cycle was getting tedious and you may as well eradicate the problem in its entirety."

As Wil thought about it, a chill ran through his core. "Is it possible the Erebus have been interfering with us for millennia without our knowledge?"

"We know they can mess with people's minds, like they did with the *Andvari*. Who's to say they haven't planted ideas in other individual's heads at key junctures over the centuries, to nudge developments in directions of their choosing?"

"It's possible."

"Could they have been manipulating the Priesthood regarding all those awful genetic interventions?" Saera asked.

He shook his head. "Honestly, it would make me feel better to know that it was alien influence rather than people willing to perpetrate such evil against their own kind, but who knows?"

Saera bit her lip. "Unless the Erebus admit it, I guess it's all speculation."

"I certainly don't like the implications, if this is the case."

"No kidding. If they've manipulated people in the past to accomplish their objectives, then who might they be working with now?"

"That's a very concerning thought." He crossed his arms.

She let out a long breath. "My instincts tell me they're gearing up for something significant."

"I have no doubt," he agreed. "Though I can't begin to assess the best way to prepare countermeasures."

"I do have one thought in that regard."

"Please, I welcome any suggestion."

She leaned forward with her elbows on her knees. "A kill switch. If we're going to install these power cores throughout the Empire and there *is* some kind of built-in trap we haven't detected, we need a way to shut down the whole network."

"Excellent idea."

"The obvious downside to that is it would take whatever is connected to it offline, too."

"I wonder if it would be possible to build in redundancy to the system? Use the new cores as the primary but have the old MPS cores as backup."

"That might be possible in some systems but not others."

"At this point, I'll take any edge we can get. I'll think about what configuration might work and pass it onto the Lynaedans to build into the design."

She started to give him a look, but he headed her off. "I know, I need to delegate, but after what happened with the transdimensional imager, it's worth it for me to be involved in some things."

"I was actually going to say that working on these engineering problems would be a better use of your time than TSS administration. Michael and I can pick up some of your load so you can focus on that."

"You sure?"

"Absolutely. You can jump back in when it comes to battle strategy, but right now, digging into technical details is the best use of your skills."

"All right. I just hope we're making the correct assumptions."

"Time will tell."

CHAPTER 9

THEY'RE WATCHING ME. I know it. Lexi saw the suspicion on every face in the Alliance's office. Their gazes followed her, singling her out from the crowd at meals and when she passed by in the halls. Maybe it was only in her head, but she couldn't be sure.

She hadn't yet been able to drag herself from her bunk for the morning. Nerves had her stomach twisted and her chest tight while her mind raced through how the Alliance would call her out on her betrayal. Would they hold her captive? Kick her out? Kill her?

She'd tried to keep her head down since the incident, working on marketing copy for the Alliance, inventorying, and her other assorted tasks within the organization. Frankly, she was surprised no one had come for her already. She'd been avoiding Oren as much as possible, since he was the most likely person of authority to question her about what she had been doing when she followed the manager to his back-alley meeting. Though no one had asked her about it, she sensed the weight of the unspoken question in everyone's gaze. It was a coordinated campaign to get her to crack—to spill all the information about her co-conspirators. Everything was falling apart.

"Lexi?"

She jumped at the sound of her name, then relaxed against her pillow when she recognized Kira's voice. "Hey," she replied, needing to force out the word through her tight throat.

"Everything okay?"

"Yeah, great!" She faked a smile.

Kira saw right through it, though Lexi hoped it would be less obvious over the security cameras. "Glad to hear it," she said aloud but then met Lexi's gaze and added telepathically, *"I haven't noticed any changes. You're good, at least for now."*

"It doesn't feel that way."

Kira sat down on the edge of Lexi's bunk, the frame letting out a groan of protest at the extra weight. *"You need to relax. Don't hide in here. Acting weird is going to bring unwanted attention."*

"It's too late. They're onto me. It's not safe here." Lexi took a shaky breath.

Kira placed her hand on Lexi's shoulder. *"Leon is working a lead. Be patient for just a little longer."*

"Okay."

"I really liked that new recruitment pamphlet you put together. Nice work," Kira said. She patted Lexi on her knee and then rose from the bed.

"Thanks."

Lexi sat on her bunk for another minute. *Get up. Just make it through the day.*

For now, she had to continue playing her part. She had to hold onto the hope that she might soon see the Alliance unmasked.

She slipped off her bunk and stood up, setting her jaw and narrowing her eyes into a resolute gaze. *This isn't over yet. We'll get them.*

—   —   —

A broad smile spread across Raena's face as she sat down to lunch in the courtyard with Ryan, scanning over a new report on her handheld. "Thank the stars!"

"Good news?" her husband asked.

"Just got the word that we've received government approval to implement my plan for floating the monuments above the dig sites at five test locations on Earth."

"Really?" he asked incredulously before catching himself and clearing his throat. "Rather, I'm glad to hear that worked out."

"It is a little crazy, isn't it?" Raena laughed. "I can't wait to see the footage of everything hovering in the air. It's going to be spectacular."

"*How*, exactly, is that going to work...?"

She waved off the question with a dismissive flip of her hand. "Repurposing some mining techniques and assistance from a team of TSS Agents. It's a big project and an unusual combination of things, but it's quite workable with the resources at our disposal."

"Well, it's good to hear it's coming together. I'll leave that to you." Ryan's shoulders were slumped slightly and he was lacking his usual spark.

Raena leaned forward with concern, her eyebrows drawing together. "Hey, did something happen?"

"More of the same," he said. "People saying that we're abusing our position and will drive the Empire into the ground."

"I can't blame them, really. On Earth, I would have thought that any family that referred to itself as a 'dynasty' didn't deserve generations after generations of wealth and power, either."

"With the realities of governance for a galactic-scale civilization, though, passing on generational knowledge makes the most sense," Ryan said. "Electing leaders for short terms would be madness."

"I know, and now that we have the approval rating system in place, we *need* to perform," she said.

Ryan tousled his dark hair. "That reality doesn't change public perception. It also doesn't help that we're isolated here on an island. I look back on my ancestors and the placement of the original Dainetris estate, and it was in the middle of the town. The Sietinen estate is remote, by comparison. But this," he made an all-encompassing gesture, "takes seclusion to a whole other level. We make all these claims about being open, and trying to be 'one of the people', but we *literally* live on a private island. Doesn't send a great message."

"That's true." She sighed. "I really don't want to move again."

"I don't believe that's the right solution. I was thinking more in terms of opening up the property to visitors."

"Oh, I can't *wait* to hear what Ivan has to say about the security risks of that." The Captain of the Guard for their estate was a touch over-protective in Raena's opinion, though that was certainly preferable to the alternative. He had spent his first year of training with the TSS, as was customary for those in service to highborn, and had become a good friend to them over the years.

"There are ways to mitigate those concerns," Ryan replied.

"I don't necessarily mean in the main manor. We could arrange for tours of the grounds and set aside a little time each day to meet with visitors."

"In other words, make us more accessible."

"Precisely. We can keep shields around ourselves. I think face-to-face time would go a long way for public relations."

"I like that idea." She smiled. "You're right, everything we've been doing has been at a distance."

"You're tackling the problems on Earth by letting people get a closer look. Maybe we need to do the same here."

"I like it."

He sat back in his seat. "I didn't expect us to get this leadership thing right from the outset, but I try to be a little better every day. I think getting a closer connection to our people is what we need to grow."

"Agreed." She held up her glass to toast. "To progress."

—   —   —

Wil had been staring at power core schematics for so long that his eyes had started to go bleary.

The design really was ingenious—so simple in its execution and scalable in a way that never would have been possible with MPS' design. He still marveled at how the Erebus had been able to engineer such a perfect system using readily available materials. If he was being honest, he was a little envious that he hadn't seen the solution himself.

In going over the design at various scales—from a miniaturized version for use in personal equipment to large units for industrial applications—he was starting to see an array of possibilities for how they could put the core into practice. Nothing, as yet, offered significant protection from the Erebus, though he wasn't even sure that was possible. In the immediate term, offering a quality of life increase for Taran citizens seemed like a worthwhile starting point.

His thoughts were interrupted by a knock on his door, followed by a telepathic caress from Saera.

"Come on in," he replied in his mind.

She opened the door and gave him a concerned smile. "You missed lunch."

"What? It's only…" He checked the time. "Oh. So I did."

"How's it going?" She closed the office door and wandered over toward his desk.

"Not badly, but not as well as I'd hoped. I'd like to have more to offer the Lynaedans when we hand over the project."

"Their engineers are quite good," Saera pointed out. "I don't think they're expecting anything other than the original design schematics the Erebus gave us and the data from our field tests."

"Meeting bare minimum expectations has never been my style."

"I've always been impressed by how you can immerse yourself in these projects."

"There's a lot to consider. It's easy to lose track of time."

Saera smiled. "I learned long ago that I'd need to compete for your attention against your latest tech project."

He chuckled and closed out of the holographic model. "You always come first."

"This isn't about me. I just want to make sure you remember to eat and sleep." She raised one eyebrow, knowing there had been many occasions where he'd neglected to do both.

"I'm not that far down the hole," he assured her. "I've just been exploring what we can do with the core."

"New applications, you mean?"

"Yeah. We've been sitting on this technology Archive from the Aesir, but half the stuff wasn't feasible to implement because of power limitations. Now…"

Saera perked up at that. "Anything of particular interest?"

"I'm not sure yet."

She eyed him. "That use of 'yet' suggests you're not going to let this go anytime soon."

"There's no clear end to this kind of project. We'll always see new ways to use old tech based on evolving conditions."

"Unless you can think of a way to put up a transdimensional wall the Erebus can't break through, we have other things to focus on now."

"Huh." Wil stared at the information with new perspective.

"What?"

He leaned back in his chair. "You just gave me an interesting idea."

"Oh yeah?" She sat down in one of the padded visitor chairs across from his desk.

"There *was* something like that in the Aesir's Archive." He navigated to the directory and found the applicable file, then opened it on the holoprojector. "Stars, was this what they've been wanting me to see?"

"What is it?" Saera asked.

"A planetary shield design. It was never implemented because of the extraordinary power requirements. The performance improvement is significant over the others— actually a transdimensional component due to a spatial distortion energy field. But the necessary upgrades to support it didn't balance out."

"That's certainly intriguing."

"But," Wil looked over the specs, "that new power core

design from the Erebus would accommodate this load with very few other modifications."

"Having a more robust shield could make a huge difference if the Erebus attack."

"My thoughts exactly. But it's more than that. The thing that makes this design so unique is its ability to be customized—think of it like tuning to a specific harmonic frequency."

"Okay…"

Wil stood up to pace as he thought through the branching connections. "Forget about making more ships like the *Conquest*… Instead, we can customize the energy output of the shield to make a wall the Erebus wouldn't want to pass through—just like the energy field of a Gate."

Saera sat up straighter in her chair. "Stars! And those shields will work at a planetary scale?"

Wil smiled. "With the new power cores, yes."

Saera shook her head. "Why would the Erebus give us technology that can be used against them?"

"They might not understand the way we can fit different devices together. And, this particular shield generator is only in the Archive, which we keep offline. They wouldn't have been able to learn about it when they scanned the *Conquest*."

"It seems hazardous using their own tool against them."

"We don't *need* to use it. But it might be nice to have it as an option."

"You mean build in a modulator to, say, a new planetary shield that would allow us to weaponize it if we came under attack?"

"Precisely."

She tapped her finger on her lips and nodded. "Now *that* is a very interesting idea."

"It's not a lot, but it could make the difference if this comes down to a fight against the Erebus."

"Any edge we can get is a prudent preparation to make. My only concern is they might see us laying that groundwork and go on the offensive."

"Honestly, I don't think they have a very good understanding of what we do. Yes, we can think of them as being omniscient in some ways, but being able to gaze at the lower dimensions doesn't mean they can correctly interpret our actions."

"Right, like how we talked before about the Erebus looking at us in the way we might regard a drawing on a piece of paper."

"And, in those terms, we can't interact with that paper beyond being able to glide a hand along its surface or use an implement to manipulate it—but we can't really be a *part* of it."

"That's true."

"Except," Wil continued, "there was something I didn't consider in that analogy. We *can* merge with the paper—when we're cut and bleed. We give up a part of our essence in exchange for direct contact as our blood infuses in the paper fibers."

Saera's eyes widened with realization. "Maybe it's the same for the Erebus! It might actually *hurt* them to interact with spacetime, in the way we would need to cut and bleed to meld with the paper. That would explain why they didn't launch an outright invasion."

"It would."

She drummed her fingers on the chair's armrest. "The question is now, what do we do with this information?"

— — —

Leon hadn't been able to relax since his last meeting with the Alliance's leadership. His instincts told him that he was venturing into dangerous territory, but his curiosity and commitment to find answers drove him forward.

He would rather avoid spending any time in the dreary research lab, but given that he'd joined the Alliance under the pretense of serving as a technical specialist, he needed to make do with the limited resources. On this afternoon, he was once again reviewing a series of models for contact tracing between individuals within a large population. He'd explained on multiple occasions that he was a geneticist and knew next to nothing about the assigned work, but they insisted he do it anyway. Consequently, the task was both tedious and stressful, as he internally questioned his competence while wishing he was doing anything else.

His work was interrupted by a knock on the doorframe. Leon swiveled around to see Oren.

"There are some people from another team who'd like to meet with you at 15:00," the lanky man stated.

"What about?" Leon asked.

"Room B-27, 15:00," the man replied, pointedly ignoring the question.

Leon's heart leaped. "Should I bring anything?"

The man walked off without saying anything further on the matter.

The true precariousness of his situation snapped into focus. A last-minute meeting communicated out loud meant they didn't want a paper trail—no calendar item to reference. Now he was getting somewhere... but it also meant he might be in trouble.

He grabbed his handheld and typed out a message to Kira: >>I miss you. Any chance I can get a kiss on your way to the bathroom?<<

They assumed everything in their personal handhelds was tracked by the Alliance, so he kept the message intentionally vague. She'd know from the signals they'd worked out that he had a potentially important piece of information to share as soon as possible.

A response came a few seconds later: >>Yeah, I could use a quick break. See you soon.<<

He excused himself from the lab. Kira was waiting for him outside the restroom. His heart lifted upon seeing her, alleviating some of his tension.

She flashed a goofy grin and wrapped her arms around him. "Can't even make it through the afternoon without seeing me, huh?"

"Working in separate areas is a cruel form of torture." A bit much, but he wanted to sell the cover story for the meeting in case anyone was watching.

"I can't stay long."

"That's okay. I just wanted a few minutes with you to get me through to dinner." He slipped his hand behind her neck. "I never get tired of looking into your eyes."

She took the hint and activated a telepathic link.

"What's going on?" she asked in his mind.

"I've been summoned to a meeting in the basement at 15:00. They wouldn't say what it was about. Oren just came by to tell me to be there."

"I don't like the sound of that."

"I have to show up. This might be the lead we've been waiting for."

Kira stroked the side of his face with the back of her finger, keeping up the appearance of a love-struck couple for the sake of the security cameras. *"I should go with you—at least from a* distance."

"They'll see you and be suspicious."

"I'll get Kacey to trade for the guard post at the top of the stairs, so I'll be close by if there's trouble."

"B-27 is in the back corner. You won't be able to hear anything from up top."

"I won't risk you."

"What are they going to do? Most likely, they just want me to go over some more genetic models."

Even if there hadn't been a telepathic link, her expression would have spoken to him clearly. They both knew that wasn't the case; the Alliance was dangerous, and there was a high probability that they either meant him harm or intended to make him a part of the new research initiative that was being planned.

"Don't go to that meeting, Leon."

"How else are we going to learn what's going on? This is the opportunity we've been waiting for. I have to do this."

Kira seemed on the verge of protest, but then she nodded. "I'd want to do the same in your shoes, so it's not right of me to argue. Just be careful."

"Always." He pulled her in for a kiss.

She gazed into his eyes again. "If anything goes wrong, I'll find you. I promise."

"We really need a vacation after this undercover nonsense is over."

"Deal."

"See you again at dinner," Leon said out loud.

Kira grinned. "Counting the minutes!"

After a quick parting kiss, Leon returned to the lab. *What am I getting myself into?*

He had difficulty focusing for the rest of the afternoon in

anticipation of the meeting. When the time finally came, he arrived at the specified meeting space a few minutes early, as was his custom. The door was open, and the four individuals inside motioned for him to enter. A man and a woman were seated, and two other men of large stature stood to either side of the door.

The musty space was configured for meetings, with six chairs placed around a rectangular table. In typical Alliance fashion, the materials were well-worn, with scuff marks along the metal frames visible even from a distance. Being underground, there was no natural light, and the only illumination came from a low-grade bulb suspended from the center of the ceiling. The resulting ambiance made it feel more like an interrogation than a friendly conversation among peers.

One of the men standing next to the door swung it closed, sealing the five of them inside.

"Thank you for joining us," a woman greeted. "Claire had wonderful things to say about you."

Leon smiled meekly. "I'm happy to assist the cause."

"We need more committed individuals like yourself who have the skills and training to make a real difference."

"I'm eager to do more." Leon took a seat in the offered chair. It creaked under his weight, clearly having seen better days.

The woman leaned forward. "Good, because we have a project for you."

"I'm interested, of course," Leon replied. *This is exactly what we wanted. I need to get them to trust me.* He wasn't sure what they were looking for in a candidate, so he hoped that being himself—aside from the truth about being undercover—would win them over.

"That's good to hear, but this isn't an optional assignment.

The Alliance needs you."

How would they force me to do anything I don't want to? He tensed. "What's the project?"

"We'll share the details once you're in position," the woman stated.

The two men standing next to the door inside the room subtly stepped closer to the opening to better block the exit.

Shite! What have I walked into? Leon's hand-to-hand combat training gave him confidence in most situations, but he recognized that he was outnumbered and in an enclosed space with no clear escape path. "Where is the assignment located?" he asked.

"Offworld."

Uh oh. Leon swallowed. "My fiancée is here. I'm happy to relocate if she comes, too, but otherwise—"

"She is not needed for this task," the woman interrupted.

"Sorry, that doesn't work for me." Leon rose from his chair and started toward the door.

The two guards closed the gap between them, fully blocking the exit.

Across the table, the woman slowly rose, a weary smile on her lips. She took a slow breath and brought her gaze up to stare at Leon. "I think you'll find that it's in our best interests to work together."

CHAPTER 10

AFTER STARING AT his screen for most of the day, getting caught up on various administrative duties, Jason headed to the gym to work out his anxiety. He had yet to receive another update from Kira and was getting worried that something was wrong. *I need a distraction.*

As Jason entered the gym, he spotted a familiar face jogging around the track.

Could it be? The unexpected person was a distraction, all right—though not at all in the way he'd intended.

Jason waited next to the track for the young man to loop around. By the time he was within shouting distance, Jason was certain it was whom he'd initially thought.

"Darin!" Jason flagged him down.

The young man did a double take and then smiled. "Oh, hey!"

His eyes had a brightness to them that hadn't been there when Jason had interviewed him at the Prisaris Station several months before, after the *Andvari*'s destruction. Apparently, Darin had taken his advice to pursue a career in the TSS.

"Good to see you," Jason said. "I didn't expect you to end up here at Headquarters." It was unusual for Militia members to train at TSS Headquarters unless they were in a specialist program, which meant Darin had either been selected for elite training or there was something else going on.

"Yeah, me either. Suffice to say, the last few months have been weird." Darin wiped sweat from his brow with the back of his hand.

"I'm sure you've been through a lot. Believe it or not, I actually did wonder what happened to you after Prisaris. You can't spend time inside someone's head and not have a little connection there."

"Heh, I guess." Darin shrugged.

"So, what have you been up to?" Jason asked.

Darin ran his hand through the hair on the back of his head, letting out a long breath. "Well, I put in my TSS application right after we spoke. I got in right away."

Jason smiled. "My recommendation may have had something to do with that."

"Thank you. The TSS has been great. It wasn't long before I started my training at the Tauron base."

"Ah, yeah, that's one of the newer outposts for Militia. I heard it's pretty nice."

"Not as swanky as Headquarters here, but yeah, it was good. Everything seemed standard for about three months, but then things started getting… strange."

Jason tilted his head. "How so?"

"I began to… sense things, I guess you could say. Little stuff at first, like picking up if someone was lying or anticipating an attack in hand-to-hand combat training. At first, I thought I was just a natural. I mean, I had been training to join the Guard, like my mom, for my entire life. I *do* have skills." Darin flashed a proud grin.

"I don't doubt it."

"Anyway, it started happening more and more—and then with stuff that training alone wouldn't explain. The thing that really tipped it over the edge was when I knew someone tripped and hurt their knee in a pair sparring near me, but when I turned to help them, I saw the injury happen."

"You had precognition of the event, you mean?" Jason asked.

"Seemingly. There were other things like that. So, my commander started getting weirded out by it, and they referred me for a medical exam. The results of the scans were even more bizarre."

Even skilled Agents don't have anything like precognition skills. I actually haven't heard of that outside the Aesir with their 'pattern-reading'. Jason crossed his arms, becoming increasingly more intrigued. "What did the scans show?"

"I won't pretend to understand the science—not that anyone attempted to explain it to me—but the gist of it, I think, is that I've gained some sort of telepathic connection to higher dimensions… or something like that."

"I've never heard of that kind of ability developing spontaneously, so I imagine the working hypothesis is that this is related to your experience with the Erebus?"

Darin nodded. "That's what I'm told. No one has a clue how it might have happened. But at any rate, Headquarters has the best medical and research facilities, so I eventually found my way over here."

"The research team must be all over you."

"It's been a wild ride, man. Or should I call you 'sir' now that I'm in the TSS?"

Jason waved off the question. "Not at all necessary when

it's just us. I can't say I'm surprised there was a lasting impact from your experience with the Erebus. Direct contact with a higher-dimensional being like that does seem like it would change things."

"Oh, did it ever! I mean, fok, I was just a random salvage-hauler kid, and now I have this weird precog-telepathy thing? I'm still trying to wrap my head around it."

"That's a pretty cool skill to have," Jason said. "I hope you're able to make the most of it."

"It was really random at first, but it's been getting a little easier to focus and get impressions about specific things." Darin let out a long breath between his teeth, shaking his head. "I wish it hadn't come from those bomaxed Erebus, though. I just about pissed myself when I saw the announcements about those spatial rifts opening up around Tararia a few months back. I thought that would be it—that we were all done for."

Jason nodded. "It was intense, not gonna lie."

"Shite, were you *there*?" The young man's eyes widened.

"With a family like mine, I can't seem to avoid being in the middle of any given crisis."

Darin chuckled. "I can see that. Stars, that must be tough being in the spotlight all the time."

"Could be worse," Jason replied. "I guess the nice thing is I usually know what's going on—even when I wish I didn't."

"Knowing the truths you can't share with anyone?"

"Yep."

He nodded. "I haven't told many people what happened to me, or that I was on the *Andvari*. The ship has become kinda famous within certain circles."

"Sometimes being anonymous is the best approach. No sense coloring relationships before someone has the chance to get to know you."

"You probably know that better than most," Darin said.

"I rarely get the pleasure of anonymity. Especially not in the TSS; the family resemblance is too strong. But it is what it is."

"I hate to say it, but I think a lot of people would kill to have your life."

Jason shrugged. "That's the problem, isn't it? People tend to think that others have it better. Except, once you get a look on the inside, you may find out that things aren't always as great as they seemed."

Darin raised an eyebrow. "Being a Sietinen isn't all it's cracked up to be, eh?"

"My family is great, don't get me wrong," Jason said. "The problem is that people make assumptions based on the name alone. I mean, my sister and I grew up on Earth, for stars' sake! We're about as far from typical nobles as you can get. I think what's more important is how you live your life, not where you start out."

Darin nodded slowly. "I'm trying. It would have been a lot easier to give up after what happened to my family on the *Andvari*, but that's not me."

"A person needs a little fight in them to get anywhere worth going."

"My mom used to say something like that—about the best rewards coming from hard work." He looked down morosely. "I always took my family for granted. I wish I'd realized how good I had it back then."

Jason gave him a sympathetic nod. "Hindsight is difficult like that. I think back to my teenage years on Earth when I complained about stupid shite, like why my parents wouldn't buy me a car, and can't help but see how inconsequential it seems now. The best thing you can do is live in the moment and try to appreciate the little pleasures."

"Wait, your parents wouldn't get you a *car*? Don't they own, like, entire planets?"

Jason laughed. "Not quite. But that wasn't the point; it was a lesson in responsibility I couldn't appreciate until much later on."

"I guess that's one of the big things about growing up, isn't it? Realizing those lessons that seemed so irritating were actually full of wisdom. My mom had a lot of those."

"Let me tell you, it's doubly annoying to come to that realization when you have parents in positions like mine. A huge portion of their careers has been spent turning arrogant teenagers into responsible adults to wield some of the most powerful weapons in the Taran Empire."

Darin laughed. "I guess it was inevitable that you'd turn out to be a model Agent."

Jason smiled. "Not that there weren't times when I wanted to rebel. Some of the best things come from living on the edge."

"With you there." Darin paused in quiet contemplation for a few moments. "I appreciate what you said about living in the present and trying to appreciate what you have. You never know what tomorrow will bring."

"Life does tend to throw us twists when we least expect it."

The young man looked down the track and then back to Jason. "I'm glad I got to see you again. Last time I was... not at my best."

"You were doing a lot better than I probably would have been in the same situation. I'm glad to see things are looking up now, though."

"I hope so." Darin crossed his arms. "This new ability still has me a little freaked out, though."

"Have you spoken about it with my parents directly?"

Jason asked.

Darin shook his head. "Just some researcher-medical types."

"I'll follow up with them—let them know we chatted. I know firsthand that sometimes reports don't do a good job of capturing the magnitude of a new development."

"Sure, if you think they'd care."

"Definitely. You may be able to tell us things no one else can."

— — —

"What's this meeting about, exactly?" Saera asked as she followed Wil toward one of the conference rooms near his office.

"Remember the sole survivor of the *Andvari* attack?" Wil replied. "Apparently, he's come to train here at Headquarters."

"How did we not hear about that?"

"A sign that the organization has reached a scale where we can no longer personally keep track of everything." Wil opened the conference room door and held it for Saera to enter.

She frowned. "That seems like a significant person we would have heard about."

"I asked Michael, and apparently he was aware. Darin is in the Militia Division, so he wouldn't have come across your desk as a new Trainee."

"That makes me feel a little better."

"What's strange, though, is he was brought here to study some newly manifested ability of precognition."

"Wait, what?"

Wil nodded. "Sounded very strange to me, too. And I don't understand why no one on the medical or research teams reported it to me."

Saera smiled as she took her seat. "I'm certain they did. How many of those reports do you actually read?"

He sat down next to her. "Point taken."

"Aside from him being a medical curiosity, why are we meeting with him?"

"I want to question him about this transdimensional connection. I've been kicking around some ideas following our last discussion, and I'd like to see if there's a link."

The door opened, and Jason entered with Darin in tow.

"Hi, thanks for meeting on short notice," his son said, sitting across the table from Wil and Saera.

"Sir. Ma'am." Darin bobbed his head respectfully before taking a chair to Jason's right.

"Darin Suro, correct?" Wil said.

The young man nodded. "Yes, sir."

"It's good to have you here in the TSS. I hope you're settling in."

"I am, sir, thank you."

"So, Darin and I had an interesting chat earlier," Jason began. "I thought you'd like to hear what's been going on with him since his contact with the Erebus."

At the mention of the aliens, Darin swallowed hard and flushed a little.

"Some kind of limited precognitive ability, correct?" Wil asked.

Darin took a quick breath. "Yes, sir, it seems that way. I'm still learning to control it, but sometimes I get flashes of a thing before it happens."

Wil eyed him. "That's quite unusual."

"Which is why I thought you might want to speak with him," Jason explained. "With the talk about the Erebus' higher dimensional existence, I got to thinking…"

He is very much my son. Wil smiled. "This is quite a complex puzzle we're trying to solve, and this may be an important piece. Tell me, Darin, did you ever experience these flashes before your encounter with the Erebus?"

"No. It started shortly after I woke up from the coma, though it took a few months before I started to realize something significant might be going on. At first, I thought it was just an issue with my vision or concentration."

There was likely some denial that had prevented him from noticing, but Wil could understand a person's reluctance to admit they were different. "When Jason reached out to me about this earlier, I decided to take a look at your medical records. There's no clear physiological explanation for this ability, though scans do read like a Gifted person actively using telepathy."

"Which is what has everyone so stumped… sir."

"Don't worry about the honorifics right now, Darin. I've never been much of a fan."

The young man nodded. "Okay."

"I know it's difficult to talk about," Wil continued, "but I hope you can shed additional insights into what happened on your ship—knowing the people involved and their general temperaments. I'm aware that you were unconscious during the events themselves."

Darin shook his head. "I don't understand what that thing was doing or why it was messing with us. All I know is that it took everything I love from me."

"I'm sorry for your loss."

"Thanks. I'll answer what I can."

"I've been particularly curious about how your engineer managed to determine what you were dealing with." Wil folded his hands on the desktop. "We had quite a difficult time trying to recreate the conditions under which your ship captured the first transdimensional image of the Erebus. I can't figure out how it happened without you blowing yourselves up. None of our attempts to duplicate the conditions produced the desired results. We had to start over with an entirely different approach."

"I wasn't awake for that." Darin shrugged. "Were your probes and ship inside an Erebus during testing?"

"No."

The young man flourished his hand. "Well, there you go."

Wil turned to Saera. *"How did we miss that?"* he asked her telepathically. *"We never* actually *replicated the original environment—we were missing that detail."*

"I can see how being inside a transdimensional entity would alter the conditions... you know, just a little."

He had to smile at her sarcastic mental tone. "Thank you for clearing up that portion of the mystery," Wil continued to Darin. "As for your own manifested ability, that's more complicated."

"Yeah, I've been hoping for an explanation of that myself."

Wil nodded. "It's been our suspicion that your coma was a result of direct contact with the Erebus as it reached down from a higher dimension to interact with you. What I hadn't considered is that a portion of the framework for that transdimensional bridge may have remained intact."

"What does that mean?"

"Think of it like digging a trench. Even when the dirt is filled back in, it's always going to be a little looser than it was before the ground was disturbed."

"I don't have any experience with trench-digging, but I catch your meaning," Darin said.

"*See? This is why I rarely use planet-bound analogies, because it means nothing to us space-reared kids,*" Wil said with an amused telepathic smile in his wife's mind.

"*Well, I thought it was quite apt.*" The situation had been reversed when the two of them met, and Saera never failed to remind him how much life experience played into a person's perspective.

"What I mean to say is," Wil continued, "that the Erebus needed to reach down from the higher dimension to make contact with you in our reality. We're not sure how they accomplish that, precisely, but it's clear it created a telepathic link with you. I suspect your premonitions have something to do with that link—that it left a tether between you and the higher dimensions above spacetime. I can't explain why you'd get flashes for some things and not others, but it sounds somewhat like the access we gain to the cosmic energy pattern when gazing into the nexus. The Aesir read those threads."

Darin scrunched his brows. "Sorry, I only tracked about half of what you just said."

"There's precedent for precognitive visions, but the way it seems to be working for you is unique," Jason summarized.

"Should I know about these Aesir?" Darin asked.

"No, they keep to themselves, and they're also frustrating and unhelpful most of the time," Wil replied. "Anyway, all of this suggests that the Erebus you encountered was interacting with spacetime in a different way than they did when they attacked the Alkeer Station and Tararia. It learned something from the encounter with the *Andvari* and shared it with the others of its kind."

"That sounds bad." Darin frowned.

"I also find it strange that you experienced a PEM failure, your crew encountered a strange array of ships, you went after a replacement PEM, and then the Erebus handed the TSS a new type of power core."

The young man's eyes went wide. "Wait, they what?"

"Yes, a 'gift', they said. It's a loose connection, but in bizarre transdimensional being logic, I can see how they may have inferred meaning," Wil told him.

Naturally, the *Andvari*'s crew had gone after a new perpetual energy module when their system was damaged, so it tracked that the Erebus may have interpreted 'power source' as being the most important thing to Tarans—being the first thing they sought when they became stranded. What better gift than to offer the thing people desire the most? It just so happened that MPS' issues intersected with that need.

Darin shrugged. "I wish I could offer a big breakthrough understanding of what's going on. I can't. I was unconscious. When I woke up, I was a physical wreck, homeless, and without my family. Now there's this new precog ability, and I don't know what to do with it."

"You've been through a lot," Saera said. "We'll try to get you answers."

"It doesn't matter. I've got a place to call home for now."

"I'm glad to hear you feel that way." Wil gave him a sympathetic smile. "This has given me some things to think about. Thank you for speaking with us. I'll reach out if I have follow-up questions down the line."

"Happy to help. And thanks for believing me. Some people thought I was crazy when I first brought up the visions."

"I've had far stranger experiences myself." Wil stood. "Take care, Darin."

"Thank you, sir."

"I'll check in with you later, Jason. I want to process this," he told his son telepathically. *"Thanks for bringing him here."*

"Sure thing."

Jason departed with Darin, leaving Wil and Saera alone in the conference room.

"That was rather illuminating," his wife said.

"Indeed. Everything keeps coming back to the transdimensional interactions, and it's got me going down some very strange hypothetical trails."

"You? I'm shocked," Saera jested.

"It makes me wonder what things would have been like for ancient Tarans when they first encountered the Erebus."

"Did they have a way to protect themselves? Did they understand how to control the energy link between the dimensions?" Saera mused.

"Right. And then I got to thinking…"

"Hmm?"

"Now, I might be making connections that aren't there, but I started wondering about Earth. Raena is helming that archaeological investigation, which might be related to the ancient war, given the suspected age of it. Okay, so that's all well and good. But then there's this facility we adopted as TSS Headquarters. Well, not *us* specifically, but you know, the Priesthood."

Saera tilted her head. "What about it?"

"The unique construction method, suspending the facility in a subspace bubble. We still have no clue how they even pulled that off, but it was brilliant. The perfect defense from interdimensional attack, which is what made it so ideal for the Bakzen War."

"I see where you're going with this. The facility predates that war by at least a millennium."

"Precisely! So why was it originally built? Perhaps because of knowledge about the ancient war with the Erebus and

Gatekeepers, before that information was lost or suppressed?"

Saera nodded. "That actually makes a lot more sense."

"There's another wrinkle, though. Part of the TSS mandate has always been to serve as stewards of Earth."

"Was that driven by the Priesthood when they founded the TSS, or did it evolve when Earth's space exploration kicked off?"

"I'm not sure, honestly. Either way, it doesn't explain how or why the Aesir built this facility. Dahl refuses to give me a straight answer whenever I try to broach the topic."

His wife sat in silence for a few seconds. "*Did* the Aesir build it?"

"I don't know. That's what we'd always assumed, but… it's a mystery." He paused. "I might need to press the issue with Dahl. If the location of this base has anything to do with this emerging ancient tech discovery on Earth, then I doubt it's a coincidence that such a specialized thing was constructed here."

"Perhaps it was intended to be an observation outpost to keep an eye on a device of great importance?" Saera suggested.

"Yeah, something like that."

She sat in silence for a while. "Was it a mistake for us to transition the facility out from subspace?"

As he had walked through the branching possibilities, Wil had wondered the same thing. "All I can say with certainty is that our ancestors knew more than we do right now. We need to learn everything we can."

CHAPTER 11

A BLARING ALARM snapped Lexi to attention at her workstation. She squinted against the glare of red, pulsing lights she hadn't known were even installed in the room.

"What's going on?" she asked no one in particular.

"That's the evacuation alarm," Shena said. "What—"

She cut off as a loud *boom* sounded outside, and the building shuddered, bits of dust and plaster raining from the ceiling.

Stars! Lexi instinctively ducked. "Are we under attack?"

Shouts sounded from the lounge room followed by the sharp crack of breaking glass.

Everything had been fine for the preceding hours of the afternoon. She'd had lunch with Kira and Leon and then gone back to work at her station. Nothing had seemed out of the ordinary until the alarm sounded.

More screams and rumbles carried from outside. A particularly loud quake accompanied another *boom* close enough to hurt her ears. More plaster flaked off the ceiling, a cloud of debris filled the air. She spat out the chalky taste.

"We need to get out of here!" Shena shouted, making a run for the nearest door.

"I'm right behind you." Lexi had no intention of going anywhere just yet. She needed to locate her friends. They'd never find each other if the sounds from outside were any indication of the chaos breaking out across Duron City.

She jogged back toward the lounge room at the intersection of the various work areas. If Kira was coming to find her from her usual post location, she'd pass through the room.

Halfway across the lounge, a powerful blast shook the building, causing the old light fixtures to spark. A section of the ceiling cracked apart, which sent a fresh cloud of dust billowing on the wind streaming in from the broken windows.

A cough sounded from the doorway and Kira stumbled into view, covered in white dust and dark smudges.

Lexi waved away the dust in front of her, to little effect. "Kira! Are you okay?" She ran to her.

The other woman had a small trickle of blood streaming down from her hairline. "Yeah, just a scrape. I'll be fine. Have you seen Leon?"

"No, not since lunch. What's happening?"

"Shite. I wish I knew. I can't find him. He was summoned to a meeting this afternoon, but he didn't come back."

"Meeting with who?"

"Alliance leadership. Something about their research."

Another explosion in the distance rocked the building foundation.

"Fok!" Kira exclaimed. "This must have been the plan all along."

"What do you mean?"

"I think the Alliance might be cleaning up loose ends."

Lexi glanced toward the window. "It sounds like the whole city is falling apart out there."

"We knew the Alliance was planning something, but I didn't think it would be *this*." She shook her head, seemingly on the verge of a more emotional display but her poise as a seasoned soldier kept her focused.

"We'll find Leon," Lexi tried to assure her. "Where was his meeting?"

"Down in the basement."

"Then he might be trapped down there. Or, there are all sorts of underground passageways leading out, so he could have been taken that way."

"If that's the case, he wouldn't have gone willingly." Kira swore under her breath. "I need to try to look for him, to make sure he's not being held somewhere onsite."

Lexi waved her arms. "The building is falling apart!"

"I won't leave him here to be buried in rubble. *If* he's here. I have to be sure."

"I'll help you look."

"No, Lexi, you should go. Now," Kira urged.

"I'm not leaving you here alone."

"I can look after myself."

Lexi crossed her arms and stared down the other woman. "I have no doubt, but that doesn't change that I'm the reason you're here. Helping the authorities stop the Alliance—or Coalition, or whatever—is the only thing separating me from the criminals behind these attacks."

"There's a lot more that makes you different."

"It doesn't matter. I want to see this thing through. I won't run away."

Kira sighed. "All right. But I can't promise I'll be able to protect you if things get dicey."

Lexi flashed a confident smile. "You're not the only one who can look after herself."

"Let's start with the basement, since that's his last known location. Maybe there's a clue."

The two women broke into a quick jog toward the staircase. The corridors were a mess of dust and minor debris that had fallen from cracks in the ceiling and walls.

No one else was visible in the building, presumably having already evacuated. That was the smart thing to do. Running deeper into an unstable building went against Lexi's gut instincts and everything she had been taught, but she agreed with Kira; they had to make sure Leon wasn't trapped somewhere.

The basement was in even worse shape than the upper levels, being of an older construction vintage. Several bricks had broken free from the mortar and now littered the central hallway. The pervasive musty smell in the space had intensified, filling Lexi's nostrils with a strong aroma of mildew and wet stone.

Lexi followed Kira toward the back of the basement to a room labeled B-27. She had never been to that portion of the facility before, but she'd heard it referenced by management. The door was cracked open and the room empty, aside from the spartan furnishings.

Kira, undeterred by the lack of people, immediately began examining the room. "Look for any computer access. We might be able to pull up recent files."

"You know how to hack?"

"Not as well as Kyle or Nia, but I can get by."

"Who?"

"Some of the best soldiers you'll ever meet." Kira spotted something and knelt down next to the back wall. "Ah ha!

Control panel for the holoprojector." She took out a multitool from her pocket and began prying off the covering.

"You just carry that thing around with you?"

"You *don't* have one?" She popped the panel off, revealing a mess of data ribbons and a crystal matrix. "This would be so much easier with the right equipment."

Lexi remained silent, having nothing to add. She watched as Kira traced the path of one data ribbon and then unplugged it. Kira pulled out her handheld and plugged the ribbon into the universal port at the base.

"Hardwiring in bypasses some of the usual security protocols. If I can find the right network opening..." She tapped rapidly on her screen. "Gimme a few secs."

After a minute of rapid typing and several expletives of frustration, she gave a victorious shout. "All right! I've got the user's login credentials who last accessed these files. Looks like they were in a project directory. I bet you anything that this is the information about that new lab."

"If they've got a new lab, they'd need people to staff it."

Kira gave a grim nod. "I have a suspicion that Leon was 'recruited' for that very purpose."

They couldn't yet rule out the possibility that Leon wasn't still somewhere in the Alliance office, but it did make sense that he could have been taken. Regardless, they needed all the information they could get on the lab. "Where is the planet?"

"Let's see... We should be able to go into the directory and— Shite! The permissions profile has been modified. They must have locked it down in preparation for their departure." Kira rocked back on her heels. "Bomax. With this lockout, these files can only be opened from a local terminal for this division. I can't get in from here."

Lexi's heart dropped. "Then there's nothing we can do. We

should get out of here."

"No, this is the clue we've been waiting for! We need those files. We have to find a terminal." Concern edged Kira's normally playful tone.

Lexi couldn't blame her. The files could very well hold the clues they'd been waiting months to uncover, not to mention Leon's possible whereabouts. "Where do we need to go?" she asked.

Kira consulted her handheld's screen. "Fourth floor, northeast corner."

Lexi did some quick mental calculations about how long it would take to get up there and the likelihood that the building would come down around her. "We should hurry."

Kira unplugged her handheld, and they ran back into the hall.

A couple of doors down, Lexi halted when she heard the faint sound of a metal chair scuffing on the stone floor. "Do you hear that?"

"Yeah." Kira pressed her ear to the door to confirm the sound. "Hey, is someone in there?"

Stifled shouts replied, unintelligible.

"Leon?" Lexi ask hopefully.

"No, it doesn't feel like him." Kira tried the handle, finding it locked.

"I've got it." Lexi reached out telekinetically and broke the lock.

Kira raised her eyebrows, impressed. "Nice trick."

"I've been holding back... a lot." Lexi swung the door inward, and the sounds of struggle inside the room got louder.

The overhead fixture was off, but light streaming in from the hallway illuminated a man tethered to a chair. He wriggled and cried out through a cloth gag.

"Hey, we've got you." Kira rushed forward to remove his face covering. "Who are you and why are you tied up?"

Lexi appreciated that Kira hadn't immediately assumed the man was on their side. She hadn't had much opportunity to see the soldier in her element, and it was freeing for both of them to now finally be able to let their fronts down.

"I'm Trent. They threw me in here when I tried to stop them."

"Do you know what's happening?" Kira asked.

"The end of this stage. They had to move up the timeline. There was a breach. They don't want any witnesses."

"Well, *we're* still alive!" Lexi declared.

"For now. The entire planet is set to go up."

Lexi gaped at him. "How do you know that?"

"Because I was the one who objected to the plan. Please, untie me."

Lexi and Kira exchanged glances, coming to silent agreement that he didn't seem like a threat. They began loosening the ropes securing him to the chair.

"Thank you," the man said, giving them a grateful smile. "They were about to shoot me when they were interrupted by one of the scientists trying to escape while they were dragging him out. Guy had some moves."

"Probably Leon," Kira said, freeing the last of the man's bonds.

He rubbed his wrists. "Well, I owe him my life—whatever little time we have left."

"What do you mean?" Kira asked.

"The Alliance's plan is to overload the planetary shield generator and force it to go critical, releasing a deadly blast."

"What?!" Lexi and Kira exclaimed at the same time.

"It will take hours," he said. "But once the chain reaction

starts, it's all over."

"There's still time to stop it," Kira assessed. "If we can get an engineer—"

"You won't find a specialist like that on this world. And they've certainly taken out all the ports by now, so we're trapped. Your best bet is finding a deep cave to ride out the initial blast." He started to move toward the door.

"Hey, come with us," Kira offered.

"No, thanks, I'll find my own way. Good luck." He ran out.

"Is it really possible to weaponize a planetary shield like that?" Lexi asked.

Kira bit her lower lip. "Maybe. I do recall hearing that they could be turned into a giant planet-killing bomb under *very* specific conditions."

"The Alliance has been recruiting engineers…"

"Those sick bastards are just deranged enough to try it. We need to get the authorities here."

"They have to know something is going on with all the madness outside!"

"Yes, but there might not be any signs of a critical shield failure yet. The sooner we can get word to them, the better the likelihood of diffusing the energy buildup before it can't be stopped."

"Make the call!"

"The communication grid is failing. I have no connectivity down here."

"Well, we need to go after the project files, and I don't know that we'll be able to get back here if we leave."

"I need you to go get those files," Kira said.

"Split up now? You can't be serious!"

"Please go, Lexi. I'll find somewhere with reception to make the call, and then I need to escort as many people to safety as I can. I'm on a mission, but it's my duty to protect civilians whenever possible."

"I don't know how to get into the files even if I can find an access terminal on the fourth floor."

"There's no trick to it. Now that we have the user information, just enter it into the system."

"Okay." Lexi's gut lurched. "I'm so sorry for getting you into this mess."

Kira laughed. "This? This is nothing! And I volunteered to be here—that's not on you." She turned serious. "We'll meet at the park near the port in half an hour. You can do this, Lexi. It's going to be okay."

She wanted to believe the other woman, but the chaos erupting around her amplified every doubt swirling in her mind. "Okay. Be careful."

"You too."

Kira ran off into the swirling smoke and dust.

Lexi took a slow, deep breath to center herself. *I can do this. This is the moment I've been waiting for.*

With renewed resolve, she jogged down the hall, toward the stairwell that would grant her access to the upper levels. Normally patrolled by security guards—though no one would admit that's what they were—the way ahead was now clear. She raced up the steps, not wanting to waste any time while the structure slowly crumbled around her. Worse than the groaning metal superstructure and flaking plaster was the warning that the man, Trent, had given: the Alliance didn't want to leave any witnesses, and they'd take whatever steps were necessary to destroy Duronis now that the planet and its people were no longer useful.

They're making this entire world a sacrificial symbol, she realized. *Get an uprise of the people all over the news and then wipe it out in a shocking act of terrorism that can be blamed on whoever makes the best narrative.*

She'd spent enough time working on Alliance marketing messaging that she could play the story out in her head, how they'd twist the tragedy and turn it into a moving masterpiece. Those in charge would show no remorse; she wasn't even sure they were capable of it. The people who had been roped into the organization were pawns to be manipulated in a giant game. She didn't know where they were going with it, and she didn't want to find out.

The best hope for stopping the Alliance was to recover as many files as possible and turn over that information to the authorities. The issues were beyond the scope of her abilities.

Getting that information, though, was on her. Kira was counting on her to come through. Moreover, she needed to do this for herself. She'd spent more than a year waiting for a chance to make a big move, and this was it.

Her legs were warm and tingling by the time she had loped up the stairs from the basement. At the fourth-floor landing, she was faced with a closed and locked security door leading to the wing she needed to access.

I've been wanting to do this for a long time.

She telekinetically yanked the door from its hinges, holding back just enough to prevent other structural damage to the already weakened building. Tossing the metal and plasglass door aside, she rushed into the northeast quadrant of the building to look for an access terminal.

The hallway was lined with offices. The desks had been mostly cleaned off, though the items that remained were strewn about in a haphazard way. Whatever order had been given, this was a rushed evacuation.

When did they clear out? Lexi thought back over the

afternoon, and she couldn't think of a time when there'd been unusual foot traffic. In fact, everything had been *normal* until the moment the alarm went off. Within three minutes of it sounding, the building had been almost empty, and the stragglers had vacated by the time they were ten minutes into the incident.

It didn't make sense. How could an entire building full of people disperse without anyone noticing?

Lexi stopped in her tracks. She was missing something.

Her desire to get answers battled with the ticking clock in her head. Another explosion could go off at any moment and bring the entire building down. Yet, she had risked her life to get this far, and she had to learn everything she could while there was still an opportunity to do so.

She ran back to the landing and busted down the other security doors leading to the different sections of the building. As she looked down the hallways, she noticed that the interior was arranged oddly. A quick run down the hallways confirmed it. There were gaps between some of the rooms; the interior walls didn't adjoin in a way that it looked like they should.

Stopping at one such area, she telekinetically punched at the walls and began ripping away sections. Her breath caught in her throat as the hole revealed a hidden stairway.

Of course! In retrospect, she felt silly for not suspecting there were secret passageways throughout the building. There were always more people at mealtimes and in the bunkrooms than she ever saw coming or going throughout the day. If she had to guess, the stairwell probably connected to the old transit tunnel system beneath the city. It would provide perfect access for planting explosives at key sites, and for moving people around without detection.

As great as that information was to have, it did little to

assist with her current task of obtaining the project files.

Clock is ticking. Move!

She ran back to the quadrant where she needed to access the terminal. She'd spent precious time running around, and her chest was tight with anxiety about getting trapped in the building.

Toward the back of the hallway, she spotted a room that still had the computer terminal intact. To her relief, she saw a docking port where she'd be able to hook up her handheld.

She made the physical connection. A network access protocol popped up on her handheld's screen. She flipped through the directory to locate the same project folder Kira had identified.

Got you! She opened it. Unlike the previous attempt, she now had access. *Now to download this data.*

Lexi began the sync. The estimated time to completion was twenty-seven minutes.

How much information is here? She groaned with dismay. Not only would that make her late for her meet-up with Kira, but she wasn't sure her handheld had enough storage capacity for the files. Unfortunately, she didn't have an external storage device on her, and the office looked like it had been picked clean. *I guess I'll take as much as I can get.*

The transfer status bar began slowly crawling across the screen. She leaned against the edge of the desk, tapping her foot with nervous energy as she watched it progress.

Several minutes passed in anxious anticipation. It was coming along well, and she had yet to get a 'memory full' error.

A large explosion boomed outside, this one further away. The windows rattled slightly, but at least the building didn't quake this time.

Her sigh of relief was cut short when the lights cut out. A

moment later, the connection screen on her handheld dropped to idle.

No! Her heart sank. Though daylight still streamed in through the windows, the illuminated displays on buildings outside had all gone dead. The power was out. A plume of smoke rose above distant buildings. *Did they take out the power distribution station?*

It didn't matter. The fact remained that the interface was now dead, and she couldn't proceed with the data transfer. She had *some* information copied, but was it the part that would provide answers?

Shite! There was nothing she could do about it now. However, there was the other lead she could follow about the hidden stairway to see where it went. There might be answers down there if they didn't have useful information in the limited files she'd been able to copy.

What do I do? There were only moments to decide. She weighed her options. The obvious solution was to stick with the plan and meet Kira at the rendezvous. However, there wouldn't be another chance to get underground and search if she passed up this opportunity. She had to risk it.

She reached out with her mind to search for Kira. *"Where are you?"* She couldn't feel the presence of the other woman in the building. Or anyone.

There was no way to pass on a message about her intentions. It didn't change her decision. If she couldn't get all the files, she could at least chase this lead.

Wait for me, Kira, she willed out to the universe. *I'm coming.*

CHAPTER 12

JASON WAS WINDING down for the day in his office when his desktop illuminated with a high-priority alert. A quick check of the incoming call showed an unregistered ident from Duronis.

An update from Kira? He accepted the vidcall. "Hi, how's it—"

"Jason!" Kira coughed as a plume of smoke swirled around her.

"Stars, what's going on?"

"Shite went sideways." She started to laugh, not a happy sound, which turned into another cough. "Field work is the best!"

"Are you okay?"

"Mostly. For now." Her expression turned serious. "It all happened so fast. One minute we were going about our regular afternoon duties, and then alarms were going off and people were panicking."

"I don't understand. What—"

"The Alliance has made its big move, Jason," she

interrupted. "They took all of the 'valuable', trusted people and got off this rock. Near as I can tell, they've left us here to tear ourselves apart."

"That doesn't make any sense. Why?"

"Because they're insane. The more disruption, the easier it is for them to work toward their ultimate goals, whatever those are."

"Slow down. What's happening?" He brought up the listing of TSS incident reports. Sure enough, Duronis was flagged with a developing situation, though no details had yet been loaded into the files accessible to him.

Kira shook her head. "These sick bastards are destroying the planet and leaving people here to die. They've taken out the food stores and the ports. Torched the farm biodomes. Blew up the power station. I expect communications will go down as soon as the backup batteries are drained."

Jason was speechless. It sounded like too much devastation to have happened in short order, but the smoke and rubble in the background of the video supported Kira's words. "Where are you now?"

"A few blocks from the Alliance office—or what's left of it. Lexi was going to try to copy some information from one of the management offices, but I don't know where she is now. She missed our rendezvous. The whole building just went up in flames."

His stomach dropped. "What about Leon?"

She let out a bitter cough. "He disappeared this afternoon. I think they may have taken him as part of that new research project we learned they were working on."

No! This can't be happening. He tried to keep the emotion from his face. She needed reassurance right now, not someone else feeding into the worry she must be feeling. "I'm going to get you out from there. Send me your current coordinates."

A notification popped up that he had received a datapacket.

"The port is gone," Kira said. "I don't know how this planet can get evacuated in time."

"In time?"

"We found a man tied up in the basement. He claimed that the Alliance has rigged the planetary shield to overload and scorch the surface. I already alerted the local Enforcers."

"How would—"

The vidcall abruptly cut out.

Shite! Is the communication network on Duronis down? Kira had told him that it could drop out at any moment. The situation was deteriorating much faster than he'd anticipated. *I need to tell Dad what she told me.*

He ran down the hall to the High Commander's office. He knocked on the door.

"Dad, I just got a message—" he began telepathically.

"I'm on a call."

"This can't wait. It's about Duronis."

"Mine, too. Come in."

Jason opened the door to see his father was on his handheld. "Mobilize everyone who's available, Michael," Wil was saying. "Do what you can." He held up his finger to indicate to Jason that he would be finished soon.

"Yes, I understand. Okay. Keep me apprised." Wil ended the call and turned to Jason. "What have you heard?"

"I got a panicked call from Kira saying that there've been a series of explosions on Duronis. Conditions on the planet are deteriorating quickly. She said the Alliance might be trying to overload the shield to take out the planet. Is that even possible?"

Wil scowled. "Theoretically, yes. It's never been attempted, to my knowledge. I got the same information relayed to me via the Enforcers—that tip must have come from her."

"Yes, she told me she made the call. If that is happening, there isn't a lot of time to get conditions under control."

"It's not just Duronis," his father revealed.

Jason froze. "What?"

"We're getting reports from all around the Outer Colonies. It's unclear what's going on, exactly. Random explosions planetside and at spaceports. No estimates on loss of life, yet, but there are certainly casualties with the scale of it. This was obviously coordinated, and highly so."

"The Coalition?"

"It's looking likely—this is bigger than the Alliance's activities. No one has yet stepped forward to take credit or state demands, though. Sowing chaos seems to be the goal, and it's working."

Jason's brow knitted. "When did these reports start coming in?"

"Within the last thirty minutes."

And he didn't tell me right away? In reality, it was perfectly reasonable that his father hadn't yet informed him about the developing situation; there were other people in the command chain to deal with these sorts of incidents. Still, this involved someone in the field he was responsible for, and he felt terrible that he hadn't known Kira was in trouble until she called him.

"We need to get Kira out of there," Jason said.

"Neither the Guard nor TSS can spare field personnel for a dedicated extraction team right now; we need to focus on evacuating civilians in case this situation with the shield pans out and we can't stop it. Kira is going to need to find a way to get herself out."

The ports are shut down. What is she supposed to do? Jason stood his ground. "I convinced her to go on this mission. I won't abandon her."

"I understand, and I appreciate your loyalty. I just can't in good conscience redirect resources to take care of one person while we're facing a crisis of this magnitude."

"Then I'll go."

"Absolutely not."

"You wouldn't say that if it was me down there, would you? Or Mom? Or Michael?"

Wil faltered. "That's different."

"I might not have that kind of personal relationship with Kira, but she trusted me to be her point of contact on the outside. It's my duty to honor that," Jason insisted. "Leave the other work to the teams. I'm just one person, but I can handle it."

His father pressed his lips into a line, weighing the options. "You're not going to take 'no' for an answer, are you?"

Jason stood firm. "Please, let me do this. I can scope out the situation firsthand and help a friend in the process."

"All right," Wil consented after a heavy pause. "Please, be safe."

"I'll see you soon."

Jason ran from the office and headed straight for the surface port. The subspace jump would take more than five hours; that was a long time for Kira to be trapped on a potentially dying world. Perhaps she'd be able to make it to a civilian evacuation center, but he didn't want to rely on that. He'd take a ship that could land directly on the surface so he'd be as agile as possible.

There was the complication that he didn't know *how* he would locate Kira once he got to Duronis, if she'd moved from the coordinates she sent, but that was a problem for a few hours from now. All that mattered for the time being was getting underway as soon as possible with hope that there would still be a planet there by the time he arrived.

— — —

Flames and a burst of debris shot into the tunnel from where the stairway door to the Alliance office had been. Lexi covered her head with her arms and ducked against the side wall of the tunnel until the clattering stopped. Her skin stung from the heat and flying shards, but she was unharmed.

Her hands shook and her breath came in ragged gasps as she coughed out the burnt air. *That was too close!*

She wasn't sure what had brought the building down in the final moments of her descent, but she likely wouldn't have made it out alive if she'd been delayed by even a few more seconds in the office after the file transfer terminated.

The universe was looking out for me today. She didn't want to count on that good fortune to last. Now she needed to find Kira and figure out a way off the planet.

As the fire became blocked by fallen debris, the tunnel fell into darkness. Lexi fumbled for her handheld in her pocket and managed to get its flashlight turned on.

She took in her surroundings. The tunnel was similar to the others she'd explored during her previous exploits with the Alliance, but this one had none of the supply racks or other signs of habitation she'd seen in those passages. The only clue that there was anything of interest to find here was the disturbed layer of dust coating the paving bricks on the floor. Hundreds of footprints had worn a bare patch along the center of the tunnel, with overlapping prints visible toward the edges.

A lot of people had come through here recently.

Where were they going? She set off to follow the tracks, trying to quiet the voice in her head pleading that missing the rendezvous with Kira was going to leave her in a tough spot.

Lexi jogged along the path, the limited light from her handheld making it feel like she was venturing into an abyss.

It was easy to track the course. Distance was difficult to gauge in the monotonous landscape, but it felt like she'd gone at least a kilometer before she encountered a rubble pile off to the side of the tunnel—the only feature of note she'd come across. The footprint curved toward the pile and disappeared into it.

Bomax! That's my exit. If she had to hazard a guess, the port was on the other side of the rubble. Unfortunately, she had no way of knowing where there might be other exits or how deep this debris pile might be. Presumably, the entire port had been destroyed, so that was... a lot.

Continuing down the tunnel to look for another way out would bring her further from the rendezvous site with Kira. Conditions on the surface were unlikely to be favorable, given what she'd seen out the windows before fleeing down the staircase, so she'd face obstacles no matter which way she went.

If she attempted to dig her way out now, at least she'd have the benefit of using unrestricted telekinesis without an audience. That seemed like the better option.

Large-scale feats of telekinesis were outside her comfort zone, but she'd had enough training to understand she was powerful. Some of her instructors' other students hadn't been able to lift more than a supply crate even after months of training, but Lexi had always been a quick study in her lessons and hadn't strained on anything she'd tried once she gotten the hang of it in her late-teens.

Summoning all of her past experience, she created a shield around herself to offer some protection in case of a collapse. Holding the shield while excavating would be a challenge, but now was as good a time as any to learn.

Lexi began dragging away rubble while holding the pile back to prevent it from filling back in. She took it slowly at first while she got the hang of it, then picked up her pace as she grew more confident in her approach. A tunnel out began to form, angling upward, just large enough for her to crawl through.

Soon, the escape passage was too deep and dark for her to be able to see what she was doing. She could feel the pressure lessening on the load, indicating that she was getting closer to the surface, but she'd need to eventually be able to see her exit point in order to complete the route. That meant crawling into the hole without knowing for certain that she would have a way out.

Stars! At least if I die down here, I'll go out in an adventurous fashion. She took the plunge.

The uneven rubble of brick, concrete chunks and bits of metal made for an uncomfortable climb on her hands and knees, but she managed to make her way up the narrow chute without too much difficulty. Several meters in, the path took a steeper upward angle, at which point the crawling turned into a climb.

As she ascended, she telekinetically probed ahead of her for any weak points in the overhead, which might indicate a thinner place in the ground for her to break through to the surface. One such place stood out, and she started pulling away material to work toward it. Unfortunately, clearing the way while also being in the shaft made for messy business.

After accidentally dropping several piles of debris uncomfortably close to her face, she carved out the area next to her so that she could direct the excavated material around her and drop it behind. The path behind her began to close up as she pushed forward.

A sudden wave of panic took hold when the reality of her situation snapped into focus. She was in the middle of a collapsing disaster zone, in a tunnel held open by questionable telekinesis skills, and no one knew where she was.

There would be no rescue if she messed up and the chute around her collapsed. She was alone.

The anxiety tightened her chest, and her heart pounded in her ears. Her breathing and pulse were all she could hear in this grave she'd dug for herself.

Calm down! You've got this. The self-assurance did little to calm her spiking nerves. She didn't *feel* confident. She was alone, and scared, and everything was quite literally falling apart around her.

But she wasn't dead yet. She had to keep fighting.

With renewed determination, Lexi resumed her ascent. Excavate. Climb. Repeat.

Half a body length at a time, she worked her way up the shaft. After several more agonizing minutes, other sounds joined in the thump of her accelerated pulse in her ears. Shouts, scuffling, thuds. She must be getting close to the surface.

The pressure pushing down on her had diminished, too—requiring less effort to hold up the ceiling with telekinesis. The nightmare was almost over.

At last, she broke through. The sight of light streaming through the exit was enough to almost bring tears to her eyes, and she took a gasping breath of fresh air that turned into a sob.

Except, the air wasn't fresh. Her lungs burned from the gulp of dust and soot, filling her nostrils with the stench of burned metal and charred flesh.

People had died here. Recently. Her stomach heaved with the realization.

Her head cleared the lip of the tunnel, and the sights confirmed her assessment.

She was near the location of the former port, which was now a steaming heap of rubble atop a blackened, shallow crater. Some kind of bomb had destroyed the structure, likely killing everyone who'd been in the vicinity.

The Alliance evacuated the people they cared about to the port, took off, and then blew up the city behind them. She wasn't surprised by the confirmation, but it wasn't the breakthrough clue she'd hoped for when she'd descended the hidden staircase. No, this was just more evidence of how vile people had a complete disregard for life.

Lexi pulled herself from the hole, taking in the horror around her.

The fires in the distance cast an ominous orange glow in the sky. Several charred heaps scattered around her still smoldered, and it took her a few moments to realize that they were corpses. The bodies had been burned beyond recognition—barely even distinguishable as people.

Another wave of emotion threatened to break her spirit. *I helped do this. I worked with the Alliance to recruit people. I'm partially to blame for what happened.*

She had enough wherewithal to not take sole responsibility. She wasn't the one who'd planned the massacre or planted the bombs across the city. But she also wasn't blameless. She'd stayed within the organization, even knowing they had evil intentions. She still played her role to spread their messaging, helped them organize their supplies. Stars, for all she knew, the shipments she'd help inventory were probably components that had eventually been combined into these weapons.

I'm so sorry. I didn't want any of this.

Remorse wouldn't bring anyone back. She could apologize and take her share of the blame, and it wouldn't change a bomaxed thing.

The only action that might make a difference now was to get the data she'd managed to copy from the Alliance's network to the authorities. There might be something useful there to point to the location of the Alliance's other operations so they could prevent future tragedy like what had happened to Duron City.

Reaching those authorities meant finding Kira. With any luck, the Guard officer had been able to get out her distress call before the power outage. If not, they were likely trapped—unless there were other ports which might still have intact ships.

One step at a time. First, find Kira.

Lexi oriented herself as best she could in the decimated landscape and figured out where the park where they'd agreed to meet up should be.

Though it was only two blocks to the park, she found the travel difficult. Between the rubble, remains of people, and overturned vehicles, she had to navigate a weaving path that took her well out of her way. She brought her shirt up over her mouth to block out some of the smoke, soot, and sickening charred scents as she snaked through the wreckage.

So many people dead. She tried to keep the dark thoughts at bay, but they kept creeping in with every corpse she had to step over or around. The small forms of children particularly difficult to see.

She moved around the crumpled hood of an overturned

car, and the small park came into view. An office building next to it had collapsed, covering most of the park in debris. The little bit that remained of the trees and grass stood out like an oasis.

Lexi's heart leaped when she saw a woman standing at the center of the green. Her short, red hair was unmistakable.

"Kira!" Lexi shouted as she ran toward her, not sure she'd ever been so happy to see anyone. "Thank the stars! I wasn't sure I'd be able to find you."

"What happened to you?" The other woman wrapped Lexi in a hug.

Lexi squeezed her tight, as though Kira's strength could fuel her. "The building blew up."

Kira frowned, releasing her. "I saw that. I was worried you might not have made it out in time."

"There was a bomaxed hidden stairway leading down from the upper levels! I spotted it when I got up there and then hightailed it out when the power was cut."

"Did you get the files?" There was so much hope in Kira's voice, Lexi was reluctant to answer.

"I'm so sorry. We lost power before I could complete the transfer."

Kira nodded with understanding, but Lexi could see the disappointment in her eyes. "Well, this entire thing is turning into a foking shiteshow." Kira assessed the surroundings, her brow furrowed. "I'd hoped to use this park as an extraction point, but the building collapse has made the area too unstable. I've directed survivors to get over to Evanwood Park—should be a large enough area for rescue operations."

"Shite, that's a long hike on foot!"

"Don't have a choice."

"Is someone coming to help?"

"Hopefully. And I highly suggest you tag along."

"I'm definitely not turning down that offer!"

They set out at a quick jog. Kira easily took long strides as they wove through the maze of debris, displaying a level of athleticism Lexi found herself envying.

Further from the port, the buildings were more intact and people were out on the sidewalks. Frenetic energy permeated every street they passed, with groups of people running and others trying to seek shelter. No one seemed to know what was going on or how best to react. Such uncertainty was dangerous; scared people were capable of anything.

"You need to get out of here!" Kira shouted. "Follow us!"

A few people heard her and started to follow, but many others scowled and went their own way.

"What happened?" a scraped-up woman asked, clutching the hand of a small child with tear-stained cheeks.

"I don't know for sure, but it's not safe here," Kira replied. "I'm with the Guard. They're sending help."

The woman looked over Kira's civilian clothes. "You don't look like a soldier."

"I was on vacation. Of all the bomaxed timing!" Kira laughed.

The woman gave her a weak smile in response. "My husband was at work. I haven't heard from him."

"Communications went down shortly after we lost power," Kira said. "Right now, you need to look out for yourself and your son."

"Where is it safe to go?" the woman asked.

"We're heading to Evanwood Park. It will be a good area for staging an evacuation," Kira replied.

The woman nodded. "I know the way." She scooped up her son and took a brisk pace down the street.

Lexi and Kira followed her, putting out the call for others to accompany them to the planned evacuation site.

"I won't leave everything behind!" more than a few people shouted back, gathering up whatever supplies they could use while sheltering within their homes.

"These buildings won't offer any protection if the shield goes," Lexi whispered to Kira while they escorted the group.

"I hate leaving people behind, but we're not in a position to force anyone to evacuate. We have to focus on helping the people who want saving."

A difficult reality but nonetheless true. Lexi glanced at the two dozen or so survivors they'd gathered in their group—only a fraction of the people they'd passed on the streets. If the planetary shield did overload and these people weren't evacuated in time, Lexi couldn't begin to fathom the scale of the loss.

How many people live on Duronis? A billion? More? She didn't know the exact figure and really didn't want to.

The trek to Evanwood Park took almost two hours. Though it was only three kilometers away, several of the people traveling with them were unable to move quickly, especially over various roadblocks in their path from destroyed structures to car wrecks. The city was an absolute mess, nothing like the thriving metropolis it had been that morning.

Seeing the rapid destruction and breakdown of normal social etiquette gave Lexi a renewed appreciation for the fragility of life. She'd seen her share of hardship and loss, but it had always been on a somewhat personal scale—family, friends. Never had she witnessed an entire planet attacked.

I stayed with the Alliance while they were planning this, and what do I have to show for it? A few files?

All she had wanted was to do good—to help. Instead,

countless people had died, and she had also utterly failed in her original mission to find Melisa. Now, she didn't know if she would ever find her friend; that trail had ended on Duronis, and what remained of the planet was falling apart around her.

"Almost there," Kira said, breaking Lexi from her reflection.

The rows of city buildings to either side of the streets opened up into a broad greenspace with a grove of low trees ringing a pond at the center. Several hundred people were already in the park, some carrying packs and others with their clothes in tatters, so bloodied it was a wonder they were even standing.

"Stars, it's either going to take a big ship or a lot of trips to get everyone out of here," Lexi said.

Kira looked over the scene with a frown. "That's the problem with evacuating a planet—there's no good way to do it. And especially without a port."

More people were flowing in from the surrounding intersections. At this rate, there would be thousands packed into the space, which wouldn't leave room for any craft to land. Getting everyone to disperse enough to make the necessary room was going to be a challenge when the time came.

"Any signs of rescue?" Lexi searched the sky for transport craft, not seeing anything.

Kira shook her head. "If any help *does* come, this is where they'll be."

"They *are* coming, though, right?" Lexi whispered, not wanting to raise alarm with the survivors.

"I need to believe so."

Not the most reassuring statement. Lexi swallowed. "Okay."

There was a very real possibility they might not make it offworld before the shield failed. She reached into her pocket, wrapping her fingers around her handheld. "Hey, Kira…"

Before she could complete the thought, the woman with the small child, whom they'd picked up at the beginning of their trek, suddenly pointed to Lexi and Kira, shouting, "They're with the Guard! They're going to get us rescued!"

The collective attention of the crowd suddenly shifted to them.

"Shite, that's not good," Kira said, barely above a whisper.

"Take me first! I'll pay you!" a man shouted.

"Please, take my daughter!" another woman shouted.

The calls for priority evacuation soon overlapped in an incomprehensible cacophony. All the while, the crowd started to close in on Kira and Lexi as people jostled to get to the front of the nonexistent line.

They started to shove at each other. A few took up the salvaged items in their hands and began wielding them threateningly to anyone trying to get too close, all the while advancing.

"You've got to help us!" a man said, reaching out to Kira.

She sidestepped him just as a woman tried to grab Kira's arm from the other side.

We can't do anything to help these people right now. We're just as trapped as them at the moment. Lexi's pulse picked up, sensing the frenetic energy in the air. These people were on the edge, and one wrong move would send them into a frenzy.

"Go," Kira whispered, nudging Lexi back the way they'd come.

"Where—"

The crowd continued to press closer, their cries for help escalating to shouted demands. Shoves turned into striking fists, and bits of rubble began flying through the air.

"Run!" Kira ordered Lexi.

Something was strange about Kira's skin—like it had taken on a silver sheen in the evening light. Metallic-looking scales began to form, little droplets coming up through her flesh to combine into a second skin, giving her a bulkier, more muscular appearance. Even her fingers elongated into claws, and her mouth opened to reveal metallic fangs encasing her teeth.

Lexi stood there, dumbstruck, as the crowd recoiled. "What the fok?"

"Go!" Kira shouted at Lexi again.

She took a couple of stumbling steps backward and then turned and ran. *How did she do that?*

Kira had hinted that she had acquired some sort of unique augmentation while in the Guard, but Lexi had never heard about anything like this. Even the Lynaedans didn't have nanotech that could enable that kind of shapeshifting—if that's even what had happened.

Lexi ran blindly down several side streets, not knowing where to go. No one seemed to be pursuing her, so she stopped in an intersection that should make it easy for Kira to spot her when she broke free from the crowd.

Not more than thirty seconds since stopping, Lexi felt a breeze to her left, accompanied by a silvery blur. Kira, still transformed, skidded to a stop next to her.

"Over here," she said, beckoning Lexi into a more secluded side street.

Lexi followed, unable to keep from gaping at her. "You're... what *are* you?"

The scales began to break apart into what looked like liquid metal, and it absorbed back into her skin. Kira flexed her joints as the final shimmer faded. Portions of her clothes were ripped where the metallic form had over-stretched the fabric.

"It's a long story," Kira said. "Let's just say I'm one-of-a-kind."

"I've never seen nanotech like that. Is that what it is?"

"Yes, of a somewhat alien variety. It's classified." Kira checked the main intersection. "Looks like I got away without pursuit."

"I didn't know you could do that. And you ran so fast... How?"

"Transdimensional energy transfer," was all Kira said at first. When Lexi gave her a confused look, Kira added, "The nanotech is stored in my musculoskeletal system, and my embedded AI, Jasmine, can activate it to form a sort of exoskeleton. That's actually why she was paired with me."

"How does all of that store inside you?"

"I'm a lot heavier than I look."

Upon reflection, Lexi realized that the bunkbeds and chairs always did seem to react to Kira like she was a large person rather than her relatively petite build. "It's incredible."

"Though not without its downsides. Feels like I've been run over by a car every time I do that." She flexed her hands. "Jasmine can only dial back the pain so much without causing other performance issues."

"Yeah, that didn't look very comfortable."

"But running at superspeed is pretty fun. You should see how high I can jump!"

A shout sounded from the main street. Kira fell silent and motioned for Lexi to crouch behind a dumpster with her.

The sound of heavy footfalls from multiple sets of feet passed by, then silence.

Kira listened for a few seconds longer before speaking. "We need to find a different extraction point. Now that we've been identified, there's no way we can hang out in that crowd without getting ripped apart."

"Can't we disguise ourselves?"

"Yeah, but…" Kira sighed. "There's a bigger issue. A rescue of this scale is going to a take a lot of time. The information you have needs to be a priority to get off-planet."

"That's what I was going to talk about with you earlier," Lexi said, taking out her handheld. She offered the device to Kira. "You should be the one to hold onto this."

"Why?"

"In case we don't make it, they'll know to search you."

"We're going to make it out of here."

"Please, Kira, take it."

Reluctantly, Kira took the device, but she fixed Lexi with a level gaze. "I'm only holding onto it for safekeeping. I'm not leaving this planet without you."

Lexi shook her head. "Do I really deserve to make it out? I *helped* the Alliance."

"None of this was your doing. It's not your fault." Kira placed one hand on Lexi's shoulder. "You want to make an impact? Then come with me so you can help us track down the Alliance's leadership with the full resources of the TSS and Guard at our disposal. This action took them from a public nuisance to a major security threat for the Empire. No more watching and observing. We're going to take these bastards out."

I guess that is the best thing I can do now, Lexi realized. Dying on Duronis wouldn't accomplish anything, but she could fight for the rest of her life to make the Empire safer for others.

"Okay," she agreed. "So, how do we get off this rock?"

CHAPTER 13

JASON WASN'T USED to spending an entire subspace jump in the pilot's chair on the flight deck of a ship. Though it would have been fine to leave the craft on auto-pilot for the voyage, he was too wound up to rest, so he opted to stare out at the ethereal light of subspace and let his mind wander.

By the time he dropped back into normal space, he was itching for action.

The craft he had selected for the mission was a survey ship, equipped with an independent jump drive and short-duration living quarters, complete with a galley and four cabins. He wasn't sure how long he might need to hang around, so the craft seemed like the right balance of easy maneuverability and adequate functionality.

Duronis was a mess, even from orbit. Patches of the planet emitted an orange glow from where the landscape was being overrun by massive fires. The orbital structures were in ruins, which would make for a significant hazard during entry and exit from the planet's surface.

Jason ran a scan of the area; two TSS ships and four Guard

transport vessels popped up on the HUD. He identified the TSS craft that seemed to be operating as the lead for the relief efforts and sent a communication request.

A vidcall opened on the holographic overlay of the front viewport.

"Agent Jason Sietinen reporting in," Jason announced. "What's the status?"

"Sir! I wasn't expecting anyone else here," a middle-aged woman replied. She was dressed in Agent black. "Agent Leotti. I've taken command of the airspace. The Guard is currently running shuttles to get as many civilians offworld as we can, but we don't have the transport capacity for more than a few thousand."

"Have you been able to determine if there's a credible threat to the planetary shield stability?"

She nodded. "Yes, and the tech specialists from the TSS *Fairview* are currently planetside working on it."

"Any estimates on their likelihood of success?"

"It's looking promising that they'll be able to stop it from going critical, but we're not all the way in the clear yet."

"What about the conditions on the planet's surface?"

"No estimates on casualties yet, but it will be in the millions. We have a ship en route to airdrop supplies near the main population centers that were most affected, assuming we can get the shield situation under control."

Okay, so there is a bit of good news. Jason nodded. "Have you heard from a Captain Kira Elsar with the Guard? She was working on a joint mission with the TSS."

"No, sir, not since the Enforcers got her tip about the shield. I was apprised of the situation. I'm afraid we haven't had the resources to spare to go look for her."

"Okay, I'm going down to pick her up myself. Keep

working on getting as many people as possible to safety."

"All right. Be careful down there."

"Always."

He ended the call and plotted a course down to the surface to the coordinates Kira had sent him.

Jason kept an eye on the scan data during the descent to the planet. Conditions on the surface were dicey; even finding a place to land would be difficult.

The comm system flashed an alert on the main console: 'Communication network failure'. It wasn't unexpected, but it confirmed this rescue would be a challenge. To coordinate with Kira about the pickup point, telepathy was his only option.

While Jason didn't love the idea of going to the planet alone, there was no way he would leave Kira stranded. That was no way to treat a fellow officer, let alone a friend. Still, he'd have no backup for the first time in his career—at least none close enough to intervene at a moment's notice. He was, frankly, shocked his father had agreed to the mission, but he was glad; he didn't want special treatment, only going on assignments that were safe and comfortable. Whatever other TSS Agents faced, he should shoulder the same burdens—and take the same risks. That was why he had been so insistent to take on this rescue himself.

He piloted the survey ship to the coordinates, relying on instruments since visibility was limited by a combination of smoke in the air and this side of the planet presently being in the shadow of night. With the power grid down, there weren't even city lights to offer guidance.

The ship finally dropped below the upper cloud layer, offering a slightly better view of the ruined metropolis. Great pillars of smoke still rose from dark pits where incendiary devices had been set off hours before. At least a quarter of the buildings had been leveled to piles of rubble. He'd never seen that kind of destruction firsthand, and there'd been few incidents on this scale since the end of the Bakzen War. This rivaled some of the worst footage he'd seen from the aftermath of those wartime attacks.

He arrived at Kira's provided coordinates, finding the space empty. The area was in ruin.

Shite, where is she? If she had made it off the planet, she would have certainly reached out to the TSS to let them know where she was. That meant she was still somewhere in the city. It had been approximately six hours since their last communication. Though she could move quickly, there was only so much distance she could cover in that amount of time. It was a reasonable area to cover.

Jason extended his mind to search for her telepathically. He'd spent time with her in person before, so he had a sense for what her energy felt like.

There were still hundreds of thousands of people in the city, and at first he was overwhelmed by the frantic thoughts of the survivors. Their terror flooded through him. He pushed it to the background, filtering out everything that didn't fit his memory of Kira's presence.

He allowed his consciousness to roam while he circled the survey ship over the city.

At last, he found her mind amid the chaos. *"Kira, where are you?"*

"Jason? Fok, you have impeccable timing." It didn't feel like talking to an Agent—she was adept at telepathy like them, but the different nature of her abilities made it more like communicating with someone without Gifts.

"I wasn't about to leave you here. Are you okay?"

"Yes, and I have a plus one."

"*All right. I'm working my way to you,*" Jason said. "*Is there somewhere I can land a twenty-two-meter ship?*"

"*Not really. The best landing site became untenable.*"

He kept his cool. "*Okay, I'll get as low as I can. Try to find somewhere elevated where you can jump in through the side hatch.*"

"*Roger. I think I have a good place. See you soon.*"

Jason traced Kira's movements with his mind, cross-referencing her location with the area map on the HUD. He saw her intention was to climb up the remains of a building that still had four floors intact and a clear space to one side.

As he brought the ship into position, he saw two small figures working their way up the rubble. Kira easily stood out with her red hair, and a brunette woman was with her.

Jason opened the side hatch with the controls in the flight deck, sending a gust of smokey air through the ship. He watched out the side viewport as Kira took up the other woman in her arms and then leaped the distance onto the survey ship—an easy bound for her augmentations.

A thud and shuffling sounded down the corridor from the flight deck as they touched down.

"Clear!" Kira shouted.

Jason resealed the hatch with the remote controls and set a course toward space.

Kira jogged up to the flight deck, followed by her companion. "Thanks for the lift! Stars, what a bomaxed day."

"Glad to see you in one piece." He glanced back at her, noting her tattered clothes. "Mostly."

"Had to shift to get out of a tight spot." Kira took the seat next to him on the flight deck.

The other woman sat down at the station behind Kira. Jason recognized her as Lexi Karis, the woman who'd submitted the video that had kicked off the entire investigation. While he'd found her pretty in the video, he was mesmerized by her in person.

Though they'd never met, he found himself drawn to her and comfortable in the way he was with longtime friends. Despite the distance between them on the shuttle, he felt a closeness.

She turned and looked directly at him, as if she had sensed him watching her. The moment their gaze met, it was like he was struck with a bolt of electricity. The world around him faded into the background. There was only her. His heart pounded in his chest and breath came short. His skin was on fire.

What in the stars? He yanked his gaze away and the sensation faded. *Was that...?*

— — —

Lexi's heart pounded in her ears. She'd never been in the presence of an Agent before, but this one in front of her wasn't what she had been expecting.

She'd heard about Agents having a certain aura about them, but this... this was something else.

For starters, the young man was strikingly handsome. Lexi didn't have a 'type' per se, but she could only imagine that he'd be to anyone's taste. She was surprised Kira was able to talk to him so casually—perhaps because she was already in a committed relationship. But Lexi felt suddenly more self-conscious than she ever had about her own appearance, aware of how much of a mess she must look after crawling through tunnels and running through a smokey city for hours.

"Oh, sorry," Kira said. "Lexi, Jason. Jason, Lexi."

"I recognized you," Jason said, stealing another glance back at her.

There was another electric bolt through Lexi as their gaze briefly met. His glowing teal eyes seemed to bore into her, his gaze filled with surprise and intrigue.

Does he feel this, too?

She broke free and stared at the floor, overwhelmed by the intensity of it. There was a hum in the air—the kind of power she'd only sensed around other Gifted, but she'd experienced nothing on this scale before. This was an exceptionally powerful Agent.

The sudden attraction felt out of place after the traumatic experience she'd just been through—witnessing death and destruction up close. She should be rocking in the corner crying. Instead, just being in this man's presence was somehow grounding, like she was being comforted by a longtime friend by simply being together in the same room.

She didn't understand it, and she wasn't in a good mindset to figure out what it might mean.

Lexi kept her gaze down until they reached space. A weight lifted from her chest as they left the atmosphere with the knowledge she wasn't going to die down there, but she also felt a sting of guilt knowing there were so many still trapped on the planet's surface.

In the pilot's seat, Jason punched in a few commands on the front console to set the ship to auto-pilot. He then swiveled around in his seat. "Okay, so what happened down there?" he asked Kira.

"I don't know much more than when we last spoke. But Lexi was able to get this." Kira pulled out Lexi's handheld from her pocket and tossed it to Jason.

He examined the device. "What's on it?"

"I was able to access the Alliance's computer network," Lexi said, finally managing to find her voice. "It's part of a project directory that might be related to a planet where the Alliance is setting up a new research lab."

"And likely where they took Leon," Kira added.

"Only partial?" Jason asked, looking at her.

None of the intensity had let up. She refused to meet his gaze. "Yeah. The power cut out before the transfer completed."

He frowned. "Hopefully, that didn't corrupt the data."

"That can happen?"

"Depending on how their transfer protocol is configured." He examined the device for a moment. "I don't want to check it out on the ship here in case any kind of virus or malware also copied over. Better to open it on an air-gapped terminal once we get to TSS Headquarters."

Lexi felt a flush in her cheeks. "TSS Headquarters?"

"Yes, we need to debrief you," he explained. "You're not under arrest or anything."

She shot a panicked look at Kira.

"It's okay," her friend said. "I've always wanted to see TSS HQ. I heard it's quite impressive."

"The best." Jason smiled. "Though I am biased with it being home and all."

"All right," Lexi agreed.

Jason pivoted his chair to face forward again. "I'm going to let everyone know what's up and initiate a jump back. Need to send any messages before we enter subspace?"

"No," Lexi said. "I don't have anyone."

He glanced back at her before turning his attention to the front console.

"Mind if we get cleaned up?" Kira asked.

"No, of course not. Go right ahead," Jason said. "I haven't

touched the cabins, so pick whichever ones you'd like and help yourselves." He evaluated them over his shoulder. "There isn't a fab on this ship so I can't offer replacement clothes, but there should be a hydrosonic cleaner in the washroom, at least."

Kira waved her arms over herself as if displaying fine wares. "I'm going to start a new fashion trend with the tattered look. Isn't it fabulous?"

Jason smiled. "If anyone can pull it off, it's you."

"I'm probably going to pass out as soon as I shower. Wake me up when we get there," Kira said, giving a salute before leaving the flight deck.

Lexi followed her out to the corridor, where Kira was palming open one of the cabin locks. As soon as the door slid open, Lexi pushed her inside.

"What?" Kira snapped.

Lexi waited for the door to close behind them before speaking. "Is that your TSS handler?"

"Yeah. What about him?"

"You never said he was gorgeous!"

Kira laughed. "Stars, Lexi, you've been in the Alliance for too long. Go take a cold shower."

Lexi's face burned. "Sorry. I've never been around an Agent before. Are they all like that?"

"No. But if you're going to make friends with any Agent, Jason is one of the best you could have."

Lexi shifted on her feet. "Is it just me, or was he staring at me, too?"

"He most certainly was." She patted Lexi on the shoulder. "Now, I mean this in the nicest way, please leave before I shove you out."

"I'll see you later." Lexi quickly excused herself.

Back in the corridor, she glanced toward the flight deck

where Jason was still seated at the controls, plotting a subspace jump. It'd been a long time since she'd been with anyone—had even *wanted* to be.

Stop getting ahead of yourself. She took the cabin across the hall from Kira's.

A shower was definitely her first priority. Then a snack. Apparently, almost dying had a way of working up an appetite in more ways than one.

— — —

Half an hour into the subspace jump, Jason got up to stretch. The auto-pilot would keep them on-course for the duration of the voyage.

Being a small ship, there wasn't a lot of room to roam, unfortunately. He wandered down the central corridor. When he reached the galley, he heard someone inside.

He was about to poke his head in when Lexi walked out.

"Oh, hi. Looking for something?" Jason asked.

"Yeah, sorry." She blushed at the sight of him. "It's been forever since lunch. I was just grabbing a snack."

"Sure. Help yourself to anything in the galley."

She smiled. "Good, because I already did!"

Jason could feel Lexi watching him, radiating the confusion he felt internally about the strong connection between them. She had the aura of someone Gifted. Tons of potential churned as a mass of disorganized chaos beneath the surface, indicating that she lacked formal training.

"Where did you study?" he asked her, captivated by her presence.

Her eyes widened. "What do you mean?"

"Your abilities. I can tell you've tapped into your potential, though not completely. You're quite strong for a civilian." He was downplaying it quite a bit. Truthfully, he assessed her potential to be in the upper Primus range. It was shocking that she'd progressed this far without anyone taking notice.

"I've, um, had a few instructors here and there over the years," she replied.

Jason stepped a little closer, gauging her reaction. He couldn't help being drawn to her, as though they were being reunited rather than just meeting for the first time. She seemed eager to be near him, too, but was clearly holding back.

"I've worked with a lot of students," he said. "You have significant innate talent."

"A fat lot of good it's done me."

"Maybe you've been hanging out with the wrong crowd if you feel that way."

She let out a bitter laugh. "Oh, you have no idea!"

There was the pain of loss in her tone. Jason recognized it because he often felt it in himself. Maybe that's all there was between them—just two wounded souls who could see in one another the hollowness left behind by tragedy.

For some inexplicable reason, he sensed they might be able to help each other heal. He spoke without conscious thought about what he was saying, thoroughly entranced by her. "The good news is, now you have the opportunity to try something new."

They stared intently at each other, standing much closer than two strangers typically would.

"Have we met before?" Lexi asked.

"No. I'd certainly remember that." He ventured a smile. *I didn't feel like this when I saw the video of her. How can I have such strong feelings for someone I just met?*

As they stood alone in the hallway, there was an almost

electrical energy between them. The closer he moved toward her, the more intense it became.

What do we do now? He couldn't imagine walking away from her, though that was the most logical thing to do. She was the key witness in an ongoing investigation, and his job as an Agent was to escort her back to TSS Headquarters.

Yet, standing so close together, his normally ever-present sense of reason evaporated. He yearned to be closer to her—this stranger who he should rationally be talking to in an interrogation room. Nonetheless, he stared at her, inexplicably intoxicated.

"I've never felt something like this with anyone before," she said softly, gazing into his eyes.

"Me either." As much as he wanted to reach out to her, he resisted.

Almost as if she knew he wouldn't make the first move, Lexi reached out and placed a hand on his chest, sending a tingle through him. "Why do I feel like I've known you my whole life?" Her hand slid from his chest to behind his neck, pulling him closer. Her warmth beckoned him.

Stars, what am I doing? His TSS training told him that he should be acting like a professional, but all of his other senses told him that this was the moment he'd been waiting for his whole life.

Jason could feel the heat of her up against him. Her breath on his cheek. The desire in those clear, blue eyes…

A glimmer of logic and reason returned to his mind.

"We need to slow this down." He was so absorbed in Lexi that it may as well have been someone else speaking. He took a deliberate step back from her before he lost perspective again. "You don't even know me."

Lexi's arms dropped to her sides. "What are you scared of?"

"I'm not scared. Just cautious."

"Sometimes, you need to let go." She took a step toward him.

He backed up to match her movement, holding up his hands. "No, there's something more going on here. I suspect you feel it, too."

Lexi looked down the hallway but didn't say anything.

There was only one explanation. "Have you ever heard of a resonance connection?" he asked.

"Yeah, but that's…" She faded out. "Is that what this is?"

"I don't think I really grasped it until now," he said.

Understanding filled her eyes, but there was still confusion and worry. "The chances of meeting this way…"

It really makes you wonder about fate. He left the statement unsaid, but her open thoughts echoed the sentiment.

She crossed her arms, and Jason couldn't help but notice how the motion accentuated her cleavage and toned stomach beneath her thin shirt.

She really is stunning. It took a significant measure of his willpower to not test out their apparent physical chemistry. But he was a high-ranking TSS officer and had a family legacy to uphold. He couldn't allow lust to cloud his judgment.

Besides, this very well could be the start of the same kind of powerful connection Raena had with Ryan or that his parents shared. Lexi could be that special person for him. The potential relationship didn't make any logical sense given the current social dynamics, but none of that mattered in the present moment. He sensed a deeper connection there that defied the circumstances of everyday life. It was worth exploring and nurturing that possibility—not a situation to rush into blindly.

Stars! This is more complication than I wanted right now.

Emotions warred within him. Lexi was beautiful, determined, and courageous—exactly the type of woman he adored. The recent past, though, made the situation tricky enough to give him pause.

Neither of them spoke as they processed what this unexpected meeting might mean for their futures.

The silence made Jason feel awkward standing in the central corridor. He opened the door to one of the unoccupied cabins and motioned her inside. "Let's talk."

CHAPTER 14

LEXI LOOKED AROUND the small cabin on the TSS transport ship as she wandered in, stopping near the two plush chairs next to a viewport. She felt incredibly warm and her pulse was racing.

Who is this guy and why do I feel this way? Being around Jason was surreal. The physical attraction was obvious, but there was more to it—like she'd just been found a piece of herself that she hadn't known she was missing.

It was absolutely crazy. She'd just met the guy. And he was a TSS Agent! There was no way anything could work out between them.

Jason followed her into the cabin and sat down on the edge of the bed. "This is totally unexpected."

"Yeah, I'll say." Lexi traced her fingers along the back of the chair, studying him; the distance he'd intentionally placed between them did not go unnoticed.

"I wish I had more of an explanation for what's going on here," he said. "We met less than an hour ago, yet I feel like I've known you for years."

"Same here."

Given that odd sense of familiarity, this didn't seem like a conversation they should be conducting from opposite sides of the room. However, when she took a step toward the bed, he held up one hand, palm outward.

"I'd love to be close to you right now, trust me, but there are some important things we need to discuss first."

"Such as?" She could think of a number of issues related to his career and her recent association with criminals, but she was curious how he would respond to the question.

Jason propped himself up with his arms angled back on the bed. "For starters, what do you know about resonance connections?"

"It's a powerful attraction."

"It's more than that," he said. "It's indicative of the potential to have a very strong bond."

Lexi's brows shot up with surprise. Telepathic bonds between Gifted people were formed through physical intimacy, as she understood it, so that seemed to be jumping ahead a bit. "Doesn't bonding require a conscious decision?"

"Usually. But in cases of resonance connections, it can happen spontaneously. I have to be upfront that I'm not in a position to take rash actions. We need to, you know, make sure we actually *like* each other before we consider doing anything more."

"And then?"

Jason shrugged. "We either throw caution to the wind and go for it, or we keep taking things slow until we're absolutely certain this is something we want long-term."

Is he genuinely considering a relationship here? It sounded like it. She'd thought that a TSS Agent would dismiss her out of hand. Except, if he felt this connection as strongly as she did, walking away wasn't an option. "How often do relationships between people with resonance connections work out?"

"All those I know about personally have."

She swallowed. "So, in the 'caution to the wind' scenario, odds are more for than against?"

"Yes."

Stars! That's it? You have an insta-love connection and your future together is a foregone conclusion? It was a lot to take in—to think that this could be the person she'd spend the rest of her life with. "If it's so inevitable, then why wait at all?"

Jason took a deep breath and let it out. "Because I'm not just a TSS Agent. I'm Jason Sietinen, twin brother to the Sietinen Dynasty heiress."

Lexi went from a state of awe to shock to confusion to concern in the span of a second. "No foking way." She retraced their interactions with new perspective. *I almost kissed a Sietinen heir. Stars!*

The hope that she'd started to feel evaporated. It was one thing to overcome the obstacle of being with a TSS Agent, but a High Dynasty heir? And the son of the TSS High Commander? That was another story.

"I have a nice heaping pile of responsibility on me that makes everything more complex," Jason said, meeting her distressed gaze with surprising calm. "Service to my family and the TSS has always been paramount. Yet, I now have this profound feeling that I need you in my life, and I'm having difficulty reconciling that with the fact that I don't even *know* you."

He... wants this? Lexi worked her mouth, not sure what to say.

"Rushing into anything isn't smart," he continued after a pause. "Nonetheless, I know the power of these kinds of connections. It's not something I can ignore."

Her pulse pounded in her ears. "I know how I feel about you, even though it doesn't make sense. Then again, I've never really been one for careful consideration."

"I've had to work at that, myself." Jason got up from the bed and came to sit down in the chair across from her. He leaned forward with his forearms resting on his thighs. "Lexi, I believe there's something real here between us. If it is what I think it could be, I don't want to mess it up."

Her heart leaped at the thought, but it seemed too good to be true. She stared out the viewport at subspace. "How could there ever be anything with us, given who you are and me being... who I am?"

"You might know my family by name, but you don't know them. It's not as big of a barrier as you might think."

I doubt that. She ran her fingers through her dark-brown hair. "I don't get it. How do these 'resonance connections' even happen?"

"In some cases, it was the result of nanotech from the Priesthood as part of their grand genetic engineering scheme, but for other people it's natural. Some kind of genetic instinct. I couldn't tell you what's going on with us. I feel it, though. More strongly than I ever would have thought possible."

I never thought I'd experience this for myself. I wasn't even sure it was real. Lexi met Jason's gaze. "My sister experienced it with someone, too. A former TSS Agent."

"Really?"

"She's much older than me," Lexi explained, hesitant to get into too many details. "The guy was discharged after the War and went to find her. They'd met briefly while he was on his internship. Couldn't let her go."

"Yeah, that's how it tends to be."

Lexi had seen what that resonance connection had done to her sister and how it had shaped her life. Trying to fight the feelings didn't work.

Even though this seems impossible, that doesn't mean I shouldn't try. Lexi folded her legs up to sit cross-legged in the chair. "All right, if we're going to be stuck with each other, then we should probably dive into this getting-to-know-you thing."

Jason smiled. "Right. Yes." He settled back in his seat. "Basics. What, if any, do you consider your homeworld?"

"That's not an easy answer." She didn't mean to be evasive, but it was the truth. *Could we have started with* anything *else?*

He seemed a little taken aback by her terse response. "I know from your file that you were born on Cytera."

She shrugged. "I was less than a year old when we fled."

"I understand there are lots of people with strong abilities there. It partially explains yours."

This is really not where I want to begin. "I was never properly trained like you," she deflected.

"But you're not *un*-trained, clearly. Between fleeing as a baby to getting involved in the Alliance, you must have quite the life story."

Lexi was all for getting to know Jason, but discussing her past was one topic where she needed to ease in. "You first," she said and raised her brows expectantly.

"Oh boy." He let out a long breath. "Well, a few years after the Bakzen War ended, my parents moved down to Earth to raise my sister and me out of the public spotlight. It wasn't until I was sixteen that I even found out about the Taran Empire, let alone the whole 'secret prince' angle. Raena, being much more politically minded, went off to Tararia and I stayed with the TSS. For the last decade, I've done little more than work. I'm tied for the highest Agent score on record, with my dad, though

I wasn't officially tested. The one person I was close to through it all died not that long ago. So let's just say it's often lonely at the top."

Lexi blinked at him for several seconds before speaking. "Wow, that's quite the highlight reel."

"There's been some bad. Mostly good. It's strange, though. Growing up on Earth, I couldn't have imagined this kind of everyday life. Now, I can't fathom how it could be any different."

His experience was almost the polar opposite of Lexi's—stable, supportive. It was everything she'd always dreamed about on the lonely nights when she'd curled up behind a crate in an alley with an empty stomach and her backpack as a pillow. "Are you close with your family?"

"Very."

"That must be nice." A touch of bitter envy crept into her tone.

"What about yours?" he asked.

"A foking shiteshow, for the most part." She shook her head. "What do you know about Cytera?"

"Just an overview that came up when reviewing your file. It sounds like they often arranged pairings to augment bloodlines with abilities, and it resulted in a sort of caste system?"

"Yep, that's Cytera for ya. My family was wrapped up in it at a pretty high level." She wanted to leave it at that, but Jason's intent gaze urged her to continue. *I may as well throw it all out there up front.*

She took a deep breath. "To put it politely, my family fell from grace, and my older sister turned to a life of crime to get by. She's a half-sister, actually. She wasn't Gifted, but I was because of the way the Generations worked out with our different moms. When shite went sideways and the planet's government started to break down, I was taken off-world. My sister eventually tracked me down, but she wasn't in a position to raise me so I bounced from place to place. I was pretty desperate by the time I fell in with the Alliance, and having a reliable bed with three square meals a day was nice even though I'd joined up to search for my friend. Melisa is pretty much the only person I have left."

Jason took in the story, his gaze compassionate. "We'll do our best to find Melisa."

"And now Leon is missing, too." Lexi winced. "It seems like things always turn to shite when I get close to someone. Be warned!"

"Having past misfortunes doesn't mean things can't work out in the end," Jason assured her.

"Easy for you to say. Life was handed to you on a silver platter."

He didn't reply at first. "Regardless of my family's power or influence, I've still put in the work to become the best TSS Agent I can be. But you're right, I've never had to worry about going hungry or not having a safe place to sleep. And more than that, I was lucky to have supportive parents. I can't imagine how difficult it must have been growing up how you did."

She shrugged. "It gave me grit. So there's that."

He nodded. "One of the best traits a person can have."

"They've probably taught you a lot more valuable skills in the TSS."

"Some. But grit is something you either have or you don't. It's tough to train into a person later in life."

"And you? Ever had your resolve tested?" Lexi asked.

A pained expression flitted across his face. "I consider

myself someone who'll fight for survival if I'm backed against a wall. I bet you could teach me a thing or two, though."

She smiled slightly. "Maybe."

He shifted in his seat. "You mentioned earlier that you've had a few instructors. How'd you get that training for your abilities?"

That was another topic she wasn't too keen to discuss, but it made sense that a TSS instructor would be curious. She raised one shoulder and let it fall. "I've worked with various people here and there. I spent a month with a woman from Valdos at one point who gave me some tips."

The planet was one of the few places that had never caved to the Priesthood's ban on telekinesis, so the use of abilities had remained a core component of their culture. Once the restrictions had been lifted, many people had left Valdos to help teach others about the suppressed parts of themselves. Working with Reva had been the first time Lexi hadn't felt ashamed of herself.

Jason sat up with interest. "My grandmother did her TSS internship on Valdos."

"Hey, small galaxy."

They fell silent.

It did seem like a small galaxy in that moment. Trillions of people, and yet the two of them had met through happenstance. Resonance connections were rare. Them being brought together was special.

"You don't have to be alone anymore," Jason said, meeting her gaze.

I want this more than I've ever wanted anything. She wasn't yet convinced it was possible. "How would this even work? Would I have to join the TSS?"

"There are options. But I know for certain that I want to

get to know everything about you."

"You might not like what you discover."

He smiled. "Only one way to find out."

—   —   —

One of Raena's favorite things was to solve problems, but she hadn't expected her solution about Earth's historical sites to lead to even greater difficulties.

"What do you mean they won't move?" she asked Trevor. She had a fair understanding of what he'd just told her, but clarification didn't hurt.

"The people have assembled on the pyramid and are now sitting down without any signs of getting up," the young man restated.

Okay, so our marketing campaign didn't land with everyone. She'd known they would encounter resistance on Earth, and she was ready for it. They were in it for the long game. The work held too much potential importance to abandon, no matter what they went up against.

"Are they locals?" Raena asked.

Trevor laughed. "No, that's the frustrating thing. Just a bunch of tourists claiming to speak on *behalf* of the locals. Except, the locals are fully on board with our investigation, and they have offered up a number of volunteers to help us. They're as curious to find out about the history as we are."

"What's the deal with the protestors, then?"

He frowned. "My guess? They're either looking for attention for the sake of it, or they're plants."

Raena rapped her fingers on her desk. They hadn't been able to disprove the hypothesis that the same group behind the uprising in the Outer Colonies wasn't also organizing protests on Earth, so this latest demonstration at the excavation site very well may be part of the larger disruption plan.

"Why this location?" she mused. "Has there been trouble elsewhere?"

"Not so far," Trevor replied. "This could just be a particularly passionate group."

Or, this site is the most important and they're trying to delay us while a shadow faction completes their own investigation. Raena was hesitant to share her suspicions outside her trusted advisory group, so she kept the thought to herself for now. "You said these people are tourists and not locals. Are we sure they're even from Earth?"

Trevor's eyebrows shot up with surprise. "I can't say I've looked into it."

"I know you're already swamped. I'll get someone to take on the background checks."

"What makes you think they're not Earth natives?" he asked.

"A hunch. For the time being, can we make progress at another site?"

He smiled. "Actually, that was the real reason I called. We've already found something in Belize."

"Oh yeah?"

"This is going to sound a little crazy, but we think it might be a ship."

She sat up straight. "What?"

"The ground around it hasn't been disturbed for at least ninety thousand years."

That's pretty close to the timing of the alleged 'missing link' in the human evolution record. Were Tarans actively guiding development of the life on Earth? She leaned back in her chair. "That's a very interesting discovery."

Raena had been taught that Earth's development was the product of primordial panspermia and that Tarans had interacted with those natives later on, eventually settling on the planet and branching off into modern humans. To her knowledge, there had been minimal physical evidence of those early years of Taran involvement with Earth, so most of the history was an educated guess. Most of the panspermia hypothesis made sense to her, but the independent development of humanity's ancestors had always struck her as a little suspect—and why anyone would ever interbreed with more primitive apes.

This evidence of a ship on Earth ninety thousand years ago changed things. It lent credibility to an alternative hypothesis that modern life on Earth had been intentionally designed in some fashion. After all, many historians suspected that ancient Tarans had been traveling the stars for millions of years, and there was a strong tradition of genetic engineering in the Taran culture. It was possible that Earth had been a giant experimental playground and some of the scientists had eventually gone to live with their creations. Experimental gene therapy would certainly explain the jumps in hominid development over the years.

For that matter, there were a number of oddities across the planet. *How many other species on Earth might be the product of genetic experimentation?* One very specific duck-billed, egg-laying mammal came to mind. *Maybe it was a joke, after all!*

"Really brings a different meaning to the 'Lost Colony' nickname for Earth, doesn't it?" Trevor said.

"A very interesting spin, indeed." Her mind raced through the implications for both the history she'd learned on Earth and what she'd been taught as a new citizen of the Taran Empire when she was a teenager. Actual physical evidence was going to change a lot. "Have you gained access to the ship?"

Trevor deflated a little. "I may have oversold what we found. There's a hull, which is in amazing shape. However, it looks like it was stripped clean before it was buried."

No secret information stash about our past, then. She nodded. "Find out everything you can. And we'll work on getting those people off the other site so you can proceed. I suspect this ship isn't the only buried artifact we're going to find."

CHAPTER 15

JASON'S STOMACH WAS in knots by the time they reached TSS Headquarters. On the one hand, he was overcome with joy unlike anything he'd ever experienced just being in Lexi's presence. It was incredible to feel so energized by simply standing next to someone.

Conversely, he was terrified about what his parents were going to say regarding their connection. When he'd set off on the mission to Duronis, it was to extract Kira. He didn't think he'd be coming home with someone who could very well be a lifelong partner. Not to mention the factor of her having been a part of the very terrorist organization they'd been investigating—though the argument could be made that she wasn't ever really a *part* of the group and was more of a civilian vigilante.

He took a deep breath. It was too much to process right now. One moment at a time. First, they'd debrief, and then they could take the personal stuff from there.

Lexi was tense the entire elevator ride down. Her eyes kept shifting to the side, as if something was going to jump out to attack her from the walls. Kira, meanwhile, was fascinated by every detail.

"I've always wanted to visit this place," the Guard officer said. "I hear you have all the fancy things."

"I don't know about that," Jason replied. "It's no Tararian estate, but we do have it pretty good here. I can't imagine being anywhere else."

At that, Lexi glanced up at him with a questioning gaze. Their prospective future together would no doubt be an ongoing discussion, and Jason's position as a TSS Agent and presumptive future High Commander was one of the biggest factors. He liked the idea of Lexi potentially joining the TSS—or at least staying at Headquarters with him—but he didn't know how reasonable an ask that would be.

Thinking about it made him envious of his sister and her husband; Raena and Ryan had a political future laid out for them that fit perfectly with their resonance connection. By contrast, his relationship with Lexi meant trying to find common ground while coming from two different existences. Not only was he unsure if his family would approve, but it was possible Lexi herself would walk away because of her distrust for Taran institutions. The next few hours and days would be very telling.

Jason reached out to Lexi's mind. *"I've got your back,"* he told her.

"Easy to say now, before you've heard the rundown of everything I've done."

"Have you intentionally hurt anyone who wasn't trying to do something harmful to others?"

"No."

"Then I don't need to know anything else."

The elevator stopped at Level 1, and Jason cut off the

telepathic conversation. Any Agent would be able to detect a telepathic exchange in progress, even though they wouldn't know what was being said, and he didn't want anyone to think that he was trying to coach Lexi.

His parents were waiting for them in the lobby.

"Hey," Jason greeted. "I brought some friends."

Kira smiled at Wil and Saera. "Sir. Ma'am. It's great to meet you. I've heard so many good things."

"As we have about you," Saera replied with a warm smile of her own.

"Welcome to TSS Headquarters," Wil added. "I appreciate you taking risks on behalf of the TSS and helping us protect the Taran people."

"There's still a long way to go on that." Kira's smile faded. "I'm afraid we've let this one escalate in an unfortunate way."

"Through no fault of your own," Wil said. "There's something bigger than what you were tracking on Duronis. The people behind it are very good at covering their tracks. But we'll root them out."

"There's one group I want to find, in particular."

Saera nodded. "Yes, and we'll do everything we can to get Leon home safely."

Kira dropped her gaze. "Yes, ma'am. Thank you."

Wil and Saera then turned their attention to Lexi. They studied her for a moment, then looked to Jason and back again.

His parents were probably two of the most perceptive people alive. Jason didn't need to say anything for them to know what was going on.

"Well, this is unexpected," his father said at last.

"Tell me about it!" Jason laughed. "So, that's going to be a 'thing'."

"It's a far more welcome twist than everything else we're

dealing with right now," Saera said. "Lexi, welcome to TSS Headquarters. I'm Saera, Jason's mom."

"Wil Sietinen, TSS High Commander," his father said.

"Uh, hi," she replied hesitantly. "Nice to meet you."

"We'll have a proper sit-down later," Wil continued. "Lexi, I'm looking forward to getting acquainted. However, there are some pressing official matters I need to discuss with Jason."

"We can get you set up in temporary quarters down on one of the Militia levels," Saera offered.

Jason turned to Lexi. "Or you can go to my place instead, if you prefer."

Lexi looked surprised but appreciative. "Sure, sounds good. Thanks."

His parents didn't quite hide their shock, but they gave respectful nods of assent.

Kira looked over Jason and Lexi with an amused smirk.

"Kira, please report to Medical for a physical. Standard procedure post field op," Saera said.

"Yes, ma'am."

"While Kira is doing that, I'll get Lexi settled and then meet you in your office?" Jason addressed his father.

"All right. See you there."

Jason motioned for Lexi to follow. He summoned an elevator to take them down to Level 2.

"Are they freaking out about this?" she asked him once the elevator doors closed.

"No, they're the sort of people to roll with the unexpected. You'll like them. And I have no doubt they'll adore you."

"Okay."

He took her hand, sending an electric tingle up his arm. "I know this is a lot to take in all at once."

She gazed into his eyes. "I still don't understand how you

can make me feel so comfortable when I barely know you."

"I'm still wrapping my head around it, too. But I know how I feel about you."

"Me too. I promise not to go snooping through your drawers and stuff."

He smiled. "I appreciate that, though I have nothing to hide."

Once on Level 2, Jason escorted her to his quarters. At the door, he added her as an approved guest so she would be able to come and go. The user profile would restrict the files Lexi could access from Jason's devices, so leaving her unattended wasn't a security risk.

"Thank you for trusting me."

"We're going to need a few gestures of good faith if there's any chance of this working." He opened the door.

Lexi took in the space. "It's nice."

"Nothing special, but it's home."

"Big upgrade from anywhere I've been."

He motioned around the room. "We have an entertainment library of almost anything you can imagine, so feel free to help yourself to the viewscreen. It shouldn't be more than a couple of hours before I can come check in."

"Thanks, I'm sure I can manage."

"And that handheld with information on it was your personal device, right?"

Lexi nodded.

"We have a bunch around Headquarters for the new Trainees. I'll get a replacement for you."

"Thanks. I think the other one probably has a bunch of Alliance spyware on it, but there are some pictures and things I'd like to get from it eventually."

"I'm sure we can arrange that."

She eyed the couch. "This is pretty nice treatment for being a prisoner."

"You're not a prisoner."

"I can walk away right now?"

"No."

She flourished her hand.

"Do you *want* to walk away?"

Lexi searched his face. "No."

"Then we're in agreement."

They stared at each other. He suddenly wasn't sure why he'd opened his private space to her so soon. He felt at ease in her presence, yet he still had a barrier up that he couldn't quite let down.

Lexi stepped forward, closing the distance between them. "How long are we going to keep dancing around this?"

"I…" Jason didn't know what to say. He hadn't so much as kissed anyone since Tiff, let alone more. He knew Tiff wouldn't have wanted it that way. Even before her death, she'd want him to move on and find happiness with someone. Still, it felt like a betrayal to her memory to have those thoughts about anyone else.

Even as he tried to rationalize his commitment to Tiff's memory, he could hear her voice in his head. *"Don't be a foking idiot. You need to live your own life. Just kiss her already!"* He smiled at the perfectly rendered tone in his mind. Tiff was still, and always would be, alive and well in his memory, no matter what else he did.

Lexi smiled back, unaware of the reason behind his. She drew him to her.

He gave in.

Their lips met in a passionate kiss and he pressed his body against hers. The surge of desire to be close to her was overwhelming. But it was more than the amount of time since he'd last been close to anyone. It was her. Everything about her.

This feels so right. It was easy and natural, like they'd known each other for a lifetime. Old lovers reunited after too long apart.

When they parted, all of Jason's doubts had vanished. "Make yourself comfortable. I'll be back as soon as I can." He rushed away; if he lingered, he might never leave.

—   —   —

"That was what I think it was, right?" Wil asked his wife as they strolled to the Command Wing.

"A new resonance connection? Yes."

They glanced at each other.

"How?" Wil wondered aloud. It wasn't that Lexi wasn't attractive or Gifted, but rather the odds against a chance encounter like this were astronomical.

"I have no idea, but she's here now," Saera said. "This isn't something we can ignore."

—   —   —

Jason took the elevator back up to Level 1 and met up with his parents in the High Commander's office. His father was seated behind the desk, and his mother was in one of the two visitor chairs. Jason took the empty seat next to her.

"Before we get into the debrief, we should discuss the obvious," Wil began.

How I'm falling for our civilian informant? Jason nodded. "I know, this whole thing blindsided me."

"It often does."

The words flooded out from Jason's mouth, "I know what you're thinking, and yes, I'm well aware that this looks bad with her being associated with a terrorist organization, even though she was working against them from the inside. It's messy and not becoming of a TSS officer, let alone a dynastic heir, to be connected with someone like that. But we—"

"Jason, there's no judgment here," his father said calmly. "We know exactly what it's like to experience that kind of sudden pull to someone. It's inexplicable, unstoppable, and rarely without difficulties."

"We love you and trust you," his mother added. "While this is an unexpected wrinkle, it's ultimately a good thing."

"I'm pretty overwhelmed, to be honest," he admitted.

"It's one of those things that's thrilling and scary and rewarding all at the same time," his father said. "I don't envy you needing to navigate this development amidst everything else, but you have shown time and again how you can keep a level head."

"How is she taking it?" Saera asked.

"Confused but excited. Stars! We've only known each other for a few hours, but it already feels like a lifetime."

His parents exchanged knowing glances.

"Yep, know all about that," Wil said with a smile. "At least you have the benefit of being a little older than we were. Extra perspective to bring to bear."

"If I may offer some unsolicited advice?" his mother ventured.

Jason nodded his assent.

"With most relationships, you go into it unsure if it will work out; you test it to see if you're right for each other. In the case of resonance connections, you already know the outcome. So, rather than focusing on potential dealbreakers, you can go straight to the part of the relationship where you figure out how best to support each other.

"While that's critical in any relationship, it is exponentially more important when bonding comes into play. You share a part of yourself with your partner. You feel what they feel, and vice versa. Joy, heartache, trauma. From the moment you bond, it's all there, and the depth of those feelings will continue to grow with time.

"Each relationship is different, but from what I've experienced myself and witnessed in other Gifted couples, everything goes much better if you take the time to get to know each other before jumping straight into a bond. Talk about those heavy things you carry with you so you can lay the intellectual groundwork for the other person to understand those feelings once they become shared. Build emotional intimacy, as you would in any relationship. It'll be intense no matter what, but there are ways to ease the transition."

His father nodded. "You've been through a lot over the last year, and it seems like Lexi has had some challenges in her life, too."

The subtext was obvious, and Jason was glad his parents had left it unspoken. *I didn't lose Tiff that long ago and the loss is still fresh. Am I ready for this?*

As fast as things were progressing, he knew he *was* ready. Everything with Lexi felt 'right'. Natural. Effortless. It was the spark he'd aspired to find. That happiness and bright future didn't diminish Tiff's memory or what he'd had with her. It was time to move into the next phase of his life, as she would want him to.

"Thank you for your support," Jason said.

His mother's brows drew together with an expression of deep caring and concern that brought him back to his youth.

"We will always be here for you, no matter what. I'm so happy for you."

Stars, they're acting like I just told them I'm getting married! He realized that he actually had, in a way. Finding a resonance connection with someone invariably led to a lifelong partnership. Whenever they were ready to bond, that would make it official—regardless of paperwork. *Lexi is going to be my wife.*

Thinking about it in those terms made his head spin, so he decided that changing the subject was for the best. "All right, so back to what happened on Duronis."

His parents straightened in their seats and turned serious.

Wil folded his hands on the desktop and leaned forward. "Our tech team was able to prevent a critical failure of the planetary shield. The tampering was done in such a way that it would have been difficult to identify, so it's fortunate that Kira was able to pass on that tip."

"Though the planet wasn't a total loss, the devastation was significant," Saera said. "Casualties are currently estimated around two hundred million worldwide."

Jason took a slow, steadying breath as that figure sank in. "What about the other planets?"

"Twenty-two worlds in the Outer Colonies all experienced similar attacks within minutes of each other." His mother kept her tone professional, but the pain was there in her eyes. "The bombings focused on ports and utility infrastructure. There was similar tampering with the planetary shields, as well."

"We had been unaware of the security vulnerability that made that kind of weaponizing of the shield possible," his father continued. "I've arranged for a roll-out of an update so we shouldn't have to worry about this again in the future. It was too close to a catastrophic incident."

Jason's cheeks flushed. "That's what they wanted, no doubt."

Wil nodded. "No one has yet stepped forward, which reinforces the suspicion that chaos was the goal. We are operating on the assumption that the Coalition is responsible, though we'll need proof."

"What about the files from Lexi's handheld?" Jason asked.

Saera shook her head. "Since the transfer didn't complete, the information that copied over is jumbled and piecemeal. It's going to take time to try to reconstruct it."

A knock sounded on the door.

"Come in," his father said.

Kira entered. "I'm all signed off and fit for duty."

"Please, join us." Saera telekinetically dragged a third guest chair over to the desk.

"We were just discussing the project files from the Alliance." Jason filled her in on the status.

Kira frowned. "That's disappointing."

Considering those files had hopefully held clues to Leon's location, 'disappointing' was a significant understatement. Jason's parents were also aware of the situation, and his mother jumped in.

"Your mission didn't work out like we'd hoped, but we are immensely grateful for your investigation into the Alliance's deeper operations. We never leave our people stranded, so you can rest assured that we'll do everything possible to find Leon and get him home safely."

"I appreciate that," Kira replied. "The good news is that they wanted him for his skills, so they want him alive. That buys a little time."

"We're optimistic that we'll be able to glean enough information from the copied files to determine his location in short order. With any luck, that will also yield some insight into the Coalition's larger plans."

Kira nodded slowly. "I heard that Duronis wasn't the only planet attacked today."

"Twenty-two in total," Wil confirmed.

"Any significance to that number?" Kira asked.

"We don't know yet."

Jason groaned. "Everything related to this group is 'unknown', it seems."

"Hopefully not for much longer. Let's get back to what happened on Duronis today," Wil said. "The field offices are attempting to find witnesses to the incidents on the other planets, but we didn't happen to have field operatives working undercover at an Alliance office at the time, so you're the most reliable witness we have, Kira."

"It might be easier if we just show you," she stated. "Jasmine has the whole thing recorded. May we tap into the display?"

"Sure." Wil input the necessary credentials for Jasmine to interface with the room's integrated audio-visual system.

"Hi, nice to speak with all of you directly," the AI greeted over the speakers in a bright, friendly synthetic voice that was nothing like CACI's rigid tonality.

"Hi, Jasmine," Jason replied. He'd only had limited interactions with the AI implanted in Kira, but she was a fully sentient consciousness like any other living being. In the years since he'd met her, he'd occasionally pondered what it would be like to have another voice in his head—and had decided that he already had enough internal disagreements without adding that extra layer of confusion.

"Jasmine keeps a catalogue of my sensory experience," Kira explained. "It's not as objective a record as what you'd download from a combat suit, but you'll get the gist."

Jasmine brought up a visual and auditory record from the moments leading up to the first explosion on Duronis that afternoon. Kira appeared to be standing guard duty at the top of a staircase.

"I knew Leon had a meeting in the basement that afternoon, and I was waiting for him to come out," Kira explained. "I traded for that shift so I could be close by. They always liked to have someone standing watch at that stairwell because it was so near the main entry door."

The recording advanced from Kira's point of view as a window next to her suddenly exploded in a shower of glass. She closed her eyes and ducked as a powerful *boom* took over her hearing.

When images and sound returned on the recording, dozens of people were running toward the main door. Kira ran to look out through the window, where she saw a massive plume of dark smoke in the distance and the ruins of several buildings on the street. Flames and smoke billowed from the sites. Multiple cars were overturned in the street.

"Pause," Saera requested, and Jasmine complied. "Why the attacks here? Blowing up the port makes sense, as does disrupting the power grid. But why these random attacks on the street?"

"I've been wondering that, too," Kira said. "I believe it was to cover the evacuation. At least half the people working in the Alliance office had quietly slipped out through a hidden exit without our knowledge, so there weren't nearly the numbers in our building that there should have been. By creating a distraction in the vicinity, we didn't realize we were missing people."

"And all of the hand-selected people were already offworld by this point?" Wil asked.

"Presumably so. Assuming they took off in a shuttle from the local port, they must have been gone already because that dark smoke in the background marks where the port used to be."

"What about transit records?" Wil asked.

Saera shook her head. "Nothing registered."

"I'm pretty sure they had a bunch of port workers on the payroll," Kira said. "Doesn't surprise me one bit that there's no record of anyone leaving."

"What about locks on the nav beacon?" Jason suggested.

"Good thought, but no dice there, either," his mother replied. "It appears they were using an independent jump drive—illegally, of course."

Wil deflated a little in his chair. Jason knew his father was sensitive about that technology and sometimes regretted it making its way into the hands of civilians. Naturally, criminal elements always had a way of exploiting systems that were intended to improve lives.

"Everything after that was pretty much just us running and hiding until Jason picked us up," Kira continued.

She walked them through the rest of her sensory data from the afternoon, fast-forwarding to the significant events. Jasmine offered commentary a few times, presenting observations about the detonation patterns that suggested the bombs had been set in place well in advance, following a cohesive design.

By the time she got to when Jason had picked her up— thankfully stopping before Kira had observed his meeting with Lexi—Wil and Saera were scowling at the screen.

"They really did a number on that planet," Wil said.

"Were the others this bad?" Kira asked.

"The destruction was more confined to infrastructure elsewhere. This has the look of a personal attack," he replied.

"I suspect that Duronis was the headquarters location for the Alliance," Jasmine said. "I've been reviewing footage from the other planets, and only Naevo and Erosaen exhibit similar destruction patterns. I believe those planets may also have held strategic bases, so we may be looking at three cells operating within a unified command structure."

"Those planets are nowhere near each other," Saera observed, consulting a map on her handheld.

"They are, however, each in major transit lanes for their respective territories," the AI stated. "I believe it may be possible to narrow down likely destinations for evacuees based on this information."

"Please, run the analysis," Wil said. "It would also be helpful if you could speak with a couple of our Agents about your longer-term observations while undercover within the Alliance. Any behavioral clues you can offer might help us determine their future actions."

"Gladly," Kira agreed.

Wil turned to Jason. "Now, I believe it's time we speak with Lexi and get her side of the story."

— — —

Lexi was amazed that she could have access to every bit of entertainment the Taran Empire had to offer and still not find anything to watch. Truthfully, it wasn't the overwhelming choice that was her hang-up, but rather that she was too distracted by everything else going on.

TSS Headquarters! With the Sietinens! If someone had told her that she'd one day be hanging out on Jason Sietinen's couch, she would have dropped to the floor laughing at the absurdity of the prospect. Yet, being in his personal space felt as natural as it had to be in his presence. She kept waiting for the spell to wear off and to find herself nervous and star-struck, but there was none of that. Just comfort as a sense of 'home' she'd been longing to find for her entire life.

After spending more time than she cared to admit flipping through shows on the viewscreen she had no intention of watching, she wandered around Jason's living room looking at the few personal effects on display. Pictures of him with his parents and sister confirmed the family relation that still seemed too crazy to be possible, as well as proving that they were all ridiculously photogenic.

How are these people even real? The answer was obvious— because they had been genetically engineered to be the pinnacle of the Taran form. She'd heard about the dogma of the Priesthood and had a rough understanding of what the Cadicle was supposed to be, though to know there was a real, living person attached to the title was mind-bending. Not to mention that she now found herself with the prospect of having a relationship with the guy's son.

What's the son of the Cadicle supposed to be? Is there a name for that? Her brain felt fuzzy from all the internal questioning. She wanted to focus on the fact that she and Jason felt right for each other, yet she couldn't ignore the larger political implications of that relationship. *All those people who ever fantasized about marrying someone highborn didn't think it through very closely.*

She wandered to his desk in the back corner, where she noticed a picture of Jason with his arms around a young woman with shoulder-length, dark hair. The two of them looked happy and relaxed together, almost playful. *Who's that?*

The door beeped and then slid open. When Jason stepped into the doorway, he noticed her looking at the picture.

"That's a conversation for another time," he said. "And no, we aren't together now."

Then why is there still a picture of her on your desk? She left the question unspoken. "How'd the debrief go?"

The door closed behind him. "Just the first step in a longer process. They'd like to speak with you now."

"I figured that was coming." She walked toward him.

"It's off to a good start," he said. "The more forthright you can be, the better."

"If I knew anything meaningful, the planet wouldn't have been all but destroyed."

"You know more than you might think." He stepped closer and placed his hands on her shoulders. "We need to explore every little detail for clues about where they may have taken Leon."

"What about the files from my Alliance handheld?"

"They're incomplete. It'll take time to sort through to see if anything can be salvaged."

Lexi's heart dropped. "He wouldn't be lost now if I'd never put out that call for help."

"What happened to him isn't on you, Lexi. He knew the risks of the undercover mission, so did Kira."

She nodded, knowing the truth of the words. It still hurt, though, to know her friend was in danger. "I didn't realize what I was getting into when I joined the Alliance, and I still don't know what I'm doing."

"You think the rest of us do? I just take it one moment at a time. What seems like a good decision one moment can seem like idiocy a day later."

"You hardly seem like the kind of person to make

mistakes."

"I have my share of regrets, believe me." He glanced almost imperceptibly toward the picture of the woman on his desk.

"Am I going to be one of those?" she asked.

"To the contrary, I think you're the first thing I've ever felt so certain about."

Her heart warmed. "I know the feeling."

"Then, please trust me when I say, be yourself when you go into this meeting. Be honest and try to keep an open mind."

"Deal," she agreed.

He escorted her back up the elevator to Level 1 and into a small conference room in the Command Wing. Wil and Saera were waiting, a tablet resting on the table in front of them.

Lexi sat down next to Jason on the opposite side of the oval table.

"We'd like for this to be a productive conversation," Saera stated.

Wil slid the tablet across the table to Lexi. The screen was covered in small-typeface text with a blank signature line at the bottom.

"What's this?" Lexi asked.

"A blanket immunity agreement, retroactive to birth. Needless to say, we don't hand these out very often."

Her mouth dropped open slightly. She clicked it shut and swallowed. "Why?"

"We want you to tell us everything, without reservation. Whatever happened on Duronis is part of something much, much bigger, and we need to start putting the pieces together."

She caught Jason's gaze. *"Did you know about this?"*

"They told me a few minutes before this meeting. I highly recommend you sign it."

"Do you think I'm a criminal?"

"No one in this room does, which is why you have this offer in front of you. Not everyone in the Guard might feel the same way."

She stared at the tablet. Immunity for everything she'd done while in the Alliance and everything before. Absolved of murder in the eyes of the law. She should have been happy, or at least *relieved*, but instead she felt ill.

I shouldn't get special treatment. Is the only reason I have this because Jason has feelings for me? It's not right. She tapped the edge of the tablet. "I don't like the idea of being in your debt."

Wil tilted his head slightly. "Our debt?"

"Isn't that how this kind of thing goes with highborn? You offer me a great deal in exchange for never speaking to your precious son again so he can be free to pair up with someone more suitable?"

Saera let out a loud guffaw and quickly covered her mouth. "Sorry. One day, Lexi, you'll appreciate how hilarious it is that you thought that of us."

Wil shook his head and chuckled.

Lexi looked to Jason for explanation. "That's not what…?"

He smiled apologetically. "Let me put it like this. When my sister, Raena, met Ryan, he was working as a servant. When my dad recognized a resonance connection between them, he arranged another meeting to nudge them together."

"Ryan… as in Ryan Dainetris?"

"Lineage not discovered until after the fact," Wil clarified. "I assure you, if I had reservations about you and Jason, I would state so explicitly." He pointed to the tablet. "This agreement has nothing to do with what's going on between you two; that's your business. I told Jason a long time ago that I have no expectations other than I want him to be happy."

"We've read Kira's field reports about what she learned while undercover," Saera said. "We know several incidents transpired—situations where we suspect people died—and we're grateful to whoever stopped those bad people from doing very bad things."

"We hope to have an unfiltered conversation about those events and others," Wil added.

Lexi nodded. "All right." She signed on the line using her finger and then placed her hand on the screen for a biometric record.

Wil telekinetically pulled the tablet back to him and countersigned. "Okay, to business. Start from the beginning—from when you first heard about the Alliance."

CHAPTER 16

LEON HAD BEEN in darkness for so long that he'd lost all sense of place and time.

He was strapped to a seat inside some sort of shipping crate, to his best estimation. The air had been chilly since he'd cooled off from the fight during his failed escape attempt, and he now shivered in the blackness of his cold, silent world.

His captors had whacked him rather forcefully in the head at one point, which had somewhat jumbled his recollection of events. There'd been the meeting in the basement, and they'd cornered him. They'd then taken him to another room, where there had been a scuffle. Another man was being held, and the situation hadn't looked good for him. When Leon had made a run for it, they'd knocked him out. The next thing he knew, he had awakened in the dark box.

Whatever happened to the other guy? Is he being held like this, too?

Leon had already tried numerous times to call out for help or signs of other captives, but there had been no reply. No other sounds, even. His throat was so terribly dry from lack of water that he didn't dare waste energy calling out again.

Time passed in a dream-like state. His eyes kept wanting to make sense of the shadows, even though there was truly nothing to see. The utter silence had made him hyper-aware of his own breathing and pulse, as well as the scent of stale sweat souring the air.

A shudder broke through the void—the first sensation outside his body that he'd experienced for hours. Occasional trembles rocked him in his seat, and then there was stillness again.

The sound of bolts sliding open preceded narrow cracks of light along the edges and top seam of his enclosure, then a shock of blue-tinted illumination flooded in.

He squinted against the onslaught. "Where have you taken me?" he demanded. His eyesight was too bleached in the sudden light to see if there was anyone nearby to hear the question, but there was a good chance *someone* had opened his cell door.

"Quiet," came the response in a gruff male voice.

A moment later, two figures stepped forward, silhouetted by the white-blue beam, and ducked into the box to remove the restraints at Leon's sides.

"It's about time you let me up to take a piss." His eyes were adjusting, and he could now make out a third figure standing outside the crate.

The man stood with his hands clasped behind his back, observing Leon. After several seconds of Leon picking out the man's features through the strong backlighting, he realized that it was the same manager with whom he'd spoken on Duronis.

"This would have been much easier if you'd come willingly," the man stated.

"Why have you taken me captive?" Leon let heat into his voice, not caring what kind of impression he made. He had no intention of working willingly for the kind of monsters who'd knock out and bind someone who'd turned down a job offer.

"We have a very important project in the works, and we'd like you to assist."

"You say that like I have a choice."

"We can't very well force you to comply. However, if you'd like to walk out of this in one piece, it's in your best interest to do what is requested."

"I'll never help you."

"Perhaps losing a foot would persuade you." The man glanced down at Leon's feet. "Really, the only part of you that's useful to us is your mind, so removing the extraneous bits might be an effective means of motivation."

Leon stared back at him, dumbstruck. He'd known the Alliance had a sadistic side, but it was something else to experience it firsthand. Frankly, he didn't want to lose any limbs. Not only did he enjoy martial arts, but *walking* on his own feet was a preferred mode of transit.

His mind raced back to the conversations he'd had with Kira before they went undercover on the mission. She'd told him that keeping interrogators talking was key. Unless he got lucky, rescue was more likely than escape; he'd given it his all before, and now here he was. That meant he needed to buy as much time as possible for rescuers to locate and extract him.

Unfortunately, that meant he'd likely have to play along. The good news was that if they had captured him for his mind, then they needed a specialist. Resorting to the recruitment of an unwilling participant suggested they likely didn't have anyone else with his expertise. That offered an opportunity for it to *seem* like he was being agreeable without actually accomplishing their objectives.

"I happen to like my feet," Leon replied to the threat. "I'd prefer we talk about this like reasonable individuals."

"You're a terrible liar."

"Well, you're a terrible captor, threatening me into compliance. How else do you expect me to react?"

The man stomped forward, his eyes narrowed and lips curled back into a snarl. "I expect you to do every bomaxed thing we ask, or you have no hope of making it out of this alive."

Now that he was closer, Leon could see a red welt on the side of the man's head where Leon had landed a blow during his botched escape attempt earlier.

Well, that explains his nasty mood. Leon nodded his understanding of the man's statement. "So long as I'm in one piece, I'll complete the tasks given to me."

"Glad we could reach an agreement." The sneer twisted into a sinister smile. "Now, let's get you acquainted with your new lab."

— — —

Lexi could hardly think straight after her initial debrief with the TSS High Commander and Lead Agent. Having Jason in the room had offered a surprising amount of comfort, but it had still felt like the authority of the Taran Empire was out to get her.

Following the meeting, Jason had excused himself to go take care of some business, and he'd directed her to the mess hall to grab a meal.

Walking into the large room, she was amazed by not only the homey appearance but also the pleasant aromas. Filled with hundreds of seats, the space was furnished with real wooden tables and potted plants that made it feel like she was planetside. A large buffet to the right side of the room had a wide variety of dishes that looked like the fare found in an upper-class restaurant—nothing like the gruel she had forced down during her time in the Alliance.

As she finished filling her tray, she noticed the back side of a familiar shock of red hair. She ambled over.

"Kira?" she asked, waiting for the woman to turn and confirm.

Her friend snapped to attention. "Lexi! Thank the stars."

Lexi set down her tray on the table. "Pardon?"

"Sorry, I just wasn't sure what they might do with you. I told them you were innocent in all of this, but you never know how those statements might get interpreted."

Lexi slid onto the booth bench across from Kira. "They offered me a blanket immunity deal."

"Oh, good!"

"I took it, obviously." Lexi poked at her meal.

"Glad to hear everything is coming together for you."

"Only thanks to you. I'd still be stuck on Duronis—probably dead."

"I think you're more of a survivor than that."

Lexi shrugged. "Not like you. How you can transform…" She whistled through her teeth. The image of Kira with her silvery second-skin still sent a chill up her spine.

"You're rather impressive yourself."

"I guess we've had our share of surprising each other with hidden abilities."

"And friends in high places." Lexi shook her head. "I can't believe you didn't tell me that your handler with the TSS was the son of the most famous guy in the entire Taran Empire!"

"I don't think I'm the one he really wants to be 'handling'."

Lexi's cheeks burned. "Oh, do *not* go there."

Kira burst out laughing. "Your face! Oh, my stars."

"Is it really that obvious there's something between us?"

The Guard soldier laughed harder when she looked at Lexi, clutching her midsection as she leaned back uproariously in the booth.

"Shh! People are staring at us." The situation hardly seemed funny to Lexi. Perhaps this outburst was just a bizarre manifestation of Kira's stress about what had happened with Leon. She decided to let her friend wear herself out.

"I'm sorry." Kira tried to catch her breath. "I really didn't think you were going to meet your future in-laws like that."

"What?! No..." Lexi felt the flush in her face intensify.

She hadn't thought about where her relationship with Jason was headed. At the moment, she only knew that she really liked the guy and that he seemed equally taken with her. The thought that a long-term relationship would mean family dinners with High Dynasty leaders hadn't sunk in.

Kira reached across the table and patted Lexi's hand. "You'll do just fine. For what it's worth, I've heard nothing but good things about them being genuinely nice people."

Lexi snatched her hand away and crossed her arms. "Coming from the person who's apparently been on a first-name basis with a Sietinen all this time."

"It wasn't relevant."

Lexi gaped at her. "But he's..."

Kira shrugged. "I grew up on Valta. My system wasn't even a formal member of the Empire until four years ago. I don't really get starstruck by the Taran elite."

"I guess."

"There's something you should understand about the

Guard, the TSS, and whatever other military," Kira said. "When you're a soldier, that's first and foremost. It's you, your team, and your superior officers. Yeah, we're in the service of the Taran people so we *technically* report up to the Taran High Council in a tangential capacity, but they have no say in our day-to-day operations. Taran nobles are a distant afterthought. If they're doing their job well, we shouldn't even know they're there. They're people, like anyone else. Why worship them?"

"I wasn't 'worshiping'." Lexi sighed.

"Relax, I'm just messing with you." Kira waved her hand playfully. "Seriously, though, just be yourself. Don't overthink it."

"I *wasn't* until you got started on all this."

"And soon enough you won't care again. It's a special thing to find someone you click with."

Lexi nodded. "Yeah, it is. But this is all *crazy*!"

"Not gonna lie, when I saw you two start making eyes at each other..." She grinned and clicked her tongue.

"I'm glad my life-altering predicaments are offering you such amusement."

"Oh, best entertainment in months!" She turned serious. "Stars know I need a distraction right now."

"Kira..."

The other woman shook her head. "You don't need to say it. I know we'll find him."

I meet someone just as the person she loves most goes missing... What do you say to that? Lexi swallowed. "Yeah, we will. We're in this together."

"In the meantime, enjoy your new lover-boy."

"I have every intention of doing just that."

—   —   —

Jason rubbed his weary eyes, realizing that he'd been up for more than a full day. On top of the mission debrief, he'd had his normal responsibilities to take care of, and he'd lost track of time.

Going back to his quarters to rest sounded amazing. However, that now came with the complicating factor of Lexi being there. The thought was both exciting and reassuring in a way he hadn't expected.

He palmed open the door, and Lexi rose from the couch to greet him. His heart warmed at the sight of her. *I could get used to this.*

She stepped toward him and then pulled him into her arms the moment the door was closed. Her lips found his and she pressed against him. Everything else vanished in her presence.

When they parted, he was breathless and still wanted more. She was intoxicating.

"I know it's only been a few hours, but stars, I missed you," she whispered in his ear as she held him.

"Me too."

Lexi pulled back and stared into his eyes at arms' length. "I've had a lot of time to think about it today, and I want you to know that I'm all in with giving us a chance."

The alternative had never been a viable option in his mind. "I feel the same way. Now that I know you exist, I can't imagine not seeing this through."

She smiled up at him. "Please try to be patient, because being open and vulnerable is a new thing for me."

"I will." Jason took her hand and led her to the couch. They sat down, angled with their knees touching. "Though we still need to get acquainted properly, I look forward to much more with you." He looked over her perfect figure but managed to keep his focus. "I want to set us up for the best life together that we can have, so before we take any next steps, there are some things we should talk about."

"Yes. Get to know each other."

"Exactly. And, specifically, I need to confess that having you here in my quarters is great and also a little bittersweet."

She held his hands. "It's okay. You can tell me anything."

He searched for the right words, glancing at the picture of Tiff on his desk. "I was in a relationship for a long time. You could call it 'friends with benefits', but it was more than that. After nine years, it had run its course and it was time to move on. She took a post at the Alkeer Station days before it was destroyed in the Erebus attack."

"Shite! Was she…?"

He nodded.

"Oh, Jason, I'm so sorry."

"It is what it is. Even though the nature of our relationship had changed by then, and it was never romantic love, it was still a huge blow."

"Yeah, I can only imagine."

"Worse, I was there on the *Conquest* with my dad when it happened. I was in the middle of a remote telepathic conversation with her, and then…" He faded out, unable to say it. That sensation of sudden emptiness came over him again with the memory of that awful day.

"Fok… wow." She bowed her head. "That wasn't that long ago."

"Yeah, seven months. I've come to terms with it, but there are moments, you know? And since most of our time together was spent in here…"

To his surprise, Lexi didn't appear uncomfortable with the thought. Instead, she squeezed his hands and nodded with understanding. "I'm not in any rush."

"I appreciate that. And to be clear, what I had with Tiff wasn't anything like the start of what we have."

"You don't need to explain. I feel it, too."

He brought one hand up to stroke the side of her face. "You're absolutely incredible."

"Being around you makes me want to be a better person. Historically, I've actually been kind of a bitch."

Jason laughed. "I find that hard to believe."

"I've had the kind of life that makes a person cynical."

"I want to hear all about it, whenever you're ready to share."

"I'm getting there. Maybe that's a Day Two conversation."

They both laughed.

"Stars, this really has progressed quickly." He shook his head.

"It has, but I can't imagine anything else."

"Me either."

She leaned in and kissed him tenderly. "Thank you for telling me about your friend."

"I wish you could have met her. She would have loved you."

"I'm glad." Lexi paused. "Are you sure you're okay with me staying here?"

"Yes, if you are. Tiff spent time here, but it was always *my* place, not 'ours'. I hope, though, with us that could be different."

"As long as you're here, there's nowhere else I'd rather be."

CHAPTER 17

"THIS IS INCREDIBLE," Raena told Trevor as she reviewed the latest field report of the findings on Earth. The initial ship hull had indeed been the first of many extraordinary discoveries, and this latest find looked like it would make all of their efforts worthwhile.

Raena had always thought that the technology on Earth was advanced while she was growing up, but the Taran Empire had given her access to so much more. In particular, visualization technology was significantly more sophisticated, especially when it came to looking through solid objects. A long history of space exploration and mining had given Tarans a suite of imaging and materials analysis tools, which were perfect for the current investigation on Earth.

The team had been analyzing areas of interest to determine the places that were worth excavating. What they were now finding underground, buried for tens of thousands of years or more, was nothing short of revolutionary for the understanding of both human and Taran history. Now, with the top sites identified, it was even more impressive to see those ancient treasures unearthed.

"The pictures don't do it justice," Trevor said as he flipped the feed on their vidcall to a visual recording.

The holoprojector above Raena's desk rendered an immersive scene of a lush jungle with such vivid detail that she could almost smell the damp earth and feel mosquitos buzzing around her head. At the center, a perfectly round section of the jungle landscape had been raised upward on an antigrav platform, supporting a collection of small pyramids that had long since been reclaimed by trees and vines. That portion of the ground encompassing the monuments was now floating eighty meters in the air, the antigravity drives casting an eerie blue glow on the underside of the support disk.

Raena smiled. "How are ticket sales for the floating city tour?"

Trevor chuckled. "Line out the door—figuratively speaking. If only they knew what we were working on behind the stealth shield." He began playing the holovideo recording.

Raena braced herself as the camera operator stepped underneath the platform. Though she knew the technology was reliable—and she herself was nowhere near it, only observing—there was something disconcerting about a former city being suspended overhead.

At the threshold, there was a silvery shimmer as the camera passed through to the inside of the worksite, hidden within a camouflaged shield. To an outside observer, the platform was suspended in the air above a patch of empty ground. In reality, a large-scale excavation operation was underway, and the exterior appearance was effectively a massive work tent cloak. Select government officials knew what was really going on inside, but they didn't need casual tourist observers taking pictures that would undoubtedly lead to rampant rumors.

The exposed ground where the jungle floor had been uprooted had been stripped back in tiers surrounding a hole that disappeared into the depths. Various retaining walls and other support structures kept everything in place.

"We didn't make that central hole," Trevor revealed. "It aligned with one of the pyramids. Some sort of access point, though it was invisible from the outside."

"Where does it lead?"

"To crazy town."

The video fast-forwarded to the camera operator standing at the precipice of the hole, which was now ringed in scaffolding. The opening was approximately fifteen meters in diameter and it was at least four times that deep.

"The scaffolding is ours, but the walls are original," Trevor explained.

The video zoomed in on the shaft's surface, which appeared to be a sort of shimmering stone Raena didn't recognize. It was carved with branching grooves filled with copper or a similar metal, giving the appearance of a circuit board.

Raena gaped at it, aware she had lost her dynastic heiress poise. "What?"

Trevor shook his head. "As I said, my lady, we weren't expecting to find anything like this."

The video quickly advanced again through the descent of the spiraling scaffold. At the bottom, it resumed normal playback speed as the camera approached a crystal sphere resting on a pedestal at the center of the shaft. The sphere was a meter in width, and its vertical support was covered in the same circuitry-like carvings.

"We don't know what it does yet," Trevor said. "It's clearly some kind of device."

"Age estimates?"

"Many tens of thousands of years."

What in the stars went on here? Raena stared at the bizarre scene, not sure what to make of it. Clearly, Tarans had left behind all of their technology when they settled on Earth. This could be anything from a weapon, to a shield, to an information repository.

"Capture as much data about it as you can and send it to TSS Headquarters," Raena instructed. If anyone could make sense of the strange device, it was her dad.

"Yes, my lady."

Raena's desk flashed with an incoming call from her grandfather.

"Hey, Trevor, is that it for now?"

"Yes, the rest is in my report."

"Great. Thank you for the update. Talk soon." She ended the vidcall with Trevor and switched over to the incoming feed from her grandfather. "Hi, sorry for the delay. I was in the middle of something."

Cris smiled back at her from the viewscreen on the wall. "No need to apologize. I hope all is well."

"Stars! You won't believe what we just found on Earth." She filled him in on the latest discovery.

He took in the explanation without much outward expression. When she finished, he nodded thoughtfully. "Hmm. I wouldn't have expected that."

"It sounds like there's a lot more Taran history on the planet than we'd realized."

"Are you sure it's Taran?" he asked.

That prospect hadn't occurred to her. "No, actually. They haven't done much testing yet."

"The device reminds me a bit of the images I saw of the

Gatekeeper sphere, but that might be a coincidence."

"Or, perhaps the races once worked together," Raena said.

"Also a possibility. The Erebus were a threat to them both, so maybe they collaborated after the ancient war."

"I'm curious to hear what Dad thinks about it."

"Me too," Cris said. His expression darkened. "Unfortunately, we have considerations closer to home right now."

She wasn't used to seeing him look worried. "What's going on?"

"Those coordinated attacks in the Outer Colonies have been getting a lot of media attention, understandably. That messaging is working its way through the Middle and Central Worlds. They're scrutinizing Tararian leadership, and specifically our long-term operational plans to continue supporting the ever-expanding Empire."

Raena frowned. "What's the issue? Business is good. Financially, we're in great shape."

"Yes, that's not the concern. There is a matter of succession and the continuity of power."

She was about to ask him to clarify when it struck her what he meant. Raena and Ryan were young and healthy, but they had no named scions to continue either Sietinen or Dainetris. "Ah."

"I swore I would never become my parents and be concerned about such things, so please don't take it as me trying to push you to speed up your timeline. I just mean it as a statement of fact about *why* people are making the sort of statements you've been seeing."

"It makes sense," she admitted. "I guess it's been on the backburner with everything else going on. Honestly, Ryan and I haven't talked about it."

"And, under normal circumstances, a couple your age wouldn't be in any sort of rush. Nor should you be now."

"Except, most scions have an heir of their own by their mid-twenties."

"Traditionally, yes. But your father was twenty-eight, so…"

Wow, it's amazing my parents managed to see us through high school at their super-advanced age, she thought sarcastically. She had no doubt that her grandfather meant well and wasn't trying to pressure her, but the statement got her thinking. A baby—or *babies*, more likely—hadn't entered into her planning for the foreseeable future. However, she realized that it should be discussed with her husband sooner than later.

"Point taken," she told her grandfather. "In the meantime, how do you suggest we proceed?"

"Your new discovery on Earth might actually be just what we need. A reminder about a shared history across the Taran worlds, that we're in this together. I encourage you to expedite your plans to open up tours of Morningstar Isle and to begin rolling out promo packages about these new links with Earth."

"As much as I want to share that work, I think we need to do more investigation before we post anything publicly," she said. "These artifacts could be dangerous, or they might be part of a tool to use against the Erebus, and we wouldn't want to tip them off."

"That's a good point." He sat in quiet consideration for several moments. "Okay, then let's proceed with the tours, and I'll see if I can get our relief efforts in the Outer Colonies more screen time. DGE has done more than anyone else, but Makaris has spent the most time in the spotlight. Sure, food is necessary, but there wouldn't have been half as many people evacuated yet if Ryan hadn't sent those ships."

"Some reporter has to be willing to take on that story," Raena agreed.

"Be ready for interviews. I'd like to start getting you more face time."

"Oh, joy." She smiled at him. Really, she didn't mind public relations, but it was best not to be overly enthusiastic or she might find herself doing nothing else.

"You're well on your way to becoming a great leader, Raena. You're exactly what the Empire needs."

"I hope so. I feel like I'm constantly playing catchup, having been outside the culture when I was growing up."

"That's what makes you so perfectly suited for this role, though. I hated it when your parents took you away to Earth, but they saw it was for the best, and now I understand why. You approach everyone as equals. Find common ground. That's what we need now more than anything."

"I try."

He smiled. "The media loves a modest leader. Keep this up and we'll be just fine."

— — —

Wil reviewed the latest information from his daughter on the holoprojector above his desk with Saera.

"A series of buried ships and underground structures, huh?" Saera shook her head incredulously. "And here I thought all those ancient aliens theorists on TV had done too many mind-altering drugs."

Wil chuckled. "There must have been so much vindication the moment we revealed the existence of the Taran Empire."

"There were many multi-hour TV specials. I checked." She flashed a playful smile.

"But all of this is strange." Wil turned serious. "There have been touch-points with Earth throughout Taran history, it seems. First was perhaps millions of years ago, and then significantly more involvement over the past hundred thousand years or so."

Saera shrugged. "Stewards for the planet."

"Certainly, but why bury so much in inaccessible places?"

"Well, we lock away plenty of things for safekeeping. It seems they made a concerted effort to leave behind advanced technology, so everything would have been sealed away."

Wil didn't yet have enough information about the strange device in Belize to determine its purpose, but it was clearly designed to handle the flow of a large amount of power. That kind of signature would stand out from a distance, so it made sense its builders would use subterranean construction practices to take advantage of the natural insulating properties of the ground.

The design was intentionally hidden, definitely not a random thing that had been lost. *It was preserved, sealed away...*

The pieces began falling into place. "That's it! Oh, my stars..." Wil sat up straight in his chair. "It was an ark."

"Wait, what?" Saera looked at him with a mixture of intrigue and confusion.

"Earth was an ark. Think about the timeline. The location. The cultural diversity. Raena's recent discoveries confirmed that colonists from various Taran worlds all settled on Earth, and it's highly suspected that they genetically engineered aspects of life on the planet. What was never clear was *why*.

"Now, I can't help but wonder if the reason they fled to Earth long ago was to form a settlement far away from Tararia, so that the Taran race might continue if anything happened to the Central Worlds. Given that technology is what had sparked the original conflict with the Erebus and the Gatekeepers, it makes sense that they would leave behind those temptations when founding this new world. The ancient Tarans brought with them elements of their cultures from their original homeworlds, but everything else was intentionally forgotten so that they could be a truly independent colony."

"That... actually makes sense," Saera said slowly. "Holy crap, I never thought about it that way before."

"There wasn't reason to."

"It doesn't explain the strange structures on the planet, though. What else were they hiding?"

"Well, if the ancient Tarans settled Earth—a secret colony—as a contingency plan against a war with the Erebus, perhaps they also hid some of their knowledge, or means of protection."

"Like some kind of old-fashioned planetary shield?"

"Honestly, we have no idea what technology or capabilities Tarans from that era possessed," Wil said. "We have considered the advent of subspace travel to be relatively recent, within the last couple thousand years. However, Tarans are millennia old, in one form or another, and the civilization has had its rises and falls. It's entirely possible that they once possessed technology that makes our modern methods look rudimentary."

"In other words, what's down there might be really valuable."

"Or it could be nothing. I'm just throwing out random thoughts here."

Saera crossed her arms. "In any case, it sounds like that excavation just became a top priority."

"Indeed. And it explains why there's been a pervasive

stewardship of Earth throughout history."

"I wonder if all those people who've made fun of 'that backwater planet Earth' would feel bad if they learned humans were the fallback plan to repopulate the galaxy?"

"Something tells me that would not go over well."

She nodded. "And I suppose we don't know for sure that was the intention. Your speculation makes sense, though."

"More so than the other hypotheses about Earth I've toyed with over the years," Wil said.

"An ark." She shook her head. "I guess those mentions of spaceship-like craft in religious texts had some basis in reality after all."

"And the powers of the gods. Sounds an awful lot like Gifted people to me."

"Yeah, I had a similar thought when I first learned about abilities. It does seem like divine magic—especially after a story has been passed down for generations, with each narrator adding their own embellishments."

"For sure," he agreed.

"Makes you wonder what happened to those abilities over time." Saera tilted her head in thought. "Earth wasn't subjected to the same genetic experimentations that caused the Generation Cycle in the rest of the Taran population, was it?"

Wil shrugged. "Not as far as I know. Maybe the blending with the natives eventually weakened the gene expression of those traits."

"It makes me wonder, though…" She faded out, then continued when Wil gave her a quizzical look, "The Priesthood went to great lengths to design a perfect genetic partner for you, with the intention of creating a patch to fix the Generation Cycle. Of the trillions of people to choose from to be a part of that solution, they picked my dad—a half-human from Earth.

Maybe something in that ancient Taran genome that's evolved into the modern human is the key to solving it all."

"An ark is also a genetic archive of a different sort," Wil mused.

"Yeah. I dunno, I might be over-thinking it."

"We may never know for sure, but we are certainly armed with more information now than we had before."

Saera nodded. "What does that mean for this device? And whatever else they might find."

"We study each discovery and continue filling in the pieces," he replied. "We're just beginning to scratch the surface of our history. Somewhere, buried in the past, might be the key to our future."

— — —

After the rudimentary lab at the Alliance office, Leon was amazed by the sophistication of this new facility. If he'd been a willing worker, he would have loved the place—both for its crisp, clean aesthetic and the variety of high-end equipment. As it stood, though, the shiny finishes made it no less a prison.

"You will complete the tasks given to you. No more, no less," stated the manager, whom Leon had learned was named Edward. The man had never had a particularly pleasant demeanor on Duronis, but now his expression was set in a permanent glare.

"Am I supposed to work alone?" Leon asked.

"For now. Unless you can prove you are cooperative." Edward deepened his scowl. "If you're worth the air you breathe, you won't need assistance."

Granted, Leon's line of work was suited to him being an 'individual contributor' rather than anything requiring multiple hands and eyes, but he had hoped there would be others in the lab. Aside from it being nice to occasionally bounce ideas off someone—since he'd no doubt need to do *some* actual work during his captivity—it was also much easier to get away with covert actions when there was someone else around to draw some of the attention. Being alone meant all surveillance would be solely on him; he wouldn't be able to get away with anything under those conditions.

Edward activated the main workstation on the island at the center of the lab, which was marked with a corporate emblem for 'SPEAR Tec'.

What's SPEAR Tec? Leon wondered. He'd never heard mention of the name during his time in the Alliance. Perhaps it was another division within the Coalition's umbrella?

Edward navigated to a file directory. "Everything you will need is in here." He opened up a brief and displayed it on the holoprojector.

Leon stared at the bizarre data set. "What is this?"

"Figure it out. We need a stable tether by the end of the week."

"A what?"

Edward left Leon alone in the lab without giving an answer. The lab door locked behind him, trapping Leon inside.

Fantastic. Doing nothing would immediately get Leon in trouble, and he had a feeling that their threat to remove non-vital limbs wasn't a bluff. Besides, he needed to understand what they wanted him to do before he could effectively stall or sabotage.

He turned his attention to the information on the console. At first, the disparate pieces didn't make any sense for being together on a single project. It was related to the snippets that he had been shown during the meetings on Duronis, connected to a genetic predisposition for Gifted abilities. He knew from his other work that the real point of interest was the transdimensional connection between a Gifted person and the energy in higher dimensions. Even that much was emerging science that was at the edge of his field. The only reason he knew anything about it at all was because of Kira's unique nanites, but that had only ancillary relation to this work.

Leon flipped through the assignment notes, trying to figure out what, exactly, they wanted him to do.

The brief was all over the place: Map the genome for a set of a dozen individuals. Isolate the genetic markers for transdimensional energy connection. Create a gene therapy to activate those markers in the test subjects, regardless of their base genetics. Develop a way to remotely toggle the transdimensional connection on and off in one specific person.

They want me to do this alone? And in less than a week? It was an insane task. He had his doubts whether it was even possible, regardless of time and resources. The checkpoints in the process sounded like someone had made them up without having any idea how such things worked in reality.

That settled it. He was thoroughly screwed any way he sliced it.

He looked around the room for signs of a camera; there was no way he wasn't being observed. After a visual sweep of the corners, he caught one mounted above the door in a hidden recess.

Leon stared into it. "What you're asking is impossible. You can't spontaneously give a non-Gifted person abilities. If that was possible, they would have solved the Generation Cycle problem years ago. The only thing that might be possible is to simulate a bond, like quantum entanglement between two specific genomes."

There was no reply at first, and then a woman said over a speaker, "Do that."

Nothing more.

Shite, now I've done it. Leon groaned to himself. He didn't know if he could actually accomplish the task he'd suggested, let alone in an expedited fashion. *Now I get to figure out how to do this without handing over a bioweapon that could destroy the galaxy.*

CHAPTER 18

WITH HIS DEBRIEFINGS complete and his reports filed, it was time for Jason to resume his usual duties as a TSS Agent and instructor.

Normally, returning from a mission and getting back to his routine would be a comfort. Now, with Lexi here, he wished he could take leave and spend more time getting to know her. From just hanging out to showing her around Headquarters, he'd enjoyed her company over the last few days—so much so that the idea of not being around her saddened him.

After silencing his morning alarm, Jason wrapped his arms around Lexi and held her close in bed. Sleeping next to her felt as natural as their first kiss. Though being in the same bed for the last three nights without it progressing beyond cuddles had taken considerable willpower, he enjoyed these quiet moments of simply reveling in each other's company.

"It's so early," Lexi moaned, burying her head under a pillow.

"I wanted a little extra time with you before I had to head out for the day."

She scooched closer to him. "No chance we can just lounge around all day together?"

"I wish. I've got class."

"Going off to instruct bright, inquiring minds… I feel like a total deadbeat compared to you."

Jason rolled over to look her in the eyes. "I'll say it as many times as I need to. I don't care where you came from or what you've done."

"I know, and I'm grateful for that."

He kissed her. "You've been thrown into my world, and that's a lot of adjusting."

"Yeah. I'm trying to focus on what's here between us and ignore the rest for now."

"Good plan."

"So, what happens now?" Lexi asked.

"We try to figure out our new day-to-day lives together."

"How do we deal with you being a TSS Agent, and me… not?"

Jason nodded in silent thought, weighing how to respond. "I don't expect you to join the TSS, but that is an option if you want to."

"I doubt you take people with my kind of history."

"Not usually. However, there are options for working with the TSS that don't entail being an Agent and going through that training."

"You mean like a civilian contractor?"

"Something like that."

"I don't know." She shrugged. "I might consider it, depending on what I'd do."

"That would be a longer discussion."

Lexi looked down.

He stroked her shoulder. "Hey, there's no pressure with

any of this, okay?"

"You can say that, but it's not true."

"No, really, I—"

"You don't care? I believe you, and that's great. But I think your family may see things differently."

Jason sighed. "Lex…" He interlaced his fingers with hers. "They are more understanding than you may think. Even if they aren't, though, I don't care. I *will* find a way for our lives to mesh."

She took an unsteady breath. "It's scary to feel this way about someone after so short a time."

"For me, too. But we're in this together, and we'll navigate each of these challenges as partners. Sure, we come from different worlds, but that doesn't mean our future can't follow the same path."

Lexi leaned her head against his chest. "Thank you. I really am trying to keep an open mind about my place here. Everyone has been so welcoming. The feeling out of place thing is all in my own head."

"It took me a while to feel at home here, too."

"I've always thought home is more about the people you're with than the place."

"Very true."

She brought her face close to his. "I feel like I've found that with you."

He leaned in for another kiss, savoring the contact. If every morning could begin like this, good times were ahead.

Eventually, he dragged himself from bed and got going for the day. His flight class wasn't until the afternoon, but he had a lot of papers to review before then. While he disliked assigning that kind of work, report-filing and other administrative tedium was a fact of being a good Agent, so he owed it to his students to include writing projects in the training curriculum.

Not long after he'd gotten settled into his office, a notification popped up on his desktop summoning him to his father's office. *I can't go one day without something unexpected coming up.*

The door was open when he arrived at the High Commander's office, and his father waved him inside.

Wil telekinetically swung the door closed behind him. "I know you're busy, Jason, but I wanted to chat about some things."

Am I in trouble? He tentatively sat down in his usual chair. "Sure."

"How are things with Lexi?"

"Good. I mean, it's only been a couple of days, but it seems like a lot longer than that."

"I know that feeling." He paused. "I expect the next few months will be transformative for you."

"Why?"

"Finding a partner has a way of giving a new perspective."

Jason leaned back in the chair. "Ah. Well, this isn't the first time I've dated someone since becoming an Agent."

"No, but this kind of partnership is different, isn't it? More like having a part of yourself that exists outside of you."

Jason didn't know how to respond, so he remained silent. The fact remained that he'd only known Lexi for a short time, and they hadn't bonded yet. She was important to him, surely, but he didn't see how their relationship would fundamentally change how he would go about his duties.

"I don't expect you to understand now," his father continued, "but there's a unique challenge that comes from being close to someone when you're in a position like ours. As commanders, we're used to putting the needs of others before ourselves. It's often like that in a relationship, too. That partnership can be a source of strength when it's healthy, but it can also be a distraction."

"I get that." A little defensiveness worked its way into Jason's tone. This would no doubt turn into a lecture about how he shouldn't allow being with Lexi to compromise his career advancement.

"No, I'm not trying to dissuade you. Quite the opposite," his father said. Though Jason hadn't shared his private thoughts, the sentiment must have come through in his expression.

"What, then?"

"I mean to say that we often carry great burdens as leaders, and shouldering that alone can be too much to bear. Having someone to help us through the toughest times can make all the difference. It's not a matter of career *or* relationship, but rather how the two can complement each other. Care for each other. The stronger you are as a couple, the better you'll be able to perform as a commander when the pressure is on. Be able to lean on each other to stay grounded."

"Oh." *Well, that's not how I thought that was going to go.*

"It'll take time to build up your trust in one another, no matter how instantaneous the connection may feel. At this stage it's only 'potential'. You still need to put in the work."

"I plan to."

Wil smiled. "I can tell. I think meeting her has come at a good time for you."

"Yeah." Jason looked down. *Any sooner and I might not have been ready to let go of Tiff.*

"As you begin this new chapter, it seems appropriate to increase your responsibilities in other ways. To begin, I'd like you to lead the efforts related to the Coalition; identify the branches of the organization and come up with an action plan to quell the threat."

Jason ran a quick mental calculation of the amount of time that was likely to take. There was no way he could take it on in addition to his current duties. "I appreciate you trusting me with that, but with classes and—"

"Teaching has been excellent experience for you. I think you're ready to apply those skills in a new capacity."

His heart sank. He *enjoyed* teaching, and the flight lessons, in particular were his only chance to get out into the void. "Is there any room for discussion?"

"We're very alike, Jason. I hated it when the High Commander told me I had to be an instructor, and I hated it when he told me it was time to stop working in theory and to get out into the field to put everything into practice. It's only with the benefit of time that I can look back and see that those nudges came at precisely the right moments. I hope you'll believe me when I say one day you'll be able to thank me."

Jason had no reason to doubt his father, and he certainly respected him. The rebellious edge his TSS training had worked so hard to quiet still nagged that he should resist these orders. He had a good thing going right now, especially with Lexi. They could have fun together and keep it low-stress.

Yet, he realized that he truly had matured beyond that way of thinking. He wanted to grow and to push himself. Teaching and going on one-off missions was safe. To reach the next stage of his career, he'd need to step outside his comfort zone. A formal task force command was a big deal.

"I relish the challenge," Jason said. "I think this is an assignment I can invest in." *With Lexi's experience, I certainly have the motivation to track down the Coalition members and prevent them from hurting others.*

"That's good to hear." Wil smiled, pride in his eyes. "I'll be here to support you in any way you need."

"Thanks. I'd like to at least finish out the week with my students. Do you know who'll be taking over?"

"I believe your mother has some people in mind. You can coordinate the transition with her."

"Okay. Will do." Jason rose.

Wil stood to face him. "Jason, I want you to know that I'm not giving you this assignment just because you're my son. You've earned it in your own right."

"Thank you."

"With that said, you *are* still my son, and I'd like to get to know Lexi. I hope we and your mom can all get together soon."

Jason nodded. "Yeah, I'd like that."

"Good. Enjoy this final week with your students. It's really not a goodbye, just moving on to other things for now."

"I will."

—   —   —

A buzz at the door pulled Lexi from the couch. It seemed strange to answer the door of someone else's residence, but Jason wasn't around and it would be even weirder to pretend she wasn't there. After all, the person might be there for her.

She checked the security camera feed and saw Kira outside, tapping her foot impatiently.

Lexi opened the door. "Hey."

Her friend smiled. "Still staying here with Jason? I take it things are going well?"

Lexi gave her a coy smile. "Yeah. No complaints."

"Well, I hate to pull you from your romantic bliss, but I

need your help."

"Sure."

"They've given me access to the transit data from all of the planets that were attacked in the Outer Colonies," Kira explained. "I could use another set of eyes while I sift through it."

"Yeah, I'm happy to assist." *Anything to help find Leon.*

She was also thankful to have a task to pass the time. Jason had a life here at TSS Headquarters, but she needed to find a way to contribute herself.

"I have a room reserved where we can work."

"One sec." Lexi jogged over to the coffee table to grab her new TSS-issued handheld, and she turned off the viewscreen. Hopefully, Kira hadn't noticed the paused sappy romance vid on the screen. There was something about a new relationship that always made her mushy.

"Time to do some real work," Kira said as they set off down the hall. "The Alliance liked us to look busy, but I don't think either of us really *did* much."

"No, the whole thing was a joke."

"I've become convinced that it was by design," the soldier continued. "I hate to admit it, but they are masters of deception. They kept so much going on at the surface level that it distracted everyone—including me—from the real work happening behind the scenes."

"Why even put up that front?"

"Plausible deniability."

"I'm so sorry Leon got pulled into a real project."

"If he hadn't, we might not have learned anything about their larger plans. I know we'll find him." Kira's tone was confident, and it reassured Lexi that there was truth to the words.

The work room had a touchscreen table at its center and a larger viewscreen integrated into the back wall. Compared to the secondhand furnishings found throughout the Alliance office, the room seemed swanky.

"Wow, the TSS has really got it made," she said.

Kira eased into one of the padded chairs at the table. "I'd always heard that they were posher than the Guard, but stars! Seeing everything firsthand puts it into perspective."

"I guess having generation after generation of highborn leaders has an impact."

"Nah, that organizational culture goes back way further than the Sietinens," Kira said. "They used to report directly to the Priesthood. I hear those robed freaks liked everything all fancy."

"Probably to distract people from the horrible things they were doing in the shadows."

"Likely. I'm just happy to be off Duronis. I never expected to stay that long."

"Me either." Lexi slumped into her chair. "Now, I've gotta see it through."

"I should have pulled us all out when I realized they were working on something in secret," Kira murmured. "I didn't handle it well in the field—way too much waiting around."

"Isn't that how deep undercover works? Spend time building trust?"

"Except it didn't work. And I should have realized months ago that I wasn't making sufficient progress. They played us, and it got people killed."

And Leon captured. Lexi picked at the hem of her shirt. "Rehashing what might have been doesn't help now."

"That's right." Kira activated the tabletop and viewscreen. "Let's figure out what to do going forward."

Lexi looked over the information as Kira brought it up on the screen. There were all sorts of transit logs in addition to chronological data about civil disturbances related to the main attacks and subsequent fallout.

"Duronis seems to have had the worst of it," Kira said. "However, these twenty-one other planets have had their share of disruption over the past year. It all seemed separate until there were these attacks that happened simultaneously."

"Anything else in common?" Lexi asked.

"There's no common name or branding to link them."

"The Alliance customized its campaigns down to the neighborhood level. I'm not surprised there's nothing connecting the organization world-to-world."

"The *themes* are similar, though." Kira brought up a couple examples on the viewscreen. "The common thread is seeking independence from centralized government. Trust in local representatives to lead."

"The Coalition wants its own people."

"No doubt."

"And all those experts they've been recruiting… those are the kind of skills that would help build a new world."

"Or *re*build." Kira's face darkened. "The project Leon was working on was some kind of genetically-keyed weapon. Something like that could wipe out certain life while leaving other things intact."

Lexi's gut lurched. "That's a very disturbing thought."

"I haven't told you everything I've learned about the Alliance," Kira revealed. "I do truly view you as a friend, but I had a mission to fulfill. Some information was too critical to trust to a civilian without Command approval."

"And now?"

"Now we're out of that infernal place and you know more

about it than anyone on our side. I hope you'll work with me going forward, as full partners, to find Leon and stop the people behind this violence."

"Yes. Of course, I will. I would have been hesitant to trust someone like me, too."

"This whole thing has turned out to be much bigger than either of us realized." Kira looked over the expansive star chart on the holodisplay.

"I never would have joined the Alliance had I realized what was going on. I really thought they were just going to campaign for better wages, or whatever, and my friend would be somewhere on Duronis."

"Stop trying to justify your actions, Lexi. I get it. In your position, I probably would have joined up, too."

"Okay. Sorry."

Kira pointed to the screen, getting down to business. "If you look at all these worlds, they do have a few things in common. Foremost, they're all developed Outer Colonies planets with thriving interstellar commerce. Secondly, none of them are self-sustaining."

Lexi caught on. "Which is interesting, because all of the Alliance's messaging was about complete independence."

"Right. Get people to withdraw, but they'll still need to get their necessities from somewhere."

"Enter the Coalition—standing by to serve as an organizer between the worlds." *That really would be a smart move.*

Kira scoffed. "Wouldn't surprise me in the least to learn that was their plan."

"We've already made a lot of assumptions about what's going on, but let's chase that logic. Say they're planning to swoop in with a solution for these remote worlds that will get them away from centralized Tararian rule. The Coalition itself would need a base of operations."

"That could be anywhere in the galaxy." Kira swept her hand over the vast expanse on the holoprojector. "It seems they're working with black market independent jump drives, so we can't begin to map out possible locations."

"All right, maybe not for where the leaders might be based, but what about the location of this bioweapons lab? There have to be *some* factors that would narrow it down."

"I was thinking that, too. Jasmine and I have been working with CACI to develop a few scenarios. I wanted to see if anything jumped out at you, based on your experience with supply receipts and inventorying." Kira changed the information on the screen to show several possible flight paths off of Duronis and other worlds.

"Hi, Lexi, I'm Jasmine," the AI said over the room's speakers. "Kira has been my voice, but it's nice to finally speak with you directly."

"Yes, likewise." The sudden presence in the room caught Lexi by surprise. She knew Kira had an embedded AI, but it was easy to forget since they'd never interacted directly. It made her wonder how many times Kira had been having conversations inside her head while she appeared to be sitting quietly.

Jasmine continued, "I have cross-referenced the supply shipment logs you were able to share with Kira, which has yielded a partial pattern of supply routes. I have compared that to flight paths recorded with the Duronis ports and the other worlds that were attacked to see if there were any destinations in common."

"That sounds like a whole lot more than I could do," Lexi said.

"What I cannot account for is the personal component.

That's why I suggested to Kira that we involve you in this analysis."

"I also enjoy your company," Kira added.

Lexi tilted her head, not sure what the AI and her friend wanted. "Is there a specific question in there?"

"These ten planets are the most likely candidates to have clandestine operations going on," Kira said, bringing up summary briefs on each of them. "Does anything jump out?"

Lexi glanced at the profiles. "No."

"You could look a little harder."

"Yeah, but what's the point? If you've already narrowed it down to ten planets, that's a totally reasonable number to investigate. Can't you or a few Agents just go down and scope it out?"

"No. We need hard proof and a clear action plan before we can make a move or we might spook them, and then we might lose all leads."

Lexi examined the profiles again, more closely this time. Still, none of the cursory information jumped out. They were all sparsely inhabited worlds with breathable atmospheres and bio-optimized ecology—nothing that would require specialized equipment that may have passed through her inventory system.

"I'm sorry, Kira. I wish I could help, but I don't have enough to go on."

Her friend nodded, her disappointment obvious. "I figured it was a longshot. I still think we might be able to locate something in a manual review of the logs."

"I'm all yours. Let's find some answers."

— — —

Offloading the Coalition investigation to Jason freed up Wil to refocus on the manufacturing and distribution of the new power cores and planetary shields. Jason had set them up for success with that, and the legal representative, Sabrina, had taken the deal with the Lynaedans to the finish line.

Though Wil was grateful to have Jason as the diplomatic face of the efforts, the fact remained that his son hadn't inherited Wil's passion for engineering. Whenever Wil tried to get into finer technical details, he could see the moment when Jason's eyes glazed over—and that was barely beyond Step One. It wasn't that he didn't have the intellectual capacity, just no interest.

While Wil knew he probably *shouldn't* engage in that kind of detail work as High Commander, designing new tech was his favorite way to spend time aside from being with his family. Participating in hands-on projects was one of the few indulgences he allowed himself, and this work with the power core was no exception.

With a formal manufacturing agreement in place, they now needed to finalize the production design. Wil had offered several possibilities to the team of Lynaeda's top engineers assigned to the project, and they had countered with their own revisions. He'd glanced at the plans when the message had first landed in his inbox and then promptly tossed it aside to deal with later when he'd seen several erroneous assumptions within the first five seconds of his review. Now, the uncomfortable discussion with the engineers couldn't be delayed any longer.

Reluctantly, he opened up the faulty core design specs and made a few notes about the things that would need to change before they were ready for production. As prepared as he could be, he put in the call.

The lead engineer on the Lynaedan side, Derik, answered right away; when communications went directly to a neural interface, there weren't many excuses for missing a call. "High Commander Sietinen, what can I do for you?"

"Hi, I was hoping to go over these engineering plans with you. I'm actually going to be overseeing this project myself."

"I must say, I never thought I'd have the opportunity to work directly with a living legend."

We'll see how long the celebrity adoration lasts once he realizes I want to undo all his work. Wil smiled. "And I've been curious to see Lynaedans perform their craft."

"Well, this core is a little outside my area of expertise. Most of our projects are related to cybernetics."

Good, so maybe this won't come as quite so hard a blow. Wil glanced down at his notes. "I've been impressed with the recent work on bioelectronic interfacing to mimic telepathy. I hope some of the technology the Aesir have shared with us will one day be available in the lives of our citizens."

"As do I."

"In the meantime, this power core has the potential to revolutionize life in a different way. I oversaw the field trials with DGE, and I have some observations that have bearing on the latest design interactions."

"Yes, I'm happy to go over it," Derik said.

Wil braced himself. "What you've suggested won't work."

The engineer exhaled quickly, sounding more surprised than offended. "I didn't think you telepaths were capable of such bluntness."

"I hear that's the Lynaedans' style. Personally, I prefer a direct approach."

"Then we'll get along quite well. Please, explain where I went wrong."

Wil walked the engineer through the problem. To Derik's credit, he caught onto the issue quite quickly. The error had been rooted in a single assumption that happened to have far-reaching impacts, so once he understood the original flaw, he immediately set about correcting the other problems.

"I'm embarrassed to have missed this," he said once they'd gone over the full set of plans.

"Happens to the best of us," Wil said. "I'm glad it was such a simple fix. I didn't realize all the issues had stemmed from that one thing."

"This device has a totally different operating protocol than the other tech I've worked with. It's good you've spent more time with it."

"Threw me off, too, at first. I guess it's no surprise that aliens would give us an alien design."

Derik was quiet for a long moment. "You have a lot of plans for this core, considering how new and untested it is."

"We have tested it. Thoroughly."

"Yes, as much as can be done in the given amount of time," the engineer said.

Wil couldn't refute the statement. He *had* run it through every test he could think of, but there was no way to replicate a longitudinal study other than to wait years. The only reason he was rushing the implementation was because the hybrid design of the new power cores and the Aesir's shield tech might be their only viable defense against the Erebus. It didn't sit right that they were diving in with limited information, but it still seemed like the least-bad alternative.

"Our speed is proportional to importance," Wil said. "This core will support the largest infrastructure upgrade project the Empire has undertaken in centuries."

"A sign of the prosperity of present times, I suppose."

Wil inclined his head. "It's amazing what we can accomplish when all available resources aren't being funneled toward an ongoing war."

Derik studied him through the screen. "But there's a new conflict brewing, isn't there? Shields like this aren't preparations for peace."

Wil didn't want to lie. "There's always one issue or another. We have the opportunity and means to improve safety on a number of worlds, so it seems prudent to take action."

"A very diplomatic answer."

"And necessary for someone in my position."

Derik nodded. "Understood. I'll make these revisions to the plans and get you updated copies for approval later this afternoon."

"Thank you. I'm looking forward to working with you." Wil ended the communication and leaned back in his seat.

The modified plans hadn't gone entirely unnoticed, it seemed. He didn't get the feeling that the Lynaedans would spread rumors about a potential ulterior motive for the new technology rollout, but all it would take is one reporter to put the pieces together and there could be major conspiracy accusations floating around. They'd need to keep the project details confidential. Too much was riding on this plan for it to fail.

CHAPTER 19

JASON'S HEART ACHED at the sight of his students' disappointed expressions.

"When's your last day?" Alisha asked.

"Stars, it's not like I'm moving to another galaxy!" Jason jested. "But this is it, the last class. I do have good news, though. Tom Alric is going to take over as your instructor. He normally only teaches advanced courses, but I told him how amazing you are and he's agreed to make an exception."

Their faces brightened at that. It wasn't every day that students got to train with real war heroes, and Tom's exploits during the Bakzen War were known to just about anyone who considered themselves half a pilot. His flights had been featured in at least a quarter of the training videos.

"I know you'll all do great," Jason continued. "And you can always message me if you ever have a question or issue."

"It's been a pleasure working with you, sir," Bret said.

The others echoed his sentiments.

Jason beamed at them. "Even if I never have another training group, I'll be happy to have ended on such a high note."

He said his remaining goodbyes and then quickly retreated to his quarters before Alisha could corner him. She'd never quite let go of her teacher-crush, and that had become even more awkward over the past several months of his singleness and subsequently Lexi entering the picture.

To his surprise, Lexi wasn't there when he got home. He took the opportunity to shower and change out of his flight suit.

As he was returning to the living room, dressed and beginning to unwind, the door clicked open.

Lexi startled when she saw him. "Oh! You're back already."

"Yeah, last class so I ended early. What have you been up to?"

"Still helping Kira. I think we've got it down to five planets where Leon might be, but it's still a lot of guesswork." She sounded tired and her eyes were a little unfocused, likely from staring at a screen all day.

"I'll join you tomorrow. I'm full-time on the Coalition investigation from here on out."

Lexi sauntered up to him. "Speaking of which, any updates on the data from my old handheld?" she asked.

He shook his head. "Not good news, I'm afraid. The tech team has been able to recover some files, but there doesn't appear to be any information that will aid in the investigation in terms of location data."

She frowned. "I was afraid of that."

"It was worth a try. Not every plan works out."

"Yeah."

"They'll get your old handheld back to you soon so you can pull off any personal files you'd like—all the Alliance tracking has been disabled."

"Thanks," Lexi said. "As disappointing as it is that the data wasn't helpful, I'm looking forward to working with you."

"Me too. Though I'll miss working with my students and getting the flight time. I dunno. It'll probably be a good thing in the end."

She bit her lip. "Did your dad give you this assignment because of me?"

He shrugged. "It may have been a factor, but I'm sure that wasn't the driving force. He's been trying to get me to take a more active leadership role for years now."

She drew him in for a kiss. "Well, this is the start of a new chapter. We should celebrate tonight."

"Actually, I have other plans for us. We've been invited to dinner with my parents." They'd been bugging him about a get-together for days. Jason had been inventing various excuses in order to give Lexi time to acclimate, but he'd been ambushed by a 'celebrate your promotion and introduce us to this new girlfriend-like person of yours' offer and couldn't refuse this time.

Lexi wiped her hands over her eyes. "Oh, no. I knew this was coming."

He rubbed her shoulders. "Hey, it'll be fun."

Her terrified expression indicated that she believed it wouldn't be anything of the sort. "I'm not used to interacting with the elite."

"It's a family dinner."

"With none other than Wil Sietinen!"

"It's dinner with my dad and mom," Jason insisted.

Lexi shook her head. "I'll go. But nothing you can say will convince me this is a casual event."

"Well, it *is* very casual. No dressing up or anything."

She took a deep breath and let it out. "When are we doing

this?"

"Right now."

"Now?!"

"Precisely for the reason that you won't have further time to overanalyze and build up the event more than you already have. They just want to get to know you."

"All right, I guess we're doing this."

— — —

Lexi couldn't very well refuse the offer to attend a social dinner with Jason's family, but that didn't make her stomach any less knotted. *This whole thing has to be a test to see if they approve of me.*

She felt at ease with Jason, and were he anyone else, she'd be confident they were off to a great start in their relationship. As much as she wanted to believe that their vastly different backgrounds didn't matter, the reality was that Jason had a legacy to live up to. Lexi, meanwhile, had spent most of her life as a borderline criminal. That hardly seemed compatible with a family renowned for its leadership of the TSS.

At Jason's insistence that the meal was a casual affair, Lexi tried not to overthink her plain outfit of a long-sleeve shirt and pants—some of the fabricated clothing she'd been offered upon arrival in TSS Headquarters. The items were light gray, which she'd determined was the color for first-year Agent Trainees. It was yet to be determined if there was an implication in the clothing.

Jason seemed completely at ease as they headed over to the private gathering. Of course, he wouldn't be stressed; they were a close-knit family.

Her palms were sweating by the time they reached the

door.

"There's nothing to be nervous about," Jason assured her, noticing her discomfort.

"Easy for you to say."

He hit the chime on the door.

Wil answered a few moments later. "Hi," he greeted. "Thank you for joining us."

"I appreciate the invitation, sir," Lexi replied.

He smiled and shook his head. "Please, you can call us by our first names. Formality has a time and place, but not here."

"All right. Thank you."

Jason placed his hand on the small of her back, offering a measure of reassurance.

This is so weird. Can people like them really be so normal? She was careful to keep her thoughts guarded, knowing of their advanced telepathic skills. With a turn of her stomach, she realized that they could probably read her innermost thoughts without her knowing, if they were so inclined.

"Hey, relax," Jason said in her mind. *"They'll see what I see in you, trust me."*

As they entered the residential suite, she noticed that it was larger than Jason's place. In addition to the couch and chairs, there was also a dining table set for four people.

Figures the High Commander and Lead Agent would have nicer quarters. She looked over the space but didn't see any personal effects. *That's odd.*

"Oh, this isn't our place," Wil said when he noticed her looking around. "Actually, this is where I grew up. My parents had two suites combined so they'd have room for an extra bedroom when I was young. Saera and I are still in my original quarters, and this suite is reserved for visitors or gatherings like this."

"Oh." Lexi's face felt incredibly warm. "Jason had said you were born into the TSS, but I didn't realize it was so literal."

"It wasn't a bad childhood, but not one I wanted for my own kids," Wil said.

Saera walked over to join them from where she had been tending to the table. "Hi, Lexi, it's nice to see you again. I hope you've been settling in."

"Yeah, it's good." She wasn't sure what to make of the 'settling in' part. *Are they expecting me to stay here?* Then she realized how silly it was to wonder that. Of course they were. Jason was here, and he wasn't going to leave the TSS. If the two of them were going to be a couple, then she would need to make a life for herself here.

Wil exchanged glances with his wife. "Let's have a seat," he suggested.

"Good idea." Jason sat down across from his father.

Lexi took the chair opposite Saera with Wil to her left. The table was filled with various serving dishes. Delicious aromas beckoned her.

Everyone began dishing up food from the serving dishes, covering a range of mains and sides. It was likely the same fare found in the Mess, but somehow the presentation and company made it seem much fancier.

The combination of inviting scents and being in the presence of the three powerful Agents had Lexi's head buzzing. *What do I say?*

"I can't believe you're real."

That was *not* what she had intended to say. The words spilled out before she could stop herself. What she'd wanted to communicate was how amazing it was to be in this incredible place with people she'd spent her whole life reading about, and how they were being so gracious to invite her into their personal lives when she was a nobody. No, instead, she'd thoroughly planted her foot in her mouth.

Her cheeks burned. "Sorry, I mean…" She faded out. *Nope. No way to salvage that.*

Wil chuckled. "I know you must feel overwhelmed right now."

"You're…" Lexi decided to embrace the awkward. "You're Wil Sietinen! You're famous! And your family…"

He took a sip of water. "We can't choose what family we're born into. I happened to get lucky, but none of my friends are highborn. I hope you can come to look at us as Jason's parents rather than anything else."

The words rang true and genuine. Though Lexi was still on edge, she did feel a bit of her tension dissipate. "I'm trying. Still, I have to ask, is it true that you're the smartest person alive?"

Jason almost spat out his drink.

Wil laughed. "Yes, that's what they tell me. I appreciate that you're forthright with your curiosity."

"He's being modest, as usual," Saera interjected. "The things he's been able to piece together stumped the greatest minds for hundreds of years."

"Not all of that was a matter of intelligence."

Saera loaded her fork. "Sounds like something a modest, super-smart person would say."

"I won't deny that I've had some significant breakthroughs. The independent jump drive changed a lot of things."

"There's quite a black market for those drives in the Outer Colonies," Lexi said.

Wil shook his head. "That's what I'd always hoped to avoid. The technology is potentially dangerous in untrained hands."

"I haven't heard about people getting lost in subspace or dropping out inside planets," Lexi told him. "The saving of transit times is just too valuable to ignore."

"Which is why it's continuing to be adopted in broader circles. Still, I worry about well-meaning technology being used to do harm."

Lexi looked down at her plate. "Yeah, I know all about having the best intentions."

Saera was quick to jump in. "So, this must be quite a change of scenery for you. Have you spent much time with other Gifted people?"

"Not many. Especially not at one time," she replied, thankful for the change of topic.

Saera nodded. "It feels different, huh? Especially with these two." She nodded to her husband and son. "You get used to it, but it always stands out. Elsewhere seems... empty."

"It's even more pronounced in places like the Aesir cities. Everyone in their population is Gifted," Wil added.

"What's the deal with the Aesir?" Lexi asked. "I've heard them mentioned a few times. Sounds like they're super-powerful."

"A common misconception," Wil replied. "It's not so much that their abilities are stronger. Rather, the people are more... attuned."

"What does that mean?"

"There are certain energy patterns throughout the universe. Think of it as various threads, some of which overlap and pull on each other. Select members of the Aesir have learned how to interpret these energies to glean insights."

"Sounds a little..." Lexi shook her hand and made a soft warbling sound.

"I thought that, too, until I gazed into the nexus and had a vision of my own," Jason said. "I still don't know *how* it's possible, only that it is."

His father nodded. "It's an ongoing journey to learn more about ourselves. In many ways, the Erebus have given us a whole new perspective."

They talked a little more about Wil's latest theories regarding the nature of their abilities and the potential transdimensional connections that could explain their power. It was fascinating for Lexi, though not at all how she imagined typical family dinner conversation. Then again, this wasn't a typical family.

As they finished up with a dessert of decadent chocolate cake, Wil suddenly turned serious. "Much like we continually learn more about our place in the universe, I'm also intrigued to hear more about the different Taran worlds. It sounds like you've traveled around a fair amount, Lexi."

She tensed. "Yeah, a couple dozen places, probably. It was difficult to stay in one place after I left Cytera as a little kid, but I'm sure you've looked at my file." *So the interrogation begins.*

"I prefer to speak with someone rather than to go strictly off what's written in the record. Rarely does a document capture the full picture."

"Where do you see yourself going with your life?" Saera asked.

Jason set down his fork. "That question might be a little too loaded for the moment."

"Well, uh…" Lexi floundered. "I'm kind of playing it by ear right now."

"You have very strong abilities for someone with so little training," Wil continued. "Do you know much about your family history?"

"Not a whole lot."

Wil studied her. "There's no way to ask without this sounding like an odd request, but may I have your permission to complete a genetic analysis?" he asked.

Lexi nearly choked on her bite of cake. "Excuse me?"

"Dad!" Jason hissed.

Saera sighed and shot her husband a warning glare.

"I know it's strange and intrusive," Wil continued, "but I assure you it's not for any devious ends. I have a hypothesis I'd like to check out."

Jason gave him a semi-disgusted look across the table. "What, exactly?"

"It's related to the focus on genetic lines on Cytera. When I first heard about the planet, I was under the impression that the advent of their caste system was newer—within the past several hundred years. However, I now suspect that it's, in fact, a remnant from a bygone era. A world lost in time."

"It's a foking shiteshow of a world, that's what it is," Lexi grumbled.

"I understand the sentiment, and I don't disagree. However, the level of details in the genetic records is second to none. It may offer some insights into other issues we've been trying to solve for a very long time."

Up to the recent turn in the conversation, Lexi had thought things were going rather well. Sure, the topics had been a little more esoteric than she was used to, but everyone was congenial. She now realized that it had been a distraction to get her defenses down so they could go in for the attack.

Lexi exchanged glances with Jason.

"*I'm so sorry,*" he said in her mind. "*I have no idea where that came from.*"

"*I do.*" Lexi turned her attention to Wil. "May I speak bluntly?"

"Of course," he consented.

"You also want to check me out to make sure I'm actually a good match for your son." It was a statement, not a question.

He looked down momentarily before meeting her gaze. "It's understandable that you don't trust my intentions; I wouldn't, either, after what you've been through. I've already told Jason, and I'll tell you now, that I fully support him in however he chooses to proceed with a relationship. I know the power of a resonance connection firsthand, and I've seen what it does to people when they try to fight it. Needless to say, it's a lot more pleasant for everyone involved to just embrace the feelings and figure out the rest."

"I don't see what my genetic history has to do with anything." Lexi's shoulder blades itched from the tension in her back. It took all of her self-control to keep from storming away from the table.

"You're absolutely right, Lexi, lineage doesn't define us," Saera said.

Wil nodded. "But it does play a factor in who we become, as much as we might not want it to. It's not the only component, by any means, but certain realities can't be ignored." He paused, looking over Lexi again. "I'm sorry to have spoken out of turn. I have a rather unique perspective on things like genetics and destiny."

Lexi crossed her arms defensively and leaned back slightly in her chair. "The Cadicle."

"Yes. Not a title I enjoy."

She shrugged. "Doesn't seem so bad being labeled a hero."

"There's a lot more to it than that. Even if I'd never seen a map of my own genome, it wouldn't change that I have abilities that go far beyond normal Taran comprehension. Being uneducated about that potential would be ignorance; it wouldn't change me."

"And you think my lineage on Cytera might be equally illuminating?"

"Potentially. Either you learn nothing and you're no worse off, or you could gain an entirely new sense of yourself. What's there to lose?"

She did have to admit that she was curious once he put it in those terms. But it still seemed like an invasion of privacy. Though she didn't know what might be revealed, it just felt strange to know someone wanted to evaluate her based on codified data.

"I can't stop you from performing whatever analysis you want," she said.

"I don't ever want someone to feel like I'm going behind their back. My authority doesn't absolve me of common decency."

"Well, I'm sure you can get away with doing whatever you want." Lexi was well aware that her tone had taken on a hostile edge, but she wasn't about to sit idly while she was treated like the product of a lab experiment.

"It is precisely because I have so much power that I work so hard not to abuse it," Wil replied. "I apologize. I overstepped with the request. Truly, my only aim is to help you better understand yourself." The explanation sounded genuine enough, and Lexi detected no attempts to deceive her.

Jason glanced over at her. *"He means it,"* he said in her mind. *"He gets 'ideas' sometimes that go off the rails."*

"What if we don't come back as a good match?"

"It wouldn't change anything for me. If there's a chance that this kind of analysis can help you understand your history, it may be worth doing."

Lexi took a deep breath. "If you want to do an analysis, go

for it."

"Are you sure?" Wil asked. "I don't want you to feel pressured."

Too late for that. She shrugged. "Like you said, adding a new label to something doesn't change what was there all along."

"It's true. Some people will step up as leaders no matter what circumstances they were born into. Other times, we're forced to take on a role we never wanted."

"You seem like one of those 'natural leader' sorts," she said.

Wil shook his head. "I'd rather spend all day in an engineering lab. The influence I have now was thrust upon me; I never wanted it."

Lexi looked to Jason for confirmation, and he just shrugged. She eyed Wil. "From what I've heard, you're quite the decorated military commander."

"It's interesting what information filters out to the rest of the galaxy. They call me a 'savior', but 'destroyer of planets' would be a more fitting title, if the masses knew the truth."

Saera dropped her fork on her plate and sighed. She cast Wil a 'don't do this' look, accompanied by the hum of a telepathic exchange.

Jason stared down at his meal, shifting uncomfortably in his seat.

"What I mean to say, Lexi," Wil continued, "is that we all have the ability to effect change. Some more so than others. We have a duty to our fellow citizens to treat each other with respect. We have a duty to our friends and family, to have each other's backs in times of need. And we have a duty to our civilization—to our Taran race, to preserve our way of life for future generations. These different scopes of responsibility are sometimes at odds with each other, and fulfilling our obligations can mean compromising on tenets we would hold firmly in any other context."

She looked down, reflecting on what she'd done in the last year with—and working against—the Alliance.

"You wondered why I offered you that immunity deal, absolving you of any wrongdoing," Wil continued. "It's because you—like so many others—have been a victim of circumstance. You had to do awful things no person should have to endure. Context matters. You've helped prevent further injury to innocents. What more can you hope to do?"

"It doesn't change the fact that I killed people," she mumbled.

"So have all of us in this room. I, personally, have the lives of billions on my hands." He gave a pained shrug. "Had those actions been perpetrated outside the context of military command, I would have been executed a long time ago. Instead, they call me a hero. I've never felt like one. Fulfilling my duty, my responsibility, doesn't change the weight I bear for my actions. Just as your legal absolution hasn't alleviated your own conscience. Only time and perspective can do that."

Saera cast her husband another sidelong glance. "I'd apologize, but this is typical. You may as well get used to the random philosophical ponderings sooner than later."

Jason nodded his agreement and resumed finishing his cake.

"I don't think I'll get used to *any* of this anytime soon." Lexi let out a long breath. *Dinner with the Sietinens?! How is this my life now?*

"It takes less time than you may think," Saera said. "Just remember that above all else, we're people. Maybe it's how I grew up, but I never saw the point in idolizing celebrities or people in positions of power. When it comes down to it, everyone needs to breathe and eat or we die. And we'll die eventually all the same. There are way more important things in life than dwelling on your own inadequacies or others' good fortunes."

Lexi nodded. "Totally agree. That's a good way to talk yourself into an airlock."

"I don't expect you to trust us from the start; that needs to be built. But I do hope you keep an open mind about us," Wil said.

She smiled slightly. "I can do that."

Wil looked down at his plate for a few seconds before returning his attention to her. "I know we've thrown a lot at you—and this situation is… challenging in many ways. What I'd like to make clear, though, is whatever you two do, or don't, in making a life together is yours to decide. I do care about this family and the people we bring into it. However, when it comes to legacy, credentials—political, genetic, or otherwise—are irrelevant. What matters is a person's integrity and loyalty.

"You, Lexi, put your own safety at risk to look for your friend. You took action to protect innocents when bad people were plotting in the shadows. That's real character. I don't care where you're from or what that genetic evaluation might reveal. You've earned my respect based on your actions."

She flashed an appreciative smile and bobbed her head. "Thank you."

"See?" Jason said in her mind. *"I told you they'd like you."*

"All right, maybe this won't be so tough after all."

— — —

Wil settled onto the couch next to Saera, happy to be back in their quarters and unwinding after the somewhat awkward family dinner.

"Really, Wil? Asking for a genetic test over dessert?" Saera eyed him with one brow raised.

"It came out a little more bluntly than I'd intended."

Saera sighed. "It's not about *how* you asked, but the very idea…"

"I do have my reasons," he said before she could further articulate her protest. "I think you'll agree it's worth looking into once you know a little more about the world."

"Such as?"

"For starters, they have their own genetic record system that rivals the Priesthood's. Apparently, some of the family lines go back a very long way—to before the Priesthood's interventions in the broader population. The High Dynasty designation didn't come around until that time. Rumor has it that some of the Gifted families who'd settled on Cytera were some of those vying for leadership roles in the Empire.

"The Priesthood never relied on one plan. I can't help but wonder if Cytera may have been a backup world for if their genetic engineering plans didn't pan out how they hoped on Tararia."

Saera leaned back on the couch. "Wow. So there really could be something significant there. You think Lexi might be a descendant of one of those families?"

"Given her inexplicably strong resonance connection with Jason? I'll just say that in my life, there was never coincidence. I'm afraid our children inherited that reality, as well. Sure, the Priesthood was destroyed, but their plans had been woven for generations. There's no reason to believe those threads would fizzle out just because there's no longer anyone pulling the strings."

His wife nodded. "Fair enough."

"That said, I'm all for people determining their own paths. No matter what the analysis reveals, she and Jason can choose whatever life they want, together or not."

"I do like her. There's no doubt she's spirited. Smart, too."

"Agreed. I'm glad we got the chance to talk with her more without it being a formal interview."

"She might feel differently about whether or not it was an interrogation."

He winced. "Yeah, sorry about that. I'll smooth things over later."

"If you were anything less than 'oddly intense', she probably wouldn't have believed you were taking the meeting seriously."

He chuckled. "Fair point."

Saera propped her elbow on the back of the couch and rested her head on her hand. "Are you prepared to defend this new relationship on Jason's behalf?"

"Yes, I would never stand in the way of Jason's happiness. Do you have doubts about Lexi?"

"This whole thing caught me by surprise, but I think she's actually perfect for him in a lot of ways."

"I agree. He'd get bored with a straitlaced rule-follower."

"Lexi is definitely not that." Saera raised her eyebrows. "She has more than a few blemishes on her record, immunity agreement or not."

"The media could try to slander her if word gets out about their relationship."

"They've made a big deal about far less."

"Yes, true." Wil weighed the options. "It wouldn't be difficult for us to expunge anything that might tarnish our family by association. However, that would be a blatant abuse of power—and we'd come under a different kind of scrutiny."

"We definitely don't want it to seem like we're trying to cover anything up."

"Really, we've done a lot worse over the course of our professional careers in the name of duty. A handful of petty crime convictions as a minor isn't that big a deal."

"I'm more concerned about the reaction to her not being highborn."

"I don't care what the other Taran elite have to say on the matter."

"Oh, yeah, I couldn't care less about those judgmental snobs." She crossed her arms. "Still, Lexi might be a tough sell to the extended family."

"I must admit, I'm more uncertain about my parents' reception than I would have been in the past."

She nodded. "They're under a lot of political pressure right now."

"Regardless, they've never cared much about lineage," Wil said. "I mean, they were great champions of my relationship with you from the beginning—since well before we knew about your mom's dynastic ties."

"Still, it was different with us; they won't look at Jason's situation the same way. We were both in the TSS, and I was excelling as a Primus trainee. Back then, your parents' top concern was your well-being in the TSS. I helped with that, so naturally they encouraged us to be together."

"Whereas Jason isn't on the verge of collapse, like I was."

"I know he misses Tiff—as anyone would remember a lost friend—but he's in a good place emotionally. There isn't a case to be made for this relationship being *necessary* in the way ours was for you."

"Nonetheless, there's no denying a resonance connection. My parents understand what that feels like."

"Which is why they won't outright forbid them from a partnership, unlike what your grandfather said about us."

The statement sparked a painful twinge in Wil's core. He'd tried not to let his dad's strained relationship with his own father influence his interactions with his grandparents, but he'd found himself at odds with them, as well. How could he have been close to people that elected to ignore their Gifts when those abilities were at the core of his own identity? Not to mention, they considered bloodlines paramount when choosing a life partner; love didn't enter the equation.

"My grandfather represented everything that's wrong with the highborn way of thinking." Wil shook his head. "And though he denied it up to the end, he tried to keep us apart even when he knew the power of a resonance connection firsthand. My grandparents had one, too—the Priesthood's genetic intervention had made sure of that, so they'd end up together."

"In all fairness, I'm not sure they ever experienced something like what we have. Their bond eroded after your uncle died; we all know it. They never recovered from losing their first child."

And the same thing could have happened to us if I hadn't found a way out of the darkness after the Bakzen War. He didn't need to speak it aloud. It was in Saera's eyes.

"I'd do anything to help Jason have what we do," Wil said.

"As will I. So, what can we do to frame Lexi as a sensible choice?"

CHAPTER 20

"WELL, THAT WAS an interesting dinner." Lexi was ready to curl up in a ball on Jason's bed by the time they got back to his quarters.

He'd been frustratingly quiet the whole evening. Though he'd come to her defense, it was almost like he was gauging her reactions right alongside his parents. She hated feeling like a specimen.

Still saying nothing, Jason wrapped her up in his arms the moment the door closed. The warmth and steadiness of him recentered her. For a few moments, nothing besides him mattered.

He unfurled his arms slowly and gazed down into her eyes. "No one could ever say anything that would change how I feel about you. My parents live in a very strange bubble of reality where asking certain things about people is normal when it would be a ridiculous question to anyone else. I promise, as terrible as it sounded, it wasn't meant in a judgmental way."

"Yeah, I got that eventually. But shite! What a way to pivot mid-conversation."

"My dad likes to think of himself as being well-socialized, but he has his quirks. May as well accept that now."

"I got that." She flopped down on the couch.

"You did great. They really like you." Jason sat down next to her.

"You sure about that?"

He smiled. "When you're a family of telepaths, there aren't a lot of secrets. Believe me, we'd know if there was a problem."

Lexi snuggled up next to him. "You're lucky you get along with your family so well." She paused. "Actually, you're lucky to *have* a family."

"I know I am."

"It's strange. You don't realize how much you've missed until you see what others have, you know?"

He squeezed her around her shoulders. "The important thing is you're not alone anymore. Our past experiences shape us, but they don't doom us to a set fate."

"Doesn't make it easy to escape."

"That's all about your mindset. Be open to change—and to happiness."

"All this 'one big community' talk in the TSS seems too good to be true."

"I think a lot of people feel that way when they first land here. Eventually, they realize it's genuine."

"Yeah?"

"It's a found family. My parents have been at the heart of this place for a long time. She doesn't talk about it a lot, but my mom had it kind of rough growing up. It seems like she's made it her personal mission to make sure that everyone can find a safe, supportive home here, no matter where they come from or what they've been through."

"That's a really nice sentiment."

"And my dad is close with his parents, but the TSS was always his extended family more than his grandparents or uncles and aunts on Tararia. A lot of people look at those on the top like some kind of celebrities, but it can be lonely. My dad has always looked to create a sense of close community whenever possible."

"I'm sure it was tough growing up as a kid here, but that kind of loneliness still sounds a whole lot better than my youth—never knowing where my next meal would come from."

"That's true. Still, there's a burden to responsibility, and having a soft bed doesn't lessen that pressure. Without a supportive community, it would be easy to be crushed by that weight."

She squinted at him, pursing her lips. "Okay, what am I missing?"

"About what?"

"You. You're too perfect. There has to be some sort of hidden flaw that I'm missing."

"I'm *not* perfect."

"I dunno, from where I'm sitting, you seem to have everything going for you. Handsome, smart, nice. No one is that well-rounded."

He studied her. "Perhaps the issue is that you haven't spent enough time around the right people."

She frowned. "No, everyone has issues. I'm concerned that I haven't spotted yours yet."

"Keep in mind, I'm a TSS Agent."

"And that's a flaw?"

"No, no. What I mean is, the Agent training program is designed to smooth out the issues that most people deal with. We learn how to keep a cool head, encourage critical and creative thinking, physical fitness. If I come across as put-together and capable, it's because I had great instructors who taught me how to be a well-rounded person."

"I dunno. Sounds like something someone who secretly eats people would say."

He laughed. "Now you're just being absurd."

She sighed. "I like you too much. Every time I've had strong feelings for someone, it's turned out that they're not who I thought they were."

"Trust is one of the big things we work on while training as Agents. A lot of people come to the TSS having lost someone or having been treated as an outcast because of their abilities. It's one of the reasons we place such a strong emphasis on community here."

"Are all the other Agents as balanced as you?"

"For the most part. There's extensive screening during the TSS application process to weed out the hotheads and those who don't have enough natural aptitude to be trainable in the way we need. Our medical science can address almost any physical challenge, but there's only so much you can do to change someone's mindset. If they don't *want* to be here, to learn and grow, that's often a losing battle."

"I don't know how you're going to put up with me. I'm not all… 'refined' like you."

"I think you're wonderful just the way you are."

"That's because you don't know me well."

He crossed his arms, an amused smile brightening his eyes. "All right, since you're so hung up on people's hidden issues, what's yours?"

"Oh, I'm flawless!" She smirked.

"That's how you're going to play it, huh?"

She sighed. "No, I… That trust thing you talked about

earlier definitely hits home. Case in point with me doubting you without having a reason to."

"Letting people in is difficult. Especially if you've been let down before."

"I'd say having a good portion of my family murdered and then spending my entire life running might have something to do with my mindset."

Jason took a few moments to respond. "I think your resilience is incredible."

"But here I am, trying to self-sabotage because you're this amazing guy and I can't let myself just be happy for a change."

"You're in luck, because I'm not that easy to scare off." He wrapped his arm around her. "What's here between us isn't superficial. We can grow into that trust."

"I want to, but I don't know how."

He took her hands. "Every relationship is different, and every couple needs to figure it out for themselves. We will. Together."

"See? You're still being so bomaxed *nice*! It's kind of infuriating."

"Only because I've had a taste of loss, and I know what tricks that darkness can play with your mind. We don't have to be alone anymore. I want to know everything about you, Lexi. The *real* you, not whatever front you share with people."

"What makes you think I put on a 'front'?"

"I'm telepathic, remember?" He smiled. "Kidding. It's… little things I've noticed when you're around others versus when it's just the two of us."

She sighed. "Well, you're not wrong. I dunno. It's tough to open up."

"And there's no rush. I just want you to know that I'm in this for real."

"Of anyone I've met, you might actually be able to understand."

"About what?"

You can't keep it bottled up forever, she told herself. *If not him, then who?* For the first time in as long as she could remember, she *wanted* to talk about the things she'd tried so hard to bury. If they were going to have a future together, there was no point delaying the conversation; either he'd accept it, or he'd run away.

She met his questioning gaze. "What outsiders hear about Cytera isn't an accurate portrayal of what's gone on there. Gifted people like us were a valuable commodity—as in prized possessions. And those fortunate enough to have active abilities in their bloodline were a force to be reckoned with."

Jason sat back, listening. His attentiveness drove Lexi on.

"Like any planet, certain families rose to power. Any reasonably intelligent person can see it play out on countless worlds—a valuable product or service propels a company into the spotlight, and the owners pass it down to their children, and so on. Eventually, the people running the show don't remember what had made their business relevant and successful in the first place, they just feel it's their *right* to be in that position of power."

She swallowed. "And, of course, once a person has power, they become obsessed with ways to keep it. They distrust anyone who might take it away. In such an environment of paranoia, being able to see into others' minds becomes a valuable asset."

Jason nodded with understanding. "So, Gifted can read minds—and also avoid being read."

"Exactly. And the stronger the abilities, the more someone could get away with deceiving others to achieve their desired ends."

"Placing a premium on the bloodlines with the highest potential."

She nodded. "Yep, you've got it. And, of course, that's the problem with the Generation Cycle. Eventually, you reach a point when the ability expression will disappear. What's a powerful family to do when that happens?"

"Either find a new way to stay relevant, or…"

"Adopt," she completed. "And thus the market for Gifted children was born." She let out a bitter laugh. "Lucky me, I was born to a 'consistently productive' line."

"Shite." Jason's brow knitted.

"But no, I didn't grow up in that mess. My parents were sick of the whole thing and decided to resist. It got them killed and me handed off to a family friend, who managed to get me offworld as a baby. But, life can be hard in the Outer Colonies when you're on the run and have a target on your back. I had my irises altered as soon as they started to glow, which helped keep me hidden. When someone decides that you're 'theirs', they'll go to great lengths to track you down."

"No wonder you moved around so much."

She nodded. "Even though I was offworld, I was still valuable. Like those in the Valdos System, Cytera didn't quite play by the rules when it came to abilities. On the surface, it was all about telepathy and using those secret readings for subterfuge, but you don't hold power for generation after generation with mental prowess alone. Every leader needs an army. Who better to defend one's domain than those Gifted with the invisible force of telekinesis?"

"That's pretty much how the TSS came about," Jason assessed.

"Yep. Well, the person who got me off the planet was a

trainer for one of those secret armies. When I came of age, she taught me how to use my Gifts—I kind of glossed over that when you'd asked me where I got my training when we first met. Though it was a far cry from TSS Agent training, I can get by."

"What happened to this mentor?"

"We parted ways."

"May I ask why?"

The memory still brought a flush to Lexi's cheeks. "A difference of opinion about how we should use our Gifts. She felt that using telepathy for personal gain was justified, after what we'd been through. I argued that substituting a random person for those who'd wronged us wasn't fair."

"I must say, I fall on your side of that argument."

"No surprise there." She smiled at him. "At any rate, I set out on my own when I was nineteen. I met up with Melisa soon after, and we started to carve out a life for ourselves for the next few years. Then, she set off for Duronis to check out this 'great new opportunity' and was going to pave the way for me to follow her, and then the whole mess with the Alliance started. You know the rest."

Jason nodded. "What about the intervening years after you left Cytera and before you met Melisa?"

"Not a lot to tell. We were chronically poor and on the run. When the regime on Cytera started to crumble, all those former hired goons had nothing better to do than become bounty hunters for their slighted masters. Between telepathy and their training, they'd root out any runaway they could get their hands on."

"Hence your eye-altering and staying on the move."

Lexi felt a stab in her gut as she looked into Jason's mesmerizing glowing irises. The luminescent teal was one of the most stunning things she'd ever seen. She could have had that every time she looked into the mirror with her own pale blue eyes, and she hated that the circumstances had forced the modifications.

"Eyes are the easiest way to identify Gifted." She shrugged. "They know to check for contacts. The people who smuggled me out wiped my genetic ID from the database, so the hunt was all about visual appearance. I needed to have my best chance of staying undetected."

He nodded. "I'm sorry."

"It is what it is."

"I'm almost positive there's a way to reverse the alteration, if you're interested."

Her heart lifted. "That would be amazing. But I don't have the credits for that kind of cosmetic procedure."

"Cost is not a factor."

Of course, a Sietinen would think that way. She didn't know what to say. The last thing she wanted was to be thought of as a mooch. She genuinely cared about Jason, fully independent of his family's wealth. As long as she stuck with him, she could have anything she'd ever wanted. Though she had no idea exactly *how* wealthy the Sietinen Dynasty was, it was likely measured in the quadrillions—so far beyond the scope of normal life that it made her head spin.

"I'm not looking for handouts," she said.

Jason shook his head. "I didn't remotely mean it in that way." He worked his mouth, seeming to search for the right words. "I grew up on Earth with a perfectly normal upper-middle class childhood. I went straight from that into the TSS, where I've always been surrounded by people from all different backgrounds—most of them less than well-off. I have the Sietinen name and genetics, but my life perspective couldn't be further than that of a typical High Dynasty heir. It would be amazing to be able to spend that wealth on something meaningful." He took her hands. "I'm growing very fond of you, Lexi, and I can't think of a better recipient to benefit from the privileges of my position."

"Why don't you give it all away?"

"Believe me, it's been discussed. It's not as easy or as good as it sounds, but that's a discussion for another time."

"I should warn you, I'm really bad at accepting gifts. Too many brushes with people who have ulterior motives."

"I don't have an agenda."

Lexi could sense the truth in his statement, and yet she still found herself holding back. She *wanted* to trust him, yet it felt like she was living in a fairy tale and the spell might break at any moment.

"I want to give it a little time," she said.

He brushed the side of her face. "Take all the time you need. I'm not going anywhere."

— — —

Leon hated being trapped. Not only was he physically locked in the place, but he was being directed in a way he detested, and he couldn't do anything about it without risking his life.

What kind of monsters would want a weapon like this? He didn't enjoy the glimpse he was getting into the minds of psychopaths. The work he'd been forced to undertake went against everything he knew to be decent and good.

For the last week, he'd been locked in the lab for twenty-hour shifts, given meals only when he'd completed certain tasks. He wished he would be able to tell Kira that he hadn't broken, but the lack of sleep and threat of harm had prompted him to take his assignment seriously. He told himself that if *he* did it, he could make it safe. He would know how to disable the weapon once he got free.

Except, there wasn't a way to engineer in a failsafe. They were talking about genetics—people. The weapon controls would be tied to a person. That *was* the failsafe. If the person in control had evil intentions, there wasn't any way for Leon to engineer that out of them.

The entire situation made him sick. He was working on a way to turn someone into a living conduit to the higher dimensions, a key that would be destroyed in order to unleash whatever came through.

This was so much worse than a disease, like he'd pictured when he first heard of the bioweapon. SPEAR Tec had started with that foundation and then taken it to such extremes that the original idea was almost unrecognizable. What they wanted was a precision tool. What they were making was a potential planet-killer.

Leon hadn't believed such a thing was possible until he began running simulations. He'd figured that the task the Alliance had set before him was doomed to failure, but then the reality of it set in. A genetic tether *could* be accomplished, in a roundabout way. It would take someone naturally Gifted—or at least of a bloodline with the potential, even if the abilities were on an inactive Generation. That potential could be channeled into a single explosive expression, supercharging every molecule of a person's being with higher dimensional particles. It would burst them from the inside.

He had no idea what such a detonation would do to the surrounding environment, but he could only imagine it would be horrific. What didn't make sense is *why* the Alliance was interested in this work—something so far afield from the disease bioweapon they'd set out to create.

Did they realize they could make something much more powerful and just went for it? Or do they not understand what this will do? He was missing a piece of the plan, but he didn't know what. Frankly, he didn't *want* to know.

By the end of his latest long shift, his eyes were sore and his head ached. He massaged his temples with the heels of his hands.

"There's no way to make this stable," he spoke to his ever-silent overseers. "You can initiate a transdimensional link, but there will be no way to control it."

"You have done well." The reply boomed in the room, catching Leon by surprise. They hadn't said a word to him since the first day when he got the assignment, aside from chastising him when he wasn't doing anything.

The only thing he'd done so far was replicate a small portion of research he'd conducted with the Guard. He'd spent extensive time studying the transdimensional energy connection of Kira's nanites, which drew the energy required to transform into her special second-skin. It was possible to open up that kind of connection in normal cells… it would just immediately kill a person. They'd written off the research as a dead-end and left it at that.

Leon had hoped that by demonstrating what a terrible idea it was to his captors that they might let him go. To say that he had 'done well' suggested he had made a grave error in judgment.

Obviously, I'm not thinking straight! I'm not getting enough sleep and I've been staring at this for so long that I can barely see. So much for acting smart. Kicking himself wouldn't fix the problem, yet he couldn't prevent his thoughts from spiraling.

He was so very tired.

The door clicked unlocked. Leon tensed. He still had at least two hours left in what had become his usual work schedule.

Edward entered. "Come with me."

"Where are we going?" Leon asked.

"Another lab."

Another? He thought it best not to ask about 'what' or 'where' since he was unlikely to get a favorable response, and he wasn't in the mood for getting yelled at again.

He followed Edward into the hall, where he was met by two large men who fell in behind him. Had he been rested and had any clue where he was, he might have considered taking them on in an attempt to escape. However, since that was unlikely to end well, he decided it best to continue playing along.

Edward stopped outside a door at the end of the hall and palmed it open. He held out his arm to indicate Leon should enter.

Cautiously, Leon stepped inside. To his surprise, he saw half a dozen other people inside working at the various computers and scientific analysis stations. They looked up with surprise at his arrival.

There are other people? What have they been doing?

When Leon's gaze met the other scientists, he got the distinct impression that up until very recently they'd thought they had been working alone, too. More than likely, each of them had been given a discrete component of a larger assignment. With a sickening lurch of his stomach, Leon's mind began racing through the possibilities of what it could be. None of them were good.

"That's all of you," Edward stated. "Please complete the task at hand."

The door sealed shut behind Leon.

He gave the other scientists a cautious smile. "Fancy meeting you here."

One of the young women chuckled and a couple others sighed. The remaining individuals remained stoic, worn down by worry and fatigue.

"What's your specialty?" the woman who'd laughed asked him.

"Genetics, though I think I'm here mostly because of my work on the biological expression of transdimensional links," he replied. "I'm Leon."

"Carla. Molecular chemistry."

The others introduced themselves, as well—all specialists in niche areas of biology, chemistry, and physics.

The strange mix of fields didn't make sense until the quantum physicist, Brandon, explained what they had been brought together to work on. "They're creating a living weapon," he revealed. "Previous research has given us the means to form its essence in a higher dimension, where it can pull energy to interact with our reality. Right now, it isn't stable in spacetime, so it can't be deployed with any precision. Our task is to link the weapon with a handler—a Keeper—who will serve as a conduit and controller for its interactions."

Leon gaped at him. "What will this weapon do?"

"It will spread like a disease, breaking down molecular bonds following the instructions from the Keeper," Carla said. "It will be the perfect weapon—able to target the organic matter in an environment without causing harm to anything else." Her dark eyes had taken on the sheen of someone in awe, but Leon couldn't tell if she was horrified or excited.

Breaking down molecular bonds? It sounds like this 'disease' would turn any living thing it touched to dust! Suddenly, Leon understood how the genetic tethering research was, in fact, related to a bioweapon—and he'd been coerced into giving them a major component of that plan.

Regardless, there was another serious matter. He had told them how to create a link, but it wouldn't function in the way they envisioned; he was certain of that fact. His overseers hadn't listened to his warnings, but maybe these scientists would. "I can't speak to the rest, but there's no way a person can support this kind of sustained transdimensional link or 'control' anything. It would kill them," Leon said.

"That's not an issue," Brandon replied. "Having a means to allow the weapon to enter spacetime is the key. Any other loss falls under acceptable casualties."

Okay, these people are not *my friends.* He couldn't be sure about everyone yet, but Brandon, at least seemed fully on board with the disastrous plan. The way Carla was nodding along to Brandon's explanation didn't indicate disgust, so she was more likely than not already in the Alliance's pocket. The others hadn't yet spoken so Leon wasn't sure where they stood; however, it was unlikely he'd be able to rely on help from anyone.

"They brought the rest of us together this morning," Carla said. "Apparently, they were waiting on you to deliver one final piece for us to complete our work. They've been eager to try again after the previous experiment failed."

Oh, stars, they've tried this before? Leon's stomach turned over. "What happened with that one?"

"They haven't said exactly. I got the impression that they had a different approach for that weapon and are trying something new this time," she replied. "All I know is that the first iteration was unstable, and when it accidently triggered, the results weren't what they'd wanted."

"This new method is far more thorough," Brandon added.

Leon didn't want to clarify what was meant by 'thorough'; all of the possibilities were awful.

His concern intensified when he noticed Brandon navigate on his screen to one of the genetic models that Leon had been tooling in his private lab.

"The conditions in this model aren't sustainable," Leon warned again. "Don't do this."

Brandon raised his eyebrows in challenge. "We already have."

Leon froze. "You've...?"

Brandon indicated a partitioned area along the back wall.

Leon approached the viewing window, a pit growing in his stomach. He looked inside at a woman strapped to a chair. *Stars, no!* He took a shaky breath. "What is this?"

"She's Gifted; the perfect test candidate for the tethering." Brandon began adjusting controls on a console.

I won't be a part of this! Leon yanked open the door to the other room and ran inside to the captive young woman.

She had a blank look in her eyes, as if she'd been drugged.

Leon leaned close to her. "Hey, I'm here to help you."

She turned her head to the side, gazing at him in a way that made it seem like she was staring past him.

Looking at the young woman, a thought suddenly struck him. "Are you Melisa?" he whispered.

The woman blinked slowly. "No. Rachel."

Well, it was worth a shot. He shook his head. "Rachel, I'm going to try to get you out of here."

It was a hollow offer. He had no idea how to get free himself, let alone to escape with someone who, in her current state, could barely string together a sentence, let alone stand.

Before he could think about what to do, hands grabbed

him roughly and pulled him back. He fought against the sudden restraint, only to feel cold metal against his neck. Though he couldn't see what type of weapon it was, the implement would no doubt definitively end any attempt to escape.

"We're all professionals here," Brandon said in Leon's ear. "Let's act like it."

The hands released Leon.

He stood there in silence, his pulse pounding. *I can't leave her like this. They're going to kill her!*

Even so, he didn't know what he *could* do for the young woman. They were both prisoners here. He had no way out.

Brandon prodded Leon out from the smaller testing room back to the observation lab. "Where are we with the lock, Nora?" he asked.

One of the other women in the group of scientists replied from her station. "Synchronizing the energy fields now."

Leon watched the team, trying to piece together what was going on. His best guess was that they intended to turn Rachel into a 'Keeper' to direct the actions of the transdimensional bioweapon. They had mapped her genome and had linked certain genetic markers to tether her to the living weapon. Were it not for the alien tech and extradimensional oddities he'd witnessed over the past several years, he would have thought such a feat impossible. As it stood, though, he was seeing the reality play out before his eyes.

"Link established!" Nora reported.

Scientists at the other stations began shouting out various readings and status reports. Leon only half-listened, more concerned about what was happening to Rachel in the other room.

She started to writhe in her seat, the restraints biting into her flesh. Her skin was flushed and had a radiance to it that could have been beautiful were it not for the agony twisting her features. Energy was building within her, every cell becoming supercharged with power flowing from the higher dimensions.

Leon kept a close eye on the readouts. The numbers were creeping upward without any sign of stabilizing. He did the math. If this rate continued, Rachel would certainly die. Not only that, but the energy would need somewhere to go. It would be released as a single explosive charge with enough power to take out the facility. In fact, if the connection didn't automatically sever, that reaction could conceivably spread.

"Shut it down," Leon urged.

Brandon ignored him.

Leon stepped closer. "It's not safe. Shut it down."

"We have everything under control," Brandon said.

"No, you don't. Have you looked at these numbers?"

"This isn't your area of expertise. Leave it to us." Brandon turned back to the work.

"This woman is the only stopgap, and that control will cease the moment she dies. It doesn't take a doctor to see that you're killing her!"

"There are always sacrifices—"

"You're not listening to me!" Leon shouted. "If she dies, there will be nothing to hold back that energy well. You will rip open a gash in spacetime to the higher dimensions, and it will disintegrate everything it touches. You won't just kill her, you'll kill *us*."

Finally, the words seemed to land. Brandon looked at the readouts with fresh eyes. "They said this was the way to do it..."

"I don't know what in the stars they were thinking, but this isn't a bioweapon—it's a foking transdimensional energy bomb! There is no way to do any of this 'safely'," Leon insisted.

"The entire concept is an affront to science."

"Maybe we *should* shut this down," Carla voiced in Leon's support. "We need more testing to learn how to regulate the energy transfer so we can stabilize the bridge."

In the other room, Rachel was close to glowing. Her breath came in ragged gasps, and she was trembling uncontrollably.

"Stop this now, or you won't be able to," Leon said, about to push the other man aside and take over the controls himself, even if that meant the guards shooting him.

"Shut it down, Brandon." Carla's tone was calm but firm. Her eyes, however, were darting between the controls and Rachel, clearly running her own assessment that things were about to get beyond their control.

With a grunt, Brandon tapped the requisite commands into his console to terminate the test.

Immediately, Rachel stilled in her chair, eyes closed and panting. The glow faded from her skin.

Carla leaned against her console and took an unsteady breath. "That was close."

"It shouldn't have been. You shouldn't be doing this at all!" Leon backed away from the equipment, his cheeks burning.

He was about to rush over to help Rachel in the other room, but two of the other scientists were already on their way in to tend to her.

"There are always risks with progress," Nora said.

"You call this 'progress'?" Leon scoffed. "This is perverse madness."

Edward stormed into the lab. "Why did you abort the test?"

Leon rounded on him. "This 'test' was going to kill all of us. I told you this won't work in the way you intend it to."

"So make it stable." Edward spun on his heel and left without another word.

Un-foking believable. Leon quivered with rage. There was no regard for the sanctity of life. He was in a waking nightmare.

"You heard the man," Brandon said. "Let's analyze this data and see what went wrong."

How about 'everything'? Can't they see this is fundamentally flawed? Leon shot Carla a desperate look for help, silently pleading with her to back him up that they were going down a disastrous path.

She shook her head, almost imperceptibly. "We have to. It's what we're here to do."

In that moment, he realized that she did know this project was immoral. She also recognized that opposition would mean a swift death sentence.

I'm trapped, but I'm not alone. He gave Carla a nod of understanding. There was nothing they could do for now except get back to work.

CHAPTER 21

THE RESEARCH TEAM on Earth was nowhere near finished with their investigation, but the information they had uncovered so far had forever changed Raena's perception of history.

She looked up from her tablet at Ryan across the lunch table from her. "This is huge. I need to talk with my dad."

"What's the latest?"

"That weird pit they found in Belize? It wasn't the only one. It looks like they're part of some kind of ancient energy grid."

"Have you sent the survey data to the TSS?"

"Yeah, a little while ago." Her handheld buzzed. "And here he is!" She grinned at Ryan and accepted the vidcall, placing the device on the table so they would both be in frame. "Hey, Dad."

"Hi, Raena, Ryan. I just looked over the report. You have no idea how timely it is," her father said.

She tilted her head. "Is that so?"

"We've been finalizing the designs for the power cores and new shield generators to start production. The crazy thing is, I recognize some specs on those devices you sent."

Ryan's mouth dropped open. "How? Aren't those pushing a hundred thousand years old?"

Wil nodded. "Yes. And it seems to be an older iteration of a design that ended up in the Aesir's technology Archive."

Raena leaned forward, her forearms resting on the tabletop. "What does it do?"

"It's a large-scale spatial distortion generator. But here's the thing: in the Aesir's write-up, it was considered only theoretical."

"What's a real one doing on Earth, then?" Raena asked slowly.

"A very good question to which I don't have an answer."

"Huh." Ryan rocked back in his seat. "This keeps getting weirder and weirder."

Raena pursed her lips. "Do you think the devices on Earth are functional?"

"They're very old and have been sitting unused for an incredibly long time," her father said. "I would be quite dubious if it powered on with no difficulty. Not to mention, I wouldn't try. We have no idea what it might do, despite our best guesses, and it may never have been operational in the first place."

"Yeah, it *was* buried," Raena realized.

"It fits with my new ark theory, though," her father continued. "I think Earth may have been set aside as an isolated colony to preserve the species in the event something happened to the core Taran civilization."

The assertion caught Raena off-guard. It *did* fit shockingly well with the new discoveries about her home planet. "I take it you have a whole breakdown of how that hypothesis maps to the archaeological record?"

"Yes, and I'd be happy to go over it with you another time.

For now, my point is that it's becoming clear why the TSS has always had a mandate to watch over Earth. The Priesthood might not have had all the details, but they certainly had some information that underscored the historical relevance of the planet."

Maybe it's not a coincidence at all that they arranged for Mom to be born there. It made Raena's head hurt to think about—millennia of planning and manipulation to guide the development of a galaxy-spanning society. "I'll keep passing on the information as I get it from the investigation teams."

"Thank you. I'm amazed by the synergy here. It goes to show that there really is a bigger pattern to our experience."

"Speaking of which," Ryan said, "do you have any updates on the attacks in the Outer Colonies?" The hits on the ports, in particular, had been a blow to DGE, so he'd been following the situation closely.

"I've assigned the ongoing Coalition investigation to Jason," Wil revealed. "Have you spoken to him recently?"

"Not for a couple of weeks," Raena replied.

"Oh. Well… maybe put in a call and get an update."

"Is everything okay?"

"Yeah, nothing bad. I think he could benefit from your perspective right now, that's all."

She nodded. "Okay, I'll check in with him."

"I'm going to finish going through these notes on Earth," Wil said. "Thank you again for sending along the information right away. This is exciting stuff."

Raena smiled. "It is. I hope your other projects go well. Talk soon."

"Love you both. Take care."

"You too." She ended the vidcall and looked at Ryan, slack-jawed. "Earth was a backup for Tararia?"

He crossed his arms. "What does it say that that's one of the *least* surprising revelations lately?"

She laughed. "I have no idea."

"Hey, what do you think your father was hinting about with Jason?"

"Maybe he got a promotion or is working on something new?"

Ryan shook his head. "I don't know, the way he said it made it seem more... personal. I wonder if he met someone?"

"Huh. Maybe. It would be good for him." She knew he'd been struggling with Tiff's death and the loss of that relationship. It had been several months, so it would be wonderful if he was ready to open his heart again. "He deserves to be happy. He likes to come across as a loner, but he's always been at his best when he's with a partner."

"We can all use some stability and companionship in these uncertain times."

Raena looked down at her hands before meeting his gaze. "On that note, there's something I've been meaning to talk to you about."

"Hmm?"

"It's finally happened. My grandfather broached the subject of 'legacy' last week."

Ryan swallowed. "Oh."

"No pressure, really, just that it's something we should start thinking about."

"He's not wrong. It's crossed my mind more than once recently."

It has? She raised an eyebrow. "Not that I'm opposed to the idea, but I've had other things to think about."

"Of course. And I wouldn't say I've given it a *lot* of thought. Still, I'm coming up on thirty, and now that DGE has its legs under it, it would be nice to have a path for the company's future."

"That's pretty much what my grandfather said." She sighed. "It's ridiculous that 'thirty' is a ticking-clock threshold when we'll live to be well over one-hundred."

"Being highborn is weird. I don't think most civilians these days have kids until their late-thirties or forties, based on what I've heard."

"Yeah." Raena crossed her arms. "None of this should come as a surprise. We knew in no uncertain terms that agreeing to this political path meant being beholden to the expectations of others. All the same, I didn't appreciate the magnitude of that mandate back when I was a teenager."

"Are you having regrets?"

She hastily shook her head. "Not at all. I look forward to having a family with you—it would just be nice to be able to do that on our own timeline."

"Like you said, there's no rush. We can find an opening in that detailed timeline of yours."

"Well, it's pretty packed, so it will be a matter of *making* time. But yeah, we can talk about it more once things calm down a bit."

He took her hand. "We should also be prepared for the possibility that things won't get easier. I'm not saying it's a priority this second, but at some point, we may need to take that step even if circumstances aren't ideal."

"I know. So long as we have each other, we'll figure it out."

— — —

Since the startling revelation about the ancient technology that Raena's team had unearthed, Wil had been revisiting his other recent observations with a new perspective. In particular, he found himself contemplating other instances where former Taran leaders had potentially built backup plans into their systems.

There was definitely a pattern emerging, such as Cytera's genetic records to complement the Priesthood's Genetic Archive on Ryla. There were also smaller instances of things he'd never considered before, like Lower Dynasty operations that mirrored the High Dynasty industries. Those businesses had always been considered 'subsidiaries' of the High Dynasty infrastructure, but once he dove into it, he realized that they were structured far more like wholly independent companies. Most notably, each of those critical 'backup' corporation's interests had received funding directly from the Priesthood at one point or another in the past several hundred years—specifically earmarked for infrastructure improvements.

He did have to give the Priesthood credit for their planning on that front. The recent issues with MPS had revealed just how fragile the High Dynasty corporations could be if something went wrong, so having some manner of redundancy in place was critical. Unfortunately, it seemed that even the Priesthood hadn't foreseen a shortage of voydite; MPS had kept that hidden very well.

The other major secret that was now coming to light was the awful treatment of Gifted people on Cytera. He'd barely heard mention of the planet before, and it wasn't until Lexi's appearance that he'd had sufficient reason to look into any details. From what little he'd learned in the interim, there had clearly been a failure on the part of the Taran government. While the policy was to allow each world to govern itself, it was the responsibility of those in charge on Tararia to ensure that all citizens were protected, especially children. To find out that groups of people had been essentially sold into slavery generation after generation was a shocking and horrific discovery.

How did we miss this? Wil felt especially to blame as the leader of the TSS—the organization that was the face for those with abilities and had been such a strong advocate for ensuring Gifted were treated as full citizens. *They were hunted and used like the Priesthood abused their test subjects. We failed them.*

It appeared that the caste system had finally broken down around the time that Lexi had fled the planet as a baby. That predated Wil's leadership of the TSS. It would have fallen in the post-Bakzen War years when his father was serving as interim High Commander, when there had been so much cleanup on worlds decimated by the enemy that internal civil disputes hadn't been a priority.

That's not an excuse. This went on for hundreds of years. He hated when hindsight revealed a different course of action—when help could have been offered back when people needed it most.

Though the worst of the injustices on the planet may already have been rectified, that didn't mean that there weren't still problems to address. And mysterious backgrounds to solve.

What is your legacy from this planet, Lexi? What went on there? Her genetic trail might reveal more than any news article about the planet's history.

Lexi's genetic profile was on record from her medical exam following her extraction from Duronis. Wil had felt bad about his ill-timed and blunt request at dinner, so he'd delayed running the analysis, as curious as he was about what it would reveal. Having been so often classified by his own lineage, he tried not to reduce others to those terms. Now, though, there was too much in play with his son and the political state of the Empire.

Wil initiated the genetic mapping on his desktop, first running it as a pairing match with Jason. He had few doubts about what it would say.

The analysis completed in three minutes. As expected, it revealed a strong match—not as perfect as his own with Saera or to the level of Raena's with Ryan, but well above the average level expected through a chance encounter.

But this was *random. It couldn't have been planned in the way the rest of our lives were. Or, could it?*

The strong match affirmed the feelings they had for each other—an instant and profound attraction. Bonding would be a natural extension of that, once they gave in.

On top of that, Lexi's ability potential far exceeded his expectations. She showed as being at a 9.4 estimate, which would tie her with Saera if it was fully realized. The TSS rarely saw trainees much above 8. It was a shame she hadn't come to the TSS as a teenager to maximize that promise—though based on the skills she'd demonstrated on Duronis, she was far from untrained.

Wil's true interest, though, was in Lexi's lineage. That part of the analysis took longer, running a search for genetic markers through the generations of records from across the Empire. Cytera's own internal archive hadn't been merged with the central database, so he couldn't follow her recent family lines. However, that didn't matter for his purposes. He wanted to see if there might be any connections to ancestors back much further.

A handful of distant genetic matches popped up for shared markers in the Lower Dynasties. There was a clear shared history there, supporting the hypothesis that former nobles had gone to Cytera and formed their own insular society. All of the arranged pairings on the planet had been selected for bloodlines with the strongest ability expression, so her high potential made sense.

A knock on Wil's door pulled him from his ruminations.

"Come in."

Michael entered quickly, carrying a tablet. "An intriguing field report just came in—reports of new arrivals on a remote colony world." He brushed his hand along the tablet to display its readout on Wil's desktop.

The genetic analysis was replaced by the report about a planet known as Quel. It only had approximately eighty thousand colonists at present, people who agreed to be the first settlers on a newly bio-optimized world. Such recently transformed planets often suffered from extreme weather and tremors, so only the most intrepid, or desperate, people would choose to be part of the initial wave of colonists. However, the low population and location outside the standard transit lines made the planet a perfect place for people to hide out—people like the missing members of the Coalition who'd departed Duronis hours before the attacks.

"The proximity makes sense," Michael said. "It's less than a day's transit from Duronis, even with a civilian jump drive. If they were using an independent jump drive like we suspect, it's within easy jump range of all the attacked worlds."

"What's the word on the new arrivals?"

"Multiple ships dropping off personnel and supplies before taking off. People sporting advanced tech. They've got security that, and I quote, 'looks like a private army'."

Wil sat up straight. "Those could very well be our people. To whom do we owe this tip?"

"One of the locals. They're protective of their home and

weren't too happy about all the new neighbors."

"And thank the stars for that."

Wil cross referenced Quel against the course mapping that Kira and Lexi had been analyzing with Jasmine over the past week. Sure enough, it was one of the worlds they had narrowed down as a prime candidate.

He pushed back in his seat. "Well, I said that we needed a solid lead in order to warrant a ground-op rescue. I think this qualifies."

"I'll get a probe sent over to capture current imaging and energy mapping to see if there are any bases outside the known population centers," Michael said. "Who would you like leading this?"

"Jason is on everything Coalition-related now. Let's hand it over to him."

Michael nodded. "I'm glad to see you giving him more responsibility. He's earned it."

"I was tossed into the deep end when I was way younger. We all need those sink-or-swim moments."

"I have a ground ops team in mind who'd be perfect support on this."

"Make the preparations."

— — —

"This seems too easy." Jason looked over the information on his father's desk. "How do we know we can trust this tip?"

Wil transferred all of the information to Jason's access credentials. "Michael is gathering further intelligence to corroborate the lead. We must remember that there are good people out there who look after their homes."

Jason nodded. "It's been a while since we've had positive

news come our way. I can't help being suspicious."

"It's always smart to question information. In this case, I believe we got lucky. After what we've been through recently, I'll take it."

"Getting down to the surface on a planet with this minimal a population is going to be tricky. I think a stealth shuttle makes the most sense."

"Wait on the detailed scan to make those determinations. Michael should have it to you soon."

Jason nodded and headed out.

He'd been on plenty of missions—had even taken the lead on several—but those were one-offs. This was the first time he was going on a mission as part of a task force that he was also managing. It would set the tone for all of the work to root out the Coalition and its members going forward. Dwelling on that might mess with his head and make him overthink his actions, so he tried to focus instead on the specific objectives he needed to accomplish.

His first step was to loop Kira in on the new information. He pinged her handheld and requested she meet him in his office.

While he waited for her, Jason pulled personnel files and craft specs to select his team and equipment for the upcoming rescue mission. It was only a preliminary selection since they had yet to plan out the tactical details. However, he thought it prudent to have the available resources in mind while planning the op.

Kira arrived just as he was sorting the ships and personnel into a few different configurations to fit various entry scenarios.

"Hey, what's up?" she greeted.

"We got a tip. I think we now know where they took Leon."

She tensed, her gaze focused and intent. "Where?"

"A remote colony world called Quel."

"That's one we've been looking at closely. It's so far out that there hasn't been good scan data to work from. No obvious signs of activity from what we could see."

"The TSS has sent a probe to check it out. I should have the results soon."

Kira's eyes narrowed. "Why didn't anyone tell me that was an option? We would have checked out each of the worlds we've been investigating."

"Because the breadth of data we're collecting is essentially spying on private citizens, and we can't do so without cause. Being in a flight path isn't a crime. Setting up a secret base that the locals didn't authorize is enough of a reason for us to take a look."

"Yay for land use codes." Kira seemed less than thrilled. She crossed her arms, her foot tapping anxiously.

She wants to rush in to get Leon. I would, too, in her position. He flipped his staffing work around on the desktop to show her. "We need to be calculated about this. I hope we're going to be dealing with a single site. Field reports indicate there's no armed aerial presence, just a ground force."

"Infiltration is my specialty." Kira seemed a little more upbeat at that thought.

Jason's desktop pinged with an incoming data dump. It was accompanied by a note from Michael: >>Scan data from Quel. Let me know who and what you need to get the job done. I have a group of capable mission candidates if it would help you.<<

>>Send over a list. I'll need good people,<< he replied and then smiled at Kira. "Perfect timing. The TSS Head of Ops just sent me the surveillance we were waiting on." He projected the

data on the holodisplay.

The planet Quel appeared above his desk, rotating slowly on the illuminated three-dimensional image. Every topographical detail was rendered in stunning realism, from polar ice caps to what promised to be fertile plains to the north of the equator on the main continent. The only settlement of any meaningful size was nestled at the foot of a mountain range running along the northwestern coast above the plains.

Jason toggled to a combination thermal map and electromagnetic activity overlay to look for signs of other activity. The TSS probe had just completed the scan within the last half hour, so the information was as up-to-date as they'd be able to get this far from their target. Besides the city, one additional spot stood out on the hybrid map, indicating an active area to the northeast of the main settlement. It was in the mountains, making it difficult to access but also a great place to hide something like a secret lab.

He pointed at the site. "There. I bet you that's where the Coalition set up their new shop."

Kira grabbed the holographic image with her hands and zoomed in on the location. The resolution refreshed at increasingly lower elevations until they were looking at a small building on the surface.

She smiled. "Well, well. How modest a structure for having that much energy output."

That energy pattern extended well beyond the footprint of the building, indicating an extensive underground facility. The orbital scan wasn't capable of creating a detailed underground map with that much interference, so they'd be going in blind in that respect. However, they had a singular ground target and could form their strategy around the choke point at the facility's entry.

"All right, I'll need to present a tactical plan to Command. Let's figure out the best way to approach this."

— — —

Lexi paced through the living area of Jason's quarters. Kira had run off from their investigation session, saying only that there was news. It had been two hours and she had yet to hear anything.

The door clicked and slid open, startling her. Jason entered.

"Hey." She rushed over to him. "What's going on?"

"We think we've found the Alliance—or Coalition—hideout."

Her heart leaped. "Leon?"

"No confirmation who's there, but we're hopeful. It looks to be an underground lab."

"Where is it?" Lexi asked.

"Quel. It's not a place I'm familiar with."

She frowned. "It's on the list of planets I've been compiling with Kira, but I hadn't heard of it before then."

"Somewhere remote and unknown makes sense. They no doubt intend to do some nasty things."

"Certainly have shown that time and again."

"We'll have to go in blind. There's not time to do proper reconnaissance."

"Though you can't take anything at face value, anyway." She spread her hands. "The people within the Alliance would smile to your face and then have no problem ordering the death of innocents."

"I like to think that people aren't born evil, but you have to wonder sometimes." He headed to the bedroom.

"You've probably seen some bad things in the TSS, huh?" Lexi asked, following him.

"I don't do a lot of field work, honestly." He pulled out a travel bag from the closet. "I've been lucky to be surrounded by good people, for the most part. But I saw true corruption up close while we were ousting the Priesthood. Being near those monsters… It was a good lesson in what happens when corrupt individuals remain unchecked in positions of power for too long."

"I suspect the leaders of the Coalition are in a similar situation—on a smaller scale, of course."

"Lust for control makes people do crazy things." He started to place clothes in the bag.

She tilted her head and looked at him. "You're not like that, though. You have more power than most, but you don't seem interested in it."

"Maybe it's because I grew up as a commoner. Being in an influential role seems to bring more bad attention than good. I'd rather work behind the scenes and help people when I can." He zipped up his bag.

"I really appreciate that about you." She looked at the bag. "Are you leaving now?"

"Not quite yet, but I want to be ready to head out as soon as we have mission approval."

Lexi bit her lip. Watching him pack and prepare, it didn't feel right for him to go off. He had been given the assignment, but this wasn't his fight. It was hers. She had a responsibility to make sure her friend made it to safety.

"Jason, I want to go with you."

He shook his head. "No, it's too dangerous."

She stood firm. "I appreciate that you're trying to look out for me, but this relationship isn't going to work if you try to coddle me or tell me what I can or can't do."

He met her stern gaze. "I'm sorry, I didn't mean it that way. The reality is that you don't have military training."

"So? I can handle myself."

"I have no doubt, but—"

"It's my risk to take. Kira and Leon are my friends, and I want to help reunite them. Besides, everyone keeps talking about how the TSS is so shorthanded right now. She motioned to herself. "I'm at your service."

He sighed. "We might not have known each other for long, but I can already tell that it's not worth arguing with you once you've made up your mind."

"Good-looking *and* smart." She eyed him appreciatively. "This may work out after all."

"I'm not guaranteeing you'll go in on the raid with us, but you can at least come on the transport ship."

Good, plenty of time to talk my way onto the team. Lexi smiled. "Deal. Let's go get 'em."

CHAPTER 22

SINCE HE HAD gone to work with the other scientists, Leon had been pushed at an even more grueling pace. *Don't they know that we need rest so our brains can do this kind of work?*

Or maybe that was the point. The Alliance realized that they were asking otherwise good, well-meaning people to do awful things, so keeping them sleep-deprived was a way to break their natural moral compass. Get someone tired and cranky enough, and they were more likely to be compliant when promised a proper night's sleep once it was over.

Even Leon could feel his resolve breaking. His brain kept telling him why he had to be strong and how he couldn't complete these tasks. Yet, he found himself knitting together the pieces all the same, adjusting his work to fit with what the other scientists were doing. He may as well have been outside himself, watching someone else perform the actions he'd sworn he would resist to his dying breath.

He was so groggy that it took him several seconds to realize that Edward had entered the room.

The shrewd man stood at the center of the space, waiting

for everyone's attention. "I hope you're making progress, because we need to be ready for another test by this evening," he announced.

Why the sudden rush to the timeline? Leon wondered.

Normally, there would be no elaboration, no reasons. For once, however, Edward wasn't finished. "There's been a breach. The location of this facility is no longer secure."

It was the greatest news Leon had ever heard.

How did they find out we were here? The Alliance had been so careful with all of their plans that it seemed unlikely there'd been a slipup at this juncture. The only reasonable explanation Leon could think of was that they weren't alone on this planet—whatever and wherever it was. Perhaps one of the locals hadn't taken too kindly to the new arrivals.

"We are going into a lockdown of this facility," Edward said. "Our leadership is expecting a full report on the viability of this new tool by tonight. If it proves feasible, we will continue the work elsewhere." With that, he left the room again.

The scientists began whispering to their neighbors in hushed tones. Only Brandon and Leon remained silent, eyeing each other from across the room.

Leon stared down the man in challenge. *It'll be over soon. You've lost.*

"You heard the instructions. Finish your tasks," Brandon barked, ripping his gaze away from Leon.

There wasn't much left for Leon to do. He'd already begrudgingly helped the other specialists zero in their locks on certain genetic markers and then find the correct resonance for the unique energy field of their test subject. He couldn't stall or delay further, short of smashing equipment—and doing that would be a quick way to end up dead. His best bet was to wait out rescue and let the TSS deal out the justice.

Still, he might be able to persuade some of the others that they didn't need to go along with the remaining work and could call it quits now. If enough of them refused to continue, there might be safety in numbers.

Leon leaned over next to Carla, pretending to make adjustments on his console. "Are you worried about what we're doing here?"

"It's science. A little danger keeps things interesting." Her expression told a different story than her words. Eyes wide and face flushed, she had the look of someone who was handling a live bomb with no idea how to defuse it or when it might go off.

"We don't need to do this," he said quietly. "If we all stop what we're doing, they can't do anything."

She swallowed hard. "They can, though. To us."

"We can't live in fear like that. Think about what we're doing! This could kill everything on a planet. Do you want that guilt?"

"I don't know, it—"

"Are you finished over there?" Brandon asked from across the room.

"Who put you in charge, anyway?" Leon snapped.

"Someone needed to step up who understands how all of these pieces fit together. I wouldn't expect you to understand that kind of big-picture thinking."

Leon rounded on him. "At least I'm not blinded by ambition. You're so wrapped up in trying to do this that you didn't stop to ask if you *should*."

"And why shouldn't we? This is the foundational technology to revolutionize how we connect. Creating quantum entanglements between people—think of how it could bring couples closer. Bonds across space and time."

"This is nothing like the natural bonding between Gifted people. That's a partnership. This technology is about one person having complete control over another—the way you want to make a handler for this extradimensional monster. Don't pretend that this isn't anything other than a scheme for control."

"Oh, it *is* for control," Brandon said. "It's a tool to rend control from the corrupt leadership on Tararia and take a stand for independence."

"Do you really think the 'leaders' of this organization are entirely altruistic? They want to seize power *for themselves*."

Brandon scoffed and turned back to his console. "One step at a time. Complete the preparations."

Leon looked to Carla for help, but she wouldn't meet his gaze. He searched around the room for anyone else willing to stand up for common sense and decency. "How are all of you okay with this? This technology isn't even *close* to ready!"

"There is no progress without testing," Brandon said, not looking up from his work. "If you don't want a part in this, then shut up and leave us to our business."

Leon's only move was to keep talking in an attempt to slow them down. "What you're proposing isn't even a test in a scientific sense. You're attempting a demonstration of undeveloped technology. You're not treating it with any respect."

"It is *you* who has no respect. Do you not understand the gift we have been given?"

The phrasing caught Leon off-guard. "What do you mean?"

Brandon smiled. "A discovery of this magnitude would have taken generations' more research. We have been given the keys to design our own destiny."

Wait... what is he saying? Leon shifted on his feet. "Who developed this tech?"

"We have great benefactors. Respect them."

Leon backed away, suddenly getting the impression that there was much more going on here than he'd realized.

The man had the glazed look in his eyes of a zealot. It was impossible to reason with someone or get a straight answer when they were so invested in their singular perspective on an issue.

"I won't have any further part in what you're doing," Leon said. They could mutilate him or kill him, but he wouldn't help these monsters perfect a weapon. He'd already done too much.

Leon was about to make a run for it when the door opened. Before he could make a move, muscular arms wrapped around his chest and pinned his arms to his side. No matter how much he struggled, he couldn't break free.

"That wasn't smart of you," Edward stated, coming into Leon's field of view. His face was even more pinched than normal. "You *will* behave. We're not finished with you yet."

—   —   —

Wil took in the information as Jason walked him through the tactical approaches for the raid on Quel. "This is a good plan, Jason, but I'm not sure if it's the best approach. Did you work on this with Kira?"

"Yes. What's the issue?"

"The involvement of the Guard. I hate to say it, but the local Enforcers have probably been paid off."

"What?"

Wil shook his head; he'd been over that ongoing issue with

the Tararian Guard's leadership, and there wasn't an easy solution. "I've already spoken with Admiral Mathaen, and there's not a lot we can do to prevent bribes aside from frequently rotating duty stations. Unfortunately, that can just mean more people are getting wealthy and there'll be more compromised Enforcers to turn on us."

"Or, we could get people who'll turn down those kind of payoffs," Jason countered.

"It's not that simple. Rarely is it only a matter of money. Criminals have a way of finding their target's weak point—threatening loved ones or blackmail. As much as we tell people that they should report any threat to their superiors, sometimes they go their own way all the same."

Jason scowled. "Okay, so we can't rely on local backup. Where does that leave us?"

"I suggest you instead bring as many Agents as we can spare from Headquarters. All the field personnel in that sector are still wrapped up with the attack aftermath."

"All right, that will require some reworking. Should I put together a list, or—"

Jason cut off when Wil's desk chirped with an urgent communication request.

"Sorry, it's Dahl. Hold that thought." Wil accepted the call. "Hi, Dahl. I'm in the middle of—"

"We must speak at once," the Oracle stated.

Wil considered ending the call right there without an explanation. He was sick of dropping everything for the Aesir only to have them make vague insults and refuse to answer his reasonable questions. "I'll call you back when I'm available."

"You must stop what you're doing immediately. We have just learned about your plan, and it will have dire consequences."

"Which plan?"

"The power cores."

Jason rose slowly. "I can handle the rest of the planning…"

Wil had no doubt his son was capable. In fact, it was probably better for him to do it on his own to reinforce his increasing autonomy. "Take whoever and whatever you need. Good luck. And be careful out there."

Jason nodded and saw himself out.

Alone in the room, Wil returned his attention to Dahl. "I don't appreciate your forceful intrusions."

"This matter could not wait. I believe you are making a grave error."

— — —

With his father otherwise occupied, Jason jogged to his office to revise his tactical approach. He sent messages to Kira and Lexi to come meet him so they could revisit the details together.

They showed up within minutes.

"What's the latest?" Kira asked.

"We have our go-ahead, but we need to change tactics to keep it within the TSS." Jason brought up a detailed rendering on the holoprojector above his desk. "I have authorization to bring Agents, and we can take whatever ship we need. It's down to the fine details: how do we get into the facility and get the Coalition's captives offworld without anyone getting hurt?"

"I'm all for getting as many people out as we can, but my priority is rescuing Leon," Kira stated.

"Of course. We're going to do everything we can," Jason assured her.

She nodded her understanding, but they both knew getting

him out was easier said than done. They had no idea where he was, precisely, which meant storming in was risky. A recon mission would be ideal, but time and resources were in short supply.

Kira was a veteran soldier, so she didn't let it show, but fear and concern churned just beneath the surface. Jason's finely tuned senses picked up on it, and Kira shook her head when she realized he'd noticed.

"I won't let worry cloud my judgment."

"I know you won't."

Lexi frowned at the screen. "How many other people might have been forced to work like Leon? I mean, everyone else at the office seemed to be on board with the Alliance's message."

"And it's possible they all are," Jason admitted.

Kira crossed her arms. "Really, there's no way to know who's there willingly and who's been forced to work. We shouldn't barge in shooting."

"You don't need to do any shooting at all to have people show their colors and pick sides," Lexi said. "The Alliance hates people with abilities, right? So those kind of skills don't enter their planning. If you send in a bunch of Agents, you should be able to subdue anyone who puts up a fuss by either pinning them with telekinesis or using mind-control."

She did have a point. It was a bit more direct than Jason's typical approach, but perhaps it was the best way to proceed in this matter. Lexi did know the Alliance better than him, so it was prudent to listen to her suggestions.

"We can't do things like that in the Guard, but it does make sense for a TSS op," Kira chimed in. "Only issue would be if you encounter people with significant mental guards training."

"Unusual among civilians," Jason assessed.

"It's unlikely, I agree."

"With enough strong Agents, you can overwhelm anyone," Lexi said.

He shook his head. "That's not how we do things. Yes, we can easily force a person to submit, but we have a code of ethics. We don't violate minds without cause."

"Capturing people and forcing them to work as slaves counts, I'd say."

"Yes, but not every person we'll encounter is guilty of those crimes. There's nuance. A blanket application of maximum force would make us no better than those perpetrators."

Lexi crossed her arms. "It's the same thing."

He'd grown to care deeply for Lexi, and in their short time together, he'd come to appreciate that their different life experiences had given them significantly divergent perspectives on certain issues. She had always been on the run, forced to be defensive in order to survive. She'd never had the opportunity to take another tactic, so he could understand why she felt there was only one way to go about it.

"We can never fall into the mindset that everyone is the enemy just because they happen to be standing on the opposite side of a line," Jason said. "We go in and offer an alternative. Anyone is free to change sides in the moment."

Lexi scrunched up her face with a mixture of annoyance and confusion, but Kira nodded her understanding.

"Appeal to the person inside," the soldier said.

"Yes. And that's how we'll get people out." Jason rotated the map on the screen. "We're going to have limited people to pull this off, so let's make them count."

— — —

Wil took a centering breath. Whatever Dahl was about to

go off about wasn't likely to be complimentary, and Wil didn't want to further damage his relationship with the Oracle. As infuriating as he found Dahl sometimes, he was still a friend.

"All right, what's the issue with the cores?" Wil asked.

"This is not what we intended."

"Dahl, I respect you, but I can't take any more of these riddles." Wil resisted pinching the bridge of his nose. "I have tried to do my best, and apparently it's not good enough for you. Why do you keep turning to me only to tell me I'm wrong?"

"We do not have the answers."

"Then how do you know that I haven't acted well? One moment you say you trust me, and then you say that I am failing."

"We did not say that you have 'failed'."

Wil spread his arms. "You may as well have, based on how you're talking! Nothing I do is good enough. I don't know what you want from me. I told you years ago that I didn't want this responsibility, and yet you keep *insisting* that it has to be me. Why?" He was well aware how petulant he sounded, but years of frustration boiled to that single moment. They'd already rehashed this argument too many times. Calm and rational hadn't sold his message, so it was time for a new approach.

The Oracle studied him over the screen. "We fear you have looked only at the surface of what was offered and not the larger picture."

"Of what?"

"This 'gift' from the Erebus."

"Oh, I don't trust them in the least."

"And yet you are still preparing for production and intend to spread the technology across the Taran worlds."

I gave the Aesir ample chances to be involved in that process, and you refused! Wil managed to keep a level tone despite fuming inside. "I evaluated the information and made the best decision available to me."

"You should have consulted us before making unilateral decisions about the well-being of the Empire."

Wil scoffed. "I *did* try to work with you, Dahl. You declined. Repeatedly, you have told me how I don't take enough action and keep waiting for others to make decisions. Now I do, finally, forge ahead on my own, and what I do is wrong? I can't win."

"All that we have wanted is for you to see the patterns. You focus on the facts and figures in front of you. That has its place, but you can do—you can be—so much more. You have the gift of sight. You used it once, back in a time of great need, and yet you have ignored it all these years since. You continue to ignore it now, when there is a threat far greater than that of the Bakzen."

What is he talking about? After a few seconds, he realized that Dahl must be referring to the energy-pattern reading of which the Aesir were so fond. Wil had seen his personal truth in the nexus as a young man, and that had given him the insight needed to win the war. *Does he want me to go back to look into the nexus again?*

"I thought those visions were a one-time thing," Wil said.

"Visiting the nexus, yes. But that is only to establish your connection. Once you are successful, you can tap into that well of knowledge any time you like… and you never have. It has been our greatest disappointment."

"You never told me I could do that."

"That shouldn't require an explanation. You should feel it."

Wil didn't know whether to be embarrassed or angry. If

they had simply told him years ago in what way he had failed to meet their expectations, they could have avoided this whole mess. And, perhaps, he could have handled situations differently had he tapped into that alternate perspective.

Even knowing that, he didn't know how to 'read the patterns' in the way Dahl insisted was possible. He'd never felt a pull or a spark of inspiration. Stars knew he'd spent enough time astral projecting that he should have had some kind of extrasensory experience to nudge him in the right direction.

Unless... I didn't want to see it. The war had left him psychologically scarred. He'd hated himself and his power. The self-loathing had made him close himself off, and only rarely had he tapped into the true extent of his abilities.

Maybe some sort of cosmic truth had been there the whole time and he had been afraid to see it. Now, he wasn't sure he *wanted* to know that truth.

"I'm sorry, Dahl. I think I understand now. I'll need to reflect on where to go from here."

"Nothing you do now changes the fact that you have already sold Tarans to these Erebus. By accepting their offer, you have started down a path that is not easily altered."

"I still believe that our modifications to the power core are our best—"

"No, we had hoped that the Lynaedans would show you the errors of your assumptions, but it seems even they have been blinded by the Erebus' spell. You should have stood up to them, not become reliant on them!" Dahl had never shouted before. Up until that moment, Wil didn't know he was even capable of that kind of emotional display.

"What choice do we have? We need some form of protection, and this is our best chance."

The Oracle shook his head. "We fought too hard for

freedom to end up slaves to others."

"Oh, I know. We have a truce with the Erebus."

"Do you honestly believe that peace will last?"

"No, which is why I am trying to find *any* solution to offer us some protection. I also believe that we better convince them we're friends or we won't be around long enough to fight back."

Dahl shook his head. "Look at the pattern, Cadicle. Not the sole item. I can't spell it out any more clearly for you than that." He severed the connection.

What the fok? Wil slumped in his seat, feeling like he'd just run a marathon only to be beat up steps from the finish line.

As much as he wanted to write off Dahl's statements and move on, Wil couldn't shake a nagging feeling that they had walked into a trap.

What am I missing? Now, more than ever, he needed to figure it out before it was too late.

CHAPTER 23

THROUGHOUT THE RIDE on the TSS transport ship, Jason sensed everyone was watching him—not just because this was one of his first commands, but because they could feel the connection between him and Lexi. Kira and the two dozen Agents with him were all seasoned pros so they'd never say anything directly, but it was obvious to Jason that they were wondering if he was the right person to lead this mission.

It's all in my head. Just focus on getting the job done, he told himself.

Still, it was highly unusual for a civilian to accompany a tactical operation of this sort, and all of the Agents he'd selected for the mission were adept in both reading people and skilled in their abilities. The resonance connection between him and Lexi was no doubt obvious to them by the end of the voyage if they hadn't noticed it right away.

He wasn't personally acquainted with many of the Agents, but most of them knew his father quite well. One, Andy Renteria, had been his father's roommate when they were Junior Agents, so Jason had met him on a handful of occasions when he was at Headquarters. As a predominantly field Agent, Jason was counting on Andy to be his second in command for this mission.

Ten minutes out from their destination, Jason pulled Andy aside into the private conference room.

"You've spent a lot more time in action than I have, so please let me know if you see anything I've missed," Jason told him.

Andy smiled. "Of course, Jason. I'd do the same for any Agent."

He nodded. "Thank you."

The older man hesitated. "On that note, I'm surprised Lexi is here with us."

"Yeah, she's invested in seeing this thing through. I trust her."

"Okay, good enough for me." Andy clapped him on the shoulder. "I've seen your parents' relationship from the beginning, and I know how powerful the right partnership can be. I hope you find that, too."

"Thanks."

Andy held out his arm. "Let's rally the troops."

Jason took the lead back into the passenger compartment to address the team.

"This organization has been terrorizing the Outer Colonies for months," he began. "Their senseless violence has claimed millions of lives. While this raid is unlikely to dismantle the organization's leadership, it is an opportunity to thwart their development of a new weapon that could lead to even greater losses.

"Our goal is to minimize casualties on all fronts—subdue and restrain—but lethal force is authorized in the event the situation demands it. There may be hostages, and protecting those innocents is the priority. In particular, our top target is Leon Caletti; consider him a part of the TSS family, and get him home safely.

"We will break into our established teams. Since we don't know what exactly we're walking into, each team will adjust its operations to fit with the actual conditions. Maintain telepathic contact at all times. Disable operations and rescue captives. It's as simple as that. Once the immediate threat has been neutralized, we can conduct a thorough sweep for information-gathering purposes. Any questions?"

Everyone shook their heads; they'd been over the available information on the way over and were already as prepared as they could be.

"Kira, you're with me," he told her.

"I'd like to go with you, too," Lexi said.

"That's not a good idea." He added telepathically, *"I was okay with you coming on the ship, but I don't feel right about you walking into a dangerous scenario like this."*

"I might not be trained as an Agent, but I've gone up against these people before."

"Yes, and while those actions have been forgiven, you are still a civilian and should not be taking violent acts toward others in the future."

She scowled at him. *"They've taken my friends, Jason. I want to see this through."*

"Bringing you would be showing biased judgment. I can't."

Lexi paused. *"I can identify key members of the organization's leadership on sight. That makes me essential."*

He considered it. Though bending the rules, it was a reasonable justification. Even so, he wasn't keen on her walking into the heart of danger. *"I would rather you stay here."*

"Very sweet, but pass. I promise, just telekinesis for defense.

Let me be another set of eyes for you."

"*All right,*" he agreed. "Upon further consideration, Lexi can identify key persons of interest who may be on the premises, so she will accompany my team, as well."

Kira raised an eyebrow at him and glanced at Lexi.

"The more the merrier." He smiled at her and then headed toward the space-to-surface stealth shuttle berthed in the belly of the ship.

The team followed, and they geared up in anticipation of their imminent arrival to Quel.

Going in with a large group of Agents plus Kira and Lexi might be overkill, but Jason couldn't be certain about what they would find inside the facility. In the end, he'd rather have too many people than not enough.

"Slow and steady," he instructed as they piled into the shuttle that would take them down to the surface.

Kira had donned body armor since she didn't have the ability to keep a telekinetic shield in place like the rest of them. She went through her weapons checks with cool proficiency.

The Agents had little to prepare, being weapons unto themselves. They did carry sidearms just in case, but any Agent tactical team was all about telekinesis first and foremost—far more powerful and precise than any ballistic or energy weapon. Their TSS Agent outfits looked too lightweight for running into a potential combat scenario, but the fabrics were all rated to protect against kinetic and energy weapons fire; the TSS didn't advertise that fact, but every Agent knew their standard issue uniform was more than just about style.

He had Lexi put on specialized light armor, since he was unsure of how successfully she would be able to maintain a personal shield, and he would never forgive himself if she took a stray shot.

"You sure *you want to go in with us?"* Jason asked her telepathically as she fidgeted with the coveralls; though lacking the aesthetic flare of the Agent uniforms, the garment was still form-fitting enough to show off her figure.

"For the thousandth time, yes!"

There was no arguing with that enthusiasm. *"Okay. Stay close. Keep your shield up."*

He headed to the flight deck of the stealth shuttle and prepared for launch. It was go time.

— — —

Being forced to watch others commit atrocities was almost worse than doing it himself, Leon realized. The security guards had placed him in a chair in the corner of the lab with instructions to not move from the seat.

Why am I still here? He would have expected them to send him to his cell-like room, where he'd been sent to sleep for a few hours each night. The fact that he'd been made to sit in the corner like a child in timeout was certainly meant to be a demeaning punishment.

For Leon, however, it was the opportunity to watch others work without any distractions. He studied each of their movements, looking for any tells that they weren't fully invested in their tasks. Some of them were here willingly, but others were definitely forced participants.

In particular, Carla kept glancing over at him with a worried crease in her brow. She was only playing along for fear of her own wellbeing. Leon was guilty of the same thing, though apparently he had a lower tolerance threshold than her. This wasn't the time for moral judgment; she was his best chance at having a friend to help him get out of here.

Leon was plotting how best to stage a diversion when a heated conversation caught his attention on the other side of the lab.

"People are coming. They say it's the TSS," he overheard someone say.

Leon's heart leaped. *Thank the stars!* He may yet live to see tomorrow.

He considered trying to make another run for it but thought better. More likely, he would be shot or injured trying to break free than actually make it out. If the TSS really was on their way in, they could subdue the opposition without any trouble.

That line of thinking came to an abrupt halt when Edward entered. "Change of plan. What better way to test our new weapon than to eliminate our encroaching enemy?"

Are they seriously going to try to control this 'weapon' to attack only the TSS raid party without hurting us? It was an absolutely absurd notion. The only thing it was going to do is get all of them killed.

The other scientists in the room got to work prepping for another test. In the back chamber, a dark-haired tech was tending to Rachel.

Edward stepped into the room to say something to the tech and then left. The tech's reply was inaudible.

"No, we're doing it now," Edward continued the conversation on the comm. "I don't care what you think! Do it!"

Leon wasn't sure what specific order had been given, but it clearly wasn't good. Rachel was again strapped to the chair in the testing room, still—thankfully—with a distant expression of blissful ignorance about what was being done to her. The lab tech was wringing his hands nervously, his deep brown eyes darting between the woman and Edward through the window in the main lab. "You're not going to hurt her, are you?" he asked over the intercom.

Edward glanced at Rachel. "Whatever happens, happens."

The tech shook his head. "No, this isn't what we—"

Edward slapped the console in front of him. "Do your job or get out! I don't need your sniveling."

The man shrank back at the outburst.

"We will proceed with the linking," Edward ordered. "Prepare the subject."

Leon shifted in his chair, wishing he was anywhere else right now.

Edward sneered at him from across the room, his lips curled with a declaration of smug victory.

The scientists took their stations, and Brandon began barking out orders as the self-declared leader of the group. Results-minded Edward didn't seem to care who took the lead so long as the work was being accomplished on his increasingly aggressive timeline.

Having been in the chair for several hours with a poor view of most workstations, Leon wasn't sure how much had changed in the group's approach to the task since the last test. He remained convinced that there was a fundamental flaw to the theoretical framework itself, so no amount of fine-tuning would change the issue. It was simply impossible to force a bond like this without an adverse reaction—much like an organ couldn't be placed in a foreign body without a tissue match and anti-rejection therapy.

The scientists entered commands on their stations. In the testing room, Rachel began to writhe against her restraints. Once more, her skin took on a strange flush that seemed almost like a glow.

As her tremors increased, a strange buzz of energy filled the room, hurting Leon's inner ears. His head felt fuzzy, as if the neurons in his brain were vibrating in tune with the frequency. The odd sensation distorted his senses.

I shouldn't be able to feel anything with this test. Something is wrong.

The thought was a vague feeling at the back of his mind. He struggled to process the observation.

I need to go.

That thought was clearer. Actionable.

Everyone else in the room seemed to be fighting against the same mental blocks. They stood motionless, as if in a trance.

The buzzing beckoned for Leon to stay still and accept his fate, as well. Except, an impulse deep within him screamed that he needed to get away.

This is your chance. Get back to Kira!

He bolted upright to his feet, almost knocking the chair over in the process. The other people in the room were still frozen in place, their eyes unfocused as the oppressive buzzing intensified.

"Get out of here now!" he shouted. "You'll die if you stay here." Leon ran toward the door, which was no doubt guarded on the outside.

Surprise was his best weapon, coupled with years of sparring with some of the top soldiers in the Guard. Hopefully, it would be enough.

He hit the door release. It was still unlocked since Edward was inside the lab. The guards would no doubt think it was their boss exiting. Leon used that to his advantage.

The moment the door slid aside, Leon reached through and grabbed the first guard's arm, twisting it around to pin the man's face against the wall. He then kicked to his side to strike the other man off-balance. The two seemed to have been entranced by the buzzing, which was still audible outside the lab but wasn't quite as intense the further out he went.

He landed firm blows on the two guards to knock them unconscious; there was no way to know how long they'd be out, but he didn't intend to be there long enough for it to matter.

He took off down the hall. After a moment, he heard quick footfalls behind him.

"Wait!" Carla called out. "I'm coming with you."

Leon's heart lifted.

The lab tech and three of the other scientists soon followed, including Nora. He was disappointed that half of the group remained behind in the lab, but that was their choice.

"Do any of you know the way out?" Leon asked the group.

"No, but we're in an underground facility," Nora said. "We need to go up."

Up. Good, I can work with that. Leon waved them onward. "Come on! Let's find a way out."

— — —

Lexi kept a tight grip on her armrests during the shuttle flight down to Quel's surface. The voyage itself was so smooth that she barely noticed a sensation of movement, but she was anxious about what was to come.

What are we going to find in there? What have they been doing? She couldn't change her past role in helping the Alliance, but she could now help prevent further tragedy.

In his seat on the flight deck, Jason was stoic and focused. He'd trained for these kinds of tense moments for his entire adult life, and she had no doubt he'd be nothing but professional for the duration of the mission.

She was surprised he had agreed to let her accompany the TSS team. Though she had confidence in her own survival abilities, it was no doubt unusual for a civilian to come along. It spoke to his growing trust in her more than any words ever could.

This is a chance to prove I can be a worthy partner. It wasn't so much about proving it to him but proving it to herself. She'd let her Gifts be an afterthought for most of her life, and now it was time to embrace every aspect of her being.

The pilot set the shuttle down a mere fifty meters from the small shack marking the entrance to the underground facility. With its special stealth tech, it would be all but invisible on standard scans. Even so, it was possible the Alliance had still spotted the main transport ship when it dropped out from subspace and moved into orbit; they had to proceed as though the enemy knew they were coming.

"Okay, let's do this," Jason said. "Cody, stay with the shuttle and prepare to get us out of here in a hurry if needed."

"Aye, sir," the young Agent acknowledged from the pilot's seat while Jason and Lexi moved back to the passenger transport area.

The Agents stood attentively, awaiting their commander's go-ahead.

"Andy, you can do the honors." Jason gave a nod to the older Agent.

"My pleasure." Andy motioned for the five other Agents in his team to join him at the rear of the shuttle, ready to make their exit. They would be the lead infiltration team to clear the path for the rest of the unit into the facility.

Lexi sensed the energy around each of the Agents where their protective shields encompassed their bodies. Her own shield seemed a little unsteady by comparison, and she was happy Jason had insisted she wear something more robust than street clothes.

I'm going to need to learn how to do what they do! That might be a bold ambition considering these Agents had been training since they were teenagers, but she made a vow to try.

Andy hit the rear hatch release, and the back wall of the craft folded down to form an exit ramp. He took the lead as the group of Agents made a run for the entry.

The building's door ripped from its hinges in a single, smooth movement. A moment later, the Agents disappeared inside.

Jason got a distant look in his eyes for a moment. "All right, top level is clear. Let's move in."

Lexi fell into step behind him as they jogged through the calf-high grass to the entryway. The sun was getting low in the sky, casting long shadows from the mountain range surrounding the valley. A crisp breeze swirled by, carrying a scent of damp earth and ozone.

Her senses were hyper-alert, looking for any potential threats in the landscape. So far, it seemed clear.

Cries of surprise and rending metal carried from inside the building as the advance team worked its way inside.

Jason led his team in first, followed by Kira and then Lexi.

The Guard soldier had a multi-handgun drawn, set to sonic stun; a toggle allowed it to also fire kinetic rounds. She had showed it to Lexi during the voyage over, and based on her rundown of the features, Lexi got the impression it was her favorite weapon.

I'll stick to my mind, thank you. Lexi telekinetically knocked aside a rock in her path as if to prove a point.

She passed through the open doorway and into the shadow

of the building. The hallway inside was illuminated but seemed dim compared to the afternoon sunlight outdoors.

Four Coalition guards were bound and propped against the wall near the entry door, three with their eyes wide in a mixture of fear and surprise, and the other seething with palpable disgust and rage. The latter was no doubt one of the Gifted-haters that had been so common within the Alliance. Lexi was sure to shoot the woman a nasty glare as she passed by.

The corridor beyond was featureless aside from sconce lighting, just bare concrete walls and a metal support structure at three-meter intervals. The hall was five meters across, which seemed conducive to staging items for transport down the solitary elevator that stood six meters down the corridor, where the building burrowed into the hillside.

Andy and his team were waiting outside the doors.

"I don't like the 'one way in and out' deal," Jason said. "Any signs of a stairwell?"

Andy nodded toward a smooth section of wall next to the elevator entrance. "It feels like there's a void through here, but we haven't spotted a control switch."

Jason turned back to look at the bound guards. "Where is the stairway entrance?" he asked. A hum of energy surrounded him—a subtle telepathic command, nothing too invasive, but enough to encourage a response.

"Baseboard on the right," one of the scared-looking men said.

His angry female companion shot him an accusatory glare.

Andy kicked at the baseboard in the indicated location. After a couple of tries in different spots, a section of the baseboard depressed and the wall next to it popped open.

With a nod from Jason, Andy and his five Agents slipped

through the opening and began descending the poured concrete staircase.

Two of the Agents from the third team following Jason's group inside broke off to stand watch at the entry. The remaining Agents fell in behind Lexi as they entered the stairwell.

Musty air assaulted Lexi's nose the moment she passed through the hidden door. This was obviously not a well-used mode of access, and the facility clearly wasn't new construction. Perhaps the Coalition had repurposed an old outpost from the planet's early colonization history.

She wound her way down the switch-backing stairs for four stories, halting when she noticed the Agents up ahead had stopped to examine a side door—the first they had encountered in the stairwell. The steps continued downward for another two stories.

A light buzz of energy in the air indicated a heated telepathic conversation was underway between several of the Agents.

Jason closed his eyes. A hum of energy swelled around him, unlike anything she had experienced before. There was an intensity to just being in his presence under normal circumstances, but to actually feel him tapping into his power was incredible. She sensed him extending his consciousness throughout the facility, looking for other people and potential threats. While most trained Gifted could perform such a search on a limited scope, she had never witnessed anyone able to expand their senses in the way Jason was doing. There wasn't a hint of straining; this was routine and easy for him, making it that much more impressive.

He returned to himself and opened his eyes. "Three levels, guards on all. Most activity on One, and there's something I can't identify on Three. There aren't many people here."

"This must just be a small research site," Kira assessed. "Everyone else from offices on Duronis and the other planets must have gone elsewhere."

Lexi got the impression he had said that only for the benefit of Kira, because another telepathic conversation ensued. The medium was so much faster, it was inefficient not to. Lexi was a little disappointed that he hadn't included her in the telepathic network, but these people knew how to work with each other and understood tactics she'd never been in a position to learn. Grateful to even be here, she left them to the planning.

They must have reached a decision because eight of the Agents continued down the stairwell; two stopped at the next landing and the remaining six continued to the bottom. When they were in position, all three doors suddenly ripped from the wall and were tossed aside out of the way.

The Agents all rushed in. Sounds of struggle were quickly silenced.

Lexi's heart pounded in her chest. *This is getting intense!*

She followed Jason and Andy's team through the first door. Unlike the ground entry level, this interior branched out in three directions—straight ahead and to either side. The Agents split up to cover the different areas.

Lexi followed Jason and one other Agent at a distance along the left branch.

The Agents halted a short way down the hall, just shy of an intersection. Several Coalition guards flew from around the corner in front of them, flailing. For a moment, Lexi thought that they had been thrown or jumped, but then she sensed they were under telekinetic holds; the two Agents had sensed their presence and taken proactive action.

While the Agents began securing restraints on the guards, another man suddenly jumped out and took aim with a pulse handgun.

Lexi instinctively gripped the assailant in a telekinetic vise. By the time Jason had looked up, she had already levitated the man in the air, high enough that his toes couldn't brush the ground.

Jason looked at his Agent companion. "I told you there was another person."

The other man shrugged. "There wasn't anything going on in his head. They were standing so close together, I thought it was just one really big guy."

Lexi gently twisted her captive's arms behind his back, using just enough force to exert authority without the risk of hurting him.

Jason raised his eyebrows. "Nicely done."

Lexi beamed. "Told you I could handle myself." She applied a tie from the pouch on her tactical belt and secured him to a fastener on the wall.

"I never had any doubts."

"Jason, over here!" Kira shouted from down the main hall that had been straight ahead from the level's access point.

They ran back to her, leaving the other Agent to tend to the Coalition guards.

Two Agents were telekinetically holding a dozen more armed guards, and Kira stood next to a doorway on the left.

She motioned into a room. "I think we've got captives."

Lexi and Jason jogged over to take a closer look. Inside the room, five people were confined in holding cells; a sixth cell was empty. The men and women were standing at the front barriers of the enclosures, hands pressed against the transparent walls. Their mouths were open in shouts of distress, though no sound was audible through the barriers.

Lexi gleaned the surface of their minds. They were all Gifted, and it appeared they had been subjected to all sorts of tests. Whatever the Coalition was working on, these were the subjects of their experimentation.

Melisa? She searched their faces, but none of them were her missing friend. Either she was already dead, or there were possibly other facilities like this.

Jason entered the holding room and was working with another Agent to locate the controls.

The captives sobbed with relief as the doors opened.

"Thank the stars!" one cried out, stumbling forward.

"We'll get you to safety," Jason said. "Who are you? How did you get here?"

A man from the middle cell was the first to answer, "I was picked up on Veraria. I think I've been here for a week, maybe two."

"What have they done to you?" Kira asked.

"Tests. Hooked us up to equipment, scanned us, took blood and cheek swabs." He took a shaky breath. "I don't know what they were planning, but they weren't treating us like people. We were *things*."

"What about that empty cell?" Jason nodded toward the unoccupied chamber. "Is there anyone else?"

"She's been gone for the last day," an older blonde woman who'd been in the adjacent cell replied.

Lexi's stomach turned over. *Holding people captive? Experimentations?* Whatever was going on here was a new level of horrible. Coupled with the rumors of a new bioweapon, she didn't imagine the Coalition expected any of these 'test subjects' to make it out of the facility alive.

"Delia, why don't you escort these people up to the

surface," Jason said. "I just got word from B Squad. Something strange is happening on the bottom level, and it's spreading."

CHAPTER 24

YOU'RE ALMOST FREE. Just a little further. Leon repeated the mantra in his head to stay in the moment. The oppressive buzz in the air was closing in around him.

He had no idea what might be happening back inside the lab, but it obviously wasn't going according to plan. Nothing in the scientific models had indicated that anyone other than the test subject would experience physical sensations related to the transdimensional bridge being opened through Rachel. It should have been a quick process.

No, something else was going on here, and he didn't want to be anywhere close by. Based on the previous test's energy escalation rate, this current test was now past the point of no return. No shutting down, no turning back. Evacuating the facility was the only move.

Leon ran through the maze-like halls of the facility with the four other scientists and lab tech who'd had the good sense to get out. They'd already taken several wrong turns and needed to backtrack.

When he rounded the corner into a new hallway, his heart

jumped. Approaching ten meters up ahead were a man and a woman dressed all in black, the A-line cut of their overcoats unmistakably TSS.

A yelp of joy lodged in his throat. He took a ragged breath and ran forward at a quicker pace.

The woman's glowing hazel eyes held a spark of recognition. "Leon Caletti?"

He nodded emphatically. "Yes. These other scientists were taken to work for the Coalition, too. I don't know them, but they want out."

He didn't feel comfortable vouching for the people since they had continued to help with the project even after they knew the horrible intentions for the research. The TSS could sort out the morality of it and levy charges as they deemed appropriate once their investigation was complete. For now, all that mattered was getting everyone as far away from this place as possible.

"You're safe now," the male Agent stated.

"No, we're not," Leon waved his arm behind him to indicate the location of the lab. "There's another experiment underway right now. I think it's going to blow this whole place up, and it's already too late to stop it."

"Is that what this energy field is?"

"Yes. They're trying to open a transdimensional bridge through a person."

The Agents exchanged concerned glances.

"Is there anyone else down here?" the male Agent asked.

"The people who caused this mess in the first place. Everyone who wanted to get out is here." His cheeks flushed. *Whatever happens to everyone else is on them. They deserve it after what they've done.*

There were a few seconds of silence, and both Agents got a

distant look in their eyes—likely a telepathic exchange, from Leon's experience of the tells.

"Everyone this way," the woman said the moment her focus returned. She set a quick pace down the hall in the opposite direction of the lab.

After three turns along corridors, they reached a stairwell, where they encountered four other Agents coming from different directions. The group entered the stairwell and raced upward two stories. At the landing, Leon spotted the one person he'd hoped to see more than anyone else in the universe.

"Kira!"

Her face brightened at the sight of him, and she ran forward and embraced him.

"Stars, I've missed you." He held her close—not the most comfortable hug, given her body armor.

When they parted, she gazed into his eyes. "I knew you would be okay."

"Yeah, well, none of us will be for long if we stay here."

"What do you mean?"

Leon recognized the man who'd spoken as Jason Sietinen; he was surprised to see him personally on a field op like this. Then he noticed Lexi standing behind Jason.

"Lexi! How did—" He cut off, realizing the details weren't important right now. He refocused. "Listen, the crazy people in charge of this facility are doing another 'test' right now. The tech isn't remotely stable. I think this entire facility is going to go up."

"Then we need to stop it," Jason said.

"You can't," Leon explained. "I've seen the models. At this stage, there's no diffusing it. Once the energy is released, the transdimensional bridge will collapse because its tether to spacetime will be destroyed." He didn't want to spell out that the anchor was a person.

"How big of a blast are we talking?" Jason asked.

"I have no clue! But you guys can make telekinetic shields, right?"

Jason looked to his fellow Agents and they nodded. "All right, we'll isolate this facility from the outside."

"Now come on! I don't know how much time we have." Leon grabbed Kira by the hand and urged her to run.

It was no doubt a difficult decision for the Agents to withdraw rather than diffuse the situation. However, Leon knew it was the right call. Rachel was already dead, no matter what. At least this way, the entire rescue party didn't need to die.

Leon kept the information to himself about the captive in the test chamber. He didn't know Jason well, but he suspected that the Agent would have run into the lab in an attempt to save her, regardless of the dangerous realities of the situation. Everyone who could be saved was already out. Those left in the lab had made their choice to see this horrendous 'test' through to its completion—and it would be their end.

— — —

Jason raced with the group up the stairs toward the planet's surface. He recognized that Leon was holding back information about what was really happening on the lower level. However, he also trusted the man when he said that they needed to get out now.

Jason checked through the telepathic link with the other TSS Agents that everyone knew they were evacuating. They hadn't searched the entire facility, but he'd performed a remote sweep using his abilities and didn't detect other people beyond those on the lower level where Leon had come from and those they had already freed; the captured guards had already been escorted out. While not an ideal situation by any means, he couldn't risk harm to the rescue team. They would look for other survivors after the explosion. The important thing now was to get in position to get a shield around the facility to prevent damage to the nearby city.

At the top of the stairs, the group ran down the entry corridor heading outside. The bound guards had been secured in the shuttle already. Likewise, the captives liberated from their cells were safely strapped into passenger seats.

"Get on board!" Jason instructed. He hung back at the entry door to make sure everyone was out of the facility before him.

Lexi lingered.

"Go!" he urged her.

"You're not going back in, are you?"

He had considered it. There *were* still people here, enemy or not, and he didn't feel right about leaving anyone in harm's way. The Agent code of conduct demanded a respect for all life. Besides, the leadership of this facility might be valuable to interrogate about the Coalition's other activities.

Leon was halfway to the shuttle with Kira. He glanced back over his shoulder and stopped when he noticed Jason wasn't following them. "What are you waiting for? Come on!"

"I don't want to leave anyone behind," Jason replied.

"Jason..." Lexi urged.

"This isn't a bomb with a set timer," Leon said. He came back toward the building entrance and dropped his voice to just above a whisper. "They've turned a person into a higher-dimensional conduit. All of that energy is going to explode when the vessel can't hold it any longer. That could happen in any moment."

"The 'vessel' is a person," Jason realized. "The missing test subject."

Leon's grim expression said it all.

"I have to go help—"

Leon gripped his arm. "She was dead a long time ago, even if the body doesn't know it yet. There's nothing you can do. But we have to get out of here if we don't want to get caught up in the blast."

"What is it going to do?"

"I don't know, but it won't be good."

The top responsibility is to those who can be saved. He hated this part of the job—making calls about life and death. It was an unavoidable aspect of command, but it never got any easier.

Jason looked between Leon and the door back into the facility. "Let's get everyone to safety."

They all made a run for the shuttle. Steps away from the back hatch, a discordant hum filled the air, emanating from the underground facility. It continued to intensify.

"Oh no! We're out of time." Panic filled Leon's eyes and tone.

"Strap in," Jason told them as they ran ahead. He was the last into the shuttle. He slapped the hatch controls on the way inside. "Cody, take us up! Hold at a two-kilometer elevation."

The placement was a bit of a guess, but he figured that would be a high enough vantage from which to project a telekinetic shield without being so far up that he couldn't be precise in his movements.

"I'd offer to help, but I have a feeling I'd just hold you back," Andy said in Jason's mind.

He smiled at the other Agent from across the passenger

area. *"I've got it. But I appreciate the offer."*

Jason summoned his power and visualized a bubble forming around the facility below, isolating it from the rest of the planet. He fed energy into it, making its walls as robust and impenetrable as he could. He hadn't drawn this much power for a long time—not since his last use of the *Conquest's* telekinetic energy weapon.

His senses were heightened in that state of draw, making him aware of the other Agents assessing his shield with their own enhanced senses. They were impressed and confident; whatever was about to transpire on the surface, it would be contained.

He held the shield, waiting. Leon had made it sound like everything was about to—

The force of the blast caught Jason by surprise. He held the shield in place without faltering.

Except, the decimation ripped right through the shield as if it wasn't there.

Jason gaped at it in disbelief. *How did…?*

He tried to sense what was going on with the explosive blast and why it had so easily bypassed the shield. Any physical matter and kinetic force should have easily been absorbed.

But that's not what we're dealing with… he realized with horror.

The blast had disintegrated all of the organic matter in its path. The grass was replaced with bare dirt, the former trees were only evidenced by a hole in the ground where their root systems had been, and there was no way to tell from orbit how deep the damage had gone. The ground was almost certainly unstable, as a result. And the radius of destruction was continuing to widen.

"I don't know how to stop it," he whispered, as much to

himself as anyone on board.

The other Agents watched the grim reality of the situation unfold, unable to offer any suggestions. No one had expected this. If Jason couldn't contain it, then *no one* could.

The radius of destruction was still spreading outward, turning the organic matter momentarily to gray ash as it broke down before it dissolved completely. With nothing to control its destructive force, any organic compounds in building materials and other manufactured items would likely be destroyed, as well.

"Take us up!" Jason ordered. *Stars, no! Why is this happening?*

The pilot directed the shuttle upward, quickly and steeply enough that it took a moment for the stabilizers to adjust to the new trajectory, causing a brief jolt and sensation of his stomach dropping.

He stumbled to the nearest empty seat and strapped in. The viewport next to him offered a partial view of the devastation growing outward from the facility, expanding at a rapid rate toward the city.

Please, stop. Not the colony...

The wave hadn't slowed down in the least. Jason had to look away as it reached the edge of the civilization. It would be over in a matter of seconds.

He choked back a shaky breath, knowing he needed to be the strong leader for his team. Nothing needed to be spelled out. They all knew they were witnessing the total destruction of a world. Its population wasn't large, but they were all innocents.

"I don't understand," Leon murmured. "The bridge shouldn't have been sustained for long enough to reach this far. It should have been a zone of a few hundred meters, tops. I don't…"

The young man seemed on the verge of tears. Kira kept her lips pressed into a thin line, but Jason saw the confusion and pain in her eyes. They came from a small, remote world not unlike this one, and the loss no doubt hit close to home.

Lexi had unmitigated disgust painted on her features. She'd been rallied against the Alliance—and its Coalition parent organization—for over a year, consistently disappointed by their selfish disregard for life. She had shared her feelings with Jason during their bedtime chats, and he'd gotten the impression that she had felt they were at a turning point where the Coalition was going to begin losing. No more death and destruction.

All of that had gone to shite. This wasn't a victory for either side—just senseless loss of life.

No one said anything else for the remainder of the shuttle ride back to the transport ship. When they docked, the other Agents filed off into the main ship in silence.

"I need to see," Jason said soberly.

Leon nodded. "Me too."

Kira and Lexi wordlessly nodded their agreement.

The four of them headed to the flight deck, where the Militia officer pilot was observing the planet on the holodisplay.

She met Jason's gaze when he entered. The slow shake of her head said everything.

The planet was now nothing but a baren wasteland, reduced to its base geological features. No life remained.

"No…" Leon gasped. "They were trying to make a targeted disease…. How did it take out everything? It shouldn't have spread like that. How did it encompass the whole planet?"

Kira wrapped an arm around him, offering what little

comfort she could through the physical contact.

Jason's chest was tight and his throat hurt to swallow as he held back his anguish. *Is there anything I could have done if I'd gone back inside?*

He'd been certain a shield could hold back any kind of decimation. He'd trusted his abilities. He was wrong, and now all those colonists were dead. The innocents who'd called in the TSS to help in the first place.

We made this worse for them. Would the Coalition have rushed their test if we hadn't come here today? He'd never know what might have been different, but he felt the blame of it as if it was entirely his fault.

Lexi placed her hand on his back and gazed up at him. "No one could have known what this weapon would do."

"We should have evacuated everyone before moving in," he murmured.

"And blow our approach?" Kira said. "No, this is just one of those shite situations where things go bad and there's not a bomaxed thing we could have done to change it."

Jason knew all too well about those. He'd lectured about it to his students, and he'd lived it for himself with what happened at Alkeer. Hindsight gave clarity, but it didn't change the facts. Decisions made on incomplete data weren't bad in the moment, and he wasn't to blame.

"If we hadn't evacuated when we did, we would have been caught up in that blast, too," Kira pointed out. "This isn't on you, Jason."

Then why do I feel so responsible? Nothing they could say would make him feel better anytime soon. He needed to talk about the incident with his father; if anyone could give an honest perspective, it was him.

"Make a record of all the scan data from the incident,"

Jason instructed the pilot. "This information is now classified until further notice."

"Yes, sir," she acknowledged.

Jason had seen enough. "Plot a course back to TSS Headquarters and jump as soon as the scan data is sent to Command." He left the flight deck.

Lexi, Kira, and Leon followed him out. He wasn't sure where to go, so he stopped in the corridor and closed the flight deck's door.

"I still don't entirely know what we saw," he said. "It looked like all the organic matter was un-made, like what happened on Alkeer. If this is the same thing, the Coalition is messing with the energy that is literally the foundation of everything. No one person with our corporeal limitations can control it. What we do as Gifted is only scratching the surface of what's possible with that higher dimensional power."

Leon shook his head. "Those scientists thought they were invincible."

"I saw it with the others on Duronis," Lexi murmured. "They believed they were above natural law—that it would bend to their wills."

"Another planet destroyed because of hubris." Kira scoffed with disgust.

Jason's stomach turned over as guilt welled in his chest. He kept replaying Alkeer's destruction, when Tiff's presence had been ripped away.

Lexi took his hand, sensing his struggle. *"Hey, I've got you."*

Her physical touch and the presence of her in his mind kept his thoughts from spiraling further. *"I'm glad you're here, Lexi."*

"You did everything right."

"Sometimes, that's not enough." He swallowed the lump in

his throat. "What happened here today isn't something we want getting out onto the public news streams. If people knew that there was a weapon capable of destroying life on a planet in this way, and that it's in the hands of a terrorist group, there'd be mass panic that could tear apart the Empire."

"The information may have been destroyed with them," Kira said.

Leon shook his head. "I don't think so. They were reporting to someone offworld. I'm sure there are data backups."

"We must proceed with the assumption that this could happen again," Jason said. "We still don't know who is behind this or what their end goals are."

They all nodded somberly.

"Where does that leave us?" Kira asked.

"We don't speak of it. We file our reports and the truth gets locked away at the highest clearance levels."

She nodded her understanding. "I'm all for never speaking of it again."

"What about the locals?" Lexi asked. "There were people on the orbital station."

"The TSS will talk with them and see what aid we can offer, though nothing will make up for this loss."

"I'm so sorry, Jason," Leon said. "I really had no idea…"

"I know. None of us did." Jason took a steadying breath. "I've gotta say, this first command hasn't gotten off to a great start."

"On the plus side, it can only get better from here." Kira gave a surprisingly lighthearted shrug.

Jason was amazed by her ability to take things in stride. He'd admired that about her since their first meeting, and the more time they spent together, the more he saw her resilience in action. It was a necessity in this line of work. Loss—horrible loss, sometimes—was a fact of the job. It would either get a person down or they would find a way to let it fuel them to be stronger.

"I guess I would have set an unreasonably high bar if I'd solved all of our problems right from the get-go," Jason jested back. The attempted levity pained him in the moment, but he knew it was best to keep things in perspective; he had a long fight ahead of him, and he couldn't give up now.

Kira took Leon by his arm. "Well, we've got a few hours before we reach TSS Headquarters, so please excuse us while we unwind after this shiteshow of a day."

"Thanks again for getting me out of there," Leon called over his shoulder.

"And, Jason, don't forget you owe us a fancy date night!" Kira said as she led Leon into one of the guest cabins.

"I remember."

The cabin door slid closed.

Lexi turned to Jason when they were alone in the corridor. "This is what I dealt with every day in the Alliance. Those two can't keep their hands off each other."

"How can they even think about that at a time like this? A planet was just destroyed."

"People deal with stress in different ways. In a way, I can understand just wanting to be close to someone you care about, to remember you're alive."

"Yeah, I guess there is that."

She wrapped her arms around him. "There's no one else I'd rather be with right now."

"Me either." He savored her presence. "We're going to track down the people who did this and bring them to justice, Lexi."

"I know we will. And we'll do it together."

— — —

How did this happen? Wil took in the devastation on the video feed from Quel. His son was safe. Leon was rescued. The loss could have been worse, but it was still horrific.

He'd received word from Jason's ship that they were on their way back to Headquarters. They had been successful, but this was far from a victory.

Saera entered his office. "I just heard." She closed the door behind her.

"I doubt they made this weapon on their own. A transdimensional bridge that can break apart matter?"

She nodded. "It has the Erebus written all over it."

"How did they get involved with the Coalition?"

"No idea, but this explains why we haven't heard from them much since calling a truce."

It's not a truce if they're working with a rogue faction to design planet-killing weapons. Wil had no doubt that Quel was just the beginning if this was the new scheme. *What are the Erebus planning? What do they intend to gain?*

"On a more optimistic front, the new power core production started today, right?"

New planetary shields won't do any good if a weapon like this is released from within. Wil nodded. "Yes, I suppose that is a bit of good news."

Saera sighed. "I hate this feeling, too, Wil—constantly playing catchup. Of not feeling in control."

"This enemy doesn't think like us. They don't move like us. I don't know how to get ahead."

"You've solved the unsolvable before. I believe in you."

But how many people will die while I figure it out? Wil knew it wasn't all on him, yet he was the TSS High Commander. A war hero. The designer of the revolutionary jump drive. Everyone was looking at him for answers again, whether he liked it or not. "Thank you. I could never do this without you."

She smiled playfully. "I know."

He had to crack a slight smile at that. No matter how grim the situation, she always knew what to say to keep his thoughts from going too dark. "We'll prioritize getting the new shields in place. If the Erebus *are* working with the Coalition, a large-scale assault is no doubt coming."

"Agreed." Saera sat on the edge of his desk. "I wish we had a way to definitively test the shields without... well, a direct Erebus attack."

"It's the unfortunate nature of our position. We can create theoretical models and explore the elements of the universe through our own perception, but nothing within the scope of our existence can compare to how the Erebus experience their reality. I don't know if any of our predictions about their abilities will hold up."

"Well, we know that the *aesen* can be directed away from them," Saera said. "The Erebus wouldn't be hurt by the Gates if they had full control over the energy flow; they wouldn't allow their own essence to be taken if that were the case. So, they do have limitations to their control. We have that going for us."

Wil considered the thought. It was true; Tarans might have a chance to take advantage of that limitation. He thought through the possibilities. "The only thing I feel fully confident in right now is that the *Conquest* and the ships like it can hurt the Erebus if used in proximity to their being. However, there have been too many assumptions made in the models about these new planetary shields for me to be confident that it will be an impenetrable barrier."

"At this point. I think it's reasonable to think in terms of 'slowing down' rather than stopping completely. Even putting up a fence is better than an unmarked property line."

"Fair. And I do believe that the augmented shields will give us that much, at a minimum."

Saera drummed her fingers on his desktop. "It still doesn't make sense to me why the Erebus gave us this tech. They had to have predicted that we would use it to power our own defenses. Do they not care?"

Wil shook his head. "More than anything, I wish I knew the catch. But I've been over every millimeter of the design and completed every conceivable test, and I can't find any evidence of the device having a hidden trap."

Saera bit her lip.

"What?" he asked, recognizing the look she got when she'd made a worrying realization.

"We tested the individual units. But what testing have we done related to a *group* of the power cores?"

"Several, at planetary scale. Everything checks out."

"And bigger than that?"

Wil's heart skipped a beat. "You mean interstellar?"

"Yeah."

"No, I don't believe anyone has run those models. With everything looking stable at smaller scale, it didn't seem important."

She crossed her arms. "What if that's the point?"

"Stars, if that's…" Wil faded out as he jumped on his desktop to begin drafting the models for a galactic-scale assessment of the energy fields once all the cores were active.

The results of the analysis confirmed their fears:

collectively, there was a unique energy field created when all of the power cores were active.

"This is why the Aesir warned us about having too many close together. What they meant about looking at the big picture," Wil realized. "I was wrong. Not a little error, but I fundamentally missed the mark with this whole thing."

"Wil, don't—"

"No, Saera, I foked this one up in the worst way. We're backed into a corner. If we halt installation of these upgrades, then we have no defense at all. I don't know what this energy field might do, but I bet you it's not an accident. Why do the Erebus want this?"

Saera looked over the data, unable to refute that they were at a crossroads of two horrible options.

Wil shook his head. "We're trapped, and it's my fault."

"The rest of us signed off on this move."

The worry and anger welled in his chest. "I should have seen this coming. It's my job to see what others don't, and I helped make all of this happen."

"We were in an impossible situation and acted in the best way we could with the information available. We can proceed with the installation. There's the kill switch if things take a bad turn."

"That will shut off the planetary shields in their entirety. Do we abort the installation and stick with the tried and true that will do *nothing* against the Erebus, or do we take the risk with this new design on the off-chance that it *might* give us an edge more than it does them?"

"Going into this, we knew there was a calculated risk." Saera looked a little queasy despite her assurances.

"We could have accepted the core and let it sit in a warehouse. I pushed for disseminating it to all of the Taran worlds, made all those announcements, figured out how to integrate these other systems with it. I turned it into a showpiece, and it's the heart of a trap."

Saera gripped his shoulder. "How we got here doesn't matter. We need solutions."

"After missing this, I don't trust myself."

"Well, you need to get over that, because we need you."

He looked down, unable to meet her gaze.

"Hey, *I* trust you." She cupped the side of his face. "We have to focus and get through this."

Wil swallowed. "You're right." He took a deep breath. "We're already too invested in the upgrade process to turn back now. We'll need to take our chances."

"I agree. We'll look into this other energy field and see if we can figure out what it might do. Perhaps there's a way to mitigate the effects."

Solutions, yes. Wil refocused his mind. This wasn't the end, just another roadblock. There was always a path forward—he just needed to find it.

CHAPTER 25

HAVING KIRA IN his arms again was the greatest gift Leon could imagine.

"I really thought I was done for back there," he whispered into her hair.

"Nah, you'd never go down that easily. You're way too stubborn." She ran her fingers along the base of his neck and kissed him.

He lost himself in her for a moment, happily forgetting where they were and what he had just been through. The last week had been a nightmare, and just when he'd thought he was waking up, it had taken an even worse twist.

I told Jason not to worry. He would have evacuated the city or done something else to keep those people safe. Everyone died because I wanted to get away and never look back.

The guilt and doubts had been weighing on him since the moment the blast had first ripped through Jason's telekinetic shield without meeting any resistance. That moment had revealed that Leon hadn't had a clue about what they were really dealing with. No one had, apparently.

The SPEAR Tec researchers within the Coalition had been trying to make a targeted bioweapon, but instead they manufactured a mass planet-killer. He suspected that the leadership would try again, using what they had learned from the mistakes of this and the previous incident.

If they do make another attempt and succeed, what would that weapon be able to do? He didn't have answers.

The scientist in him yearned for an explanation, but his traumatized psyche wanted to stay far away from the Coalition and its profane science. He wasn't yet sure which side of him would win out in the end. For now, he did his best to focus on Kira and remember everything that was worth living and fighting for.

"What are we going to do now?" Kira murmured into his chest.

"Go back to TSS Headquarters for a long debrief, I expect."

"No, I mean after that. After all this time away, it feels weird to think about going back to the Guard base and taking whatever assignment might get thrown my way."

"I miss my lab at Orion Station a little," Leon admitted. He had a good team back at the base, and they'd been through enough challenging projects that they'd gelled, bonded by mutual respect. That could be tough to find.

Kira frowned. "It hasn't been the same for me since my promotion. I dunno. Maybe it'll all feel comfortable and normal once we get back there."

Leon kissed the top of her head. "You know I'll go anywhere with you. I want you to be happy."

"I don't want you to sacrifice your career for me. There've been enough upsets."

"My work is transferable and replaceable. You are not."

She squeezed him. "I really don't know what I did to

deserve you."

"I think I got rather lucky myself." He pivoted to look into her hazel eyes. "I love you more than anything, Kira. If you want a change of scenery, I'm all for it."

"Thinking I'd lost you… it made me realize that what's most important to me now is the people I'm with. Since my team was broken up, I haven't had my Guard family. I don't know if I'll find that again."

"Yeah, you will. In the meantime, you'll have to settle for me."

She scrunched up her nose. "I *guess* that will have to do."

"Do you have anything else in mind?"

"I dunno. We'll see how it goes. I wouldn't mind working with the TSS more; it's been nice being around other telepaths who understand what it's like to be inside someone's head."

"They have all the resources the Guard has to offer, and more."

"Oh, stars, and the food! Especially after the Alliance slop… Shite, you're not going to believe the menu in the Mess."

He smiled. "You make a compelling sales pitch."

"But they might not be interested in *me*, so don't get your hopes up. I don't really know what I'd do, to be honest."

"Concerns for another time," Leon said. He kissed her. "Right now, being back with you is the only thing that matters."

— — —

Raena closed her eyes and turned away from the screen. *So much loss. When will it end?*

When she opened her eyes again, she noticed Ryan was still taking in the scene on the viewscreen next to his desk.

"We swore to protect our people, but what have we done

to keep them safe?" Ryan shook his head and slumped in his office chair. "More civilians caught in the crossfire of greed and corruption."

"No one expected a betrayal like this—for them to work with an internal enemy." She sat down on the edge of Ryan's desk next to him.

"What happened to pretending the Erebus are our friends?"

Raena had never genuinely felt that way, and Ryan knew it. "We don't know for sure that the Coalition is working with the Erebus."

"But it certainly seems that way, doesn't it? Nothing else explains that weapon on Quel. It's unlike anything of Taran design."

Raena was reluctant to admit that there might be a rogue faction within the Empire in possession of dangerous alien tech. *Our greatest threat might come from within. How do we know who we can trust?*

Ryan took her hand. "I know. I don't want to think about it either, but denial won't help us resolve this issue."

She nodded. "We need to find a way to unite our people. We can't let these actions continue to divide us."

"Agreed. Right now, this isn't a society I'd be proud to hand over to future generations."

"We need to change that, but I don't know how."

"No more secrets," Ryan said, squeezing her hand. "We need to finalize security and start bringing guests here as soon as possible and show that we aren't the self-absorbed elitists everyone expects us to be."

"I wish we could share the new revelations about Earth, but we need to keep that part quiet for now," Raena said.

"How much longer do you think the investigation will

take?"

"Weeks. Months. I'm not sure yet. We're sending more people next week to assist with the excavations. There's a lot left to uncover."

He nodded. "I hope it goes well. We might need that secret weapon soon—if that's indeed what's buried down there."

"A weapon could either bring Tarans together or turn this social divide into a chasm that will be impossible to bridge."

He gazed into her eyes. "I won't let that happen. Whatever it takes, we'll find a way for all of our people to move forward together. I want a legacy our future children will be proud to inherit."

"There are always going to be people who won't want to get along with others," Raena said.

"And we'll take those in stride. The important thing is that we show up for the people who need us the most."

She nodded. "Let's get to planning."

—   —   —

Jason went to meet with his father immediately upon his return to Headquarters. When he entered the High Commander's office and saw that it was just the two of them, he wasn't sure what it meant.

"Dad, I—" he started as soon as the door was closed.

"Have a seat, Jason." Wil's neutral tone didn't give away if this was a reprimand or something else.

Jason sat in silence, waiting for his father to continue.

"I've been over the scans and all the footage. There was absolutely no indication of a planetary-scale threat, or even of a regional concern. Your precautions at the facility were reasonable and proportional."

He only nodded in response.

"I know that doesn't make it any easier. And I also know how reactions to other events can get projected. The similarity isn't lost on anyone. The frightening thing is that the Erebus and the Coalition might be working together."

Jason had tried to avoid drawing parallels between Quel and Alkeer, but it was inevitable. Life in both places had been un-made in moments, without any warning that such destruction was even possible. Only, the incident on Quel was worse—an accident resulting from willful ignorance as people had tried to wield powers beyond the scope of their understanding.

None of us knew this experimental technology could be just as destructive as the Erebus. He'd already tried to reassure himself more than once, but the guilt kept sneaking back.

"It appears our enemy has decided to be friendly to our face while plotting against us with those who should be our allies. We're being played from two sides."

"What do we do about it?"

Wil shook his head. "We continue making preparations to protect ourselves as best we can, but we must be even more vigilant."

"The Coalition might be working with the Erebus! 'Be vigilant'? We need to *do something*!"

"What more can we do right now? We're still waiting for a clear lead to point us to the organization's leadership. We will interrogate the guards you brought back from Quel, though, they are likely so low-level that they won't know anything of substance. It's a slow process because those we're pursuing know how to cover their tracks extremely well."

"You'd think alien collaborators would stand out."

"They specialize in deception," Wil pointed out. "Though

we have extraordinary abilities, the galaxy is immense. There are many places to hide within the confines of the Empire and beyond."

To hide, and to grow stronger. The more time that passed, the greater the potential threat. Jason could see in his father's eyes that he was thinking the same thing.

"We're in uncharted territory, Jason," his father said. "I had once thought the Erebus might be some kind of cosmic overseers. But no, they're just powerful beings, as fallible as any other."

"The suspicion that they're teaming up with Taran terrorists doesn't bode well."

Wil shook his head. "It doesn't. Unfortunately, we have no way to know if the Erebus all feel the same way—if they're some kind of collective consciousness or individuals. Some may mean well, and others may be selfish, while others may seek vengeance."

Jason didn't have much hope that any Erebus would come to Tarans' aid, now or in the future.

"As it stands," Wil continued, "the Erebus have levied judgment on our race because of actions taken by our long-gone ancestors. We Tarans don't punish the friends and family of a criminal, and I hold others to that same standard. So, until the Erebus are willing to acknowledge that Tarans are autonomous people and each person must be weighed by their own merits and actions, they will remain a threat. Nothing about them is inherently worthy of our reverence. We must put our own people first and foremost."

"And any Taran who acts in the interest of the Erebus over their own people is on their own, as far as I'm concerned," Jason said.

Wil inclined his head. "I hope it doesn't come to that kind

of choice."

"I fear it already has." What Leon had told Jason about the activities on Quel suggested that the people involved were acting against their fellow Tarans. Perhaps they were obeying an Erebus master.

"In any case, we have a long road ahead of us," Wil said. "I'll be counting on you to help see us through what's to come."

"I'm ready," Jason said. *I hope I'll have Lexi's support. I'd rather not face this on my own.*

"Thank you. Your mom and I have been working on some ideas for restructuring the TSS to be more agile. Stay tuned for updates."

"Okay."

His father looked him over. "I know this last year was difficult, but I doubt it's going to let up any time soon. It can be good to know who you can lean on when things get really bad. Cultivate those relationships while you have the chance."

Is he talking about Lexi? Jason tested the waters. "Rushing in too quickly can be a mistake."

"Some things you know right away. Waiting only delays the inevitable."

Well, that seemed definitive enough. He nodded. "You're not worried about how others might react?"

"I don't want to influence your personal decisions one way or another. I just want you to know that you have my full support in all respects no matter what you decide."

"Thanks, Dad." He hadn't expected an explicit blessing regarding his relationship with Lexi, but it was nice to know there wasn't any concern there. *There's no reason to hold back any longer.*

They said their goodbyes and agreed to meet up soon to strategize further about how to approach the next phase of the

Coalition investigation. For now, Jason needed time to decompress after the difficult day. He returned to his quarters, feeling slightly better about what had transpired.

As the door slid open, his heart lifted at the sight of Lexi on the couch. *I've missed coming home to someone.*

Jason smiled at her as he stepped inside. "Well, the meeting went better than I expected." He kicked off his shoes. "In some ways, it might have felt better to be yelled at for doing something wrong. To instead be told that sometimes shite just goes sideways and you've gotta move on doesn't lend itself to catharsis."

"Yeah." Lexi was lacking her usual vibrance. She sniffed and crossed her arms.

"Hey, what's wrong?"

Lexi shook her head. "Sorry, I've been thinking about Melisa. I let myself get my hopes up that maybe she'd be in that place. But I need to accept the possibility that she might be dead."

Jason sat down next to her. "Does it feel that way, in your gut?"

"No, and that's what makes it so difficult. For whatever reason, I feel like she's still alive."

"Then I wouldn't give up hope."

"Something's not right, though." She scrunched up her face. "I sense she's somewhere, but… distant, somehow. I can't explain it."

"Well, I don't pretend to understand how we experience connections with others, but I can tell you that it's real. So, if your instincts tell you she's alive, don't give up on her."

"It's been so long. Why has she gone this long without reaching out to me if she's okay?"

"These people know how to control others. They tried to

cut you off, too."

She swallowed. "They did. And it was easy for me to let them because I was used to being alone." She met his gaze. "I don't want to be like that anymore."

"Good, because I've been thinking about how I want to grow closer to you." He traced his fingertips along her hand. "In every way."

She shifted closer to him. "Aren't you concerned about bonding?"

"After today, I know this is right."

She placed a hand on his chest. "No more holding back?"

"I'm all-in if you are."

Lexi pulled him into a passionate kiss.

Her warm hands were under his shirt by the time they reached the bed, helping him strip it off. She took off her own before lying down, pulling him with her.

He was drawn to her, needed her, more than anything else.

"You're sure about this?" he asked.

She smiled up at him. "You said it was bound to happen. Why wait?"

He'd already committed to her in his heart. He had the day they'd met—even if it had taken him a while to confirm that instinctual connection. There really wasn't any reason to stay apart.

He gazed into her eyes. "There's no one else I'd rather be with."

Her lips found his, and the rest of the universe faded into the distance.

— — —

Lexi lay back on the bed next to Jason, feeling a level of

contentment she hadn't thought was possible. Yet, she'd expected to feel... different.

It doesn't seem like we bonded. Would I feel a change?

She rolled her head to the side to study Jason. The adoration in his gaze back at her melted her heart all over again.

He shook his head, seemingly with disbelief. "Wow. That was…"

"Pretty incredible, I must admit."

"Have you ever been intimate with another telepath?"

"Not like this."

Jason nodded. "It's always more intense—since you experience everything with your partner. Even so, this was special."

"I don't have a good point of comparison, but I know what you mean. It was like I've known you for a lifetime and this was a reunion."

He ran his fingertips along her back, sending tingles all the way to her toes and fingertips. "That's a good way to put it."

"Still," she said, "I was expecting some sort of discernible moment of change with the bond. Actually, I don't feel all that different."

"No, there wasn't a spontaneous bond," he confirmed. "There's not a guarantee it will happen."

"So all that waiting we did before was for nothing?"

He brushed her hair away from her eyes. "I'm still glad I got to know you better before jumping into bed. I don't consider any of it wasted time."

"Yeah. I don't, either."

"Honestly, I suspect the caution against spontaneous bonding is more applicable to younger people who aren't as in control of their abilities. Young love sparked by a resonance connection—rushing into things as teenagers. I could see how emotions would get out of hand and the bond could be formed out of subconscious desire rather than by making a conscious choice."

"Meaning, it'll take an intentional decision to make this official?" she asked.

"Likely. Though, I wouldn't have minded if the link formed on its own."

"It still might." Lexi propped her arm under her head. "This was only one time, and I must confess that I'm still reeling from what happened on Quel."

"Same. There's no rush. I'm looking forward to growing with you—and getting closer—at whatever pace feels right."

"Yeah." She ran her hand along his chest. "I guess today was a good test for how we work together under pressure."

"You were great out there."

"Thanks. You were pretty impressive yourself."

He smiled. "We make a good team."

"I was thinking the same thing." She paused. "I'm still trying to figure out what my life would look like here, with you and the TSS."

"Yeah, there's a lot to consider." Jason took her hand. "But I'd really like to figure it out."

"Me too. But it does scare me. This isn't my world."

"The TSS isn't anyone's world when they first get here. That's what makes it a special place—we each make it our own," he said.

"When you got here, you were with your family."

"True, but there's a lot more to the community than my parents. And all of them will welcome you, too. You just need to be willing to take the chance."

"I am."

"You're not alone anymore, Lexi. We're here for each other."

"Thanks." She bit her lower lip and shook her head. "You. This. It still feels like a dream."

"Not every unexpected twist in life needs to be a bad thing."

"Yeah? I suppose I got dealt a bad hand early on that made me jaded."

"Understandably. But that's all in the past now. I'm looking forward to exploring our future together."

She kissed him deeply. "I suppose we have time to tempt fate some more before getting back to the outside world?"

"Absolutely."

CHAPTER 26

THE INCIDENT ON Quel wasn't the worse loss of life Wil had seen, but it was among the most senseless. The parallels to Alkeer Station made it that much worse. "Those poor people."

Saera had sat quietly while he reviewed the latest update on the clean-up efforts. "I know, it's a tough one.

"The orbital station has broken free. Looks like they're going to try their hand at being a floating city until they can find a new place to call home."

Saera nodded. "You've got to respect their grit."

"Indeed."

"There's the other issue, though—how Leon said that this incident wasn't the first," Saera said.

Wil had been particularly distressed to hear that during the debrief. "I haven't been able to figure out where the previous test might have been conducted. The Enforcers have responded to a lot of incidents and don't always know what they're looking at. Plus, they were probably bought off to call it a natural disaster, or whatever."

"Then we may never know."

He shook his head. "I wish I could say this would be the end of it. The researchers took a new approach on Quel after their first attempt failed, and that also was a disaster. People like this will keep trying until they succeed."

"How would such a weapon even manifest? Would it be more like a disease or a total wipe like what happened on Quel?"

"I hope we don't ever have to find out," Wil said. He'd faced many destructive forces over the course of his career, and it never got easier. Nor should it. Losing an entire planet wasn't a situation he ever wanted to become numb to.

Saera met his gaze. "It's a terrible feeling to be in this position of authority where we're supposed to know what's going on, but instead we learn how much we don't know."

"We do the best we can."

"Always looking ahead." She let out a long breath and consulted her tablet. "Have you been able to find out anything about SPEAR Tec—the lead Leon mentioned in his debrief?"

"It would have been tricky to track down, but we got lucky. Or, rather, everything is disturbingly connected."

"How so?"

"There's a good chance that the SPEAR Tec logo Leon saw is an abbreviation for Steyn Pharmaceutical Experimentation and Research, which is already under investigation for black market drug-running and piracy. Remember the undercover operative we sent out several months back?"

"Oh, *that* operative?" Recognition filled Saera's eyes. "I feel really silly for not making the connection to that name sooner."

"Took me a while myself. But it gets better. The leader of the Steyn operations goes by 'Maggie'—short for Magdalena. Magdalena Steyn."

"That's it, then." Saera sat up straight. "She could be the

ringleader for the Coalition."

"Perhaps, but I don't think she's working alone. As much as I'd like to suggest to Jason that he use his new taskforce to take out the Steyn family and their operations, we need to make sure we eliminate the *entire* criminal network. There are a lot of unaccounted for people from Duronis still in the wind, not to mention those from the other planets."

"So we continue to observe."

"That's my recommendation—for now."

She nodded. "Jason won't be happy about sitting on this lead."

"Learning to bide time until the moment is right to strike is an important lesson."

"For sure. I'm a little concerned to see where this goes."

Is it possible it will trace back to Monsari? The pieces were lining up that way. Such a powerful dynasty had both the connections and financial resources to fund an interstellar initiative of this magnitude. It would explain why they had turned down the power core manufacturing—they already had other plans to strike out on their own. To dismiss that much income potential and influence, they had to have an even bigger play in mind.

He shared the thoughts telepathically with Saera, and she swallowed. "That's what worries me, too."

"How much else that's been going on might be related? The demonstrations on Earth? Narratives in the media?"

Saera looked over the notes on her tablet again. "On that note, there have been a series of disappearances. Young, unattached drifters… with abilities. They fit a similar demographic profile to Lexi's missing friend and several of the captives liberated from Quel."

Wil exchanged a worried glance with his wife. "That also

sounds an awful lot like the Priesthood's profile for its subjects."

"I had the same thought."

"I hate to think anyone was inspired by their 'work'."

"Or, we didn't get all of them."

"That's a possibility I've been reluctant to acknowledge." The fall of the Priesthood had been initiated on Tararia and the TSS had done its best to pick up stragglers on other worlds, but there was no way to guarantee they'd all been apprehended.

"We might need to change our assumptions."

Wil wasn't quite there yet, but he would see how these new developments played out. "Aside from their profiles, is there anything linking the women?"

"Nothing we've been able to find yet. Honestly, I wouldn't have seen a connection if it wasn't for Lexi telling us about Melisa."

"Definitely a lead worth chasing, nonetheless."

"Agreed. Since it's potentially connected to the Coalition, I'll pass it over to Jason," Saera said, making a note on her tablet.

"If they do find any connection between the disappearances, we should get someone out in the field as soon as possible to look into it."

"Speaking of which, have you heard from our operative with Steyn?"

He shook his head. "No—not that I expected to. We might have to wait a while on that one."

"I don't like how big this thing is getting, Wil. The more rocks we overturn, the more darkness we find. Has it always been like that, or were we just too distracted by other things to see it before?"

"I don't know. But we need to address it now. The rot from

within is as great a threat as any other we've faced."

She nodded. "We're going to need more good people to cover all these bases."

"I'm working on it. In fact," he checked the clock on his desktop, "it's just about time for one of those conversations."

Saera stood up. "I'll leave you to it."

"Thanks for the update. I'll see you tonight."

When Saera opened the door to leave, Kira was standing in the hall about to knock. "Oh, hi!" the Guard officer said.

"Come on in," Wil beckoned for Kira to enter.

Saera looked back over her shoulder and gave a nod of approval. *"I can't think of a better person to have on our team. Lock her in."* She gently closed the door, leaving Wil to the private meeting.

"What can I do for you, sir?" Kira asked.

"Please, make yourself comfortable, Kira." He motioned to the chairs in front of his desk. While she got seated, he continued, "You have quite the fascinating story. A unique form of telepathy due to the biology of your homeworld. The alien nanotech that's granted you such impressive abilities. Your pairing with Jasmine. There truly isn't another soldier like you."

She smiled coyly. "Well, someone needs to get things done around here."

He laughed. "I can see why your teammates have spoken so highly of you."

"Just doing my job, sir."

"And what, ideally, would you like that job to be?"

The question seemed to catch her by surprise. "Whatever is needed."

"Please, speak freely. I am well aware of what it's like to be the odd one out. What is it that *you* would like to do with your considerable skill set?"

She sat in silent contemplation for several seconds before responding. "I would like to be the person who's called in to save the day when no one else can."

"That's a very honest answer."

"I joined the Guard because I wanted to make a difference. My homeworld wasn't even a formally recognized colony of the Empire until after I'd been in the service for a decade. I always wanted to be a part of something bigger than myself. And I wanted to be the best."

"You do have an exemplary record."

"In the Guard, yeah. But compared to the TSS? There's nothing I can do that your best Agents can't do better."

"That's not quite true."

"I can shape-shift, move really fast, and read minds with direct eye-contact. Comparatively, Agents can blow up things with their mind and effectively 'stop time' to move across a room in the blink of an eye. They'd win every time against me."

"Not all Agents can perform the more advanced feats. You'd outpace many."

"As flattering as that is, there's no point in pretending that any mission would be better off replacing a Primus Agent with me."

Wil couldn't deny the truth of the statement. While Kira was remarkable, and she was able to go places where a Gifted person would otherwise be found out, that didn't change that she had limitations. The breadth of abilities a trained Agent could bring to bear were superior in most ways.

However, Kira had more to offer than just her raw physical capabilities.

"You do have something that no one else does, Kira: an understanding of how different abilities are applicable in a given situation. You are at the intersection of the skill sets championed by both the Guard and TSS. No one else in the Guard has experienced firsthand how telepathy or super-speed can be incorporated into tactics."

She considered the statement. "I guess I do have a unique perspective."

Wil leaned forward, folding his arms on the desktop. "I want to offer you a new role, that's neither Guard nor TSS. It would fall under the new Taran Unified Force—one of the first positions officially under that umbrella. You would be a mission coordinator, of sorts, reviewing the most sensitive assignments and strategizing the best approach with others."

"That's a generous offer. I'm honored." Despite her words, she wasn't smiling.

"I sense some hesitation."

"To put it bluntly, sir, it sounds like a desk-job, and I'm not ready for my days in the field to be over quite yet."

He smiled. "On the contrary, it's an opportunity to select which missions are worth your time to go on. One of the perks of command is that no one can tell you 'no' when you say you want to tag along."

She caught on, a bright smile lighting up her face. "In other words, I get to have my hands in a little bit of everything."

"Precisely."

"That sounds rather perfect." Her smile faded slightly. "Where would this new position be located?"

"We're still working that out," he admitted. "Admiral Mathaen and I have talked about establishing a new TUF office on Tararia, so that's a possibility down the line. For now, we've agreed to keep it here at TSS Headquarters."

"You do have a nice place here."

"Since I can guess what your next question will be, I'd also like to invite Leon to stay on as a member of the TSS research team. He has a lot to offer. As we continue to build out the TUF's infrastructure, I believe he'd be a strong candidate to eventually head up its research division."

"I don't think it would take a lot of arm-twisting to get him to agree to that."

"And what about you?"

She beamed. "Where's my desk and my first assignment?"

— — —

Heading to a TSS officer's office would have made Lexi anxious under most circumstances, but the fact that the Lead Agent was Jason's mom made the situation all the more nerve-wracking.

Does she know we've committed? Though they hadn't yet sealed their bond, there was a start of one. She didn't know how much of that would be obvious to other Gifted who knew the signs.

Saera was behind her desk, and she motioned Lexi inside. The Agent closed the door and tinted the outer glass wall opaque for privacy.

Lexi gulped. *Stars, what am I walking into?*

"How's everything going, Lexi?" Saera asked.

"Good. Great."

"This isn't an interrogation. You can relax."

Saera had been nothing but kind to her, but that didn't make it any less awkward for Lexi while she was still trying to get a handle on her relationship with Jason, let alone navigate the larger family dynamics. It was too much to handle right now that the TSS Lead Agent was shaping up to be her future mother-in-law.

"What did you want to meet about?" Lexi asked.

"In short, your future."

Oh, stars, here we go! Lexi swallowed. "Jason and I are still figuring things out, but I care about him a lot."

"I can tell."

"I can't imagine not having him in my life now that we know each other. I might not be the Taran noble you'd hope for him to end up with, but I'll do everything I can for us to be happy together."

"That's good to hear," Saera said. "And related to that—"

Lexi held up her hand. "I already know what you're going to say about marrying into a High Dynasty family, and how everyone is super nice, and accepting, and there's nothing to worry about. But that's easy for you to say, as someone who's actually highborn, even if you didn't grow up that way. But what Jason and I have is special, and I don't know what lies ahead for us, but I'm hopeful. It doesn't matter what others think."

Saera cracked an amused smile and folded her hands on the desktop. "That's a good attitude to have. But actually, I wanted to talk with you about your Gifts and training."

"My…" Lexi's face burned. "Oh." *Shite, did I just ramble about all of that for no reason? I practically said we were getting married, and we haven't even remotely talked about that yet!*

"I understand that you have some advanced skills," Saera continued, thankfully moving past the other subject without further commentary. From the look on her face, she sensed that Lexi needed a lifeline. "I'm curious if there are skills you'd like to refine further."

Lexi gladly took the offer to change the subject. "I thought abilities didn't develop beyond a certain age?"

"It's true, gaining new skills with our Gifts becomes more

challenging the older we get, but the important thing is to have tapped into the potential by your mid-twenties, which you certainly have. Beyond that, the potential fades, if it's never utilized. But to augment your capabilities, you're still well within the window."

"I don't want to be an Agent."

"I wasn't going to suggest that." Saera looked her over. "As Lead Agent, one of my responsibilities is to oversee the training program. Now that telekinesis has been legalized, there are a lot more people like you emerging from the proverbial woodwork who've received some ad hoc training but nothing formal. The TSS is in a position to offer a sort of… continuing education program to help refine those skills."

Lexi crossed her arms, not sure whether she should be intrigued or if it was a trap. "Okay."

"I thought you might like to take part in a pilot program— offer insights and help refine the curriculum and course setup to make it something that would be appealing to civilians."

The proposal caught Lexi by surprise. She sat in uncomfortable silence for several seconds. "That's an interesting suggestion."

"Sorry, I didn't mean to blindside you," Saera said.

"I should be used to it by now. This last year has been a doozie."

"I can sympathize."

"Shite, yeah." She flushed. "My problems are nothing compared to what you must face on a daily basis in the TSS."

Saera shook her head. "Don't diminish the challenges you've overcome. It took a lot of bravery to go after your friend and infiltrate the Alliance. I'm a firm believer in offering credit where it's due."

"I still haven't found Melisa. Total bust on that mission."

"However, you've brought a severe issue to our attention through your investigative work, and we owe you that."

"These civilians that you want to train... Would you use them as informants?"

The Lead Agent studied her. "Some, perhaps. That's not the driving motivation for this new initiative, though."

"I like the idea of helping to teach others about their abilities, but Melisa is still out there. I need to find her... or at least learn what happened to her. I don't want to give up that search."

"We will help with that." Saera paused. "Your friend isn't the only disappearance."

"What? Who else?"

"A number of other young women. All Gifted."

Lexi's heart dropped. "The Alliance? Or, Coalition. I don't know what's what with that."

Saera shook her head. "The missing women are from various worlds in the Outer Colonies, most far from Duronis. It is possible the larger Coalition is involved, but we don't have enough information to establish a clear connection."

"Where might they have all disappeared to?"

"We don't know, but we're going to find out."

"I want to help."

Saera folded her hands. "I appreciate that, but we have other people for this investigation. You can do more good in other ways. Help us with this training initiative. I promise, we'll have a dedicated team working to find your friend and the others. It'll be rolled up under Jason's larger task force, so there will be plenty of opportunities for you to stay up to speed."

Lexi considered the offer. It was a good deal. "I don't have experience as a teacher," she admitted.

"Easily rectified. You can offer a lot of perspective in other areas. I think this could be a very good partnership."

She couldn't argue with that. It was an opportunity to have a defined role, and it would keep her here with Jason. On the whole, she couldn't imagine a better arrangement. "Yeah, I'm game."

Saera smiled. "Welcome to the team."

—   —   —

The pieces were falling into place. Jason hadn't expected half the turns, but he was grateful to have such good fortune. He'd been excited to share the news about Lexi with Raena when she'd called to check in, and he was happy to see his sister so thrilled for him.

With the training coordinator role his mother had designed for Lexi, the biggest questions about how she could fit into his life at TSS Headquarters had been answered. They each had challenging positions that would keep them busy, and they'd have each other to come home to every night. It was everything he'd hoped to find in a partnership.

However, there remained one major step: the decision to bond. He'd hoped that it would be spontaneous; now, knowing they'd need to make a conscious decision, it was more pressure. *Wait, or go for it?*

Jason was reminded again of that crossroads as Lexi finished telling him about her preliminary concepts for the civilian training program. Curled up on the couch next to him, she had a new vibrance about her—energized by having a clear sense of direction. The passion in her tone and expression made her even more alluring.

"It's going to be a lot of work," she was saying, "but I'm looking forward to making these resources available. I could have really used a program like this myself a few years ago."

"I love the idea. You're perfect for it."

"Just because I'm doing this, that doesn't mean I don't want a part in the investigation into the Coalition."

"I very much hope you'll be involved," Jason assured her.

"I'm looking forward to working together."

"Me too. I hope you don't get sick of seeing me all the time."

She smirked. "I don't anticipate that happening."

He inched closer to her. "That's good to hear, because I'd like to see what we can have together if we stop holding back."

Lexi met his gaze. "That's a big step."

"I don't want you to feel rushed or pressured. I just want you to know that I'm ready now, to share myself completely." He'd thought about it a lot over the past week. What he'd had with Tiff was as close as he'd ever gotten, but that relationship was always missing that extra... something. With Lexi, it was all there—and it could become even more.

"I keep waiting for this feeling of perfect bliss to subside," Lexi said. "All I want is to be close to you. It's been so short a time together, and yet I can't imagine not having you in my life."

"Both of us are used to kind of being loners, it seems."

"I'd call it 'self-sufficient'."

"Well put."

She bit her lip. "Except, I don't want to be anymore. Not since meeting you."

"Me either."

Lexi was perfect for him in so many ways. Good-hearted and street smart. He looked at her not being highborn as a positive rather than a detractor. It was the makings of an exceptional partnership where they could learn from each other and grow.

Lexi smiled and shook her head. "This still feels like a dream."

"There've been enough nightmares. I'll take the change of pace." The Coalition was still growing in the shadows. The Erebus were likely plotting a major assault. The coming months and years would no doubt hold the greatest challenges Jason had ever faced, but knowing he'd have someone by his side made it far less daunting.

"Finding a place—or a person—where you can seek comfort when everything else around you is going to shite. I guess that's what this is about, isn't it?" Lexi mused.

"Yes. And so much more." He stroked the side of her face.

She grasped his hand in hers. "I feel like I could take on anything with you."

"Good," he kissed her, "because we're in for a bomaxed big fight."

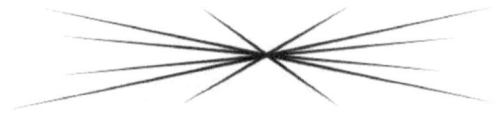

THE STORY CONTINUES *EMPIRE DEFIED...*

Some alliances were never meant to last...

Dark forces are working in the shadows within the Taran Empire. When a series of attacks hit the Outer Colonies, it becomes clear a new war is brewing.

As Jason and his family try to track down the perpetrators, they soon learn that their enemies pose a greater threat than they could have imagined. The Taran Empire's fight for survival is about to begin.

ADDITIONAL READING

Cadicle Space Opera Series by A.K. DuBoff
Book 1: Rumors of War (Vol. 1-3)
Book 2: Web of Truth (Vol. 4)
Book 3: Crossroads of Fate (Vol. 5)
Book 4: Path of Justice (Vol. 6)
Book 5: Scions of Change (Vol. 7)

Mindspace Series by A.K. DuBoff
Book 1: Infiltration
Book 2: Conspiracy
Book 3: Offensive
Book 4: Endgame

Verity Chronicles by T.S. Valmond & A.K. DuBoff
Book 1: Exile
Book 2: Divided Loyalties
Book 3: On the Run

Shadowed Space Series by Lucinda Pebre & A.K. DuBoff
Book 1: Shadow Behind the Stars
Book 2: Shadow Rising
Book 3: Shadow Beyond the Reach

In Darkness Dwells by James Fox & A.K. DuBoff

AUTHORS' NOTES

Thank you for reading *Empire Uprising*! This was a fun but challenging book to write.

Connecting this book (and series) to the broader Cadicle Universe is one of the biggest challenges I've faced as an author. It is so rewarding to see all the pieces come together, but wow, it takes a lot to coordinate everything!

In particular, this portion of the series connects closely to the Shadowed Space series written with Lucinda Pebre. The intersections will be most apparent in the next book, but I needed to make sure everything was set up properly in this volume. And I am so excited to have all the pieces come together!

The other challenging aspect of this book was the science aspect of it, explaining the Erebus, aesen, and Gifted abilities in a way that is interesting and plausible. I've received a lot of questions over the years about how everything works, and it's been wonderful finally expounding on those foundational ideas in this series.

My amazing beta readers have been a critical part of getting this book ready. I so appreciate them looking over the drafts multiple times and being a sounding board for ideas. Many thanks to John, Gil, Charlie, Jim, Doug, Steve, Heather, Marc, Leo, David, Kaj, Louise, and Liz.

Thank you also to Angel and my other proofreaders for helping to add the final polish. I appreciate everything you do!

Special thanks to my husband, my parents, and the Fox

family for all their love and support during the writing and editing process.

Thank you again for reading this second novel in the Taran Empire Saga, and I hope you are enjoying this expansion of the Cadicle Universe. Until next time, happy reading!

GLOSSARY

Timeline of Key Events

All dates are adjusted for the standard Earth calendar

~98,000 BC - Ancient war and signing of the peace treaty between Tarans, the Gatekeepers, and the transdimensional aliens

AD ~50 - Priesthood's rise to power as a governing entity on Tararia

AD ~1000 - Taran Revolution period, following the split of the Priesthood when the Aesir left Tararia

AD 1587 - First skirmishes of the Bakzen War

AD 2016 - Invention of the Independent Jump Drive

AD 2025 - Official end of the Bakzen War; destruction of the Bakzen homeworld

AD 2050 - Fall of the Priesthood; transition of Dynasty corporations into public entities

AD 2054 - Reactivation of Gatekeeper tech

AD 2055 - Reopening of the rift/tear and reappearance of the transdimensional aliens

Key Terms

Aesen *(Ay-sen)* - The foundational energy of the universe; pure energy capable of being shaped into any form. *Aesen* energy exists in a higher dimension and can be drawn upon to perform feats of telekinesis.

Aesir *(Ay-seer)* - A group of Tarans who broke away from the Empire around 1000 AD (Earth years) to engage in metaphysical pursuits, such as reading cosmic energy patterns. The founders of the Aesir were all former members of the Priesthood and possess strong telepathic and telekinetic abilities. The Aesir are isolationist and long-lived, possessing advanced technology lost to the rest of the Empire during the Priesthood's corrupt reign.

Agent - A class of officer within the TSS reserved for those with telekinetic and telepathic gifts. There are three levels of Agent based on level of ability: Primus, Sacon and Trion.

Ateron *(at-er-on)* - An element that oscillates between normal space and subspace, facilitating high levels of telekinetic energy transfer.

Baellas *(bAy-las)* - A corporation run by the Baellas Dynasty, producing housewares, clothing, furniture, and other textiles for use across the Taran civilization. Additional specialty lines managed by other smaller corporations are licensed to Baellas for distribution.

Bakzen *(Bak-zen)* - A militaristic race that lived beyond the Outer Colonies. All Bakzen were clones and possesses varying levels of telekinetic capabilities.

Bakzen War - A centuries-long conflict waged primarily by the TSS in a secret spatial rift.

Cadicle *(Kad-i-kl)* - The definition of individual perfection in the Priesthood's founding ideology, with the emergence of the Cadicle heralding the start to the next stage of evolution for the Taran race.

Course Rank (CR) - The official measurement of an Agent's ability level, taken at the end of their training immediately before graduation from Junior Agent to Agent. The Course Rank Test is a multi-phase examination, including direct focusing of telekinetic energy into a testing sphere. The magnitude of energy focused during the exercise is the primary factor dictating the Agent's CR.

Dainetris Dynasty *(Dayn-ee-tris)* - One of the seven High Dynasties, the Dainetris Dynasty was considered lost for nearly two hundred years. After members of the family spoke out against the Priesthood's corruption, the Priesthood destroyed the family and buried the city that served as their seat of power. The Dynasty's status was restored in 2050, and a new seat of power was established on the Priesthood's former administrative island, renamed Morningstar Isle after the flower in the Dainetris crest.

Earth - A planet occupied by humans, a divergent race of Tarans. Considered a "lost colony," Earth is not recognized as part of the Taran government.

Enforcers - The police force of the galaxy; a division of the Tararian Guard.

Erebus *(Ayr-eh-bus)* - A race of transdimensional aliens capable of manipulating *aesen* at the foundational level to create and un-make matter within the spacetime dimension. The beings can reach down into spacetime through dimensional rifts and are capable of telepathic manipulation.

Gatekeepers - An ancient alien race with advanced portal tech. Little is known about their native form beyond that they are higher-dimensional beings and create hybrid versions of themselves to interact with spacetime reality, including Taran hybrid vessels.

Generation Cycle - Also known as the Twelve Generation Cycle. A genetic mutation in Tarans where seven generations will express no telepathic or telekinetic abilities, followed by five with those Gifts—the strongest expression being 10th Generation. It is believed that the genetic line descending from the Cadicle may hold the key to developing a genetic patch to fix the mutation. The Aesir left the Empire before the dissemination of the gene therapy that resulted in the Generation Cycle, so they do not suffer from the mutation; they do not intermingle with other Tarans for this reason.

Gifts - The colloquial term used to describe a variety of telepathic and telekinetic abilities, ranging from simple mind-reading, to object levitation, to manipulating energy fields on small or large scales. These Gifts typically emerge between the age of sixteen to eighteen. Before the Priesthood's fall, all but telepathy were illegal; since then, telekinesis has been legalized for non-violent applications. The TSS remains the foremost training institution for those with abilities.

High Commander - The officer responsible for the administration of the TSS. Always an Agent from the Primus class.

High Dynasties - Seven families on Tararia that control the corporations critical to the functioning of Taran society. Each have a designated Region on Tararia, which is the seat of their power. The Dynasties in aggregate form A High Council oligarchical government for the Taran Empire.

Independent Jump Drive - A jump drive that does not rely on the SiNavTech beacon network for navigation, instead using a mathematical formula to calculate jump positions through normal space and the Rift.

Initiate - The second stage of the TSS training program for Agents. A trainee will typically remain at the Initiate stage for two or three years.

Jump Drive - The engine system for travel through subspace. Conventional jump drives require an interface with the SiNavTech navigation system and subspace navigation beacons.

Junior Agent - The third stage of the TSS training program for Agents. A trainee will typically remain at the Junior Agent stage for three to five years.

Lead Agent - The highest-ranking Agent and second-in-command to the High Commander. The Lead Agent is responsible for overseeing the Agent training program and frequently serves as a liaison for TSS business with Taran colonies.

Lower Dynasties - There are 247 recognized Lower Dynasties in Taran society. Many of these families have a presence on Tararia, but some are residents of the other inner colonies.

Makaris Corp *(Mak-ayr-is)* - A corporation run by the Makaris High Dynasty responsible for the distribution of food, water filters, and other necessary supplies to Taran colonies without diverse natural resources.

Monsari Power Solutions (MPS) *(Mon-sayr-ee)* - A corporation run by the Monsari Dynasty, responsible for power generation systems for the Taran worlds, including geothermal generators, portable generators, and reactors to power spacecraft. Their foremost product are the Perpetual Energy Modules (PEMs) that function in the most critical systems.

Rift - A habitable pocket between normal space and subspace. The largest rift—specifically known as *the* Rift—is located at the site of the former Bakzen homeworld, a wound left by the destruction of the planet at the end of the Bakzen War. It is thought to be a place where the veil between dimensions is thinner.

Sacon *(Sak-on)* - The middle tier of TSS Agents. Typically, Sacon Agents will score a CR between 6 and 7.9.

Sietinen Dynasty *(sIgh-tin-en)* - High Dynasty overseeing the Third Region of Tararia, responsible for the SiNavTech navigation network. Considered the most influential of the Taran dynasties due to the family's ties to the TSS and responsibility for the Empire's transportation infrastructure.

SiNavTech - A corporation run by the Sietinen High Dynasty, which controls and maintains the subspace navigation network used by Taran civilians and the TSS.

Spatial Dislocation - The act of physically transitioning from normal space to the brink of subspace, either by means of a jump drive or telekinetic abilities.

TalEx - A corporation run by the Talsari Dynasty, managing mining operations and ore processing across Taran territories.

Tarans *(tayr-ans)* - The general term for all individuals with genetic relation to Tararian ancestry. Several divergent races are recognized by their planet or system. Humans are of Taran descent.

Tararia *(Tayr-ayr-ee-a)* - The home planet for the Taran race and seat of the central government.

Tararian *(Tayr-ayr-ee-an)* - Someone from or residing on the planet Tararia.

Tararian Guard - The military and peacekeeping arm of the Taran Empire. The military side is known colloquially as the Guard, and the personnel on the policing side are known as Enforcers.

Tararian Selective Service (TSS) - A quasi-military organization with two divisions: (1) Agent Class, and (2) Militia Class. Agents possess telekinetic and telepathic abilities; the TSS is the only place where individuals with such gifts can gain official training. The Militia class offers a formal training program for those without telekinetic abilities, providing tactical and administrative support to Agents. TSS Headquarters is located inside the moon of the planet Earth. Additional Militia training facilities are located throughout the Taran worlds and there are numerous TSS bases throughout the Empire. Since the end of the Bakzen War, the TSS has also engaged in more academic pursuits so many Agents can pursue careers related to the sciences rather than being 'soldiers'.

Trainee - The generic term for a student of the TSS, and also the term for first-year Agent students (when capitalized Trainee). Students are not fully "initiated" into the TSS until their second year.

Trion *(Try-on)* - The lowest tier of TSS Agents. Typically, Trion Agents will score a CR below 5.9.

Priesthood of the Cadicle - The institution formerly responsible for oversight of all governmental affairs and the flow of information throughout the Taran colonies. During its rule until 2050 AD, the Priesthood had jurisdiction over even the High Dynasties and provided a tiebreaking vote on new initiatives. The organization perpetrated many secret experimentations on Taran citizens and was voted out of power by the High Council. All known associates have been arrested or were killed in the fall.

Primus *(Pree-mus)* - The highest of three Agent classes within the TSS, reserved for those with the strongest telekinetic abilities. Typically, Primus Agents will score a CR above 8.

Primus Elite - A special classification of Agent above Primus signifying an exceptional level of ability.

Vaenetri Dynasty *(Vayn-E-tree)* - High Dynasty overseeing the First Region of Tararia. The family operates VComm, a corporation specializing in telecommunications.

VComm - A telecommunications corporation owned and operated by the Vaenetri Dynasty.

Voydite - A unique crystalline substance used to make the nanotube casings for PEMs. The Monsari Dynasty holds a complete monopoly on the secret source of the material.

ABOUT THE AUTHOR

A.K. (Amy) DuBoff has always loved science fiction in all its forms—books, movies, shows, and games. If it involves outer space, even better! She is a Nebula Award finalist and *USA Today* bestselling author most known for her Cadicle Universe, but she's also written a variety of space fantasy and comedic sci-fi. Now a full-time author, Amy can frequently be found traveling the world. When she's not writing, she enjoys wine tasting, binge-watching TV series, and playing epic strategy board games.

www.amyduboff.com